## Evelyn reached ........ rees and stumbled on something.

She started to fall toward the hard ground, but a firm hand grabbed her elbow and pulled her behind the giant tree to her left.

"Careful," Joel murmured near her ear. He still had a hold of her arm, which meant she was now standing against his chest.

Her heartbeat ricocheted at his touch. His warm, solid presence behind her both unnerved and relaxed her.

"Thank you. I'm all right." She took a deliberate step to the side, though mere inches separated them.

Joel shifted, leaning his shoulder against the tree trunk. "Is something wrong?"

She shook her head.

He put a finger under her chin, forcing her to look at him. Her stomach flip-flopped as she peered into his handsome face. "Are you afraid of something then?"

*You,* she wanted to say. But she kept the word sealed inside.

"I'm fine, really." She swallowed hard. "Just a little tired is all."

Instead of releasing her chin, Joel glanced at her mouth. The rush of sound in Evelyn's ears grew even louder. Was he going to kiss her? She wanted him to—had even dreamt of this moment. She held her breath as he leaned forward. Shutting her eyes, she waited for his lips to reach hers.

# ACCLAIM FOR *HOPE AT DAWN*

# Hope Rising

by

## Stacy Henrie

FOREVER

NEW YORK   BOSTON

Forever
Hachette Book Group
1290 Avenue of the Americas
New York, NY 10104

www.HachetteBookGroup.com

Printed in the United States of America

First Edition: December 2014
10 9 8 7 6 5 4 3 2 1

OPM

Forever is an imprint of Grand Central Publishing.
The Forever name and logo are trademarks of Hachette Book Group, Inc.

The Hachette Speakers Bureau provides a wide range of authors for speaking events. To find out more, go to www.hachettespeakersbureau.com or call (866) 376-6591.

The publisher is not responsible for websites (or their content) that are not owned by the publisher.

*To the men and women who served in the First World War: May your sacrifice never be forgotten.*

# Acknowledgments

My heartfelt thanks go to the entire team at Grand Central Forever. Thank you for your enthusiasm, for the stunning cover art, and for a beautiful finished product.

A specific and sincere thank you to my editor, Lauren Plude, for her encouragement and her knack for helping me know where to dig for greater emotional depth. My manuscripts are so much better for having passed through her capable hands. Thanks, too, to my copy editor, Joan Matthews, for her meticulous eye on this book and its predecessor.

Thank you to my agent, Jessica Alvarez, for her savviness, support, and foresight. This series, and this book in general, would not have made it off my hard drive without her help.

Thanks to my critique partners Ali Cross, Elana Johnson, and Sara Olds, for their help in all things writerly, researchy, and chocolaty.

To the readers of my Of Love and War series, especially those who've eagerly awaited Joel's story, thank you for your excitement about the Campbell family and those who've come into their lives.

Last, but never ever least, thanks to the greatest band of true-blue fans ever: my sweet husband and kids. Thanks for, happily, taking this journey with me.

# *Author's Note*

The more I've studied the First World War, the more I'm in awe of those who sacrificed their time and, in so many cases, their lives to serve their countries. In an age when antibiotics had yet to be discovered, when machine guns and tanks and airplanes were new war weapons, and when wounds were unlike any seen previously, the Great War was a distinctly unique period of conflict.

America declared war on Germany in April 1917, three years after Germany, Great Britain, and France first began fighting. Corporal Joel Campbell's life as an Army soldier in the American Expeditionary Force (AEF)—in the trenches, in battle, and in the hospital—is representative of the roughly two million "doughboys" who served overseas during WWI. The battle in which he's wounded would have been the Second Battle of the Marne, which occurred between July 15 and August 5, 1918. The war finally ended on November 11 of that same year.

The United States Army Nurse Corps, established in

1901, had more than 10,000 nurses serving overseas during WWI. Though they did not receive military rank until after the war, these nurses were an incredible force for good in nearly all stages of wartime medical care.

An Army Nurse Corps nurse who married or became pregnant—married or not—was honorably discharged. This rule changed in October 1942, allowing nurses who married to remain on active duty at the surgeon general's discretion for the period of the war plus six months.

While St. Vincent's hospital is my fictional creation, there were hospitals in France that were run by religious sisters during WWI. Though I did not find any case where Army Nurse Corps nurses assisted in such a hospital, for the sake of the story, I had Evelyn Gray and the other ANC nurses serve alongside the Sisters of Charity at St. Vincent's instead of in an Army or Red Cross hospital.

The sodium hypochlorite solution created by Henry Drysdale Dakin and Alexis Carrel was a godsend in a pre-antibiotics world. Irrigating open wounds with the Carrell-Dakin solution (or Dakin's solution) helped keep infection from growing worse and meant wounds healed in less time.

Evelyn's experience at the evacuation hospital is true to life, with its incessant mud and occasional firing upon by German gunners. Most nurses were eager to serve at the front lines, regardless of the difficulties.

A final note: My heart goes out to the countless women who, like Evelyn, have experienced miscarriage or infant loss. I share your ranks and know the pain and grief, often silent, you've known. I hope you, too, have been able to find the loving care and hope that Evelyn eventually did.

For more information about the Great War, the AEF,

or the Army Nurse Corps, I recommend the following books, which were invaluable in my research: *Intimate Voices from the First World War,* by Svetlana Palmer and Sarah Wallis (2003); *Over There: The United States in the Great War 1917–1918,* by Byron Farwell (1999); and *A History of the U.S. Army Nurse Corps,* by Mary T. Sarnecky (1999).

# Prologue

Evelyn Gray breathed in the briny smell of the sea as she fingered the five shells in her gloved palm. One for each year without her father. From beneath her velour hat, she peered up at the gray sky overhead. The cool temperature and the possibility of rain made her grateful for the warmth of her Army Nurse Corps outdoor uniform, with its dark blue jacket, shirtwaist, and skirt.

"Nurse Gray, come on." One of the other three nurses down the beach waved for her to join them in their walk along the shoreline toward the white cliffs in the distance.

Sighing, Evelyn turned in their direction. She wasn't in any hurry to rejoin their conversation. The other girls on leave with her were full of talk about home and families and sweethearts, while she had only her aging grandparents waiting for her back in Michigan. As for a beau? Her lips turned up into a bitter smile. She'd been too busy with nurse's training to worry about any of that.

She lifted the first shell—a smooth, white one—and

tossed it into the sea. "I still miss you, Papa," she said as the seashell slipped beneath the surface of the water.

*Five years today, since you left us.* She could easily picture how he'd trudged up the porch steps that afternoon after tending to a patient—he'd never established a doctor's office in town, preferring instead to make house calls or take visits in their home. He hadn't looked well, but Evelyn's medical knowledge at seventeen wasn't what it was today at twenty-two. She still wasn't sure if he himself recognized the signs of the coming heart attack.

Tossing the second shell into the water, she swallowed hard against the flood of memories. She'd gone upstairs to make sure he was lying down and found him on the floor next to the bed, already gone.

She rid her hand of the third, fourth, and fifth shells in quick succession, then brushed the granules of sand from her gloves. The wind and the ache in her heart brought salty moisture to her eyes, but she straightened her shoulders against both. No one else needed to know what day it was or how much the loneliness tore at her.

"Afternoon."

Evelyn whirled around to find an American soldier watching her from a few feet away. He wasn't overly tall, less than six feet, but his handsome face, broad shoulders, and dark eyes were an impressive combination and made Evelyn's pulse skip from more than being startled.

"I didn't mean to disturb you." He smiled, looking anything but apologetic. "Beautiful view."

The way he said it, she knew he wasn't talking about the ocean. Evelyn didn't blush, though. She was used to lingering looks and flirtations from the wounded soldiers at the hospital where she worked. Some, like this young man, were quite handsome; others were sweet; and a few pressed her to keep in touch once they left the hospital. But Evelyn put a firm stop to any such nonsense. She wouldn't break the rule forbidding fraternization between nurses and enlisted soldiers.

Being a nurse was demanding enough; doing so while pregnant or with a venereal disease would make it twice as difficult. Not to mention she would be discharged if it were discovered she was with child. No, nursing was too important to her, and to her grandparents, to throw her job away for some soldier. Nowhere else but in a busy hospital ward, performing her duties, did she still feel close to her father.

*Time to catch up with the other nurses.*

Evelyn turned in the direction of the cliffs and started after the girls. They'd managed to cover quite a bit of distance while she lingered behind. To her dismay, the soldier fell into step beside her.

"I'm Private First Class Ralph Kelley." He held out his hand for her to shake. "And you are?"

"Not supposed to talk to you," Evelyn said in her firmest nurse's tone. "You know the rules, soldier." She tried to maintain a brisk pace across the beach, but the stones and sand underfoot made it difficult.

He chuckled as he lowered his hand to his side. "You on leave?" he asked, doggedly ignoring her rejection. "With those other nurses?"

She refused to answer, but his next question caught her off guard.

"Do you collect pebbles? I saw you picking some up earlier."

How long had he been watching her? Heat rose into

her cheeks at his intrusion upon her private mourning. "I need to go." She attempted to outdistance him again, but his feet kept tempo with hers.

"Have lunch with me."

The request, spoken in an almost pleading tone, halted Evelyn's retreat in a way his earlier attempts at charm hadn't. She circled to face him. Perhaps a gentle rebuff would serve her better than her usual abrupt one.

Before she could say anything, he spoke again. "I can't say I don't make it a habit of talking with nurses." He gave her a sheepish smile as he removed his cap and fingered the olive drab wool. "But you looked like you could use a friend back there. Like there was something weighing on your mind."

The perceptive observation took her by surprise, and she fell back a step. Could there be more to this soldier than his ladies' man demeanor? Her earlier feeling of isolation welled up inside her, nearly choking her with its hold. "It's the anniversary of my father's death—five years today." The admission tumbled out, despite the voice of reason screaming in her mind to keep walking away. "I've been thinking a lot about him lately."

"Do your friends know?" He nodded in the direction the other girls had gone.

Evelyn folded her arms against the battering breeze and shook her head. "I didn't want to spoil their time away from the hospital."

"That's rather generous." He cocked his head to study her. "Will you at least tell me your name?"

She could feel her defenses crumbling beneath the sincerity in his black eyes. "It's…um…Evelyn. Evelyn Gray."

"Evelyn."

Hearing his deep voice intone her name brought butterflies to her stomach, and the smile he offered afterward made her heartbeat thrum faster. When was the last time she'd felt this way? Probably not since she and Dale had kissed after high school graduation. Dale Emerson had been her first beau, until he moved to Sioux City, Iowa, and Evelyn had put all her time and energy into becoming a nurse. Last she'd heard, Dale had graduated from medical school and was serving as a surgeon at the front lines.

"I discovered a place yesterday that serves excellent fish," he said, his tone coaxing. "If you like fish . . ."

Despite her best efforts to stop it, a smile lifted the corners of her lips. "I think I'd like anything that wasn't cooked at the hospital. Our food there isn't much better than Army fare, I'm afraid."

Private Kelley laughed; it was a pleasant sound. "I owe it to you then, to at least provide you a decent meal while you're on leave." His expression sobered as he added, "Especially today."

Evelyn glanced over her shoulder at the three nurses far down the beach. She ought to refuse. But logic was growing less and less persuasive inside her mind. For the first time in months, she felt valued and important. This soldier's genuine notice and concern soothed the loneliness she wore as constantly as her nurse's uniform.

She pushed at the sand beneath her shoes, her lips pursed in indecision. Could any real harm come from simply sharing a meal in a public place? At least she'd be spared having to listen to the other girls prattle on about their big families and parents who were still alive. She would only be trading one conversation for another.

Inhaling a deep breath, she let her words slide out on the exhale. "Let me tell them I'll meet up with them later."

He grinned and replaced his hat on his head. "I'll wait right here for you."

Evelyn moved with new purpose toward the retreating group. She called to the girls from a distance to avoid any questions. The three of them turned as one. "Go on ahead without me. I'll meet up with you before supper."

They glanced at one another, then one of them shrugged and waved her hand in acknowledgment. A sense of freedom rolled through her as Evelyn retraced her steps to where Private First Class Ralph Kelley stood waiting.

"All set?" He extended his hand to her.

Evelyn stared at it for a long moment, then placed her fingers in his palm. With a smile, he tucked her hand over his arm and led her away from the beach.

# Chapter 1

*July 1918*

You've become skin and bones since you came here, Evelyn. And no wonder; you eat like a bird." Alice Thornton waved her fork at the half-empty plate Evelyn had slid aside. "If my mother were here, she'd try to fatten you up. Unlike the hospital cook, apparently."

Evelyn smiled, despite the queasiness in her stomach. She could imagine Mrs. Thornton—a rotund, matronly version of red-headed Alice—chasing her down with a ladle of stew in hand. Alice talked a lot about her family, particularly her three beanpole brothers who never put on pounds no matter how much they ate, much to their mother's chagrin.

That wasn't Evelyn's problem. The morning sickness that plagued her, even now in the middle of the day, prevented her from stomaching much of any meal. But she certainly didn't plan on telling Alice that.

Almost of its own volition, her hand rose to rest against the middle of her white nurse's apron. The tiny life inside her could only be ten weeks along by now, but her own life had been altered just the same. Would anyone else notice her lack of appetite, as Alice had, or her frequent trips to the bathroom?

Alice turned to chat with another nurse seated near them, giving Evelyn a moment to herself. She slipped her hand beneath her apron, into the pocket of her gray crepe dress, and felt the letter tucked there. It brought instant calm as she withdrew the folded slip of paper. Though the letter had arrived less than a week ago, she had Ralph's words memorized. Still, she liked to see the bold strokes of his handwriting and read the reassurance behind the words he'd penned.

> *I'm still in shock at your news of the baby. I find myself thinking at odd times of the day, even in the middle of a battle, that I'm going to be a father. I am going to do right by you and the baby, Evelyn. Not like my own father. As soon as I get leave again, I'm coming to the hospital there and we'll get married. I know you'll be discharged after that, being married and all, but you won't have to worry about what to tell your grandparents anymore. You can tell them you got hitched in France and came home to have our baby.*
>
> *I miss you and think of you every day.*
> *Yours,*
> *Ralph*

"Did we get mail today?"

Alice's voice broke into Evelyn's reverie. Startled, she glanced up in confusion. "Mail?"

Her roommate pointed at the sheet of paper in Evelyn's grip.

Evelyn quickly folded the letter and shoved it into her pocket, away from Alice's curious gaze. "Oh, I'm not sure. This is from last week."

"Is it from your grandparents?"

Though she wanted to answer in the affirmative, Evelyn wouldn't lie. She hadn't heard from either her grandmother or her grandfather in several months. Their declining health made returning Evelyn's missives difficult.

"It's from a...friend," she hedged. She steeled herself for more questions, but thankfully Alice accepted the response with a nod.

Evelyn hadn't yet broached the subject of the baby or her inevitable homecoming in her letters to her grandparents. She'd wait until she and Ralph were married. That way when she told them, she would be breaking the news as a new bride and not an unwed mother. What would that shock do to them? She was hopeful they'd like Ralph— that his charisma would eventually win them over as it had her. The thought of his larger-than-life personality filling the too quiet house where she'd grown up brought a smile to her lips.

"Better hurry up." Evelyn stood and picked up her plate. "I heard Sister Marcelle is doing a round of ward visits today or tomorrow."

Alice frowned and scrambled up from the table. "In that case, I'll skip the rest. Sister Henriette is likely to tell her that I yelled at Sergeant Dennis good and long this morning. But honestly, the man refuses to rest."

Evelyn's smile flattened into a frown as she followed Alice to the kitchen. She'd noticed the way Sergeant Dennis watched Alice. The man was clearly captivated by the younger girl and would go to great lengths to garner a response from her—even if it was a good scolding. Evelyn could only hope her roommate would remain blind to the man's attention. Alice didn't seem the type to disregard the rule forbidding nurses and soldiers from fraternizing, but then again, Evelyn hadn't expected to break the rule herself. Not until she'd met Ralph.

A torrent of French greeted them as they set their dishes beside the kitchen's enormous sink. The hospital cook stood at the back door, shaking her spoon at a dark-headed youngster.

"*S'il vous plaît?*" the boy entreated.

"*Non pas de pain,*" the cook responded. She slammed the door in the boy's disheartened face and muttered under her breath. Throwing a pointed look at Evelyn and Alice, she returned to her table and began whacking dough with a stick.

"Come on, Evelyn." Alice retreated back toward the entrance to the large dining hall. None of the twenty nurses at St. Vincent's liked spending much time in the kitchen with the cantankerous cook.

"I'll be along in a minute. You go ahead."

The moment her roommate left, Evelyn took both the half-nibbled rolls from their plates and discreetly put them into her free pocket. While she might not be able to stomach much food, that didn't mean someone else should go away hungry. She retraced her steps to the dining hall and let herself out one of the hospital's rear entrances. A welcoming breeze loosened bits of her dark hair from underneath her nurse's cap. Evelyn tucked them back and eyed the sky. Gray clouds overhead promised rain.

Before her, the back lawn of the hospital extended long and wide, bordered by forests of beech and oak trees. The hospital itself had originally been a château, rebuilt in the 1860s and bequeathed to the Sisters of Charity. The living quarters for the hospital staff stood to her left in what had once been the orangery and beyond that sat an ancient stone church. Though different from the clapboard building she'd attended as a child, she couldn't help wondering each time she saw the old building how many weddings, funerals, and services had been held within its rock walls. Would it see another hundred years' worth of worship and poignant moments or fall, ravaged by the war like so many other towns and villages?

Out of the corner of her eye, Evelyn caught sight of black hair as the beggar boy rounded the hospital. "Wait! *Attendez!*" she called out as she jogged after him. "Please, wait."

He stopped so suddenly Evelyn nearly ran into him. Large black eyes peered up at her from a dirt-smudged face. They looked neither sad nor angry, but resigned and weary, though the boy couldn't be more than six years old. That wizened look constricted Evelyn's heart more than the other signs of poverty about him—the cuts on his shins and the disheveled state of his shirt and trousers.

"*Parlez-vous Anglais?*" she inquired. She hoped he spoke English. Her French was still quite rudimentary, despite the months she'd spent in his country as a nurse.

He cocked his head and nodded.

"Wonderful. What's your name?"

"Loo-ee. Louis Rousseau."

Evelyn smiled. "*Bonjour*, Louis. I'm Nurse Gray."

"Got any coffin nails or chocolate?"

She bit back a laugh at the familiar term for cigarettes. "You learned English from some soldiers, didn't you?"

Louis shook his head. "*Ma grand-mère* taught me the English. But *ma mère* takes our vegetables into the market and sometimes the Americans buy some. She didn't sell much yesterday. I was trying to beg some *petit de pain* off that *tête de chou*. That cabbage-headed cook. But she just say '*non, non.*'"

The brief glimpse into the boy's day-to-day life made Evelyn all the more grateful she'd taken the uneaten food to give him. While she understood the cook and her staff had to keep an entire hospital from going hungry, Evelyn still believed a little kindness in these dark times was equally important.

"Tell you what, Louis. I didn't finish all my bread today and I'd like you to have it." She removed the rolls, which were slightly squished now, and held them out to him.

His eyes widened as he stared at the bread, then at her.

"Go on. You can have it."

He carefully took the rolls from her. One he bit into at once, but the other he held in his free hand. "*Ma mère* can eat this one. *Merci.*"

"You're welcome."

A flood of emotion filled her as she watched him lean against the hospital wall to eat the meager meal. He was clearly famished, but he ate the bread slowly. Watching him, her thoughts turned to the life growing inside her.

Perhaps the baby would be a boy—a little dark-haired fellow with an impish glint in his black eyes just like his father. She could imagine her and Ralph and their child, and hopefully the other children that would follow, sitting

on the porch of her grandparents' house—*her house*—
laughing and sipping lemonade. The loneliness she'd experienced since her father's death would disappear, and
the large, empty house would be filled with laughter and
life and people.

She'd always envied those of her schoolmates with
large families and two living parents. While she never
doubted the love her father and grandparents felt for her,
she still used to pretend she had a whole slew of brothers and sisters—a complete family. Soon, that dream
would be realized. Once she and Ralph married, she
would be a wife and eventually a mother, with a family
of her own.

"Do you have any brothers or sisters?" she asked
Louis, reluctant to return indoors. The heat and smells inside the hospital made her nausea worse.

Louis shook his head. "It's only me and *ma mère*."

Did Louis long for more family as she did? "Where's
your father?"

The boy lowered his gaze to the grass. "He was a soldier...but he got killed last year." His brow pinched with
sorrow, the same emotion tugging at Evelyn's own heart.
So many men gone...

Losing her father had been devastating, and she hadn't
been a child. Even now, there were countless moments
when she missed him with an intensity that made his
death feel as fresh as yesterday. The similarities between
her and the young boy poking at the ground with his big
toe ran deeper than she would have guessed.

Squatting down in front of Louis, she rested her hands
on his thin shoulders. "My father died, too."

"Was he a brave soldier like *mon père*?"

"In a way. He was a doctor, so he helped people fight battles of illness and disease."

Louis lifted his chin to look her in the eye. "How'd he die?"

"His heart stopped working one day."

"*Et votre mère?*"

*And your mother?* Seventeen years without a mother still hadn't erased the longing Evelyn felt whenever people asked. "My mother died when I was five years old. But she'd been sick for a long time." The word *cancer* settled on her tongue, but she swallowed it back. The boy didn't need to know and probably wouldn't understand the whole ugly truth about her mother's condition.

Louis's brow furrowed. "Who takes care of you?"

The inquiry was said with so much seriousness that Evelyn didn't dare laugh. She chose not to say "myself," despite its being the truth. She'd been taking care of herself, more or less, since her father's death. But she recognized what Louis was really asking. Did she have any other family or was she all alone in the world? She cringed inwardly at the thought of having no one. "My grandparents are waiting for me back in America."

Her answer seemed to satisfy him.

"I'd better go," he said, wiping the crumbs from his mouth with his sleeve.

Evelyn stood. "So should I. Do you live close by?"

He pointed south. "La Troumont." Evelyn recognized the name of the nearby village. "*Au revoir*, Nurse Gray."

"*Au revoir*, Louis. I hope to see you again soon."

He grinned, then spun around and darted into the trees.

\* \* \*

When he disappeared from view, Evelyn retraced her steps to the rear entrance of the hospital. It wouldn't do to be late to her assigned ward, especially if Sister Marcelle chose today to make her inspection.

Evelyn passed through the empty dining hall. The sounds of her footsteps echoing off the high walls and marbled floors accompanied her as she moved toward the opposite end. The room that now housed long tables and benches for meals had once been a ballroom.

She liked to fancy herself in a silk dress and Ralph in his Army uniform waltzing around the ornate room, her cheek to his stubbled one, his hand firm against her back. He'd murmur funny or complimentary endearments in her ear as he had when they'd danced on leave two months before. The memories made her shiver with yearning and anticipation. Perhaps after the wedding, they could find a place to honeymoon for a few days so they could dance or explore again.

Smiling at the thought, Evelyn climbed the stairs to the wards on the second floor. The stone walls of the old château kept the place from being completely miserable now that it was the middle of summer, but she still felt the air growing warmer as she ascended. At the top, she smoothed her apron. She tried to recall from her days assisting her father how early a woman's belly began expanding when she was pregnant. Four months? Five? Hopefully Ralph would be the first in his regiment to get leave, so she wouldn't be showing too much by the time he came for her.

"There you are, Nurse Gray." Sister Henriette met Evelyn outside the door of her assigned ward. The woman's face glimmered with sweat beneath her wide, white headdress. It reminded Evelyn of the sailboats she'd seen as a child on Lake Michigan.

"I'm sorry I'm late, Sister. I had a quick errand to do first."

Sister Henriette waved away her apology. "Sister Marcelle wishes to speak with you."

"With me?" Something akin to panic wormed its way up Evelyn's spine and, with it, a new wave of sickness. She hadn't committed any infractions since transferring to St. Vincent's six weeks ago. Did that mean Sister Marcelle, the hospital administrator, had discovered her secret?

"You're not in trouble, child. She only wishes to ask you about a change in assignment."

Relief made her shoulders droop and relaxed her tight jaw. Evelyn dipped her head in acknowledgment. A new assignment she could handle, though it did seem odd Sister Marcelle wouldn't simply ask Sister Henriette to pass on the information.

"She is waiting in her office. Just report back to the ward when you are finished."

"Yes, ma'am."

She strode down the hallway with new confidence, passing the open doors of the other wards on both sides. The murmur of voices and occasional laughter floated out to her. After climbing another set of stairs, Evelyn paused outside the worn wooden door of Sister Marcelle's tiny office. She knocked once and an alto voice called out, "You may enter."

After stepping inside, Evelyn stood before Sister Marcelle's large desk. Stacks of papers and ledgers stood in neat piles on one side. The only other furniture in the room was two wooden chairs, one occupied by Sister Marcelle. A large crucifix hung on the wall behind the sister. Just as Evelyn had on her first visit to this office, she avoided looking directly at the cross.

"Ah, Nurse Gray. Thank you for coming." The sister's blue-gray eyes, the same color as the dress she wore, shone bright with kindness. Unlike the other sisters, she spoke with nearly no trace of a French accent.

"Sister Henriette said you wished to see me."

"Yes." Sister Marcelle motioned to the chair opposite the desk. "Please have a seat."

Evelyn perched on the edge of the chair.

Sister Marcelle folded her hands on top of the desk. "As I am sure you are aware, Sister Pauline is in charge of Sister Henriette's wards at night. However, as the oldest sister here at St. Vincent's, she is finding it more and more difficult to manage the irregular sleep schedule. And we certainly cannot fault her." The sister's lips curved into a smile, increasing the laugh lines around her mouth. "I think she has finally concluded she is no longer as young as she was when she came here at twenty-five."

Evelyn smiled back. She'd heard from some of the other nurses that Sister Pauline mostly slept during the night shift. But she couldn't blame the older woman for dozing. Lately Evelyn could hardly keep her own eyelids from closing at the end of a day shift.

"Sister Monique will be taking Sister Pauline's place, but her sister is ill and she has asked for time away from the hospital to tend to her. In the meantime..." Sister Marcelle leaned forward, her gaze intent on Evelyn's face. "I would like to propose that you supervise Sister Henriette's wards during the night shift. The other ward nurses will report to you, and you will have access to the books and keys. It should only be a few weeks at most, until Sister Monique returns."

Evelyn's eyes widened with surprise. The sisters were in charge of all the wards in the hospital, while Evelyn and the other girls from the Army Nurse Corps served as ward nurses. The extra responsibility showed Sister Marcelle's trust and confidence in her. But would she be able to perform her best? Especially when her pregnancy sapped her stamina? She'd actually been grateful her turn for the night shift hadn't come up yet.

These were concerns she didn't dare voice, though.

"I'd be happy to help, Sister Marcelle." Her voice carried more assurance than she felt.

Sister Marcelle's ready smile appeared again. "Thank you. Sister Henriette praises your meticulous work. You have undoubtedly proven to be a great role model for all of our nurses."

Evelyn blushed, feeling less than worthy of the sister's last compliment. She trained her eyes on her lap. What would Sister Marcelle say if she knew Evelyn had broken the rules to be with Ralph, and now carried his child?

"I will need you to be especially diligent about not overusing supplies." Sister Marcelle's admonition interrupted Evelyn's troubled thoughts. She lifted her chin and gave a determined nod. No matter what physical discomforts she had to endure with this new assignment, she would do it. Anything to keep her secret safe until she and Ralph married. "We will need to use pain medications sparely at night. If you will see that the other nurses adhere to this."

"I will."

Sister Marcelle studied her for a moment, causing Evelyn to shift on the hard chair. What did the sister see? Could she read Evelyn's secret in the tense line of her shoulders or the exhausted furrows on her once smooth face?

"Do you enjoy nursing, Nurse Gray?"

The question surprised Evelyn almost as much as the new assignment. No one had ever asked her if she enjoyed what she did. "It's the same line of work as my father, when he was alive. My grandparents were very proud of him. Naturally they hoped their only grandchild would follow in his footsteps." The explanation sounded weak, even to herself. Of course she enjoyed nursing. Didn't she? If not, why had she worked so hard, for so long, at her grandparents' expense no less, to be right here. "I—I do enjoy helping others, if that's what you mean."

Her expression thoughtful, Sister Marcelle sat back. "And we appreciate your help, I assure you—"

The splatter of raindrops drummed the window behind her, but that didn't seem to be the sound that made Sister Marcelle twist in her chair. Evelyn heard it, too—the distant rumble of automobiles.

"It appears we have our next round of patients." The sister released a quiet sigh as she stood and crossed to the window. Evelyn joined her. Through the rain-splotched panes she could see the line of ambulances making their way up the curved gravel driveway.

"More than usual," Evelyn murmured as much to herself as to the sister beside her.

Sister Marcelle's face had grown somber. For the first time, Evelyn noticed the weary lines around the older woman's eyes. "We do what we can." But she seemed to leave the sentence hanging at the end, like a question. The hesitation lasted only a moment, but in those few seconds, Evelyn caught a glimpse of the burden Sister Marcelle carried as director of the entire hospital.

Clearing her throat, the sister straightened to her full height, a few inches taller than Evelyn. A tight smile pulled at her mouth. "You may return to your assigned ward for today, Nurse Gray. Can you start the night shift tomorrow evening?"

"Yes, ma'am." Unsure whether to show the religious woman deference by curtseying or not, Evelyn settled for a quick nod and let herself out the door. She hurried down the stairs to the wards. With each step, the cacophony of sound from below grew louder.

Evelyn emerged onto the second floor into a world boiling over with movement and noise. Nurses rushed in and out of the wards on the heels of the ambulance drivers, bearing mud-splattered stretchers between them, or assisted those of the wounded who could walk. The clatter of boots, the urgent commands, the scent of unwashed bodies all bounced off the stone walls and mixed together, creating a giant cauldron of sound and smell.

When she'd first come to France, the organized confusion had been overwhelming. Evelyn was used to working in a hospital where patients trickled in, not fell upon the place en masse as they often did here. Now she found the chaos almost comforting, the adrenaline a boon to her depleted energy. Her father used to say that adrenaline was the only thing that got him through those first agonizing minutes when he had to accurately and quickly assess an emergency situation and take action.

Elbowing her way through the crowded hallway, Evelyn reached her assigned ward. A quick glance told her what needed to be done in preparation for the new arrivals. Two of the empty beds had been refitted with clean sheets, but the third stood bare.

Evelyn grabbed up the remaining sheet and blankets and hurried to the bed in the far corner. The energy throbbing through her replaced any lingering sense of nausea as she heard Sister Henriette call loudly, "Bring those three in here."

She finished with the bed and pulled back the blankets at the same moment two of the ambulance drivers approached. The man on their stretcher had his eyes shut tight, his body shivering uncontrollably. His rain-dampened hair was coffee-colored, though the lighter scruff along his jaw and chin were evidence his hair wasn't that dark when dry. He had a nice-looking, unmarred face, but it was the dried blood on the lower half of his wool uniform and the loose bandage around his leg that drew Evelyn's attention.

Most of the men in her assigned ward had injuries of the pelvis, thighs, or legs. At first glance, she suspected the soldier had shrapnel wounds in his right leg, while the sling on his left arm meant a fracture or break.

She moved out of the way to allow the men to place the soldier on top of the bed. Once they rushed off, she took their place at his side.

"Hey there, soldier," she said in a soft voice. "Let's get you warm, all right?"

She unpinned the medical card from his jacket and drew the blankets up over his shaking form. As she waited for his shivering to subside, she read through his card. Sure enough, the scrawled notes indicated a broken left arm and shrapnel in his right thigh as well as damage to his pelvic area.

"I'm going to get you some water, okay?"

Though his eyes remained closed, he dipped his chin slightly, an indication he'd heard her. She procured a glass of water from the pitcher on a nearby table and returned to the bed.

"I'll hold the glass," she instructed, "so all you need to do is sip." She lifted his head gently off the pillow with one hand and brought the cup to his cracked lips with the other. He took a long swallow.

"Thanks," he murmured, but he gritted his teeth as she carefully set his head back down.

"I know you're hurting, soldier. But we're going to get you into surgery as soon as we can. Most likely by tonight." At least she hoped. There would be others with much more immediate need for a surgeon, but she wanted him to know he wouldn't be forgotten. "In the meantime, I'm going to change that loose bandage for you."

From the supply closet, she removed a fresh bandage, a pair of scissors, and a bottle of iodine. When she returned to the man's bed, she pushed the blanket aside, just enough, to reach his leg. His eyelids flew open, revealing hazel eyes, and a flush of embarrassment crept up his face as she bent to cut away the old bandage.

"Tell me where you're from, soldier." If she could get him talking, she knew it would help ease the discomfort and pain of having his injury rebandaged.

"Iowa."

"Did you grow up on a farm?" So many of the dough-boys she'd nursed here in France were sons of farmers.

"Yes."

Evelyn lifted her head to shoot him a smile. "Me, too. I'm from Michigan." Once she had the soiled bandage off, she applied some of the iodine. She'd grown used to the acute smell, though it seemed much stronger now that she was pregnant. The man flinched as the chemical met his torn flesh.

"So your name is…" She glanced at his medical card, which she'd set on the bedside table. "Corporal Joel Campbell."

*Campbell?* She read it through again as a snatch of conversation with Ralph repeated in her mind. He'd been talking about his squad leader and best friend whom he simply called "Campbell."

"Which regiment are you in, Corporal?"

He murmured the number. It was the same as Ralph's. A flicker of eagerness and concern darted through Evelyn. Campbell was a common enough last name, but what if this was the man Ralph had spoken of with respect and familiarity? The possibility sent her hope rising, until another thought jerked it down. If this was *the* Campbell, then Ralph would have been in the same battle.

The worry flared to fear inside her. Was Ralph safe or not? There could easily be a number of men with the name *Campbell* in their regiment. *But if these two men were in the same company…*

"What company are you in?" She did her best to keep the dread from her voice as she wrapped his leg with the fresh bandage.

"Company F," Corporal Campbell replied in a tight whisper.

His answer stilled her fingers. He and Ralph belonged

to the same company—this had to be his squad leader. Was Ralph here, too, or had he escaped injury? She shot a look across the room to the door. Could he be in another ward of the hospital right now? Evelyn's heart beat faster at the notion. If only she could see his handsome face and kiss those masculine lips. Assure herself that he was alive and well.

Her gaze refocused on the man lying before her. She no longer had any doubt that Corporal Campbell knew Ralph. Which meant he alone could grant her peace or confirm her worst fears that Ralph had been injured, too.

She directed her next question toward the bed to appear as nonchalant as possible. "Do you by chance know Private First Class Ralph Kelley?"

Silence from the bed sounded louder in her ears than the continuing racket in the room and hallway. She finished with his bandage and lifted her head to find Corporal Campbell staring at her. Astonishment had replaced the weariness on his haggard face.

"Are you all right, Corporal?"

Instead of answering, he countered with a question of his own. "Are you . . . Evelyn?"

A soft gasp escaped her lips before she could check herself. "Yes."

The man not only knew Ralph, but knew her name, too. She picked up the iodine and scissors and gripped them hard within her fingers. Anything to occupy her trembling hands. A maelstrom of nausea had begun churning in her stomach, making her regret what little she'd eaten at lunch.

"H-How do you know my name?"

His hazel eyes remained fixed on hers. "Because Ralph said it several times today."

He'd spoken with the man she loved, this very day. Fresh panic and wild optimism pulsed through her veins. She searched his face for any glimpse or clue of where Ralph might be.

"And?" The single word from her lips was no more than a whisper.

Corporal Campbell broke eye contact first, releasing the turmoil inside her. The torrent of emotion engulfed her body, choking her throat and filling her ears with a dull roar. Evelyn had to lean forward to hear his softly spoken reply.

"He said your name, Evelyn, right before he died."

# Chapter 2

Bright light pressed against Joel's eyelids. He sensed a bed underneath him and not the rickety cot he'd lain in at the field hospital. His clothes felt different, too, their material softer than his Army uniform. He squeezed his eyes shut tighter, trying to recall the last thing he remembered before sleep had claimed him. The motion, though small, intensified the pain radiating from his arm and leg.

He pried his eyes open, hoping for answers, and blinked as sunshine from across the room momentarily blinded him. *Where am I?*

Confused, he attempted to raise himself off the bed, but his left arm had been tucked inside a sling and was nearly useless. He managed only an inch or two before his body protested the slight movement and he collapsed, his jaw clenched.

Memories crashed over him at the same time the noise in the hospital room registered in his foggy brain—the ravine full of Germans, waiting to ambush his squad, the pain from his injuries, the jostling ride on the stretcher, his best friend's dying words.

*Evelyn.*

He'd only heard the name for the first time yesterday, though Ralph had talked quite a bit about the nurse he'd met on leave. Today, though, the name conjured up a pair of vivid dark eyes. Eyes that had filled with anguish when he'd told Evelyn the news of Ralph's death. The raw pain in her expression, and the guilt he felt at being its cause, had temporarily numbed the agony of his physical injuries almost as well as the ether they'd given him before his surgery.

"I see you've woken up, Corporal. I'm Nurse Thornton." A petite, red-headed nurse approached his bed. "How are you feeling?"

"I'll like things better when I'm back with my squad."

She gave an amused sniff as she popped a thermometer into his mouth. "Can't say I haven't heard that one before. But you're better off accepting the fact you're here to stay. At least until you can walk and use that arm again."

The second she removed the thermometer, he plied her with the question foremost on his mind. "I will be going back, right?" He didn't like the idea of being sent home early, not when he felt certain he still had the strength to lead his men, serve his country, and help end the war.

"I don't see why not," the nurse said as she jotted down his temperature in a ledger.

"When will that be?"

Nurse Thornton shrugged, snapping the ledger shut. "Depends on how compliant you are with instructions. If you take it easy, you'll probably move onto the convales-

cent home in three to five weeks. If you insist on getting
out of bed before you're ready, then longer."

He could be compliant, even if it meant forcing himself to stay in bed. Whatever it took to be out of here
faster. The sooner he left the hospital and the convalescent home, the better. He'd help finish the war, return
home, and hope there was at least one unattached girl left
in the county by then. Before long he'd have a farm and a
family of his own—a home as bustling and full as the one
he'd grown up in.

That promise, that hope, coupled with his faith in God,
had often been the only thing to keep him slogging
through another day in a foul-smelling, rat-infested
trench. Kept him running full out toward a wall of smoke
and shellfire during a battle. Kept him encouraging his
men, even as their friends were cut down around them.

What would keep Evelyn going, after the bomb he'd
dropped into her life yesterday? She'd stumbled away
from his bed toward the bathroom, he guessed, her face
pale in color, one hand clapped over her mouth. He hadn't
seen her since.

"Do you know what happened to the nurse who helped
me yesterday?" He didn't know Evelyn's last name, but
he wouldn't risk giving her first name and appearing too
familiar with her. The last thing she needed, after learning
about Ralph, was for Joel to get her in trouble.

"You mean Nurse Gray?" Nurse Thornton shot him
a suspicious glance as she whipped back his blankets.
"Why do you want to know?"

Joel refused to regret the question. After all, it was an
innocent one—he only wanted to learn if Evelyn was all
right. Sure she was pretty—very pretty—with her black

hair and red lips, but he wasn't planning on making any kind of overture toward her. First, she was his best friend's girl, even if Ralph was gone. Second, he was in full agreement with the rules about soldiers and nurses.

"She left in a hurry, like she might be sick." He leveled the nurse with his own direct look, one he'd used on his men before. "I just wanted to know if she was feeling better. And…" He searched his brain for something else. "To thank her."

Nurse Thornton removed his bandage, her wary expression fading. "Nurse Gray is fine. She's on night duty this evening, so she's resting now. You can thank her tonight."

Once she'd finished examining his leg, she left his bedside, only to return with a jar of some sort and an assortment of red tubes.

"What's this?" Joel asked.

He hated how little he knew about the workings of a hospital. As squad leader, he was briefed on his squad's responsibilities before a battle, and while the outcome was never certain, he knew exactly what was required of him and his men.

"We're going to irrigate your wounds with sodium hypochlorite, or Dakin's solution. This jar hangs above your bed and the solution runs down through the holes in the tubes." Nurse Thornton began to set up the irrigation elements. "You married, Corporal?" Her no-nonsense tone confirmed she wasn't flirting, merely making conversation.

"No, not yet."

"Got a special girl waiting for you? Someone who ought to know you're here at the hospital?"

Unbidden, Rose's pretty face and soft smile loomed in his mind's eye. She could've been at home waiting for him, but things hadn't worked out as he'd planned.

"No." The word came out harsher than he'd intended. "Just my family," he amended.

She nodded, oblivious to the memories she'd conjured up with her inquiry.

"Can you tell me how my surgery went?"

While he was no doctor, from the brief look he'd gotten at his leg yesterday, Joel felt confident the limb would heal. Which meant, God willing, he'd still be able to run as much as he wanted and work the land on his future farm.

Nurse Thornton moved to the bedside table to pick up her ledger book. "Says here they successfully removed the shrapnel from your leg and set your arm."

Optimism rushed through him, making him almost dizzy with relief. "Does that mean I get to cut down a week or two in this place?"

She rolled her eyes, but the corners of her mouth quirked up. "We've got to make sure your injuries don't get infected. Especially the one in your pelvic region. That's why we're irrigating all your open wounds."

Joel opened his mouth to ask her what she meant about his pelvis, then thought better of it. Discussing it with the surgeon, if he got the chance, would be far less humiliating than asking the details from Nurse Thornton. Whatever the issue, he couldn't imagine it would prevent him from leaving as soon as he could walk. He was in pain, yes, but he was alive.

Unlike his brother Tom... and Ralph.

He fisted his hand, choking the blanket within his grip.

The grief he felt at losing his two greatest friends would drag him down to a place of unyielding despair if he let it. Then he would never leave this bed, never return to his men, never move on with the life he'd been granted. He had to resist this soul-tearing sorrow, and the accompanying guilt at not preventing Ralph's death. It would destroy him from the inside out if he didn't.

*Stick to the plan*, he reminded himself. Get better, get out, finish fighting, and go home. Somewhere, sometime, he'd likely have to mourn, but for now, he would focus on returning to the front as soon as he could. Things wouldn't be the same without Ralph around as his right-hand man, but he'd make it through. He had to.

"Are *you* married?" he asked Nurse Thornton, anxious to occupy his mind with something else. When she paused in her work to throw him a frown, he hurried to add, "Just making conversation."

"No, Corporal. I'm not married. And like you, no special person waiting either." She checked the tubes as she spoke. "I've got three brothers in this war already. Don't see a need to be worrying about another boy gettin' hurt." She folded her arms and stared him down. "That's all the information you're going to weasel out of me today. Anything else I can get you? Something for the pain perhaps?"

He almost agreed. After all, his lower body felt as if someone had stuck several pitchforks into it and forgotten to pull them back out. But he hated the mind-numbing fog the medicine created, the inability to know what was going on around him or to him.

"No, thanks. But I'd take my personal effects."

"Sorry, Corporal. I'm not trekking all the way downstairs for one bag. I'll bring it up when we serve lunch in about an hour."

He wouldn't last an hour—not without something to drive away the painful awareness of his injuries or the memories. With a little effort, he shot her the smile his mother used to say could coax the tail off a fox. "Please?"

Nurse Thornton shook her head, but she was smiling. "Oh, all right. I'll locate your bag."

"Thank you."

While he waited, Joel let his gaze stray to the other occupants in the ward. Most slept or read. Two men across the room were playing checkers. One soldier near the opposite corner had both legs and an arm suspended by pulleys. Even from a distance, Joel could see his bleak expression.

Joel's own injuries might not be as severe or permanent, but he could understand that look. He'd seen that same hopelessness on the faces of others, had even felt it on his own the day he received word of Tom's death and again right after Ralph died. There likely wasn't a man here who hadn't felt the same way at least once.

They would return home different, too, regardless of the variety of their physical wounds. Not one of them, including himself, was the same person who'd eagerly enlisted. The war had damaged more than their bodies; it had tampered with the very fibers of their souls. Every one of them would carry home internal scars. Ones Joel could only hope and pray would ease with time and the help of God.

"Here's your bag, Corporal Campbell." Nurse Thornton set it gently next to him on the bed. "I'll bring you some broth for lunch."

*Broth for lunch?* Joel frowned in disgust. How was a man supposed to get stronger on something so thin and tasteless? Was Nurse Thornton punishing him for persuading her to get his bag or did they serve the same drivel to all the men?

"Sounds delicious," he said with a grimace.

She sniffed in amusement and left him to rummage through his bag.

He removed the photograph of his family first. The picture had been taken the day before he and Tom had left for the Army. His parents sat on chairs in the middle of the group, holding hands. The younger kids were gathered around them: Allen, Mary, Charlie, and little George. Behind them Joel and Tom stood with Livy between them. The three of them formed their own little cluster, just as they'd done as kids.

Joel studied Tom's eyes. They were lit as if he was laughing at some private joke, which he probably was. He and Tom couldn't have been more different. He liked to plan, to analyze; Tom liked to dive into a situation with no forethought, to sniff out adventure in the unlikeliest places. But he was loyal, too, and kind to a fault. Being a soldier hadn't been so bad when Joel remembered his younger brother was doing the same thing.

A lump of emotion lodged itself in his throat. He'd never expected his brother to precede him in death, not even in war. The dark-haired kid with the cockeyed grin had always been around, at least in Joel's memory. He'd imagined the two of them growing into old men together, still arguing over stupid things but loving each other just the same.

He coughed to dislodge the strangling ache and pinned

his focus on Livy's face next. His little sis was twenty years old, five years his junior, and married now. She'd written a while back to tell him she had fallen in love with a farmer—a German-American one—after she'd taken a teaching job away from home. The wedding had been planned for the beginning of the month.

Her news had taken him by complete surprise, especially given the rumors he'd heard about anti-German tension escalating back home. Any concern he felt at her marrying a German-American, though, faded completely by the time he'd finished reading Livy's letter. His sister's happiness was evident in every word. As her oldest brother, and occasional confidant through the years, he'd hoped Livy would find a man she could trust, a man who would treat her with the utmost respect. And clearly, she had.

He had written back as soon as he could, giving the approval he sensed she wanted about her decision. If his parents—and more important, God—believed she would be safe and happy with this man Joel had never met, he could trust that. His only regret was not being able to toast the happy couple at the wedding or to see his sister's radiant face.

Ready to move on from thoughts of home, Joel placed the photo back inside his bag and dragged out his Army-issued Bible. A mud stain, which he hadn't been able to wipe off completely, covered one corner, and a piece of shrapnel had nicked the top of the spine, but the pages were still readable.

He flipped the Bible open to one of his favorite stories—Moses leading the children of Israel out of Egypt and through the Red Sea. The danger racing toward them, the trust in God to move ahead, reminded him a lot of his life as a soldier here in France. Would he have had the courage and the faith to walk onto the sea bed, while walls of water towered overhead? Joel hoped so.

He was well beyond the Red Sea crossing by the time Nurse Thornton brought him the promised broth. It was every bit as bland and unfulfilling as Joel had imagined, but he slurped it all. Anything to get better.

When he'd finished, he carefully set aside his empty bowl and eyed his Bible. Exhaustion—and pain—warred within him. Should he sleep or read more? Which would distract him from the ache of his injuries? Before he could decide, a tall man with a black mustache and glasses approached his bed. Joel recognized his face— he'd seen it right before the nurse had administered the ether to him in the surgery ward.

"Corporal, it's good to see you awake." The man spoke with a heavy French accent. "I am Dr. Dupont. We met last night."

"Yes. Over the operating table. Not the most ideal meeting place."

The doctor shot him a grim smile. "How are your arm and leg today?"

The hurt might be intense, but Joel wouldn't complain. "All right. At least they'll heal."

A flicker of sorrow passed over the doctor's face as he removed his glasses and wiped them with a corner of his lab coat. "I believe we extracted most, if not all, of the shrapnel within your leg wound." He replaced his glasses onto his nose. "It should not encumber you in any way, once you have regained your mobility."

Joel gave a hesitant nod. Things were going as well as he'd hoped. Then why the unsettled feeling in his gut?

"Your arm should also be as good as new," Dr. Dupont said, "in a short time." He glanced at Joel, then away, his Adam's apple bobbing as he swallowed hard. "There is something else I must discuss with you, though. I shall bring over a chair."

The grave look in the man's black eyes turned the warm broth in Joel's stomach to ice and set warning bells ringing through his head. His jaw and shoulders tensed with apprehension as he waited for the man to carry over a chair and sit down.

"As I am sure you are aware, the blast that injured your leg also did damage to your pelvic area." Dr. Dupont leaned forward, his elbows resting on his knees. "This was noted on your medical card, but the field medics did not know the extent."

It was Joel's turn to swallow hard. Why couldn't he get any moisture to his mouth? "What is the extent?"

The doctor released a heavy sigh and stared down at his open palms. "Are you married, Corporal Campbell?"

The question caught Joel off guard. "Um...no."

"No children then?"

He fought a surge of annoyance, reminding himself this man didn't know him. "No, sir. I'm going to find a special girl after the war, then start a family."

"Then the best way I can explain your condition is this." Dr. Dupont met his gaze straight on. "While you will be able to enjoy every physical aspect of married life, when you do take that step, you will not be able to father a child."

"I...don't understand." He'd heard the words, but their meaning seemed to be garbled in his head.

"You can have a normal physical relationship with

your wife, Corporal, but you will not be able to create a child."

Joel shook his head as the doctor's grave announcement at last registered. The man had to be wrong. Joel was going to be a father someday—that was part of his plan.

"I am sorry," Dr. Dupont said quietly.

Although he wanted to lash out at the man, reject the pity in his tone and eyes, Joel knew the prognosis wasn't the doctor's fault. "Thank you for telling me."

Dr. Dupont stood, but he hesitated, his hand on the back of the chair. "You can still lead a full life, Corporal. Things like this, whether of our own making or not, have a way of turning out for the better. If we allow God to work in our lives."

The speech, however kindly meant, only fueled the anger that was fast replacing Joel's initial shock. What did this doctor know of his plans? Plans that had been full of hope and promise not five minutes ago. Now his dream of marrying and having a family had been obliterated as easily as the men in his squad had been yesterday.

He gave Dr. Dupont a wooden nod in response, then watched with relief as the man walked away. Alone again, or as alone as he could manage in a room full of men, he tried his best to breathe through the crushing emotion pressing against his chest. Why would God deny him the one thing he wanted most in the world?

Another unpleasant thought marched forward, bringing the taste of bitter regret with it. If he'd married Rose, then none of this would matter. Even if they'd only been able to have one child before he left to fight, he would've still been a father.

Resentment burned like hot ash inside him. He set the Bible on the bedside table, ignoring the pain the small action incited in his already battered body. He couldn't read anymore. His faith felt as fragile at that moment as the Israelites' he'd been reading about. For the first time in his life, he thought he understood the cost of leaving Egypt for the unknown.

Closing his eyes, Joel tried to close his mind against the questions and doubts swirling there, but he was as powerless to stop them as he was a German tank. Had he misunderstood his own heart when it came to Rose? Had he really been acting in a way God wanted when he'd ended things between them?

Instead of answers, he felt only pain and shock and gut-wrenching remorse.

\* \* \*

With one hand splayed against the beech tree beside her, Evelyn shakily drew her other hand across her mouth. The taste of bile still stung her tongue. She needed a drink of water, and then she wanted to crawl beneath her blanket and never emerge.

Since the news of Ralph's death yesterday afternoon, she hadn't been able to settle her stomach. Knots of panic, combined with her pregnancy sickness, made it nearly impossible to eat. Or keep anything down.

"Evelyn?" she heard Alice call. "Is that you?"

She stepped out from behind the tree, leaving the evidence of her now empty stomach hidden in the grass. "Yes."

Alice gave her a quizzical look. "What were you doing?"

"Just enjoying the quiet of the forest." She pasted on a weak smile. "Did you need something?"

"No. I was just headed to bed. Sergeant Dennis is wearing me out." She shook her head in annoyance. "Today he kept asking me silly questions while I tended to him. Like what my favorite flower is or my favorite book. I tell you..."

Alice's words faded into the background of Evelyn's thoughts. If only Ralph were around to complain about. *He never picks up his socks* or *he can't ever remember our anniversary*. These were things she would never know about him or confide with amusement to other women.

"You look a little pale, Evelyn." Alice stepped closer and peered into her face. "Are you sure you're up to doing night duty? I could take your shift, if you're not feeling well."

"I'm fine."

She prided herself on how even and firm her tone sounded, despite knowing she would never be completely well again. A hole, as deadly and painful as a bullet wound, had torn through her heart. The man she loved was dead, the man who had made her happier than she'd been in years. And now her unborn child would never know his father.

What would she say in answer to her child's questions? She'd known so little about Ralph's life before he'd joined the Army—all she'd cared about on leave was enjoying his company and basking in his adoration. How foolishly she'd believed there would be time later on for delving into all the details of their lives.

Instead time had turned into her enemy. Before long, everyone at the hospital would know her indiscretion.

*Perhaps I ought to request a discharge now, before the pregnancy's discovered.* The idea relieved some of the pressure in her abdomen until she thought of facing her grandparents. She feared their weakening health would never recover from a homecoming like that.

*I could lie—tell Grandma and Grandpa I was married for a short time before Ralph was killed and I was discharged.*

She dismissed the notion at once. Having committed one mistake, she wouldn't add being untruthful on top of it. She'd simply have to hide her pregnancy for as long as possible. Being taller than most girls, she might be able to get away with it, especially with the loose fit of her uniform. In the meantime, she vowed to be the best nurse she could be.

After her secret was discovered, she would have to throw her future upon the sisters' mercy and pray her work as a competent nurse would pay off. Hopefully their need for help would mean a place for her to stay until she could no longer perform her duties.

"Evelyn?" Alice's voice broke through her mental scheming. "Are you sure you're okay?"

She straightened her shoulders. She would do everything asked of her, and do it well—being pregnant wouldn't interfere with her ability to be a good nurse. "Yes. I can take my shift."

"All right. Good night, then. Good luck."

"Good night, Alice." She waved good-bye to her roommate, reminding herself that at some point she needed to counsel Alice about keeping her distance from the sergeant. While Alice clearly didn't welcome the man's attentions at present, things could change faster than anyone expected. Evelyn herself was living proof of that.

The sky in the distance had darkened to dusk as she made her way across the grass to the hospital. She'd rested the greater part of the day in preparation for the hours she'd be awake that night, but she'd been unable to sleep. She kept hearing Corporal Campbell's voice in her head about Ralph saying her name—*right before he died*. Images of the mangled soldiers she'd assisted marched through her mind, each one bearing Ralph's lifeless face.

She'd considered asking the corporal for details about Ralph's death, then skittered away from the impulse like a child from the shadows. She hated the idea of Ralph suffering. Witnessing the final moments of several soldiers had left haunting images of agony burned into her mind. No, she wanted to believe he'd died instantly or had slipped painlessly away sometime later.

Evelyn rinsed her mouth of its sour taste, then collected the keys and ledger book from Sister Marcelle. She had two wards to inspect. But which one should she begin in? Not Corporal Campbell's. She couldn't face him yet—not after rushing off to vomit in the bathroom yesterday—and not when she suspected he knew more about her and Ralph than he'd let on.

She'd start in the abdomen ward. After all, these men were typically in the most critical of conditions. There was often little to be done to help them, beyond time.

Most of the soldiers in the dimly lit room were attempting to sleep, bringing a hush to the air. While the two nurses on duty performed routine checks and recorded temperatures in the ledger, Evelyn saw to those patients in greatest need. Afterward she claimed the small table in the hallway to add her own notes to the book.

Once the ledger was up to date, she had nothing left to do but check in on Corporal Campbell's ward. Evelyn pushed back her chair, the nerves clogging her stomach again. How much had Ralph shared with Joel Campbell about their relationship? Did the corporal know about her pregnancy? The uncertainty weighted her footsteps as she entered the large room.

Only one other nurse was on duty, a brunette named Catherine Kent. Evelyn approached her as Nurse Kent finished placing a compress on a soldier's head.

"Where's Nurse Phelps?" Evelyn asked in a quiet voice.

Nurse Kent frowned. "She's not feeling well, coming down with a cold, I think. So it's only me. I'm glad you're here, Evelyn. I haven't finished looking after all the men."

"Which ones still need to be checked?"

Nurse Kent pointed to the patients at her right, which included Corporal Campbell. "Those in the ten beds there."

Evelyn stifled a groan. Of course her punishment for worrying about the man so much would be having to actually attend to him.

"I'll see to them." Evelyn hoped she sounded more cheerful than she felt.

She gathered supplies and found herself moving to the bed of the patient farthest from Corporal Campbell. Avoiding him was pure childishness—he wasn't likely to announce to everyone about her and Ralph, at least not yet. But she needed more time. His presence in the corner reminded her of more than Ralph's death; her future happiness as Ralph's wife had also died the moment she heard the corporal's news.

Squaring her shoulders, she redressed bandages, took temperatures, filled jars of Dakin's solution for those hooked to the irrigation tubes, and rearranged blankets. But the routine tasks couldn't keep her mind occupied.

Had Corporal Campbell seen her? She forced herself not to glance in his direction to find out. What would she say to him? Should she ask what Ralph had told him about her? Or pretend their conversation yesterday had never happened? Undecided, she finished with the five patients on one side of the room and moved at an angle to assist the other four, keeping Corporal Campbell for last. With any luck, he'd be asleep by the time she found herself beside his bed again and she wouldn't have to talk or answer any troubling questions.

At last there were no other patients to attend to but him. Evelyn drew in a long breath and turned toward his bed. Her pulse beat harder at her neck when she discovered his eyes were open. Upon closer inspection, though, she realized he wasn't watching her. His focus was trained on the window across the room, a grim look on his face. What anguish kept him from sleeping like so many of the other men in the ward? Was it Ralph? she wondered.

Her resolve to avoid conversation crumbled in the wake of his misery. Talking would surely help him, and as a competent nurse, she would do what she should to help, even at a cost to herself.

"Can't sleep?" she asked in a half whisper as she stepped to his bed.

He blinked, then looked up. Recognition flooded his eyes as he shook his head. "No. I guess not."

Evelyn slipped her thermometer from her pocket. "Do you want some medication for the pain? I can't give you much, since we're low on supplies, but it might make things more bearable."

"It's not my injuries." His tone was flat, lifeless.

She studied his face in the faint light of the ward. Despondency cut furrows across the otherwise handsome features. Had he received more bad news? Or was the death of one of his closest friends only now sinking in? A small tremor of remorse shook her as she realized she wasn't the only one who'd lost someone yesterday.

A sudden urge to smooth out his creased brow made her lift her hand, only to discover she was still gripping the thermometer. Heat rushed into her cheeks as she hurried to pop the instrument into his mouth.

"Let's take that temperature of yours," she said cheerfully. Too cheerfully.

As his lips obediently pressed over the thermometer, the corporal met her eyes for a brief moment. But it was long enough for Evelyn to read the intense sorrow and regret reflected there. The need to comfort, and be comforted, rushed up like a geyser inside her. If she could just hold his hand, she felt certain they could keep each other from drowning.

Her gaze dropped to his right hand, where his large fingers lay splayed against his chest. Would he find her action forward or understand the driving need to share in his grief?

Before she changed her mind, she reached out and placed her hand lightly over his. An electric sensation jolted through her. Startled, Evelyn started to withdraw her hand, but Corporal Campbell captured it beneath his and held fast. She glanced at his face, but he wasn't looking at her.

The tender touch and rapid thumping of his heartbeat through his hand to hers loosened the emotion clogging her chest and throat. Tears pricked at her eyes. She had no one else with whom she could mourn—no one else who had known Ralph or even about him. And so as much as she knew she ought to move away, Evelyn remained at the corporal's side, motionless, her eyes focused on their hands, one atop the other.

Too soon, the squeak of a bedspring from behind broke the trance that held her bound. Evelyn pulled her hand away to remove the thermometer from the corporal's mouth. The poor man had obediently kept it in.

"Your temperature is higher tonight." Her voice wobbled a bit, adding to the embarrassment she already felt.

*You're the nurse, Evelyn*, she scolded herself. *Not a mourning widow, so to speak.* "Would you like me to remove your blanket?"

"I'm fine."

The note of desperation no longer rang in his voice, but Evelyn knew he was far from fine. She'd told Alice the same lie earlier. Was there something else she could do for him?

His stubble from the day before had become a light-colored beard, giving her an idea. "Would you like a shave?"

He arched his eyebrows. "A shave? Now?"

Evelyn nodded, warming to the idea. "It might help you sleep better."

A whisper of a smile flitted across his mouth, but it was there nonetheless. "Is that the alternative to pain medication? A shave at midnight?"

Her own lips curved in response. "It could be. Though you should know, the nurses on the day shift are often more pinched for time, so it's a thorough job tonight or a quick one tomorrow."

Corporal Campbell rubbed his hand over his jaw. "I could do it myself."

"Would you like to try?" She gave his broken arm a meaningful glance.

Again, she caught the faint lift of his mouth. "All right then. I suppose I'll surrender."

With surer steps than before, Evelyn crossed to the supply closet and unlocked the cupboard where the shaving razors and scissors were kept. There had been no attempts at suicide yet, but Sister Marcelle wasn't taking any chances. After locating some shaving soap on a lower shelf, Evelyn rummaged up a bowl of water and returned to the corporal's bedside.

"Have you ever done this before?" She could feel his eyes on her as she set up the supplies on the bedside table.

She threw him a mock look of disgust over her shoulder. "You insult my nursing education, Corporal."

"My apologies. No insult intended." A faint smirk escaped his mouth. "And please, call me Joel."

Should she? she wondered, working the soap and water into lather. He already knew her first name. Perhaps it wouldn't hurt, at least when she felt certain they weren't being overheard.

Once the lather was ready, Evelyn brought over a chair and set it next to his bed. Since he couldn't sit up himself, Joel would have to lean a bit in her direction, which she hoped wouldn't further aggravate his injuries. But her tired body protested any more standing. Besides, the chair ensured she wouldn't be committing a faux pas by perching on the edge of his bed.

Evelyn bent forward and applied the mixture liberally to Joel's face with her fingertips. His light brown hair and tan skin held little resemblance to Ralph's darker features and olive complexion. Joel's jaw and chin were more prominent, too. Touching him felt different as well, stirring both feelings of familiarity and disquiet deep within her. Perhaps her idea hadn't been such a wise one. What would Ralph think of her sharing such an intimate moment with his best friend?

She lowered her hand a few inches as guilt overcame her, but she couldn't quit now. Not with lather all over his cheeks. If she got him talking, about something other than their connection to Ralph, she might feel better. "Tell me how many siblings you have."

Joel waited while she smoothed the lather over his upper lip before answering. "I have two sisters and four brothers." He cleared his throat. "Well, three brothers now. Tom was killed here in France a few months back."

This time she let her hand fall to her lap. "I'm sorry." Had he been thinking about his brother earlier? "Were you close?"

"Yes." He seemed to find sudden fascination in his sling. "We fought like any normal brothers, but he was my best friend, too. You know how it is with siblings."

Longing swept through her as she pushed the razor through the water in the bowl. She'd always wanted a brother or a sister, and so she'd been determined to give her child what she couldn't have growing up. Another wish that had died with Ralph yesterday.

"Actually, I don't know. My mother died when I was a child, so I was raised largely by my grandparents. And my father, of course. But he was a busy country doctor."

"Is that where the nursing comes from?"

"Yes. I enjoyed accompanying him when I got older." She expertly shaved the right side of his face, until little lather remained.

Sister Marcelle's question from the day before repeated in Evelyn's mind: *Do you enjoy nursing?* Had she truly loved attending to the sick in the same way her father had, or had she simply craved time with her only living parent?

"Must've been awfully quiet."

The words stung all the more because they were true. "I didn't know any different," she defended.

"I would've liked some quiet now and again," he said when she lowered the razor. Could he tell he'd hurt her with his observation? "There was always a lot of noise, but that also meant there was always someone around to play with." His tone changed to one of regret as he added, "I always expected to have a large family myself one day."

*So did I.*

The talk of families brought her thoughts around to Ralph again. Evelyn glanced over her shoulder. Nurse Kent was occupied with another patient. How many more opportunities would she have alone with Joel during the night shift? Not many, once Nurse Phelps recovered from her cold.

Emboldened by necessity, she forced her next question off her tongue as she washed the lather from the razor. "How long did you know Ralph?"

She sensed Joel watching her. "Nearly as long as I've been a soldier. What about you? Are you the girl he met on leave?"

So Ralph *had* mentioned her, just as she'd suspected.

The realization made her heart pound harder. "Yes." She forced her hands to remain steady as she shaved the left side of his face.

When she'd finished, Joel spoke again, his voice low. "He didn't mention you by name until yesterday. But he talked about you a lot."

The grief rushed in again, so sharp it stole Evelyn's breath. If she didn't keep talking, though, she would dissolve into fresh tears. "I met Ralph before I transferred to St. Vincent's." She rinsed the razor again. "We were on leave in the same city."

"I didn't join him that time." A long pause, weighted with hesitation, preceded his next remark. "When we were on furlough the time before, he spent most of it playing the charmer to several of the local girls. It wasn't something I was comfortable with, so I opted to go somewhere else the second time."

Why tell her this now? Evelyn's stomach clenched with uncertainty. Could there have been other girls Ralph fancied? She shut her mind against the idea. Whatever Ralph's past mistakes, he hadn't charmed her, then abandoned her. She'd certainly been swept up by his magnetism, but he had promised to marry her once he knew about the baby. His words hadn't been idle promises either—of that, she felt certain.

She chose her next words with care as she wielded the razor around his upper lip and chin. "I only knew Ralph a short time, but..." What else could she say? That he'd meant everything to her? That perhaps she'd foolishly given her heart to him after only a few days—never expecting he would be unable to fulfill his promise to marry her? She guessed Joel already knew those things.

She hadn't realized she'd let the razor in her hand droop until Joel snagged her wrist in a gentle grip. "Ralph changed after that trip, Evelyn. You need to know that." His voice was barely audible but earnest. "So much so, that I said something. That's when he started talking about you."

The tiniest hope flickered inside her at Joel's story, though she feared it might prove too small to sustain the crushing weight of her grief. Was it possible some divine hand had sent Joel to St. Vincent's? She would never have known Ralph had died otherwise.

A large part of her balked at the thought. She'd gone against her grandparents' religious beliefs—and her own childhood faith—in becoming involved with Ralph. Surely that meant she'd been left to her own devices. She must hold to her new plan and the knowledge she'd bettered Ralph's life, not complicated it.

"I'm glad I knew him," she whispered, once she'd finished shaving Joel's face.

"I am, too," he said just as softly as she wiped away the remaining spots of lather. "He was an exceptional soldier and a loyal friend." He flicked his gaze to the window again, and some of his earlier grief returned to his clean-shaven face. "We used to talk about settling down near each other and raising our families together. But I guess that won't be happening now…for me or Ralph."

She wasn't sure what he meant, but before she could ask, a panicked voice from across the room pierced the quiet of the ward. "No. You can't take me. Leave me alone. My legs! I can't feel my legs."

Evelyn rushed to her feet, only to pause in indecision at leaving Joel alone to weather another cloud of despair.

"Go on," he urged with a wave at the other soldier.

"I'll be back." She hurried over to join Nurse Kent at the bedside of the terrified man. He strained against the pulleys that held one arm and both legs, his eyes shut tight. Evelyn spoke in soothing tones and wiped at his sweaty face with a dampened rag, while Nurse Kent administered a small dose of morphine. After a few minutes, the soldier calmed, and eventually he drifted back to sleep.

Evelyn brushed strands of her hair off her damp forehead and went to stand near one of the open windows. The stars hung low in the dark night sky and a breeze whistled around the old building and trees. The breath of wind helped cool her flushed cheeks and settle her rapidly beating heart. At least her conversation with Joel and the adrenaline of dealing with the other soldier's shell shock had kept her from feeling too sleepy.

Her empty stomach had begun to protest, though. Maybe she could slip down to the kitchen and bring back some coffee for herself and Nurse Kent. Right after she cleaned up the supplies from shaving Joel's face. She retraced her steps to his bedside and found him asleep.

*Looks like the shave worked its magic*, she mused.

After gathering up the shaving things and locking the razor back in the cupboard, she settled the chair in a corner and sat to record her notes in the ledger. She jotted down the other soldier's nightmare and the medicine he'd been given, then flipped idly through the book.

Remembering she hadn't made a note of Joel's temperature, she turned to the page with his name on it and wrote the information down. A description of his injuries, the same one she'd read on his medical card, was written at the top of the page. Underneath them, though, a few sentences had been added by the surgeon.

*Injury to pelvic region determined. Soldier will not be capable of fathering children, but is fully functional otherwise.*

Joel would never be a father? She glanced at his sleeping figure and a profound sadness settled over her, dark and heavy. Even in the short time she'd spent with him, she'd sensed that his desire for a large family ran every bit as deeply as her own. No wonder he'd been melancholy tonight. Like her, he wasn't just grieving the death of his friend, but the loss of his hopes and plans, too.

In light of what she'd discovered, Evelyn suddenly knew what Joel had meant by his odd remark about him and Ralph being unable to raise their families together. Joel wouldn't be having a family, large or small.

*What a pair we make.*

A harsh laugh threatened to scramble up her throat, but she hid it behind a half sigh, half sob. Her grief over losing Ralph swooped in to claim her captive all over again. She would eventually return to the quiet house in Michigan with her fatherless child, and Joel would return to his noisy one, this time without the anticipation of creating one of his own.

How she hated this war and its personal intrusion on her life and plans. Not only had it robbed her and Joel of their chance to have their own families, but it had left them to flounder in a wasteland of broken dreams, too. What could the future possibly hold for either of them now?

# Chapter 3

Morning, Corporal Campbell." Nurse Thornton approached Joel's bed.

He muttered "Good morning" in return, though it was anything but. The pain and stiffness from his injuries had made sleep less than satisfying for a second night in a row, and yet he was already itching to be out of bed. Once outside, he felt certain he'd be able to breathe easier, free his nose of the constant smell of iodine, illness, and soap.

"I have a letter for you."

Joel's mood lifted at that news. "Then I've changed my mind. It's a better morning than I thought."

Nurse Thornton smiled, but instead of handing over the letter, she set about checking his temperature and his wounds. Joel tried to hold still, but the fingers of his good hand drummed a steady beat against his wrinkled blanket.

"Impatient, are we?" Her tone was teasing.

He couldn't tell her he'd been dying for something to

read, something to occupy his mind. Being Sunday, he would've normally read his Bible, but Joel hadn't opened it since hearing the news from the surgeon. He didn't want to read about others' incredible faith or their lack thereof. Not yet, at least.

"Just anxious for news from home."

"Let me start the Dakin's solution through your tubes, and then you may have your letter."

Joel lay as still as he could, in hopes of helping Nurse Thornton move faster. As he watched her, his thoughts drifted to another nurse. Evelyn. His hand rose to rub the smooth skin of his jaw. She'd done an excellent job wielding the razor last night. And her efforts had given him a chance to observe her close up.

Those big, dark eyes of hers spoke volumes of pain, fatigue, loneliness, and compassion. But it was more than that. Something deep and powerful had swept through him when she'd touched his hand last night. Evelyn had felt it, too, judging from the way she'd started to pull back. In that brief moment of contact, the grief and guilt were no longer Joel's to bear alone. And so he'd stopped her from leaving by covering her hand with his own. Their moment of shared sorrow ended too soon, but it was long enough to pull Joel free of the darkness threatening to consume him from the inside out.

The tender touch of a woman as beautiful as Evelyn had also raised his temperature. Thankfully she hadn't been concerned with figuring out the reason for the difference. Regret sluiced through him as he realized how much he'd enjoyed her company last night, however brief. He couldn't forget she was Ralph's girl. The one Ralph loved, the one who loved him, the one who'd made

Joel's best friend into an even better man the last few months.

Would they have married, if Ralph had lived? The possibility brought a fresh wave of guilt and intensified the battle brewing inside him. He felt compelled to look out for Evelyn, to ensure her well-being, and yet doing so meant she might learn his part in Ralph's death. Chances were she'd never want to see or speak to him again after that.

Nurse Thornton finally finished, bringing momentary relief to Joel's inner war when she presented him with the promised letter. Joel tore it open at once. The letter was from his kid sister Mary. He hoped for current news from home, but apparently the letter had taken some time to reach him, judging by the six-week-old date in the top right corner. Still, any news of life back in Iowa was a godsend, especially now.

Mary had scrawled line after line about school letting out, about her latest trip into town with their mother, about Livy's fiancé and the wedding plans. Joel found himself smiling as he read; he could almost hear Mary's chattering, twelve-year-old voice relaying all the gossip. Then he reached the end.

> *I'm bored to tears without Georgiana here to do things with, but she's gone to help Rose and her brother-in-law with the new baby—a little girl. Wish I could be an aunt like her! Maybe Livy will have a baby right off and I can go help them.*

Rose had a daughter? The news cut as deep and painful as shrapnel, tightening Joel's chest and constricting his breath. *She could have been my daughter.* The realization stung with equal sharpness. If he'd married Rose, as he'd planned to for years, then his injury wouldn't matter. They could have had a child together, and he would have been a father.

What would he do now, after the war? Live at home, while the rest of his siblings grew up and left to have families of their own? Evelyn's account of her solitary childhood haunted his thoughts. He couldn't live like that, with just his parents. What would happen once they became old and passed away? He'd be left alone, in a big empty house. The very idea brought a cold, clammy feeling creeping over him.

That would never do. He'd have to hold out hope of finding a woman who loved him enough to marry him in spite of his injury. They would be the adored aunt and uncle to his siblings' children. The thought lightened the pressure in his chest, but only marginally.

As a kid, Joel hadn't given much thought to his future beyond knowing he wanted to work the land on his own farm someday. But that had changed the year he turned fourteen and Vivian Jensen, an unwed mother, and her son, Les, came to live with his family.

The rest of Joel's siblings soon tired of four-year-old Les's constant questions, so Joel stepped in to play the part of "big brother." Les became his little shadow, wanting to do everything he did. Joel taught him what he knew about birds, how to skip rocks, how to run faster without tiring, how to do the farm chores. He liked the precocious little kid and his ability to grasp things quickly.

Coming in from milking the cows one night, Joel overheard Vivian talking with his parents in the parlor. "Les has been so happy since we moved here. He's always talking about Joel. I hope the poor boy doesn't mind having Les as a constant tagalong."

There was light chuckling, then his father spoke up. "It's been good for Joel, too. He's growing up, learning what it takes to be a man, to be a father. He'll do a fine job at both."

The note of pride in Josiah Campbell's voice made Joel swallow hard against a sudden lump in his throat and puff his chest out a little farther as he crept past them up the stairs. That single snatch of conversation settled into his heart and shaped his thoughts of the future.

He would be the best farmer, father, and man he could be. A man as honored and respected by others as his own father. And someday, Joel would share that same measure of pride and love that Josiah had shown him with his own sons and daughters.

*Why, God?* he silently cried out as the death of his dreams washed over him anew. *Why didn't You let me marry Rose?*

He may not have loved her, at least not in the deep way his parents felt for each other, but Joel figured that sort of devotion would come later. After all, he and Rose had known each other for years—their families expected a union between them. But even in his anger over what might have been, he couldn't deny the strong feeling he had when he'd walked over to Rose's house, intent on proposing. He'd known then, as sure as the rising and the setting of the sun, it wasn't meant to be with them, however natural the union seemed.

*Is that what I'm to think about being a father? It's not meant to be either?* Joel crumbled the letter in his hand. The crunch of the paper eased some of his frustration.

"Bad news from home?"

Joel glanced at the soldier to his left. Even seated in bed, the man looked tall.

"Your letter—bad news?" he asked again.

"Uh...something like that."

"Name's Dennis. Sergeant George Dennis." He leaned to the side and stuck his hand across the space between the two beds.

"Corporal Joel Campbell," Joel said, shaking the man's meaty hand and trying not to wince from the pain of moving.

Sergeant Dennis straightened. "Your girl up and get married?"

"No," Joel said around the tightening of his jaw.

"I tell you," the other man continued with a shake of his head as if Joel hadn't spoken, "those guys who can't go back to the front end up marrying all the girls left at home. Which is why you've gotta look for opportunities elsewhere."

Joel followed Sergeant Dennis's gaze as it settled on Nurse Thornton speaking quietly to a patient on the opposite side of the ward. "You know that's against the rules."

"Maybe it's different between patients and nurses. Besides, a fellow can try, can't he? I just want to get to know her." He twisted to look at Joel and pointed at his neglected Bible. "You a chaplain or something, lugging that Bible around?"

A chuckle escaped Joel's throat. "No. That's the Army-issued Bible. Didn't you get one?"

The sergeant scratched his hairline. "I can't remember. It say anything in there about not talking to a nurse?"

"Not that I recall."

"Then me and Him..." Sergeant Dennis pointed to the ceiling. "We're still square, even if we ain't talked in some time."

Joel chuckled again, despite Dennis's somewhat faulty reasoning. From what little Joel knew about Nurse Thornton, he had a hard time imagining her being easily persuaded to break any rules.

He didn't plan on breaking them either. The lessons he'd learned from having Vivian and Les on the farm all those years ago went beyond seeing what it meant to be a father. Observing firsthand Vivian's difficult life, Joel quickly concluded he'd never contribute to placing a woman in a similar situation. Even now, despite knowing he couldn't father a child, he would still choose to be the man, the gentleman, his parents—and God—wanted him to be.

Joel folded Mary's letter and slipped it beneath the cover of his Bible. His gaze wandered the room. He would likely die of boredom and inactivity before his injuries healed. What he wouldn't give to feel the sun on his face and the slap of his shoes against the dirt as he ran. Even the thought of baling hay or mucking stalls or driving the plow sounded heavenly in comparison to the confines of his bed and the whitewashed room.

To pass the time until lunch, he opted to look through his bird notebook. Pain sliced down his side and leg, making him grunt, as he reached to pull the book from his bedside table. When the ache lessened, he rested the book on his chest and thumbed through the pages. Each one was filled with meticulous drawings and full descriptions of birds. His sister Livy, the true artist in the family, had sketched some of the pictures, but the ones Joel had drawn himself weren't half bad.

Ever since he'd been a boy, he'd found birds fascinating. The way they flew, and lived, and ate. His mother had been the one to encourage him to take notes about the birds he saw. Most of his bird-watching had been on his own, until Les came to the farm. The young boy turned out to be as eager an observer as Joel himself, and they'd spent many hours studying birds together.

Joel had always envied the birds' abilities to effortlessly take to the skies. Especially now, when he felt tethered to the earth by his wounds and the irrigation tubes. If only he could soar right out of the window and away from the hospital. But it would never happen, now or in the future. Only in one of those airplanes he'd seen flying over No Man's Land were humans ever likely to grasp the same perspective as a bird.

Lunch arrived and, with it, his freedom from the red tubes. Joel slurped up every last bite of broth. Today there were the tiniest slivers of meat and vegetables floating in it. Not the greatest improvement, but he welcomed any change to his bland diet. After his tray had been cleared, he took up his notebook again.

A flash of movement at the window drew his attention from the drawings and words on the page in front of him. A plump brown-and-white bird with a reddish-orange breast had alighted on the sill, its head cocked. Joel had seen few birds during his time in the trenches.

Excitement pulsed through him, masking the pain that came from moving about as he tried to locate a pencil in his bag. Once he found it, he sketched a quick picture of the bird, then noted its size and color next to his drawing. He'd have to ask one of the French sisters the name, though.

Joel watched the creature hop from one side of the sill to the other. It seemed to find as much fascination in observing the men inside the crowded ward as Joel did observing it. Would it stay or fly away if he were to try to get a closer look? Either way, the effort of walking across the room suddenly felt worth the risk. The bird reminded him of happier days, and closing the gap between them would shrink the distance between Joel and home. He could also prove to himself, and the nurses, that he wouldn't be completely confined to a bed against his will.

A quick glance at the two nurses in the ward confirmed neither one was looking in Joel's direction. He pulled back his blanket and scooted to the edge of the bed. The action started a steady ache in his wounded thigh and pelvis, but he tightened his jaw in retaliation. All he needed was to make it ten, maybe fifteen, steps across the room. A simple task.

Joel twisted to face the nearby wall and let his right foot join his left on the smooth wood floor. Once he rose to a standing position, he'd likely attract attention. He would need to move quickly if he planned to reach the window before one of the nurses stopped him.

Taking a deep breath, he pushed to his feet on the exhale. The pain along his right side intensified and his knees nearly collapsed beneath his own weight. But he was standing! A tight grimace pulled at his mouth as he forced his left foot to shuffle forward along the floor. The pressure on his injured leg robbed him of breath until he could shift his balance back to his left.

He followed up the shuffle-step with a hobble forward, bringing his legs in line again.

Joel glanced over his shoulder to discover he'd made it only six inches from the bed. Disappointment swept through him, but he gritted his teeth against it. *Rome wasn't built in a day*, his dad had always said. Fisting his good hand, he began the process of taking a step all over again. Left foot forward, hobble. Left foot forward, hobble.

To his surprise, when he looked to the window, he found the bird hadn't moved. Its head was still tipped at a curious angle as it watched Joel's funny walk across the room. Encouraged, Joel shuffled forward again, and again. Sweat broke out on his brow and rolled down his face, but he kept moving. Thankfully the soldier lying in the bed beside the window was asleep.

His breath came harder now, making him shake his head in disgust. In high school, he'd played football, but it was the running he really enjoyed. After graduation, he'd taken up running the outer perimeter of the farm in the mornings or evenings, seeing if he could best his own time. He could push through a couple of miles easily, anticipating the point when his breath and pounding heartbeat were the only sounds surrounding him. But now...just crossing a room left him feeling as if he'd charged through a mile at an unrelenting sprint.

*Almost there.*

Pain, every bit as fresh and stabbing as when he'd first been hit, scoured every inch of his body. But he couldn't quit now—wouldn't quit. He wasn't the sum of his injuries. He was stronger than the pain. Much closer to the window now, Joel could see a blue-gray layer of feathers beneath the bird's orange breast that he hadn't noticed from across the room.

The large, black eyes stared up at him in curiosity and...pity? Joel frowned. The pain must be interfering with his mind. But he couldn't shake the feeling the bird felt sorry for him, and that was something he could not tolerate.

*What would you do if they clipped your wings?* he silently cried to the small creature. *If they told you, you couldn't fly anymore? You wouldn't stop trying, would you?*

The bird inclined its head to the other side as if nodding. A tight smile thinned Joel's lips. *Then you and I are alike in that way.*

Three more feet to go. A surge of confidence increased his belabored movements. He'd nearly done it—and only a couple of days after coming to the hospital. No one could pity him now. He might never be a father, but he was every bit the strong man he'd been.

"Corporal Campbell!" Nurse Thornton's loud cry startled the bird, just as Joel came within touching distance of the windowsill. The creature threw out its brown wings and disappeared from view.

As if the bird's very presence had been Joel's source of strength, he found his injured leg would no longer support him. He caught himself from pitching headlong out the window, then slid to the floor, breathing heavily. Every pair of eyes in the room, including those of the soldier by the window, was now fastened on him.

"Corporal, what are you doing out of bed?" Nurse Thornton's glare blazed with unmasked anger as she marched to his side. "If you need to get up, you are supposed to call for one of us." She shook a finger at him. "Stay put while I go get a wheelchair."

Too exhausted and demoralized to argue or explain, Joel was forced to wait there, his weakness and humiliation exposed to everyone in the ward, until she brought the chair. With his energy completely spent, he had no choice but to allow Nurse Thornton to lift him onto the seat of the wheelchair. The wheels emitted a loud squeak with each turn as she pushed him the embarrassingly short distance back to his bed.

Agony berated his body, but he clamped his teeth against the groan rising into his throat. He'd brought enough attention to himself already.

"Is there something I can get you?" she asked once she had him back beneath his cover. This time her voice sounded more contrite.

An instant cure to his injuries. A chance to switch places with Ralph—to let him live, rather than continue this half-life Joel had now. The bitterness of his own thoughts shamed him. He should be grateful to be alive.

Afraid any reply would reveal the frustration boiling inside him, he settled for a shake of his head in answer to her question.

"Then please rest." She tucked the blanket up around him, apparently noticing the way his body had begun to shake from his short excursion. "I expect such behavior from Sergeant Dennis there," she added in a low voice, "but not you. You've been my model patient. In a few more days, we'll get you up and walking, all right?"

Joel turned his head toward the wall and promptly shut his eyes. He didn't want to see the pity on the others' faces at his folly. Only a few more days, he reminded himself, until he could try again. His leg would heal soon and before long he'd be back to running. At least he had to believe that.

*But not everything will heal*, his mind argued.

He would never be a father, and he wasn't likely to marry either. He was kidding himself to think he'd find a woman who would agree to marriage when he couldn't provide her with a child to love and care for. The other choice was to find someone who felt sorry enough for him to agree to be his wife, but Joel rejected that option outright. Better not to marry than marry where he felt no deep and passionate love. It would be Rose all over again if he did.

His earlier resentment rushed in with all the force of a raging river. Joel clenched and unclenched his good hand, desperate for a diversion from his ruined plans. At home a good, hard run would have cleared his mind. At the front lines, attention to his squad and the details of battle life kept his thoughts focused. But here, confined to a hospital bed, he felt caged, a prisoner of his own grief and anger. What was he supposed to do now? The wings of his future, his hopes, had been stripped from him, leaving him to flounder, flightless, on the hard ground of reality. His only relief lay in seeking the oblivion sleep offered.

\* \* \*

Wadding up the paper in front of her, Evelyn added it to the growing pile of white beside her bed. She threw the book she'd been using as a desk onto the blanket and leaned her head back against the wall. She was supposed to be sleeping, so she could make it through the night shift without falling asleep on her feet or consuming cup after cup of coffee.

She brushed a hand over her damp forehead. Even the breeze wafting through the open window of the little room she shared with Alice failed to cool her completely. Would her whole pregnancy be like this? As a nurse, she knew the basics about carrying a child but little of the day-to-day things about being pregnant that a mother typically shared with a daughter. A fierce longing to talk to her grandmother—or her mother, as impossible as that was—knotted her throat with emotion and increased the pinching in her shoulders and neck.

Why couldn't she find the right words for her letter home? She wanted to confide in her grandparents, tell them there was a good possibility she'd be returning to the States before her time in France was up. It might ease the shock of finding her on the doorstep with her baby in tow. But every word Evelyn had penned so far seemed to reveal too much or not enough.

She placed a hand against her stomach. It would still be some weeks before she felt the baby move; she knew that much, at least. Already, though, she felt a connection to this tiny being inside her, even as her energy waned and her daily sickness continued.

Though she might wish for a different order to things, this baby was still hers and Ralph's. A living reminder of him.

"Why did you have to die, Ralph?" Whispering the words didn't make them hurt with any less intensity. Evelyn pressed a hand to her chest, where the pain had taken up residence since Joel had brought her the news.

Tears pooled in her eyes, making the dresser across the

room look as if it were trembling. She could assess and treat nearly any wound and ailment presented to her, but how did one patch a broken heart? Joel's assurances about Ralph changing brought her less comfort today. However much she'd helped Ralph, it did her little good now. Their baby would still grow up without a father, and she would be forced to return home without a husband.

The burden of her secret had increased in size from a large rock to a boulder in the last three days. Would she be crushed beneath its weight, long before her pregnancy was even discovered? Evelyn set her mouth in a thin line of determination. No, she would stick with her plans to work as hard and as well as she possibly could.

Brushing at her wet eyes, Evelyn bent down and collected the wads of paper. She would try to think of what to write later. Right now she needed to get rid of the half-written pages and their incriminating information.

She removed a match from the box on top of the dresser and headed down the stairs. Outside the afternoon sun shone warm on her back as she stepped quickly toward the forest. Beneath the trees, she slowed her footsteps and followed the sun-strewn path.

When she felt certain no one from the hospital could see her, Evelyn stopped. She placed the crinkled paper on the ground and struck the match against a nearby tree trunk. The tiny flame lapped at the pile of letters as she crouched beside them. Once the paper caught fire, Evelyn dropped the match onto the pile and watched with satisfaction as her letters burned. Her secret was safe—for now.

The snap of a branch ahead of her made her shoot to her feet. Had someone followed her?

"Who's there?" she asked in a firm tone that belied her rapidly beating heart.

"Nurse Gray?" Louis's pale face and dark curls popped up from the brush.

Evelyn released her breath. "*Bonjour*, Louis." She stomped the last of the paper ashes into the dirt and approached the boy. "Who are you hiding from?"

Louis put a finger to his lips, then pointed upward. "I'm stalking a bird," he whispered.

Arching her neck, Evelyn peered above him. Sure enough, a gray bird hopped along a branch overhead.

"What will you do with him?" She kept her voice low as he'd done. Did he plan to snatch the tiny bird and eat it? She cringed at the thought.

"I like to watch them. Maybe I will fly one day. Like those aeroplanes I see." The bird forgotten, Louis spread his arms and pretended to soar around Evelyn, snapping branches with his hands.

Evelyn shook her head in amusement. "You will have to watch out for trees, Louis, if you want to be a good pilot."

He grinned.

"Did you sell any vegetables today?"

"*Non*. Did you forget it is Sunday, Nurse Gray?"

"So it is." She had forgotten. A flicker of shame ignited inside her. Her grandparents would be at church services today, despite their bad health. Surely they expected their only granddaughter to be doing the same.

"Are you hungry?" she asked next.

He glanced down at his dirt-stained, bare feet. "A little."

"Then come with me." Evelyn held out her hand. She

may not feel comfortable attending services at the old church nearby, but she wasn't so selfish as to ignore the needs of this precocious child.

He slipped his small hand inside her palm. The feel of it reminded Evelyn that one day soon she would hold her own child's hand.

"What food does that cabbage-head cook have today?" Louis asked as he followed her up the path.

A soft laugh escaped Evelyn's mouth. The sound surprised her. She hadn't laughed since finding out Ralph had been killed. "Whatever it is, we will both accept it gratefully. That's what my grandmother always taught me."

"I remember *ma grand-mère*." Louis pulled back on Evelyn's arm so he could scoop up a pebble with his free hand. "She smiled and told stories while she sewed. I miss her. *Ma mère* does not smile anymore or tell stories."

Sadness filled Evelyn as she thought of Louis's mother, trying to make do without her husband. Evelyn now knew what it meant to have the person one loved and counted on suddenly taken away. Though she'd never met this other woman, she felt bonded to her by grief.

Evelyn cleared her throat, willing back fresh tears. There'd been enough of those today. "Why don't you tell me one of your *grand-mère*'s stories?"

Louis glanced at her, a smile on his upturned face. "My favorite is about a fox and a bird, but I do not know it in English."

"Then tell it to me in French." She wouldn't understand, but that didn't matter. He only needed someone to listen.

Evelyn led Louis out of the woods and across the lawn as he shared the story in his native language. She couldn't help laughing again when he changed the tone of his voice or made different faces to represent the various characters. By the time they reached the back door of the kitchen, she felt almost happy. Of course her problems still lurked at the edges of her mind, waiting to pounce in a quiet moment, but she allowed the short time with Louis to fill her up with some measure of sunshine.

"Wait here and I will go get us some lunch."

Thankfully the hospital cook was occupied with talking to one of the sisters. Evelyn asked one of the kitchen staff for something to share with Louis. She was given a loaf of bread and some cheese wrapped in a napkin. The meal wouldn't be large, but she planned to give most of it to Louis anyway. Her appetite still hadn't returned to normal.

"We're going to have a picnic," she declared. She steered Louis past the few soldiers who rested on lawn chairs in the sun.

His forehead scrunched in confusion. "What is a picknick?"

Another smile tugged at Evelyn's lips. "A picnic is a meal you eat outdoors." She sat in the shade of one of the beech trees and patted the grass beside her. "You typically put your food in a basket of some sort and sit on the ground or on a blanket. Then you eat all sorts of yummy things."

"Like cheese and bread?"

"Perhaps. What I like best is fried chicken and rolls and my grandmother's fudge." Evelyn breathed a hungry sigh at the thought. How she longed for American cooking and real honest-to-goodness fudge.

She ripped a piece of bread from the loaf and handed

it to Louis. He bit off a ginormous bite, but when he caught sight of Evelyn's raised eyebrows, he swallowed it and mumbled a quick apology. His next bite was much smaller.

Now for the cheese. Evelyn removed the napkin, only to have the smell of the cheese assault her nostrils and make her stomach roil. Whirling around, she vomited into the grass at the base of the tree. She drew a trembling hand across her mouth and squeezed her eyes against the sting of acid in her throat. She wasn't just a nurse sharing her lunch with a starving French boy—she was pregnant with Ralph's child and Ralph was not coming for them anymore.

"Are you sick, Nurse Gray?"

Evelyn opened her eyes. "Just a little. Would you mind asking one of the kitchen orderlies for a cup of water, Louis?"

He nodded. "You can have my bread." After dropping his piece into her lap, he darted toward the hospital.

His willingness to give what little he had brought a fresh lump to Evelyn's throat. What would become of Louis as he grew older? Would he stay funny and compassionate or turn hard and angry when he realized what the war had robbed him of as a child? Would his life improve once the battles were over?

By taking slow, even breaths, Evelyn managed to work through the wave of nausea. When Louis returned with the water, she felt less queasy.

"Here." Louis carefully placed the cup into her hand.

"Thank you." She sipped the tepid water. "I don't believe I'll have any of the cheese, so you're welcome to all of it."

Louis ate every speck of cheese while Evelyn nibbled a few bites of bread. What she didn't eat, she gave to him.

"Are you better?" he asked when all traces of their lunch had vanished.

"Yes."

He plucked up a piece of grass and twisted it, without looking at her. "You will not...not die, will you, Nurse Gray? Like *votre mère*?"

"No, Louis." She settled her hand on his thin shoulder. "I'm not going to die." At least not in the way he meant.

Louis lifted his blue eyes and gave her a lopsided smile. "Good. Because you are my friend."

Warmth, as radiant and bright as the sun shining beyond their circle of shade, spread through her at the boy's sincere declaration. "And you're my friend." Evelyn gave his unruly black curls a tussle. "I'd better go lie down now. I have to work tonight in the hospital. I'll see you tomorrow?"

Louis hopped up. "*Oui*. I will think of another of *Grand-mère*'s stories."

"I'd like that."

He sprinted across the lawn in the direction of the village. Evelyn envied his energy. She slowly climbed to her feet, taking the cup of water and napkin with her. With her stomach mostly settled, fatigue swept in to take the place of her queasiness.

Her limbs felt spongy as Evelyn plodded up the stairs to her and Alice's room. She slipped off her shoes and sank onto the bed. Twisting onto her side, she let her eyelids fall shut. Immediately worries crowded her mind like storm clouds. She pushed them away with thoughts of her time with Louis until she could no longer think.

She awoke sometime later and sat up. The clock on the dresser claimed she'd slept for four hours. Evelyn took a few more sips of water and realized the sensation in her stomach came from hunger this time, not sickness.

After splashing water onto her face in the bathroom, she donned her nurse's cap and apron and went to dinner. Even before she reached the dining hall, she could hear the rise and fall of chatter that filled the old ballroom. Evelyn filed through the line for food, then located Alice seated at one of the three long tables.

"How was your shift?" she asked as she slid onto the bench.

Alice swallowed and waved her fork at Evelyn. "Crazy as usual. Corporal Campbell attempted to get out of bed today—unassisted. I swear if that man wasn't so nice, I'd stick him on the pulleys just so he doesn't attempt that again. I've never seen someone so determined to get out of here. And return to what? Fighting at the front again? I don't understand it."

As she ate, Evelyn half listened to Alice's stories, but her thoughts were on other things. Why did Joel want to leave the hospital so badly? Like her, he no longer had the bright, hopeful future he'd envisioned. So why be in a hurry to get away? She hoped he wouldn't leave too soon. Knowing someone else was mourning Ralph's death eased her own grief to a small degree. Of course, having Joel around might also prove to be dangerous. Who else was most likely to guess her secret first, if he didn't already know it?

She pushed her food around her plate as worry soured

her appetite. Surely if Joel had guessed about her pregnancy, he would have said something already. He'd had ample opportunity when she'd shaved his face last night. The memory of his large, warm hand covering hers sent a shiver up her arms. How strange that she'd reacted to his touch in a way she hadn't felt before.

Evelyn forced another bite to keep from drawing suspicion. Clearly her grief over losing Ralph had played havoc with her emotions last night. Joel was Ralph's best friend, so naturally she would feel friendly affection toward him. What was the old saying about friends and enemies? *Keep your friends close, and your enemies closer.* She wasn't sure yet which one Joel would turn out to be, so she'd have to be more careful there.

"Then there's Sergeant Dennis." Alice's exasperated tone broke into Evelyn's troubled thoughts. "I'm liable to dump his lunch on him one of these days if he doesn't quit hollering at me for things. Even though there's two of us in there, he's always calling out 'Nurse Thornton, Nurse Thornton.' It's enough to make a girl go mad."

"It's because he likes you." The words were out before Evelyn could grab them back. She feigned interest in her food, embarrassed at the askance look on Alice's face.

"He does not. He's always arrogant and demanding."

Evelyn released a sigh and set down her fork. "That's the way he can get your attention. Just be careful, Alice."

"Be careful?" Alice lowered her voice as she leaned forward. "I don't like him back, Evelyn. Even if I did, I would never act on those feelings. That could mean being sent home." She gave an adamant shake of her head. "No, I'm going to be the model nurse and ignore his overtures. Just like I know you would."

Heat flamed Evelyn's face at the misguided perception. She attempted to swallow the bite in her mouth, but the morsel felt like a fist-sized rock going down her throat. She coughed in protest and scrambled to grab her water cup.

"Are you all right?"

Evelyn caught sight of Alice's concerned face before she gulped down the water. At last the bite dislodged and she could breathe again. "I'll be fine," she rasped out. "But I—I think I'm done." Better to make her escape now, especially if Alice returned to the ill-fated topic of soldiers and nurses.

"Okay. Good luck tonight."

Evelyn nodded and headed to the kitchen with her dishes. At the bottom of the stairs leading up to the wards, she paused to straighten her cap and smooth her apron. What would Alice and the other nurses say if they knew the secret Evelyn hid behind her impeccable uniform and sharp skills? What would the sisters think? Anxiety tightened her stomach, making her wish she'd skipped dinner after all.

*Stop worrying.* Evelyn gripped the worn wooden banister and squared her shoulders. As long as she remained at St. Vincent's, she would do her duty—just as her father and grandparents had taught and expected of her.

As she had the night before, she ascended the two flights of stairs to Sister Marcelle's office, where she collected the keys and ledger book. Tonight, though, she wouldn't avoid Joel. She wanted to see how he was faring after getting out of bed earlier. Upon entering the ward, she found Nurse Kent and a now recovered Nurse Phelps assisting patients.

Evelyn took a seat and reviewed the ledger entries
for each soldier in the ward. Alice had noted Joel's attempt to walk without help. What had possessed him
to do such a thing? Evelyn glanced in his direction and
was both relieved and disappointed to see his eyes were
closed. She liked talking with him, but she also relished
the idea of putting off a conversation to learn if he knew
her secret or not.

Satisfied with the state of the ward, she checked on
the nurses and patients in the other. All appeared in ef-
ficient working order there, too. With the other nurses
occupied, Evelyn agreed to pen a letter for a soldier who
couldn't sleep. She drew a chair beside his bed and wrote
the words he dictated to her in a quiet tone. Perhaps that's
what she needed herself—someone to tell the truth to,
who could then write it down for her grandparents.

She had just addressed the envelope when Nurse Kent
approached her.

"There's a soldier in our ward who's struggling with
his pain tonight. He insists on not having any morphine,
but he isn't going to get the rest he needs without it."
Nurse Kent frowned. "What should we do?"

Evelyn stood and carried her chair back to the corner.
"Who is it?"

"Corporal Campbell."

The name brought an instant quickening of her pulse
and a strong swell of empathy to her heart. But why?
Joel wasn't any different from the countless other soldiers
she'd attended to since coming to France. Evelyn dug her
fingernails into her palms to rein in her emotions. She was
only concerned for Joel because he was Ralph's friend
and because she knew, more than most, what he'd lost

three days ago. He'd already been through so much; he didn't need to add the agony of little sleep to it.

Evelyn blew out a soft sigh. "I'll talk to him."

"Thanks, Evelyn."

She followed Nurse Kent out of the room and into the other ward. Her shoes marked a quiet beat across the floor as she walked toward Joel. His eyes opened at her approach, but he turned his face toward the wall.

"So they got you to bully me into taking the medicine?" he said when she stopped next to his bed. "I already told them I know there isn't enough to go around. I'm not going to take medicine from some soldier who really needs it."

"And what if that's you tonight?"

He pressed his mouth into a tight line and didn't respond.

"Nurse Thornton told me about your attempt to walk on your own today."

"It wasn't an attempt. I did walk."

Evelyn swallowed a smile. The man was certainly stubborn. "Be that as it may, we are here to help you"— she lowered her voice—"not impede your progress, Joel. Which means I'd like you to take the morphine, so you can rest tonight."

"Rest is only a temporary fix," he muttered.

She wasn't sure he'd meant for her to hear the words, but they conjured up the same desire to comfort that she'd felt last night. This time she wouldn't give in, though; she would play her role of concerned nurse and that was all. "Then why are you so anxious to leave?"

"Out there..." He raised his good arm to gesture to the window across the room, but even that movement brought a grimace to his face. "I make decisions; I decide the best tactics and strategies for me and my men. But in here..." He dropped his clenched hand onto the bed. "I'm reminded every minute that there's nothing I can control or change about what happened the other day." He lifted his chin, his hazel eyes revealing the torment inside him. "I just want to be in control again—of my own destiny."

*Me, too.* She longed to say the words out loud, but she couldn't. Not without revealing too much.

The need to reach out and touch his face, to ease his inward suffering, intensified. Evelyn clasped her hands tightly together to stop herself, her fingers aching with the effort. "I understand," she managed to reply calmly, "but there are certain guidelines you need to abide by."

The smell of iodine hit her from behind. Evelyn glanced over her shoulder to see one of the other nurses bandaging a wound. Normally the scent didn't bother her, but she still felt queasy since eating dinner. That, combined with the smell and her lack of real sleep, brought a surge of nausea to her stomach.

Evelyn took a few cleansing breaths through her mouth before continuing. "In here, we ask you to listen to our tactics and strategies, just like you expect your men to listen to yours at the front lines. Tonight, that means the tactical decision of taking morphine in order to rest."

A faint smile creased his lips. "My men might take orders better from you...Nurse Gray."

She might have blushed at the compliment if she didn't feel so ill. Unclasping her hands, she pressed her fingers beneath her nose to help block the smell.

"Nurse Gray?" She looked down at him. His brow had furrowed with evident concern. "Are you okay?"

Evelyn managed a nod. "I...uh...think something with dinner didn't sit right." She lowered her hand. "Will you take the morphine?"

"Is this one of those tactics you mentioned a second ago? You feign sickness so I'll give in and take the medicine?"

"Hardly," she said, giving a bitter chuckle. Could she make it through this conversation without running to the bathroom?

"You really aren't feeling well, are you?"

Evelyn threw another glance at the other nurse, who appeared to be finished. Hopefully the smell would evaporate any minute and take her queasiness with it. "I'll be fine."

Joel looked skeptical at her halfhearted response. "You were sick the other night, too." She could practically see his suspicions and conclusions clicking into place like cogs in a wheel. Alarm churned her stomach all the more. He wouldn't guess the reason for her illness, would he?

"Please tell me if you want the medicine or not." She didn't want to stand here arguing anymore, not when she felt ready to vomit.

"I'll take it. If you'll answer a question first."

Panic, and a sour taste, coated the back of her throat. The light from the window lit up his intense gaze. "I don't know what sort of game you're playing at—"

"No game. Just an honest answer to an honest question. Then I'll accept the medication gladly."

What did he want to know? The anxiety wasn't helping her weak stomach. She ran a hand across her forehead. When had it grown so hot in here? If she refused to answer his question, would he refuse the medicine? Evelyn wasn't sure she cared anymore. Except that this was Ralph's best friend. She owed it to the man she loved to do everything in her power to help Joel.

"Fine." After making certain the other two nurses weren't paying attention, she inched closer to ask, "What is this all-important question?"

"Were you going to marry Ralph?"

Evelyn nearly laughed out loud with relief. "Yes."

Joel studied her face, but she was no longer concerned what he might see. "Even though it meant being discharged?"

"Yes," she repeated. All that fear had been for nothing. "I'll get the med—"

"But why not wait until after the war to marry?" The inquiry came out no louder than a whisper, but it thundered as loud in Evelyn's ears as shellfire. "Unless...you couldn't wait."

Evelyn's mouth felt suddenly dry, like the time she'd first tasted sand as a child. A wave of dizziness pulled at her vision. She shut her eyes and gripped the iron headboard of Joel's bed to steady herself. How had he figured it out? She wanted to walk away, but she feared Joel saying something to one of the other nurses.

When the feeling of dizziness passed, she opened her eyes and met his probing stare. "Why does it matter?" She infused every ounce of coldness into her tone. She didn't have to answer to Joel, as long as he kept silent.

He frowned. "You're not going to answer then?"

"I don't understand why it matters." She hated the note of pleading she wasn't able to completely eradicate from her words.

"Because he was my best friend." Joel twisted his face to the wall again and blew out his breath. "I just want to make sense of something, when nothing makes sense right now."

Her head screamed at her to leave, but she hesitated, torn between helping him and safeguarding her and Ralph's secret. When Joel turned back to look at her, his stare piercing, she realized it was too late to flee.

"You don't have to say it, Evelyn." His voice carried to her ears alone, but she felt as if he were shouting it from the hospital roof. Icy shards of fear caused her to shiver. She folded her arms against the rising nausea and dread. "I'm the oldest of six siblings. I know the symptoms when a woman is... you know..."

Anger whooshed in at his nonchalant tone, sweeping away the cold terror, even if only for a moment. "I answered your question, *Corporal Campbell*," she bit out with all the steeliness she could muster. Ralph's friend or not, he didn't need to act so arrogant about guessing her condition. "I'll get your morphine now."

She marched into the supply room and unlocked the cupboard door. Her shaking hands would hardly cooperate.

*If he says anything to anyone before my pregnancy is obvious...*

Evelyn shut her eyes and rested her forehead against the cool metal edge of the cupboard. She gulped in several long breaths. But her heart rate still felt too fast, her chest too tight. If she felt this way after talking to Joel, how would she ever face telling her grandparents the truth, even in a letter?

She grabbed the morphine and slammed the cupboard

door shut. The rattling of bottles sounded from within as she locked the door. She would write soon, telling her grandmother and grandfather what had happened, and that she would be home soon—but not until after the baby was born, if she had her wish. Surely the passage of time and their love would soften the blow of her news.

Without a glance at Joel, Evelyn left the supply closet and approached Nurse Kent. "Corporal Campbell has agreed to take the medication now." She handed the other nurse the morphine shot.

Nurse Kent's eyebrows rose in surprise. "Thanks, Evelyn. He was so adamant. I'm glad you talked him into it."

"You and Irene look like you have everything in order here, so I'll return to the other ward. Come find me if you need anything else."

"We will."

In the hallway, Evelyn finally felt able to take a deep, cleansing breath that pushed air all the way to her lungs. She'd played Joel's little game by answering his question and now he knew her secret. But that didn't mean she had to continue to converse so openly with him. From now on, she would avoid talking to him as much as possible. Until he either disclosed the truth about her himself or she could no longer hide her pregnancy from the rest of the world.

# Chapter 4

*The* woods around him lay cloaked in eerie stillness. Joel swallowed hard. The quiet unnerved him more than the rat-tat-tat of machine guns or the explosive sounds of shells. At least, running pell-mell toward an erupting battlefield left little to the imagination. On the other hand, the absence of noise conjured up a host of unknowns. Silence meant hidden dangers and the possibility of an ambush.

If only his men hadn't been pinned down at the beginning of the battle. Now they had to play catch-up with the infantry.

Joel scrutinized the shadows. Out ahead he'd been told there were ravines, dark and foreboding, the perfect hiding place for the Germans to wait.

Someone bumped his shoulder—Ralph. "We're right behind you, Campbell."

He straightened his shoulders and gave a decisive nod. They were counting on him to get them back to the in-

*fantry, as unscathed as possible. They'd been lucky so far, despite taking heavy fire earlier. He'd have to trust that luck—and God—would be with them again, whatever the unseen challenges ahead.*

*Joel motioned for the group to move forward, keeping them close to the trees as much as possible. When the ground started to slope upward, he signaled for everyone to stop once more.*

*Could the Germans be hiding out on the other side? Joel hated the idea of dividing his men, but their odds of surviving were better in two groups than one. Then they'd be shooting at the Germans from both sides. It was their best chance. He would lead one group, and Ralph would take the other.*

*Before Joel had even finished outlining the plan, though, Ralph began shaking his head. Irritation rose inside him. There wasn't time for arguing—they needed to reach the rest of the Army, and fast.*

*"Send Davis with those guys," Ralph reasoned. "You and I are a team, Campbell. We work better together than anyone else here. And you know it."*

*Joel hesitated, suddenly unsure of the right course. It wasn't a familiar or pleasant feeling. Should he use his position as squad leader to force Ralph into compliance? But it would be futile. Ralph did what Ralph wanted.*

*"Fine," Joel snapped. He hated Ralph's obstinacy at times, but it did make his best friend a good soldier. And right now, walking into the unknown with someone as bullheaded and loyal as Ralph didn't seem like such a bad idea.*

*While Davis and his group headed northeast, Joel guided the rest of his men southeast into the trees border-*

ing the hill. They inched through the woods as quietly as they could, though the sound of snapping branches and heavy footfalls couldn't be silenced completely.

Near the brow of the hill, Joel stopped the group. He scanned the ravine below, but he couldn't see any enemy soldiers. To the north, Davis and the others were moving into a meadow, several hundred yards off the ravine.

"He's marching too fast," Joel muttered over his shoulder to Ralph.

"Let's pick it up then."

They maneuvered down the hill. Joel held his breath as they reached the bottom. But no Germans appeared. No machine guns burst into life. Farther ahead, he could see Davis waiting for them at the edge of the meadow.

Joel blew out a sigh. Maybe he'd been too cautious. Glancing back at Ralph and the others, he smiled reassuringly.

He turned forward again, only to have the air explode around them. Joel's lungs filled with the concussion, and his body flew backward. He plowed through a bush ten feet away, landing on his left arm. He heard the ugly crunch, and somewhere his brain registered the broken bone. But the pain coming from the lower half of his body blocked out all other thoughts and senses.

"Campbell? Campbell? Can you hear me?"

Joel forced his eyelids open. How long had he been out? Davis hovered over him, his expression bordering on panic.

"There were..." Davis sucked in a hard breath. "Germans. Germans in the ravine. They launched a shell—right in the middle of...of..." He shuddered and ran a hand over his dirty beard.

*"The others?" Could that whisper of a voice be his?*

*Davis glanced away. "We're applying what aid we can, but you're the only one conscious right now."*

*The overwhelming pain fought against his mind again and won. Snatches of movement and conversation flitted through his thoughts of home and family. The agony of his broken body pushed through the numbness now and then, especially when he felt himself being hoisted into the air or bumped.*

*When he managed to open his eyes again, he was staring at the canvas ceiling of a tent. Waves of hurt rolled through him. He turned his head to look for a doctor and discovered Ralph lying in the cot next to him.*

*"Kelley?" he croaked out of his dry throat. "You alive?"*

*Ralph didn't stir. A blanket had been drawn up to his chin. Fear momentarily blocked the pain of Joel's injuries. Something wasn't right. Why wasn't Ralph moving or cussing Joel out for getting themselves shot?*

*"Kelley," Joel tried again. He put all of his waning energy into making his voice heard.*

*This time Ralph moaned. Only it wasn't a moan; it was a name.*

*"Evelyn...Evelyn..."*

*So that was her name—the girl Ralph had talked about for weeks now. The beautiful nurse he'd met on leave. There was only one reason Ralph would speak her name out loud. Tears burned Joel's eyes. "What can I do, Kelley?"*

*"Tell her..."*

*Tell her what? That Ralph loved her, that her name had been on his lips right before he died? How would he even find this girl?*

*But Joel couldn't refuse his best friend. Not now. "I will, Ralph. I will."*

*A doctor bustled over to Joel's cot, throwing out orders to the medical orderly behind him. In the flurry of having his body bandaged and his arm temporarily set, Joel couldn't see or talk to Ralph again.*

*Finally the doctor straightened. "Try to rest, son. The ambulance will be here shortly to take to you to the nearest hospital."*

*Joel tipped his head in Ralph's direction. "My buddy... Private Kelley... Can you help him, too?"*

*The doctor glanced down at Ralph and shook his head. "I'm sorry, Corporal. Your friend didn't make it."*

*The words echoed over and over in Joel's mind— "didn't make it, didn't make it."*

*Guilt every bit as suffocating and sharp as his pain overwhelmed Joel. He couldn't get enough breath to fill his lungs, and the blanket on top of him felt as hot and smothering as fire.*

*"Corporal?"*

*What did the doctor want now?*

*"Corporal Campbell?"*

The voice wasn't the doctor's; it was a feminine voice—one he'd heard before.

Joel opened his eyes and sucked in a shuddering breath. The scent of iodine and floor cleaner filled his nose and anchored his chaotic thoughts. He was in the hospital.

He peered at the figure standing beside his bed. "Evelyn..." The name slipped from his mouth before he could stop it, a remnant of the day he'd just relived in his dreams. Her eyes widened in response before she glanced over her shoulder with a frown. "I mean, Nurse Gray. You...uh...startled me."

"You were restless." Her voice carried defensiveness. "Perhaps I should have let you keep sleeping."

He pushed off his blanket and felt instant relief from the heat and sweat of his nightmare. "I'm fine. Just... warm."

"Would you like a glass of water?"

Joel looked past her to find the other two nurses in the room occupied with other tasks. So that was the reason Evelyn had come to assess his restless sleep. Not out of choice but duty. That explained her guarded tone and confirmed what Joel already suspected. She'd been avoiding him, ever since their last conversation when he'd guessed about her being pregnant.

Evelyn tapped the toe of her shoe against the floor. "If you don't want the water—"

"I don't. But do you need some?"

The tapping stopped. Even in the half-lit room, Joel could see the lines of fatigue on her porcelain face. She didn't look as pale as she had the other night, but working the night shift couldn't be easy for a woman in her condition.

"Are you planning on walking again and procuring me a glass?" Her deadpan expression might have fooled him, but her dark eyes glittered with what he guessed was a trace of amusement.

"I could...but then, you might not get the water until tomorrow morning."

A faint chuckle and a shake of her head followed his remark. "In that case, I'm fine. Thank you." She brushed some hair from her forehead that had escaped her nurse's cap. One black curl refused to stay tucked, brushing her eyebrow in rebellion. "Is there anything I can get you?"

He tried to think of something to detain her at his bedside, but he had nothing. "No. I'm all right."

"I might as well check your injuries now that you're awake."

Was she searching for a reason to linger, too? He dismissed the foolish notion. Evelyn was nothing if not professional, at least until it had come to Ralph.

Joel gritted his teeth against any embarrassment as Evelyn pulled back his blanket to examine his wounds. He still hated the personal intrusion that came with this part of hospital care.

Remnants of his dream still clung to him like cobwebs. And yet it was more than a dream. He'd been reliving the horror of that day as if it were happening to him all over again.

If he'd insisted that Ralph lead the other group, his best friend would still be alive. And now he had the added guilt of robbing Evelyn's unborn child of a father. Joel welcomed Evelyn's attention on his injuries instead of his face at the moment. He feared she'd read the searing self-reproach in his expression.

He could easily envision Ralph and Evelyn married and settled somewhere in the Midwest, a whole passel of rascally boys and pretty girls of their own. Ralph would've taught his sons how to shoot a gun and spit watermelon seeds. Evelyn would've taught her girls how to cook and properly bandage a cut. His own regrets at not being able to have a family might have been easier to bear if he'd been able to share in Ralph and Evelyn's joy.

If he only he could go back, make a different decision,

alleviate the responsibility eating at him. Especially now that he knew about Ralph and Evelyn's baby.

"I think your leg needs redressing."

Joel swung his gaze to hers. He'd been so caught up in his reproachful thoughts he'd nearly forgotten her presence. Evelyn raised her eyebrows in question. "That'd be fine," he replied.

Evelyn returned a few minutes later, her hands full of supplies, which she set on the table next to his bed. Now that he was wide awake, he figured he'd work on strengthening the hand of his broken arm. He clenched and unclenched his fingers, his eyes trained on the window, while Evelyn bent to cut away his bandage.

A sharp intake of breath followed by the clatter of metal against the wood floor jerked Joel's attention back to Evelyn. She stood frozen beside his bed, holding one hand in the other.

"Nurse Gray?"

When she didn't respond, Joel scooted higher up on his pillows. The action brought a temporary wave of pain, but he was beginning to move about in bed without constant agony from his injuries. Nurse Thornton had told him he could try walking tomorrow.

"Evelyn?" He kept his voice low. "Are you all right?"

She peered down at him, her face white. "I—I cut my finger with the scissors. I'm not sure how it happened."

"How bad are you hurt?"

"I'm bleeding. And I can't stand the sight of my own…"

Joel reached out to grip her wrist when she started to sway. "Do you feel like you're going to faint?"

"I think…I…might."

"Sit down."

She shook her head and tried to pull back against his hand. "No. I can't. It's not...proper."

Joel stifled a laugh. Of all the rules she was afraid to break, sitting on the edge of his bed had to be the least worrisome, especially given her time with Ralph. "I think it'll be fine, just this once. We don't want you hurting yourself"—he refrained from adding *and the baby*—"if you faint."

She hesitated a moment longer, then removing her hand from his, she sank onto the bed. "I—I'm sorry."

"How bad is it?"

"I can't look." She pressed her lips together and turned her head.

Joel extended his good hand. "Can I see?"

Evelyn placed her fisted hand inside his palm. Slowly he began uncurling her fingers. In response, she shivered as if cold. How soft her skin felt beneath his touch. He absently rubbed his fingertip over one of her knuckles. His heart pumped faster as the same electric feeling they'd shared the other day shot through him again. Joel glanced at Evelyn's face to see if she felt it, too, but her eyes were glued elsewhere.

*Get a grip, Campbell. This is Ralph's girl.*

Inhaling a breath of stale hospital air to clear his head, he moved her fingers to find a splotch of blood near her pinkie. Joel set her hand on the bed and reached for the bandage she'd brought for him. After dabbing the cloth against the cut, he examined her hand again.

"It doesn't look deep, but I'll tie this around the cut to help stop the bleeding." He used his teeth to rip off a smaller section of the bandage. Tying it with one hand wasn't easy, but he finally managed it. "There you go."

She lifted her hand and inspected his handiwork. "Thank you." A flicker of a smile relaxed her mouth. "Maybe you should have been a medic."

"Maybe," he said with a soft laugh. He wanted to make her smile fully, to do what he could do to ease the burden he'd unknowingly placed upon her with his decision the other day. "How did you become a nurse if the sight of blood makes you faint?"

Her smile deepened, as he'd hoped. "It sounds a bit silly, doesn't it? But it's only my own blood that bothers me. I can doctor anyone else's cuts and hurts as long as they aren't my own." She climbed to her feet, bringing instant cold to Joel's right side.

Why did he like having her sit beside him? Or talking with him? No wonder Ralph had fallen in love with her after only a day or two. Evelyn was not only beautiful, but compassionate and funny and brave.

"Will you be all right?" he asked, trying desperately to derail his own thoughts.

She nodded. "I'll get another bandage and finish up here." Her tone sounded almost curt, which meant she'd reverted back to her role of practiced nurse. The wall she'd been erecting between them since Joel had learned of her pregnancy had returned. Only Ralph had successfully broken through that barrier—and now he was gone. The tiniest spark of jealousy ignited inside Joel, but he fought it off by pushing it deeper within himself.

When she'd finished redressing his wounds, she pulled his blanket back up, but he noticed she was careful not to brush her fingers against his nightshirt. "Is there anything else you need?"

He shook his head, but Evelyn didn't move.

"Please don't say anything," she pleaded in a near whisper, "about sitting on your bed. Or about Ralph and me . . . and our . . ." A sigh escaped her lips as her hand rose to touch the middle of her nurse's apron. Was the movement unconscious?

Joel waited until she looked at him with those lovely, dark eyes. "I won't. I promise."

The relief and gratitude shining in her gaze nearly had the power to make him abandon all his well-meaning thoughts about her being Ralph's. With great effort, he forced his attention back to the window across the room. The darkened window. It was like looking into his own future.

"Good night, Corporal Campbell."

He sensed her watching him, but he wouldn't turn his head. "Good night, Ev—" He bit back her first name. "Good night, Nurse Gray."

She hesitated by his bed a moment or two longer, then spun on her heel and walked away. Joel placed his hand on the spot where she'd sat next to him, though the blanket no longer held the warmth of her presence. The sooner he left here, the better. The last thing he needed was to heap more guilt on himself by harboring an attraction for his best friend's girl.

*     *     *

Evelyn leaned against the wall in the hallway and examined her bandaged hand. The feel of Joel's capable fingers lingered like cologne on her skin. She hadn't wanted to see what was disturbing his sleep, hadn't wanted to talk to him at all after he'd guessed the truth about her and Ralph. And yet his quick jokes and genuine concern for her well-being had almost succeeded in tearing through her defenses. Especially when she'd once again felt that lightning sensation at his touch.

*What am I doing?* She moaned and pressed the bridge of her nose, a headache already building. She shouldn't be thinking about another soldier in such a way. Ralph was the man she loved, and if she could no longer have him in her life, then she wouldn't add insult to injury by breaking the rules all over again.

She lowered her hand to her back and massaged the sore muscles. Her feet ached, too, and if she didn't keep sipping coffee, her eyes wouldn't stay open.

Pushing off the wall, she went to inspect the other ward, but a surge of nausea hit her full force. When had she last eaten? Evelyn clapped a hand to her mouth and rushed into the bathroom. She made it just in time to relieve her coffee-drowned stomach into the sink. Once she finished retching, she washed her mouth and face.

The fatigue of being pregnant and performing the night shift, while also avoiding Joel, had taken more of a toll on her body than she'd thought. Her limbs felt shaky and her head had begun to swim with dizziness. Evelyn slid to the floor. Hot tears pooled in the corners of her eyes as she drew her knees to her chest and laid her chin on top.

"We need sleep, don't we, little one?" she murmured.

Her heavy eyelids drooped, taunting her to give in to the sleep she craved so badly. But she couldn't be caught sleeping. Not when she needed to be the best nurse at the hospital.

She pushed herself back to her feet and left the bathroom. When she entered the other ward, she found the two nurses on duty talking quietly in a corner of the room, instead of seeing to patients. They straightened to attention when Evelyn strode toward them.

"Is there a problem?" Perhaps they were discussing what to do about one of the soldiers.

Both nurses shook their heads. One of them, a blonde named Sophie Whiteson, blushed. "I was only telling Abigail my news. We made sure all of our patients were cared for first."

"And what is the news?" Evelyn asked, doing her best to sound more interested than she felt.

Nurse Whiteson smiled. "Sister Marcelle told me today I'm being transferred to the front lines. I leave in two days." She clasped her hands to her chest. "I can't wait. I've been wishing for this since I came to France."

"You're so lucky," Abigail Tabbott gushed. "I hope I get transferred there."

*Why?* Evelyn bit back the question. She'd never understood the other nurses' fascination, at St. Vincent's or at the other hospital where she'd worked, to serve at the front lines. While she wanted to help wherever she was assigned, she preferred doing it somewhere with regular hours and breaks, nice accommodations, and little danger.

"You never know." Nurse Whiteson gave her friend's arm a reassuring pat. "You know how the Army is—one week you're here and the next you could be at the front. You could be transferred there anytime."

The two of them moved away to check on the patients, leaving Evelyn alone—and shaken. *You could be transferred there anytime.* Nurse Whiteson's optimistic words repeated in Evelyn's head, but they had taken on an ominous, foreboding tone. She dropped into a seat at the nearby table, unable to remain on her feet any longer.

When she had formed her plan regarding what to do about her pregnancy, she'd completely overlooked the possibility of being transferred again. At any moment, she could be assigned to the front lines. What would she do then?

She could refuse to go, on the grounds that she was pregnant, but then she might not have garnered enough support from the sisters to be allowed to stay at St. Vincent's. On the other hand, she couldn't go to the front while she was carrying a child. The long hours, the cold and the mud, the Germans close by—that wasn't a place for a pregnant nurse. Neither was the harried pace of the front conducive to leniency. The Army was more likely to arrange for her passage home, once they learned about the baby, than to find her a different, safer situation.

Her headache intensified at the predicament, along with the sickness in her stomach. But now fear mingled with the nausea. Evelyn picked up the ledger book from the table, but when she tried to read the notes, her mind refused to process the information. A fresh wave of dizziness swept over her. She shut her eyes against the tilting room, unaware of anyone's approach until someone touched her sleeve.

"Evelyn?"

She opened her eyes to find Nurse Whiteson staring at her with a worried expression. "Are you sick?"

Evelyn opened her mouth to deny it, but the words wouldn't come. She felt so weary and ill at the moment she no longer cared if she were discharged on the spot— as long as she could sleep before leaving.

"You look white as a ghost. Why don't you go back to your room?" Nurse Whiteson gestured to the hallway. "There are only a few hours until our shift ends anyway. We're fine here, and I'm sure the others can get along well enough for a little longer."

Evelyn slowly rose. She could muster up the energy to finish her shift, couldn't she? But the thought of sleep—and the chance to forget about Joel and Ralph and her ruined plans—proved too tantalizing for her fatigued mind and body. "Are you sure?"

Nurse Whiteson nodded and gave her a gentle push toward the door. "Go sleep. We'll be fine."

Evelyn wanted to beg her not to tell Sister Marcelle about leaving the shift early, but that would only raise suspicion. Instead she'd get some much-needed sleep, then throw her reputation on the good graces of her fellow nurses.

She left the ward and descended the stairs, gripping the banister tight to keep from stumbling in her tired, dizzy state. Rather than winding her way to the back of the building, she let herself out the main doors. Dark still cloaked the world outside the hospital. Evelyn welcomed the coolness of the predawn against her flushed cheeks. The air tasted of dew as she inhaled deeply.

Removing her cap, she walked around the hospital and across the lawn to the nurses' building. She added her shoes to the cap in her hands and crept up the stairs. When she reached her and Alice's room, she climbed onto her bed without bothering to change out of her uniform and apron. Within moments, sweet slumber claimed her.

\* \* \*

Daylight nudged Evelyn awake. She blinked at the sunshine pouring through the slit in the curtains. Stretching, she sat up. Alice's bed was empty, as she'd expected. On the bedside table, someone had placed a plate of dried toast. An unexpected but welcome surprise. The small meal would allow her to stay out of the dining room for a while and hopefully keep the others—especially Sister Marcelle—from learning she'd left her shift early.

Evelyn picked up the plate, suddenly famished. A folded note dropped to the wood floor, and she bent to collect it. She sampled a bite of the toast, then opened the note. Alice's name was scrawled along the bottom.

*I heard you weren't feeling well. Hope this toast I commandeered from Cook will help.*

Evelyn smiled.

*I'll check in on you later when my shift is over.*

*P.S. Sister Marcelle asked me to tell you she wants to visit with you at 3:00 today.*

The single bite in Evelyn's stomach felt as heavy as a mortar shell. The head sister wanted to meet with her. She hadn't escaped the consequences of leaving her shift. She'd only fooled herself into thinking sleep would somehow change things.

A glance at the clock on the bureau confirmed she had only a few hours before her meeting. The thought revived her queasiness from earlier and she fled to the bathroom. Though the feeling eventually faded, Evelyn felt every bit as shaky and dizzy as she had before sleeping. She returned to her bed and forced down a few more bites of toast. She attempted to sleep, but every time she started to doze, she saw the disappointed faces of her grandmother and grandfather in her mind's eye.

Finally she gave up trying to fall back asleep. She removed her wrinkled dress and stained apron for her other pair. A glance at her stomach drew an audible groan from her lips. There was a slight bump there she'd been too busy or too tired to notice sooner.

Panic made her fingers shake as she pulled on a clean dress and utility apron. Sister Marcelle would likely question her health after Evelyn had abandoned her shift early this morning. What should she say in response? She couldn't hide her exhaustion and sickness much longer.

Evelyn paced the small room. The four walls seemed to press in on her, and the air felt too stale and hot. There had to be a way to avoid telling everyone the truth this soon, a way to avoid being transferred to the front. But what? She tried to breathe in deeply, but her chest felt tight. Nausea threatened again, but she clamped her teeth against it.

No wonder she couldn't think or breathe. The room was stifling. She knelt on her bed and wrenched the window open, inhaling deep gulps of the cooler outside air. On the lawn below, several soldiers sat reading or dozing in chairs. To one side, a soldier, attempting to walk, leaned heavily on a cane, while a nurse hovered near him. Evelyn peered more closely at the man. It was Joel. She glanced at the hand he'd bandaged last night. Next to Ralph, she hadn't met another soldier as genuine and kind as Joel Campbell.

She watched as he limped a few steps, then stopped to rest with the aid of his cane. Even without seeing his face

clearly, she could guess at the determination etched there.
He would do all he could to leave as quickly as possible.
Then he'd be gone. The thought filled her with a sharp
sense of sadness. She would miss his kindness and his
sense of humor and, most of all, his connection to Ralph.

What would happen to Joel when he went home, now
that he couldn't have the big family he'd always wanted?
He would still make a good husband, if he could find
someone willing to accept not having children. Perhaps a
widow with a child of her own.

Evelyn rested her head against the window frame. The
fresh air had calmed her nausea, but it hadn't assuaged
her frazzled nerves. She still had to face Sister Marcelle
and the reality of being discharged much sooner than
she'd planned. If only she and Ralph had been able to
marry before he'd been killed...

A flash of brilliance made her sit up straight. If she
married someone else, she could avoid devastating her
grandparents and being transferred, too. But who would
she marry here? Her gaze drifted out the window and
alighted on Joel. Like a kaleidoscope coming into focus,
her scattered thoughts coalesced into a plan. She would
ask Corporal Joel Campbell to marry her. He would still
have the chance to be a father, to her child, and she would
no longer be an unwed nurse with a baby on the way. She
would be helping both of them with her proposal.

The longer she pondered the bold idea, the better it
sounded. Setting her jaw, Evelyn put on her shoes and left
the room. Her heart drummed faster, almost painfully so,
as she rushed down the stairs. It would work—it had to
work. And the sooner she presented her plan to Joel and
gained his approval, the better. Then she could face Sister

Marcelle with the hope that even if she were discharged today, she wouldn't seal her grandparents' failing health by showing up unannounced and pregnant.

Outside Evelyn headed straight toward Joel. She needed to conjure up some reason to take over helping him walk, in order to talk to him. To her relief, she saw the nurse with him was none other than shy Nurse Shaw.

Evelyn tucked an errant curl back beneath her nurse's cap and smoothed the front of her apron. She must look her best.

"Nurse Shaw?" Evelyn kept her tone light and friendly as she approached the two. Joel twisted to face her. Was that anticipation in his hazel eyes at seeing her? She didn't have time to analyze it. "Have you had lunch yet?"

Nurse Shaw shot a glance at Joel and shook her head.

"I've already eaten," Evelyn explained, "so I can relieve you here, if you'd like."

The other nurse hesitated a moment. "All right. If you're sure."

Evelyn nodded. "How far did you plan to walk?"

"To there." Nurse Shaw pointed to the nearest corner of the hospital.

"Don't I get any say in how far we go?" Joel muttered darkly, but his mouth twitched with a hidden smile.

Nurse Shaw relinquished her post at his right side to allow Evelyn to take her place. "Shall we?" she asked Joel as the other nurse headed across the lawn.

He glanced from her to the hospital. "I think Nurse Shaw may have been a bit ambitious."

"Probably at Nurse Thornton's bidding. Would you rather rest?" She held her breath, hoping he'd agree. Sitting down would mean a chance to reveal her plan to him.

He eyed the distance again, then shook his head. "I'll keep going."

Evelyn swallowed a sigh of momentary defeat. Surely a few more minutes wouldn't make a difference. There was still plenty of time to talk to him before she faced Sister Marcelle.

Joel shuffled forward, most of his weight on his cane. Evelyn walked alongside him and kept close watch in case he looked as if he might fall. "You're doing rather well for your first day out of bed."

"Do you mean that?" he said, throwing her a quick look. "Or is that what you say to all your patients when they're sweating like pigs after going five steps?"

Evelyn couldn't help laughing. "No, really. I mean it."

After another four or five steps, he stopped. His shoulders rose and fell with labored breaths. The corner of the hospital stood a good ten feet away still.

"Keep going or rest?" she prodded gently.

"Keep going."

The muscles in his jaw tightened as he moved forward one step, then another. Evelyn studied his profile as she moved slowly alongside him. No one would deny he was handsome. But could she imagine Joel as her husband? She still knew very little about him, and he even less about her. And yet her plan gave them both what they wanted out of life. While it might not be a marriage born of love, she believed they could be happy. Couldn't they?

Joel edged ahead of her, his face a mask of stone, his gaze riveted on the corner of the hospital. Beads of sweat had formed on his forehead, but he plodded forward.

"You're almost there." She'd never spent time with the

soldiers learning to walk and move about again, but she liked seeing Joel's progress. "Just a little farther."

With a single cry and a slight lunge, he crossed the final few feet and slapped his hand against the gray stone wall of the hospital. His breath was coming so hard he had to bend over, but he threw her a triumphant smile first. It was the first real smile she'd seen on him since his arrival at St. Vincent's, and Evelyn felt a strange thrill in her stomach at having it bestowed on her.

"Take that," he said, giving the building a *whack* with his cane. "I'll be back at the front in no time."

*All the more reason to ask for his help now.*

She took a step backward and pointed over her shoulder. "I'm going to get a chair and let you rest here."

Without waiting for his response, she found an empty lawn chair and proceeded to drag it over to where Joel leaned against the hospital. Once she had him seated, she brought another chair over for herself.

Joel rested his head on the back of the chair and blew out his breath. "That was harder than I thought it'd be. At home I could run a hundred times that distance and not be winded."

"Give yourself time. You'll be back to running before you know it."

He murmured agreement and shut his eyes. Was he planning to sleep? She needed to talk to him—now—before her meeting with Sister Marcelle. Evelyn threw a furtive glance at the others seated around the lawn. No one was looking in their direction. This was her moment.

She scooted to the edge of her chair and clasped her hands in her lap. Any words she meant to speak, though, became lodged in her throat. The sun felt suddenly too warm, her mouth too dry. Could she really propose marriage to a practical stranger?

The bandage he'd tied around her cut rubbed against her clammy skin. She glanced down at the cloth. Not only was he kind, but Joel was also Ralph's best friend and the squad leader he'd revered. She had nothing to fear from at least asking.

She pinched her eyes shut for a moment, gathering her courage. When she opened them, she forced herself to speak. "There's something I need to discuss...with you."

His eyelids flew open and he shifted slightly toward her. "What's that?"

"You were right the other night about my...um... condition."

He didn't reply, just watched her with those intent hazel eyes.

Evelyn swiped at her forehead. Where had the earlier breeze gone? "Ralph and I were going to be married." She studied her hands. What sort of ring would he have found her? "Not only because we loved each other, but because of the..." She finished in a whisper, "Baby."

Joel nodded silently. If only she could read what was going on behind that stoic expression. She swallowed, hoping to restore the moisture to her mouth.

"No else knows, about Ralph or my situation. Not even my grandparents." The admission tasted as dishonorable on her tongue as it sounded in her head. "I'd hoped I wouldn't have to tell anyone, at least not until after Ralph and I married and I was discharged. Their health isn't what it used to be."

"What will you do now?" After his silence, the question seemed to trumpet across the lawn. Evelyn checked to be sure they were still safe from listening ears. No one appeared to be paying them any attention.

"Actually..." She tried to muster a smile, but it fell flat. "You may be able to help with that."

"Me?"

Did she mistake the smallest hardening of his jaw? Needles of fear prickled along her arms, increasing the panicked thud of her pulse and robbing the air around her of its heat. Had she misread his kindness earlier? The pause between them stretched on as doubt settled in the pit of her stomach. Could she make him understand, persuade him to agree? She had no other recourse. He must know that. Evelyn wiped her damp palms against her apron. If nothing else, Joel's friendship with Ralph would surely convince him to consider her offer.

Clinging to that hope, she leaned forward, ready to press her suit. "The way I see it, we can help each other. I want to avoid disappointing my grandparents and being transferred to the front while I'm with child. And you want a family of your own, which you can no longer have." His face remained unchanged, but she saw his eyes narrow with what she could only guess must be grief and anger. "What I'm offering is a child to call your own, Joel."

He sat very still. Long enough to incite fresh dread in Evelyn. "Are you suggesting, you and I marry, *Nurse Gray*?"

His use of her title felt as shrewd as a slap. But she wouldn't be cowed by his initial reaction. The man was allowed some degree of incredulity. "That is exactly what I'm suggesting." She drew herself up in her chair and met his hard gaze. "We may not know each other well yet, but

I believe a marriage of contentment and happiness is possible. It would fulfill both our desires for the future."

"You're mistaken if you think you know what I desire for my future." His countenance had grown as stony as the hospital behind them, his words clipped and brittle. "A marriage of convenience is not the solution."

"But it would save us both," she pleaded.

"At what cost?" Joel countered. "Neither of us deserves a loveless marriage. Can't you see that?"

She was losing his interest, if she'd ever had it to begin with. "Even to be a father?"

He shook his head. "That's only trading one source of happiness for another. I couldn't live that way, Evelyn. And in the end, I don't think you could either." She tried to muster up some relief that he'd gone back to calling her by her first name, but she felt as flattened as a punctured tire.

"What about Ralph?" It was her final attempt at persuasion.

Joel looked away, his expression pained. "You'll always have my friendship because of what you meant to Ralph." He managed to climb to his feet without her assistance. "But that's not reason enough for us to marry. I'm sorry."

He hobbled forward with the help of his cane. Evelyn let him go, too numb to care how he managed to get himself back to his wheelchair and into the hospital. Her plan had failed. She'd pinned all her hopes on Joel, but to no avail. He didn't want her.

Tears threatened to spill, but she wouldn't release them in view of everyone outside. She rose from her chair and discreetly headed for the woods. Once alone, and no longer able to hear the sounds from the hospital, she sank between the gnarled roots of an old tree and let the sobs flow freely.

"I tried, little one," she whispered, one hand on her belly.

There were only two choices now. She could leave this very minute or she could meet with Sister Marcelle and accept whatever fate was dealt her. Perhaps the head sister didn't know her secret yet. Evelyn could take whatever reprimand Sister Marcelle might issue for ending a shift early, if she could stay a little longer and put off facing her grandparents.

Determined to leave only when made to, she dried her eyes with the back of her hand and stood. Her future might be uncertain, but one thing was clear: She would never speak to or interact with Joel Campbell as long as she remained at the hospital. That decision alone gave her the courage to leave the safety of the trees and prepare herself to face Sister Marcelle.

# Chapter 5

Evelyn stood outside Sister Marcelle's office at two minutes to three o'clock. She'd procured some bread and tea earlier from the kitchen staff, which thankfully had settled her stomach. Her hands felt sweaty again and her heart beat a nervous pace, but she was resigned to face the sister's potential wrath and answer any questions as vaguely as possible.

She drew in a deep breath and let it out as she knocked firmly on the door.

"Come in," Sister Marcelle called out.

Evelyn opened the door and stepped inside. Would she ever feel at home in this tiny room, or always fear being summoned here?

The sister glanced up from where she sat writing at her table. "May I help you, Nurse Gray?"

"Nurse Thornton said you wished to speak with me."

Sister Marcelle studied her a moment. "Oh, yes." She

returned to scribbling something on the paper in front of her and didn't bother to look up as she said, "You have been relieved of your current position."

Only one reason could account for her being dismissed, without explanation—Sister Marcelle had learned about the baby. Evelyn took a halting step backward. Her knees knocked against a chair and she dropped onto it. She couldn't seem to draw a full breath. The light streaming in from the window began to fracture before her eyes. She was going to faint, right here in the head sister's office.

She clutched the edges of the chair as hard as she could until the black particles edging her vision faded. She had to know who suspected her pregnancy and had revealed it to the head sister. Surely not Joel, though he might have after their disastrous conversation earlier.

"Why am I being let go?"

"Because of your expertise."

*My expertise?* A startled laugh bubbled up toward her lips, though she managed to curtail it. Sister Marcelle didn't know about the baby. Her relief cut every bit as deep and decisive as her fear a moment ago. She could stay. The desire to throw her arms around the head sister nearly propelled her out of her chair. Instead she squeezed her hands together to stem her giddy energy. "I'm not sure I understand."

Sister Marcelle set down her pen. "Sister Monique has returned, earlier than expected. Which means we no longer need you on the night shift."

"Where would you like me then?" Hope leapt inside her, but Evelyn tried to rein in the feeling. Surely someone had mentioned her leaving early this morning. There would still be some repercussions from that decision, wouldn't there?

"Dr. Dupont has requested you work with him in surgery." Sister Marcelle placed the paper on top of the neat pile at her elbow and smiled kindly at Evelyn. "He feels the other nurses currently working with him could use your maturity and experience in improving their own skills."

For the first time in days, Evelyn matched the sister's smile with a genuine one of her own.

"Until we receive another group of soldiers, there are no scheduled surgeries at present. Dr. Dupont will let you know when you are needed in his surgery room." Sister Marcelle picked up another paper and placed it front and center on the table. "In the meantime, I would like you to serve in the recovery ward, with those soldiers who are working to regain their mobility before going to the convalescent home."

Evelyn didn't mind the new assignment, in surgery or the recovery ward. Hadn't she enjoyed watching Joel make progress today? Her smile froze as she realized exactly whom she would be working with. Joel's severe words from earlier rang through her head: *You're mistaken if you think you know what I desire for my future. A marriage of convenience is not the solution.*

Sister Marcelle's voice interrupted the bitter reverie. "Dr. Dupont asked that you head to his surgery room now, so he may show you how he handles things there."

Evelyn rose to her feet. "Thank you, Sister Marcelle."

"You're welcome, child." She lifted her pen again. "I know the night shift is not easy, especially when one is feeling a bit under the weather."

The remark stopped Evelyn in her retreat. So the head sister did know about Evelyn leaving her shift early. Sister Marcelle didn't look upset or annoyed, though.

"If you need to rest again after you meet with Dr. Dupont," the sister said, leaning over her page, "I want you to do so. I need my best nurses in tip-top shape."

"I'll see how I'm feeling," Evelyn managed to say evenly, despite her joy over the suggestion. "Thank you again."

She slipped out the door and down the first flight of stairs. In the stairwell, she paused to lean against the wall, allowing her hopes to rise unencumbered by her earlier doubts and fears. Now she would be able to get the rest she so desperately needed, instead of staying up all night. The new arrangement couldn't be more perfect, except for having to see Joel on a regular basis. Still, Evelyn felt confident she could get Nurse Shaw or one of the other recovery ward nurses to help him instead.

She pushed away from the wall and descended the stairs toward the surgery rooms, her head held high. Joel might have sabotaged her earlier plan, but she wasn't going anywhere without a fight.

*　*　*

By the time supper rolled around, Joel's exuberance over his progress that afternoon had cooled considerably. Not only did every one of his injuries hurt, but every time he thought of Evelyn's proposition, his jaw clenched in anger. The repetitive action meant his face now ached along with the rest of his body. Even the hearty stew he was allowed to eat couldn't perk up his bad mood.

He stabbed his spoon into the bowl and brought a bite
to his mouth, wishing it were some of his mother's fried
chicken and buttery rolls. The stew burned his tongue
and Joel fought hard against uttering a curse beneath his
breath. He tossed his spoon down and gulped some water to ease his scorched mouth. He'd let his supper cool
down before he attempted to eat any more. Trouble was
he didn't have anything else to do to distract himself from
his dark thoughts.

What was Evelyn thinking, asking him to agree to a
marriage of convenience? His jaw worked tight again. If
he did marry someday, it would be for love. Not simply
to have a child to pass on his name. He wanted to marry
the right woman, someone who loved him as deeply and
passionately as he did her. Evelyn certainly wasn't that
woman. Though he couldn't deny an attraction to her,
she was Ralph's, the mother of his child. His best friend
would be first and foremost in her heart, and Joel didn't
want to play second fiddle to Ralph's memory. No matter
how guilty he felt over Ralph's death.

He absently stirred his stew, hoping to cool it faster.
Now that he'd refused Evelyn's proposal, what would
she do? She couldn't hide her pregnancy forever, which
meant she'd eventually be discharged and have to confess
the news to her grandparents. The ever-present guilt rose
up, scalding him as effectively as his stew a moment ago.

At least Ralph had planned to make an honest woman
of her. Unlike Les's father. Would Evelyn and her child
end up like Vivian and Les if Joel didn't help them?

At eighteen, Vivian had been driven from her childhood home shortly after Les's birth by the aunt who'd
raised her for several years. She lived with neighbors for a

time, but eventually she and her son were forced to move on, relying on the generosity of others. Joel's mother and father heard of her plight from someone at church and offered her a place to stay as long as she liked.

Having a roof overhead and a kind family to belong to didn't completely erase the haunted look from Vivian's pretty eyes or end her quiet sobs, which Joel could hear through the walls when she thought everyone was asleep. He'd often wondered what sort of heartache and trials she'd experienced before coming to live with them.

In his last letter from Vivian, who was married and settled in another county back home with her husband and four other children, she'd written to say Les had run away and she didn't know where he had gone. Her anguish had been palpable in every penned word.

Deep regret cut through Joel at the thought of the little boy who'd been his constant companion, now a fifteen-year-old kid, roaming the world in hopes of finding his place. Would that happen with Ralph and Evelyn's child? Would Evelyn's grandparents kick her out as Vivian's relatives had done?

"It's not my problem," he muttered under his breath.

"You say somethin', Campbell?" Sergeant Dennis asked.

Joel gave a noncommittal grunt. "How's the stew?"

Dennis loudly slurped a spoonful. "Not bad. Beats the mess at the front lines, huh?" He laughed at his own remark, clearly not caring when Joel didn't join in. "What's got you riled up tonight? You and that other nurse—what's her name?—Nurse Gray have a falling-out?"

"A falling-out?" His friend's perceptiveness annoyed him nearly as much as Evelyn's crazy idea about marrying. "I don't know what you're talking about," he said before shoveling a bite into his mouth.

"All right. You play that card. But I got eyes. And the two of you seem to be thick as thieves sometimes. Not that I mind." His gaze followed Nurse Thornton's movements across the room. "Just wish I knew how to get her to talk to me like that one talks to you."

"It's not..." Joel let his words fade out. He couldn't explain things to Sergeant Dennis. He'd promised Evelyn he wouldn't say anything, and he wouldn't break that promise, no matter how frustrated he might feel.

Companionable silence fell between him and Dennis as they ate. Joel almost wished the guy would keep talking—it would keep his mind occupied on something else besides Evelyn.

She'd just have to find help elsewhere.

Joel cringed at his own callousness. Ralph had been his best friend, and if Joel had made a different decision the other day, his buddy might have made it back to Evelyn. But Ralph's death—and Joel's part in it—had robbed her of that chance. Did that mean he was obligated to help her? The possibility chafed at his already troubled mind.

He plunked his spoon down a second time, his bowl only half-empty, and placed his tray at his side. Even his bird notebook, with its fascinating notes and sketches, couldn't hold his attention.

If things had been reversed and he'd been in Ralph's position...Joel mentally shook his head. He doubted he would have found himself in Ralph and Evelyn's position. But what if there had been a special girl in his life— a dear friend or wife—and he was killed, would he want

Ralph to look after her? *Perhaps.* Although he suspected his family would want to help as well.

His parents had welcomed Vivian all those years ago and had accepted Livy's German-American husband. They even treated Tom's fiancée, Nora, much like the daughter-in-law she would've been if he hadn't been killed. But who would look after Evelyn and her child when her grandparents eventually passed on? She had no other family—no parents or siblings, as he did, to rely on.

Joel ran a hand through his hair in agitation. He'd been so certain when he left her sitting outside, with her shocked expression, that he was the one in the right. No one would expect him to take her as his wife.

Then how come he felt so blasted guilty for making her figure things out on her own?

"You ever wonder why the good things you want aren't necessarily what God wants?" He didn't realize he'd voiced the question out loud until Dennis chuckled.

"You askin' *me* for religious advice, Campbell?"

Joel ignored his friend's remark and instead considered his own question. He'd always thought marrying and having a big family were in line with God's plan for his life. Now he wasn't so sure. Did God want him to help Evelyn, possibly even marry her?

He blew out a frustrated sigh at the prospect. "So we go along with God's will, whether we want to or not?"

Dennis threw back his head and laughed. "I've been doing the opposite. But I ain't convinced it's gettin' me what I want. Maybe we both oughta try the other approach. Kind of like that guy who ran away from God. The one who got swallowed by that whale."

"Jonah?" As a kid, Joel had loved that story.

"Yeah—that's the one. He didn't want to go preach in that town like God wanted him to, so he upped and took off. We know how that turned out." Dennis twisted to face Joel. "I'm guessin' he figured out real quick down in the gut of that smelly, cold whale that doing what God wanted was a heck of a lot better than doing what he wanted. Then when he finally did get to preaching like God asked—"

"Things turned out for the best." Nurse Thornton stood between their two beds, her face a mixture of surprise and reflection. How long had she been listening? "Are you talking religion, Sergeant Dennis?" Joel noted she only had eyes for his friend at that moment.

Dennis's face went bright red. "I...um..."

"I admire a man who isn't afraid to talk about God." With that she marched away, but Joel caught the slight smile on her face before she'd faced forward.

"Looks like you just found a way to get on her good side, Dennis." Joel shook his head good-naturedly.

"Gimme that Bible, Campbell." Dennis stuck out his hand, but his attention was still focused on Nurse Thornton.

Joel fished the Bible out from under his bag—he hadn't opened it in several days—and handed it over. He didn't let go right away, though. Instead he waited for Dennis to look at him. "Don't go luring her into a friendship with false pretenses." He'd seen firsthand what could happen when things went too far between a soldier and a nurse, and he didn't want that happening to Nurse Thornton, no matter how great a guy Dennis might be.

"I don't plan to." Dennis's usual flippant mood had disappeared, his expression somber. "If I can get her to talk to me—even about religion—instead of yellin' at me, I'll be happy."

Joel relinquished the Bible to his friend. He didn't know Sergeant Dennis all that well, but he trusted the man's sincerity. Resting his head against the headboard behind him, he stared at the window across the room.

The exercise earlier, however brutal, had stirred restless energy within him. If only he could persuade the nurses to let him try walking again. The more he attempted it, the stronger he'd be and the sooner he could leave the hospital. Perhaps a short walk, to the chair across the room, would convince them he could handle greater amounts of exercise.

He called for one of the nurses, asking her to help him to the empty chair by the window. Just as he'd hoped, the short distance seemed to deter her from refusing. Joel took his bird notebook with him. After a few halting but less painful steps, he made it to the chair. The light wouldn't fully disappear for a few more hours, so several soldiers and nurses were still making good use of the back lawn. Joel scanned the trees bordering the grass, hoping to see some birds.

A movement out of the corner of his eye drew his attention. A nurse, without her cap on, held the hand of a young boy. Joel recognized Evelyn's dark curls at once. Who was the child? He watched them walk across the lawn and sit beneath one of the trees. Evelyn withdrew what looked like bread from her pocket and handed it to the boy. The lad ate the bread slowly as the two of them talked. Even at a distance, Joel sensed the amiable companionship between them.

*Evelyn will make a good mother.*

Regret followed closely on the heels of his realization. Ralph would never get to see this side of the woman he'd loved.

Would his best friend want Joel to look after Evelyn and her child?

"If I had to do things over," Ralph had said recently, "I think I would've been more like you, Campbell."

A fresh wave of shame heated Joel's neck at the remembrance. What would Ralph say if he were to show up now? Joel wasn't sure he wanted to know. His behavior today hadn't shown the kind of discipline and benevolence he'd strived to live by, especially at the front lines. If nothing else, as Ralph's squad leader and closest friend, Joel owed him. Perhaps helping Ralph's girl would assuage some of his guilt, as long as Evelyn didn't learn the truth about that day by the ravine.

Joel blew out his breath and returned his gaze to Evelyn and the boy. Her curls fell loose around her face without her cap to keep them back. What did her hair smell like? Was it soft to the touch? He shook his head at the foolish questions.

He couldn't deny an innate desire to look after her, something he suspected went beyond his friendship with Ralph. But he still knew so little about her, and getting to know her once he left the hospital would be next to impossible. He'd have to decide before going to the convalescent home what he intended to do.

*Then we'll do this on my terms.*

Joel would consider marrying Evelyn, but only after he got to know her better. Chances were he'd come to the conclusion he only needed to assist her in some way—not ask her to marry him.

Whatever happened, Joel wouldn't allow a repeat of his experience with Rose. If she hadn't been right for him, surely Evelyn Gray wasn't either, despite her pretty looks and kindness. He mustn't confuse thoughtfulness with duty either. Evelyn was a nurse first and foremost, and her proposal was a business arrangement. Nothing more.

# Chapter 6

Evelyn rinsed the surgical tools in the stream of water, brushing a sweaty curl off her forehead with the back of her wet hand. The surgical wards typically kept their windows shut for sanitation purposes, and though the rooms were located in the basement and therefore cooler than the wards upstairs, she still found the temperature too warm in her condition.

"Nurse Gray?" Dr. Dupont rubbed at his spectacles with a cloth as he approached her. She turned off the water. "You do excellent work."

"Thank you. My father deserves the credit, though." She began placing the tools on a clean towel beside the sink. "He let me assist him with a few emergency surgeries when I was in high school and whet my interest in helping that way. Still, it's been some time since I've taken part in an operation."

"Your skills have clearly returned. I am pleased to have you helping down here."

A bit embarrassed at his effusive praise, she changed the subject. "How do you think that young man will fare, without his leg?"

The doctor placed his glasses back on his nose and frowned. "I cannot say for certain, but he is lucky the gangrene did not spread."

"I imagine it will be some time before he feels lucky," Evelyn murmured, more to herself than to the surgeon.

"You are probably right." He took a step toward the door. "I am going up for a late lunch. Would you care to join me?"

She hesitated, though the man had been nothing but respectful toward her. He was at least twice her age and she did not know him at all. What would the other nurses say if they were to find the two of them eating and talking by themselves in the dining hall?

While the rules governing doctors and nurses were different than those of soldiers and nurses, she was still smarting over Joel's rejection. Thankfully she hadn't seen him since their disastrous conversation two days earlier.

"Thank you, but I think I'll finish cleaning up first."

He bowed his head in a gracious nod. "Some other time perhaps. We have no other surgeries scheduled for this afternoon, but I will find you should something arise. "

"Yes, sir." Evelyn almost wished there would be an influx of patients. The few surgeries she'd helped with had kept her mind occupied, leaving her little time to think about the uncertainty of her future.

At the door, Dr. Dupont paused. "You remind me very much of my daughter, Bridgette." He leaned against the doorjamb, his gaze distant. "She and her husband live near Sedan, under German occupation. Right before the Germans invaded, she was pregnant with their first child."

A ripple of fear walked up Evelyn's spine. Had the man already guessed her secret, and after only one day of working together? Would the sisters know before much longer?

"We have had no contact with them since. I still do not know if I have a grandson or a granddaughter." He removed his glasses again and wiped at his glistening eyes with his thumb. "When this war is over, I suppose we will know then."

Evelyn's alarm faded into relief. He wasn't telling her he knew her secret; he was simply talking about his daughter, whom he missed. The sadness on his lined face tugged at Evelyn's heart, bringing memories of her own father. "She must be equally devastated to be separated from you."

Dr. Dupont replaced his glasses. "I held out hope she and my son-in-law were together, but I have heard some of the Frenchmen in the occupied villages have been sent away by the Germans. I pray to God every night that He is watching over them."

Is that what her grandparents hoped and prayed for, too—that God would watch over Evelyn? If only He were, if only she hadn't been left on her own. "Do you have any other children?"

"A son. He is serving in the French army. I haven't heard anything from him in two months. I tell myself he must be fine and it is just our sporadic mail." For his sake, Evelyn hoped it was the slow mail system, too, and that the kind surgeon wouldn't receive the same devastating news she had about Ralph. "At least my wife is safe in our village. With both our children gone and encountering who knows what at the hands of our enemies, she has turned our home into a refuge for children. Those who have lost one or both parents. They help with the garden and chores and, in turn, receive meals or a bed, whatever they need."

Instinctively her hand rose to rest against her stomach. Her own child had already lost a parent. What would happen to the baby if something were to befall her, too? Her grandparents would only be around for so much longer. Then who would provide her child with all the love and security she'd experienced growing up, however isolated Evelyn might have felt at times?

With slightly trembling hands, she dried the tools and placed them in the nearby cupboard. She couldn't bear the thought of her child being alone in the world, relying on the kindness of strangers.

Desperate for something else to think about, to talk about, she noticed the half-empty supply shelves and seized on their existence as a new topic of conversation. "It appears you have about the same number of supplies as we do upstairs." She locked the cupboard with the keys the doctor had entrusted to her.

"We are going to need more soon, if we are to continue performing surgeries. Even our supply of bandages is growing frightfully low." Dr. Dupont released a heavy sigh and straightened. "I will bid you good day, Nurse Gray. Thank you for indulging a father's ramblings."

"I think I'll join you after all," she said on impulse. The poor man had to be as lonely as she. "Everything is clean down here and I'm starving." She meant it, too. Her usual nausea had ebbed away by midmorning and now she felt hungry enough to eat the kitchen clean.

"I would enjoy that." The man's dark eyes crinkled with a smile as he motioned for her to lead the way up the stairs.

Evelyn entered the dining room first and found several sisters and nurses still eating. She needn't have worried about being alone with the doctor after all, though after hearing the sad tale of his daughter, she no longer cared what others thought. The man simply needed someone— especially someone who reminded him of his daughter— to talk with.

After collecting their food, Evelyn followed Dr. Dupont to one of the occupied tables, where they sat across from each other. He reminisced as they ate, regaling Evelyn with stories about his son and daughter's childhood days. She listened with interest, but there were moments when her mind caught hold of the happy image of family he created and she no longer heard his words. A life with a mother and a father, and hopefully siblings, had been what she desired most for her child. To have the family setting she hadn't really experienced but longed for.

"Are you all right, Nurse Gray?" The doctor's kind gaze watched her closely from behind his glasses.

Evelyn forced a light laugh. "Yes, I'm fine. I was only thinking how idyllic life sounds in your French village."

Dr. Dupont tore a piece from his bread. "It may sound that way now, especially given all the horrors we have seen in recent years. But there were struggles, too. No life is without them."

*And I'm going through the worst of them now.*

How she longed to unburden her secret to someone. Someone who would listen and help. Someone unlike Joel.

As she tried to think of a suitable response, Evelyn glanced up to see Alice frantically waving at her from one of the dining room's doorways.

"If you'll excuse me, Doctor." She stood and hefted her tray. "Thank you for sharing your stories. I thoroughly enjoyed them. And I sincerely hope things work out with your daughter and her family."

"God willing, it is the way we would like," he said with a soft smile. "But I am able to sleep at night because I trust He is caring for her."

A feeling of loneliness enveloped Evelyn as she made her way toward the kitchen to deposit her dishes. She envied the doctor's peace of mind, especially given the uncertainty of the world at present. At one time, she'd felt confident and peaceful about her life and God's hand in it. When had that disappeared, and would she ever find it again?

Forcing such disheartening thoughts from her mind, Evelyn went to find Alice. Her roommate paced the hallway outside the dining room with agitated steps. "Alice, what's the matter?" Evelyn had never seen her in such a frenzy.

"I need your help, Evelyn." Alice stopped pacing, her expression grave. "I went to find you in the surgery ward, but it was empty."

"We just finished up. What's wrong?"

Alice kneaded her hands together. "Sergeant Dennis and a few others were moved to the recovery ward this morning."

Evelyn waited for her to elaborate, unsure why that fact would upset Alice. If anything, she would have thought her roommate overjoyed to have the gregarious sergeant out of her regular ward.

"Sister Marcelle came to find me," Alice continued in a rush of words, "right after they were moved, and asked if I would move to the recovery ward and work with those learning to walk again. Just like you'll be doing."

"It'll be nice to work together again," Evelyn offered. She liked working with Alice and had missed the opportunity they had to talk when they were on the same schedule or serving in the same ward.

Alice looked near tears, though. "Yes, but guess who the sister in the recovery ward assigned me to help today?"

"Sergeant Dennis?"

Alice gave a vigorous nod.

"Why should that matter?" Alice's strong reaction wasn't making any sense. "You've never worried about handling yourself around him before. Did something happen?"

"He said something yesterday that got me thinking." She wouldn't meet Evelyn's eyes as she added, "Maybe he isn't such an oaf after all."

Evelyn frowned. It was bad enough the sergeant had taken such an interest in Alice, but if Alice was warming up to him...Better to keep the two of them away from one another. "Would you like me to walk with him instead?"

"Yes." Alice's face brightened. "I think Sister Giselle was going to have you help Corporal Campbell, but you don't mind switching, do you?"

A victorious smile lifted Evelyn's lips. "Not at all."

Now she could keep an eye on Sergeant Dennis and continue to avoid Joel, too. It was the perfect solution.

Alice linked her arm through Evelyn's. "Thank you. I just need a little more time before I talk to him again."

"Be careful, Alice."

She couldn't help the repeated warning. Alice reminded Evelyn of herself. The way she'd been before meeting Ralph—idealistic and naïve. Though she wouldn't trade meeting Ralph, she was beginning to wish she'd stopped and considered things more carefully during their short time together, instead of allowing her emotions to dictate her decisions.

Alice laughed, drawing Evelyn's attention back to her. "I didn't say I wanted to elope with the man. But I have to figure out how to have an actual conversation with him, without one or both of us getting frustrated."

Evelyn gently squeezed Alice's arm, wishing she could tell her more. How one conversation—with a handsome, attentive soldier—could change the course of one's life forever.

*   *   *

While the recovery ward looked exactly the same as the wards upstairs, Joel had been told he would have more opportunities to go outside now that he was downstairs. If he hadn't been placed on the opposite side of the room from where he'd been before, with Sergeant Dennis on his right instead of his left, he could easily imagine he hadn't moved floors at all.

He set his lunch tray on the bedside table, using his good arm. It was still tricky maneuvering with his left arm in a sling, but he was managing all right. Now if he could get his leg working properly again—and have a chance to talk to Evelyn—he would feel a lot better about his time at the hospital.

As though materializing from his thoughts, Evelyn pushed a wheelchair into the recovery room. Nurse Thornton wheeled in another chair behind her. They both headed toward Joel's corner of the room.

He tamped down his disheveled hair with his hand, his heart beating double time at the sight of Evelyn. Joel told himself it was only because he needed to talk to her and not because he'd missed seeing her. Evelyn hadn't shown up the past two nights with the other nurses on the night shift, nor had she appeared in his ward during the day. Wherever she'd been hiding, it didn't matter. Not when he would finally get the chance to tell her he'd changed his mind about her proposal.

"Afternoon, Sergeant," Evelyn said, somewhat smugly. "It's time for me to help you outside."

Sergeant Dennis looked downright glum at her announcement—the man had clearly been hoping to go outside with Nurse Thornton. Sharp disappointment lanced through Joel as well. He peered at Evelyn as she stepped to the other side of the sergeant's bed, trying to catch her eye, but she didn't spare him a glance.

*She's avoiding me again.*

Could he blame her, though? He hadn't been overly tactful with some of the things he'd said the other day.

"Let me help you into the wheelchair, Corporal." Though a petite thing, Nurse Thornton always managed to assist him without aggravating his injuries.

"Will I be walking today?" he asked once he was seated.

"Yes." Nurse Thornton slipped his shoes onto his feet and placed his cane across his lap.

"How did it go the other day?" She stepped behind his chair, but she didn't move.

Joel watched as Evelyn pushed Sergeant Dennis out of the ward. He needed to figure out a way for them to switch nurses. "The walk went fine." Fine until his conversation with Evelyn.

Nurse Thornton began wheeling him across the room, but she seemed perfectly content to maintain an unhurried pace. Joel gritted his teeth with impatience. Was she purposely trying to go slow? At this rate, Evelyn would be halfway across the lawn in no time and his chance to speak with her would be lost. He didn't know how soon he'd see her again.

Once outside, Joel blinked in the bright afternoon sunlight. The air felt muggy against his skin. The few nurses and soldiers outdoors had retreated to the shade of the trees. Several walked the perimeter of the lawn, but they appeared to be sticking to the shadows to avoid the direct heat.

Joel spied Evelyn and Sergeant Dennis off to his left. Evelyn was helping the sergeant out of his wheelchair, a walking stick in her free hand. What should he say when they came alongside them? Before he could think of something, Joel found himself being steered in the opposite direction.

"This is where I walked the other day," he blurted out, scrambling for any excuse to change course. "I'd like to try the other side." He twisted around to look up at Nurse Thornton. "If you don't mind," he added with a smile.

She stopped pushing the chair, her gaze drifting over

her shoulder to where Joel could see Evelyn and the sergeant walking slowly beside the tree line. "There's more shade this way."

"A little sun would probably do me good," he offered.

Did he sound as desperate as he felt? Apparently. Nurse Thornton made no response, other than to continue pushing his chair away from Evelyn.

What else could he say to persuade her to turn around but not raise her suspicion as to the reason why? She'd seemed rather happy with Sergeant Dennis the other day, and yet now, she acted determined to get away from him.

*That's it.*

"The sergeant isn't so bad once you get to know him," Joel said, glancing up at Nurse Thornton with what he hoped was a casual expression.

Her cheeks turned the same shade as her hair. "I don't know what you're talking about, Corporal. I'm in charge of this chair and I say we're going where you were the other day."

Joel let her think she'd had the last word until she stopped the chair near the hospital corner he'd whacked with his cane two days earlier. She came around the chair to help him up, but he didn't offer her his good arm.

"He only wants to talk with you," he said quietly. "Be your friend. Nothing more. He's even been reading the Bible."

Joel nearly wished the words back when a look of hopefulness flitted across Nurse Thornton's face. Was he orchestrating something wrong, all for the chance to talk to Evelyn? He quickly dismissed the thought. He believed Sergeant Dennis's intentions were honorable when it came to Nurse Thornton.

She released a sigh, her gaze wandering to the other side of the lawn. "I don't know what to say to him now. Not after I've disliked him so much." A faint smile lifted her mouth. "It's easier to yell at him."

"He may still need it."

Her smile turned full. "I would agree. But is it wrong to want to be his friend?"

Joel studied the cane resting across his knees. Could an injured soldier and a nurse strike up a friendship? If not, then the course he was about to take with Evelyn— if she agreed—would also be wrong. And yet he wasn't convinced either one of them were violating the rules.

"I don't think it's wrong. Not here, at least." Joel met Nurse Thornton's earnest look. "Once he leaves the hospital, that's a different story. It could be a long time before you see each other again. Is that something you can live with?"

She hesitated, her mouth twisting with indecision. Joel admired her all the more for it. She wasn't about to rush into anything. If only Evelyn had been a bit more that way, but he couldn't judge.

"I can do that," Nurse Thornton said at last, her tone firm with self-assurance.

"Then I say we get you over there."

She laughed before her demeanor grew somber once more. "I'm the one helping you today, Corporal. So I will decide which side of the lawn we use." The twinkle in her green eyes belied her no-nonsense tone. "We will be heading to the other side," she announced as she marched to her place behind his chair.

Nurse Thornton pushed him across the lawn at a much faster stride this time. Joel gripped the chair arm with his free hand and tried to keep his cane from sliding off his lap. When she made up her mind, Nurse Thornton certainly put all her energies into it—no halfheartedness with her. Other than a passing thought about falling out of the chair and reinjuring his arm or leg, he was pleased, too. He'd figured out a way to talk to Evelyn.

After stopping his wheelchair beside the other one, Nurse Thornton helped Joel to his feet. Evelyn and Sergeant Dennis had walked a good ways down the lawn already, but Joel was determined to catch up. He moved as quickly as his leg and cane would allow, ignoring the pain that began after his first hurried steps.

"Slow down," Nurse Thornton said with a chuckle. "You don't need to move so fast on my account. We can catch up to them when they turn around."

Joel didn't want to ease his speed, but he did so to keep her from suspecting the real reason for his urgency. The slower steps also meant a reprieve from the ache in the lower half of his body. He willed himself to be patient. Evelyn wouldn't be able to avoid him much longer.

It wasn't long before she and Sergeant Dennis turned around and began moving back in Joel's direction. He knew the instant Evelyn saw him. A frown pulled at her mouth and she promptly glanced at the grass, the trees, the sky. Anything but him. Clearly she meant to pretend he wasn't there, walking toward her.

With less than twenty feet between them, Nurse Thornton finally spoke up. "Nurse Gray? I forgot I promised Sergeant Dennis that I would help him today. And I never break a promise." She shot a look at Joel as she voiced the last few words. He guessed at what she couldn't say out loud—she would pursue a friendship with Sergeant Dennis but nothing else.

The surprise on Evelyn's face matched that on the sergeant's. "Are you sure? We're almost done."

Nurse Thornton waved away her excuse. "I know, but I told Sergeant Dennis the other day that if he behaved, I would be the one to help him with his first attempt at walking."

Evelyn glanced at Sergeant Dennis. "I apologize, Sergeant. I didn't realize you'd made prior arrangements." She gave him a pointed glare, then shot a similar one at Nurse Thornton. Joel wasn't sure whom she appeared to be more annoyed with—the other nurse, the sergeant, or himself. Or all three equally.

"She did promise." Sergeant Dennis sounded fairly contrite, though he kept his head up, his gaze riveted on Nurse Thornton.

"Then I suppose I will have to acquiesce." Evelyn motioned the sergeant forward.

Dennis didn't spare Joel a word or a glance as he passed by. Joel chuckled. Perhaps he'd tell his friend later that the true thanks went to Joel for orchestrating the opportunity for the sergeant and the red-headed nurse to talk. Nurse Thornton fell into step beside Sergeant Dennis, but Evelyn remained where she stood, her hard stare boring holes into a nearby tree.

Irritation rolled off her like a heat wave, encompassing Joel within its fury. She had every right to be angry with him. He only hoped she'd stick around long enough to hear what he had to say. With the aid of his cane, he shuffled toward her.

# Chapter 7

Evelyn's cheeks burned with anger and embarrassment as she watched Joel's slow advance. Her relatively calm stomach had started churning the moment Alice had declared she wanted to walk with Sergeant Dennis. What had happened to change Alice's mind? She'd been so adamant about not talking to the sergeant, and Evelyn had been only too happy to comply with the plan to switch soldiers. Now the very person Evelyn had thought she'd successfully eluded was coming toward her.

What would she say? Or worse, what would *he* say?

Joel stopped in front of her, standing close enough that she could feel the warmth of him in spite of the shade. His hazel eyes were lit with the same intense determination she'd seen in them before. Parts of his light brown hair stuck up here and there, despite his attempts to smooth it earlier. She had a sudden urge to rumple it more, to wreak a little havoc on his normally controlled demeanor. His dismissive tone from the other day repeated in her mind, giving her the needed courage to speak.

"I will walk with you because that is my job, but I do not have to listen to you." She moved to his side, so that anyone looking would see nothing amiss. But she made sure to add in a fierce whisper, "I don't want you to say a word. Not a single word. If you so much as repeat anything you said the other day, I will leave you to figure out how to get back to the hospital on your own. Is that clear?"

He nodded silently, a look of apology crossing his face.

*He should be sorry*, she thought as they began walking.

After only a few steps, Joel stopped and turned toward her. "Evelyn, I've changed my mind."

She glowered up at him, appalled at his tenacity. "Weren't you listening? You are not to talk." She lifted her finger and jabbed it against his chest. A rather nice, solid chest. She forced her thoughts back to his belligerence. "I promise you, Joel, I'll leave, if you say one more…" She lowered her hand in surprise as his words finally penetrated her annoyance. "Y-You changed your mind? What do you mean?"

He glanced at the trees beyond her shoulder. "I've changed my mind about your…um…proposal."

Evelyn studied his face, trying to read deceit there. "Why? You made it very clear the other day you had no intention of helping me."

His eyes flicked to hers, then away, but she caught the regret reflected there. "I apologize for some of the things I said that day."

"Some?"

Joel shook his head, a smirk on his mouth. "All of

them. Okay?" He struck out again, without waiting for her, but she easily fell into step beside him. "I've done a lot of thinking since our conversation."

Evelyn did her best to squelch the hope building inside her as she waited for him to elaborate. He hadn't agreed to anything yet, though if he did, all her problems would be at an end.

"I want to help, Evelyn." He slowed his steps. "Next to my own brother, Ralph was my best friend. I owe him...for many reasons."

Evelyn folded her arms against a prick of disappointment. She ought to be overjoyed. Why should he have any other reason for helping her than his friendship with Ralph?

"What about the baby?" She kept her voice barely above a whisper, though there wasn't anyone near their corner of the lawn. "Is that important?"

Joel twisted to face her and faltered in his next step. Evelyn hurried to steady him with a hand to his arm. She meant to release him right away, but she paused and peered up into his eyes instead. They were more gold than green today.

What would it be like to have this man as her husband? To have him look at her with adoration and love, instead of guarded concern?

She broke eye contact first and lowered her arm to her side. *You're being silly*, she told herself. *You need his help, not his love. That isn't what he's agreeing to.*

"I promise to look after the baby," he said, easing Evelyn's worries until he spoke again. "Whatever happens, I will help you, Evelyn."

This didn't sound like an agreement to her plan. Her

earlier anger swooped in again, bringing with it fresh fear and snuffing out any glimmer of anticipation. "You said you'd changed your mind. Are you or aren't you going to marry me?" She hated the candid words, but she had to know. Everything depended upon his answer.

"I'm willing to consider marriage. That's what I meant about changing my mind." He ground the end of his cane into a clump of grass. "But I think we need to get to know each other first. Don't you?"

"Well, yes, but what happens then?"

"I was told yesterday that I'll be moved to the convalescent home in two weeks. I think we ought to take that time to figure out if…" He plodded forward again. "If marriage would work between us."

Too stunned at this sudden change in events, Evelyn remained frozen, unable to move. Joel advanced another few feet before he noticed she wasn't next to him anymore. He slowly turned around, his eyebrows lifted in question.

"What if you decide at the end of those two weeks that marriage won't work for us?" She hurled the words at him, hoping to wound him as he'd wounded her the other day. "What am I to do then, Joel?" She would end up right back where she was at present—still unwed and pregnant and in danger of being transferred or discharged at any time.

"This is a decision we both need to make." He retraced his steps back to her side. "If we *both* feel marriage isn't the answer, I'll think of some way to care for you and your child. Either way, you don't need to be afraid of the future anymore. I promise."

Her anger deflated in the wake of his assurance. She

didn't like his terms. She preferred to have his pledge—now—that he would marry her. But she would have to trust him to keep his word. Something that wasn't easy for her. Everyone she'd ever truly trusted had left her to fend for herself—her mother, her father, Ralph, God. Joel Campbell might do the very same.

She breathed a long sigh, knowing she had no other choice. She would trust him and hope that in a few weeks' time he would agree to marry her.

With some effort, she managed to bestow a light smile on him. After all, if she hoped to win him over as a potential wife, she might as well start by appearing happy. "All right, I accept your proposal."

\*     \*     \*

Joel was beginning to regret his quick march across the grass to catch up with Evelyn and Sergeant Dennis earlier. That and his continued strolling had turned his injuries into one large mound of pain. His heart beat faster at the exertion and sweat had formed around the collar of his shirt. He hoped, with Evelyn's help, he could reach the wheelchair before he collapsed.

"I think we ought to head back."

"Of course." Evelyn moved to his side, keeping herself next to the cane he gripped tighter and tighter with each step.

A noise in the forest drew him up short. Instinctively he placed himself in front of Evelyn. Who was crashing around in the brush?

Evelyn peered around him at the trees. "Louis? Is that you?"

A dark-haired boy emerged from the shadows, a grin on his face. Joel recognized him as the child Evelyn had been talking with the other day.

"Nurse Gray!" Louis bounded onto the grass.

Evelyn's lips rose into a genuine smile. The action kindled warm light in her dark eyes and made her whole face appear radiant. No wonder Ralph had been eager to abandon his old habits for her. One smile was probably all it took.

"Louis, I want you to meet someone. This is Corporal Joel Campbell."

With one arm in a sling and the other maneuvering his cane, Joel settled for a nod instead of shaking the boy's hand. "Nice to meet you, Louis."

"You are a soldier?"

"I am."

Louis cocked his head. "Where is your gun?"

"I don't have it now, not since I was injured."

"Injured?" The boy's black eyes widened. "But you are okay?"

Joel didn't think Louis wanted a lengthy explanation of his injuries. He opted instead to say, "I'll be back with my men soon."

Evelyn glanced at him, then away, her expression conflicted. He could guess at her thoughts. What would happen between them before he returned to the front lines? Would they agree to marry or would he find some other way to help her?

"*Ma père* was a soldier," Louis said, his voice soft and reverent as though he were in a church. He kicked at the grass with the toe of his bare foot. The emphasis on *was* wasn't lost on Joel. He could easily surmise what the boy hadn't wanted to say.

"I'm sorry, Louis." He shifted his cane to squeeze the lad's shoulder, noting how the bones were easily felt beneath the thin shirt. "I bet he was a courageous man. And he must have felt all right about going to heaven, knowing you'd be a brave little man in his place."

The boy tipped his head to look at Joel, undisguised hope written on his dirty face. "I help *ma mère* at the market, and I do not cry anymore if supper is small."

A swell of compassion lodged itself in Joel's throat at the boy's words, and he coughed to clear it. Louis reminded him of his littlest brothers, George and Charlie, though he looked even younger in age than either of them. How would his brothers cope with living in a war-torn country without their father and with little food at home?

"I need to get Corporal Campbell back to his wheelchair," Evelyn interjected, "but you can walk with us, Louis."

Joel threw her a grateful smile as he repeated his steps back to the wheelchair. Though standing didn't aggravate his wounds as much as walking, he still felt exhausted. And he wanted to make it back to the chair in one piece.

"What were you doing in the woods, Louis?" Joel asked to distract himself from the fatigue and pain pulling at every muscle. The boy carried a book in one hand, so perhaps he'd been reading.

"I was coming to see Nurse Gray." Louis lumbered along beside them, making whirring noises under his breath. "Oh, and finding a bird."

"Louis likes birds and airplanes," Evelyn explained.

Joel paused in his next step to keep his cane from clipping Louis's heel when the boy darted to his other side. "You like to watch birds?"

Louis nodded.

"Then I have a book you might like."

"What book?"

"It's a bird notebook. My sister Livy and I sketched a lot of the birds we saw at home and I wrote things down about them." From the corner of his eye, Joel caught the appraising look Evelyn tossed him. Her interest made him momentarily forget the conversation and his hurting body. Could he imagine this woman as his wife?

"Can I see it?" Louis asked.

"See what?" Joel frowned, trying to remember what they'd been discussing.

"The bird book?"

"Yes, in fact you might be able to help me with something." He appreciated how the boy slowed to match his own laborious pace. "The other day I saw a brown-and-white bird with a red-orange breast. It landed on the windowsill of the ward. Do you know what it's called?"

Louis laughed. "That is easy. It is a *rouge-gorge*. A redbreast. A robin."

"Ah. We have robins in America, but they look different. Ours are larger and more black than brown. I'll write the French name down in my notebook when I go inside."

"Can I see the book now?"

Joel cracked a smile, despite the deepening sweat on his neck and forehead. He would never take walking for granted again. "How about tomorrow?"

"Okay."

When they reached the wheelchair, which Joel felt certain had been moved several dozen yards back from where he'd left it, Evelyn helped him sit down. "It looks like you have a book, too, Louis," she said, setting Joel's cane across his knees. "What is it?"

"It is one of *Grand-mère*'s English books." The volume he held up showed signs of being well loved. Joel read the black type printed on the front—*Around the World in Eighty Days*.

"Jules Verne." He smiled at Louis. "That's a good one. Do you like it?"

The boy's skinny shoulders rose in a shrug. "*Ma grand-mère* read in French so I could understand, but that was when I was little. I cannot read the English."

"Would you like me to read it to you, Louis?" Evelyn offered. "I can take you in first, Corporal."

Joel shook his head. "I don't mind staying outside. Now that I'm sitting."

Evelyn settled onto the grass and tucked her feet beneath her nurse's dress. Louis flopped onto his stomach beside her to listen. Opening the book, Evelyn began to read in a clear but soft voice about Phileas Fogg. Joel watched her, enjoying the chance to study her unawares. He'd noticed the weariness emanating from her face and shoulders the other day, but in this moment, she looked content.

She glanced up from the page and smiled at Louis. It was a brief exchange, but long enough to show the tenderness she clearly felt for this young boy. She cared about Louis and enjoyed spending time with him. Would Evelyn ever feel that way about him? Joel wondered.

He squashed the foolish thought. His plan centered on getting to know her, in order to figure out how to assist her. And since marriage was not likely to be the means by which he helped her, feelings were inconsequential.

"Corporal?"

Evelyn's voice jerked him back to the present. He'd missed most of the story.

"It's time I get you back." She rose to her feet in one fluid motion and handed Louis his book. "We might be able to read more tomorrow, if there are no surgeries."

Louis grinned. "I would like that. Good-bye, Nurse Gray."

The boy sprinted for the woods, but stopped when Evelyn called out, "Would you like some bread, Louis?"

"*Non. Ma mère* had a good vegetable day."

"It was nice to meet you, Louis," Joel said, lifting his hand to wave. "I'll try to remember to bring my bird book tomorrow."

"Okay, Corporal." He waved back, then darted into the trees.

Evelyn steered Joel's wheelchair around and pushed him back toward the hospital.

"He seems like a nice kid."

"He is." Joel could hear the smile in her voice, even if he couldn't see it. "Thank you for talking with him. I think he's lonely. From what he's said, he was very close to his grandmother. She died some time ago, and then he lost his father. Now there's only him and his mother."

Joel glanced up at the sky as she pushed his chair. The sun had shifted behind some clouds, taking a bit of the heat with it. Too bad Evelyn couldn't stay out longer—it would be nice to have more time to get acquainted with her.

"I suppose Louis and I are sort of alike." She laughed, but the sound resonated with hollowness. "Not much family left in the world."

The loneliness behind her words stirred Joel's sympathies. "I promised I would help you, Evelyn. And I meant it."

A deep sigh sounded above the creak of the wheels. "I know. Thank you."

His earlier question about what it might be like to have her as his wife returned to his mind. Evelyn's uniform might hang like a sack around her, but he imagined the loose fabric hid a rather nice figure. What would it be like to wake with her beside him, knowing she was his? To see that beautiful face relaxed in slumber?

Tightening his grip on the cane in his lap, Joel banished such imaginings from his mind. He wouldn't propose—or consider proposing—to the wrong girl again. When he did ask that most important of all questions, he wanted to do so with the greatest love and anticipation, for a woman he cared for more than any other person in the world. He wouldn't propose out of obligation, even to someone beautiful or kind.

Which surely meant Evelyn was not that woman.

# Chapter 8

Joel stared at the ceiling, the buzz of insects and conversation wafting through the open window across the room. He wished he could have forgone resting and stayed outside, but he'd insisted on attending church services that morning. With the assistance of one of the nurses and his cane, he managed to walk to and from the stone church behind the hospital. The moment he returned to the recovery ward, though, he felt every inch of the distance he'd traversed and every second seated on the hard pew.

He shut his eyes, but sleep eluded him. The nurse on duty sat writing at the table in the corner. There were only two other patients in the ward besides himself. Everyone else was enjoying the Sabbath day outdoors, including Sergeant Dennis. Taking a cue from the nurse, Joel decided to pen a letter to his parents. He'd written them the other week about being wounded, though he hadn't detailed all his injuries. It wouldn't hurt, though, to reassure his mother that he was healing and share his progress of the last ten days.

"Can I have some stationary?" he called out, loud enough for the nurse to hear but not so booming he woke the other two soldiers who were sleeping.

She brought him paper and a pen. Joel wrote a few lines about starting to walk again and attending church. Then he paused. What else to say? Should he tell them about Evelyn? No. Better to let things play out first, figure out how he planned to help her, before he made any mention of her to his parents.

He glanced out the window at the few patients seated near the building. Was Evelyn busy in the surgery ward? Joel hadn't seen her this morning or yesterday either. He didn't like the thought of not talking to her for the second day in a row.

*Because my time here is limited*, he rationalized. *We need to get to know each other, so I can decide what to do.* His desire to see Evelyn was nothing more, nothing less.

He brandished his pen once more and reread the words he'd written. Footsteps echoed through the silent ward. Joel glanced up to see who had come inside the room and found Evelyn walking toward his bed. She looked every bit as lovely as she had the other day, that unruly curl falling onto her brow and her red lips lifted in a soft smile. Happiness flooded him at seeing her and he couldn't stop the feeling from leaking onto his face in the form of a grin.

"Afternoon, Corporal." She threw a look over her shoulder at the other nurse before she stepped closer to his bed. The girl appeared to be engrossed in whatever she was writing. "I can't stay long. We have another surgery scheduled when lunch is over. But..."

Joel waited, his curiosity mounting over her reason for coming. She reached into her pocket and withdrew something he couldn't see.

"Louis and I went walking in the woods yesterday."

She'd seen Louis yesterday, but not him? Joel wrestled his jealousy into submission. The boy had no one else to really look after him. Of course Evelyn would be most concerned about Louis.

"We found something that I thought you might like." She opened her fingers to reveal a bluish-green feather resting on her palm. "Louis told me the name of the bird he thought it belonged to, but I can't remember the French name."

Joel studied the beautifully colored feather. Evelyn hadn't been required to bring it to him; it wasn't her duty, like shaving his face or rebandaging his wounds or pushing his wheelchair. She'd remembered his interest in birds from the other day and came here specifically to see him.

Her smile drooped at his silence. "I know it's small..."

"No, no. It's perfect." He picked up the feather, allowing his fingers to linger against her palm as he did so. Her skin felt as soft to the touch as the feather's downy plume. "It's a pretty color. Thank you."

Evelyn's face brightened. "I thought you could put it in your notebook." She lifted the book off the bedside table, where he'd placed it earlier, and set it on the bed.

Joel flipped through the pages until he located a good spot. He placed the feather inside and smiled at Evelyn. "As a kid, I'd put the feathers I found in jars, much to my mother's dismay when canning time rolled around."

Evelyn laughed. It was the first full laugh he'd heard from her, and he loved the sound. "That's a funny thing to put into jars."

He feigned a scowl. "What? Didn't you ever collect anything?"

"Flowers." Her brown eyes grew wistful. "I used to press flowers in this thick book of my grandmother's. I'd pick them from our garden or sometimes patients of my father would let me take a few from their flowerbeds."

"Where's that book now?"

"Probably in my room back at home. I haven't thought about it in a very long time." She crossed her arms loosely over her apron. "I used to love looking through that book and seeing all those flowers preserved. It was like I could make something beautiful last forever." She lowered her gaze to her shoes. "Unlike my mother or my father."

Joel wished he could rise and enfold her in his arms, offer her comfort. Would he ever be able to penetrate the loneliness and heartache she wore so persistently?

"How did it happen?"

The abrupt question confused him. "What?"

"Ralph. How did he die?" She trained her eyes on his face. "I'd like to know."

Guilt filled Joel's throat, nearly choking him. He'd expected the question, but that didn't make it any easier to answer. Especially after her kindness in giving him the feather.

If only he could tell her everything, share every horrid detail from that day...But surely she would blame him, as he did himself, for Ralph's death. If Evelyn grew to despise him, he'd never have the chance to help her or repay his best friend for costing him his life.

He had one other reason for not telling her the entire truth. If he shared the awful turn of events with someone else, especially Evelyn, Joel would have to face the grief he'd stuffed deep down inside himself. The grief of losing his best friend just months after his little brother had been killed.

Joel swallowed the regret and sorrow, and instead kept his attention riveted on the book in his lap. He would share enough to fulfill her need to know, but not so much as to condemn himself.

"We were ambushed by the Germans. Half our squad was hit by a shell." He kept his voice devoid of emotion as he spoke, afraid of betraying the true depth of it. "Ralph made it to the field hospital, but he didn't live long after that. It was there I heard him say your name."

Evelyn's face had grown pale, and there was a shimmer of tears in her eyes. "Thank you...for telling me."

"I'm sorry," Joel offered lamely, even if she wouldn't understand he meant so much more than an apology for Ralph's passing.

He was sorry for not insisting his best friend lead the other group. Sorry for bringing Evelyn the news that the father of her unborn child had been killed. Sorry it wasn't Ralph she could be marrying soon.

"It's all right." Evelyn let her arms drop to her sides. "It wasn't your fault."

Could there be more ironic words? They lanced through him with all the force of a bayonet. If she only knew... The truth, raw and bitter, raced toward his mouth.

*No.* Joel clenched his jaw. He wouldn't open himself up to that kind of helplessness, whatever happened between him and Evelyn.

"I need to go." She fell back a step from his bed.

"Thanks for the feather," Joel said, relaxing his face.

She offered him a brief smile and spun on her heel. He watched her disappear out the door of the ward, then opened up his book to where he'd placed the feather. Joel ran his finger over the delicate softness. Such a tiny object, but its presence—and Evelyn's offering of it—had the power to undo his carefully laid plans.

\* \* \*

Evelyn locked up the supply cupboard in the surgery ward and pocketed the keys. She'd assisted the doctor with two more successful surgeries, but they were out of bandages now. Dr. Dupont had asked her to procure more from another ward, if possible. Evelyn knew all too well that the other wards were running dangerously low on supplies, too. If she took bandages from them, what would they use?

She brushed a lock of hair from her forehead, switched off the lights in the surgical room, and locked the door. Dr. Dupont had already left to check on some of the patients before supper. She could think of one patient she wouldn't mind seeing. If only to talk about the feather she'd given him.

Who had gone walking with Joel the past two days? Had he thought about her? She hoped so, while at the same time, telling herself it didn't matter. They were only supposed to be getting to know each other.

Then there was her worry over Louis. Had the boy come looking for her yesterday to read more of his grandmother's book? Had he had enough to eat last night?

Perhaps she could find some time to see both him and Joel after supper. But first, she had to think of a way to produce bandages out of thin air.

As she made her way upstairs, Evelyn tried to remember which parts of the hospital she hadn't seen yet, places where she might find bandages. The upper floor, where Sister Marcelle had her office, contained several other rooms, unused as far as Evelyn knew. Maybe there were old supplies stashed in one of them. First, she'd need permission to go searching, though.

She traversed the stairs to Sister Marcelle's office and found the woman exiting the small room. "Nurse Gray." The head sister smiled. "How are you getting along in surgery and in the recovery ward?"

"Very well, thank you." Evelyn wished she could express the real depth of her gratitude. Five days of regular sleep and meals had greatly decreased her nausea.

Sister Marcelle motioned toward the stairs. "Will you walk with me to the dining room? You can explain on the way what I may help you with."

"Actually, I'd like permission to search the rooms on this floor for extra bandages."

"Are you running low in the surgery wards?"

Evelyn nodded. "We don't have any left—not after today's surgeries."

The sister clasped her hands together and lowered her chin, causing her white headdress to dip with the movement. Several moments of silence passed before Evelyn realized Sister Marcelle was praying. Unsure what to do, Evelyn stood still, her gaze shifting from the stairwell, to the floor, and back to the stairwell. At last, Sister Marcelle lifted her head.

"I will continue to petition the Lord for supplies, which I feel certain will come in due course." Her expression radiated confidence. "They are so greatly needed. However, I believe we are to learn something during this time of deprivation, Nurse Gray."

Evelyn held her tongue, choosing not to give voice to her skepticism. It didn't seem fair for a lesson to come at the expense of wounded men who were likely to suffer if the needed supplies failed to arrive soon. Was Sister Marcelle saying there might be a lesson to learn in the midst of such suffering? A stray thought crept forward in Evelyn's mind. Did God have something He wanted *her* to learn through the suffering Ralph's death had brought upon herself and her unborn child?

Before she could analyze the question further, Sister Marcelle spoke again. "You are welcome to search these rooms." She motioned down the hallway. "I do not remember placing any supplies in them, but one never knows. Will you be coming down to supper first?"

"No." Evelyn shook her head. "I promised Dr. Dupont I'd see if I could find something beforehand."

"He praises your work. We are most fortunate to have you here, Nurse Gray." Her blue-gray eyes peered kindly at Evelyn. "I hope you will be with us for a long while."

She was beginning to wish the same—the hospital staff, and Louis, were becoming a sort of ragtag family to her, unlike any others she'd worked with previously. But no matter what she wanted, she would not be allowed to stay. Even if Joel consented to marry her, and she very much hoped he would, she couldn't remain in France as a married nurse.

"Do not forget your supper," the sister said as she headed down the stairs.

"I'll be along soon."

Evelyn opened the first door down the hall and walked inside. The room was slightly larger than Sister Marcelle's office. A number of kerosene lamps stood in neat rows along one wall, a memorial to the days before electricity had come to St. Vincent's. The only other furnishings in the room were a stack of crates on the opposite wall. Evelyn peered into the top one—it was full of books. She ran her thumb along the dusty covers. With her rudimentary knowledge of French, she could read only a few of the titles. Perhaps there was something to interest Louis, though.

She glanced in the crate on top of the second stack. A slim volume with an English title caught her attention. It was a reading primer, like the ones she'd used in school. Evelyn extracted it from the other books and wiped off the dust with her apron. If she could teach Louis to read English, he could enjoy his grandmother's book when Evelyn wasn't around.

Finding nothing else of interest, she took the book with her and moved on to the next room. This one was even more sparsely furnished than the first. A chair, missing several rungs from the back, sat opposite an iron bed frame with no mattress. If the hospital received another large influx of wounded soldiers, they might have to convert these rooms into wards as well.

*At least until Joel and the others in the recovery ward leave for the convalescent home.*

The thought brought an equal measure of relief and fear throbbing in her heart. Once Joel left, their fate would be decided, for better or worse. Either way, Evelyn had to admit she would miss him. And not just because of his connection with Ralph. Joel Campbell was kind and funny and handsome. If circumstances had been different, she could imagine being courted by him for real and marrying him for love, instead of convenience.

*But circumstances aren't different*, she reminded herself firmly.

She made quick inspection of the final two rooms on the left side of the hallway. Both stood empty. Evelyn shut the last door and moved across the hall to the opposite four rooms.

The emptiness in the air reminded her of the spacious farmhouse at home. While she had plenty of happy childhood memories, there were other times as a girl when the emptiness of the large house had pressed in on her and she'd wished for more company than her grandparents and father. If she and Joel returned, as husband and wife, there would still be only one child in the house. And like Evelyn, her child would grow up and go off into the world one day, leaving them behind.

Releasing a sigh, Evelyn did her best to ignore such depressing thoughts and entered the next room. This one and the one after it were also empty. The third held another collection of crates, larger than the ones with the books, and a dusty radiator. Inside the crates Evelyn discovered yards of material from what appeared to be old curtains. There were blue ones and lacy ones and thick velvet ones. The hospital's current curtains were dark in color, designed to block inside light from being seen by the Germans.

Evelyn sifted through the rest of the crates. Another

contained a bundle of sheets, yellowed with age. She lifted one out and tugged at the material. It held firm, despite being old. Surely these could be cut up and laundered for bandage material.

What about the curtains? She discarded the lacy ones—they wouldn't provide enough absorption—but the blue ones and possibly the velvet might work as bandages, once they were cut into strips.

After gathering all the usable material into a pile, Evelyn peeked inside the last room. It stood devoid of anything but dust. She shut the door, bringing herself back to where she'd begun. Only this time, she felt encouraged. Surely they could make good use of the material she'd found.

Rather than carting the cloth to the dining hall, Evelyn set the pile on the floor outside Sister Marcelle's office and hurried down the stairs. Sister Marcelle and Dr. Dupont would be overjoyed. The old sheets and curtains would help everyone eke by until new supplies arrived. Perhaps the men in the recovery ward could cut the material.

Evelyn entered the noisy dining room, its ornate walls echoing with conversation and the clatter of dishes. She picked up a tray of food, Louis's primer still in hand, and searched for Alice, but her roommate wasn't there. Perhaps she had been detained in the recovery ward. Evelyn did locate Sister Marcelle, talking with another sister near one of the doors. After setting her tray and the book on one of the tables, she approached the two sisters. She waited at a polite distance until their conversation ended.

"Well, Nurse Gray," Sister Marcelle said, turning toward Evelyn as the other sister left the room, "did you find anything we might put to use?"

"I did."

The sister arched her eyebrows.

"There were a bunch of crates with old sheets and curtains in them. I pulled out what I thought we could cut up and use as bandages." Evelyn smiled with excitement at her success. "I thought you might want to look at the material, so I set it outside your office."

The laugh lines around Sister Marcelle's eyes crinkled as she returned Evelyn's smile. "I would be happy to inspect the material. I compliment your ingenuity. You have reminded me that prayer, followed by action, is the best way to find answers. I believe God inspired you to look up there."

Evelyn's cheeks flushed. She didn't know whether to thank the woman for her compliment or argue with her over the conclusion that God was behind Evelyn's idea. Surely He hadn't inspired her. And yet she couldn't rid herself of the hope completely.

"I thought we could ask the men in the recovery ward to cut up the material."

"Yes, that might work." Sister Marcelle gazed at something across the room. "I will think on it. Thank you again, child."

Evelyn whirled around and returned to her food. Her supper had cooled, but she didn't care. Her important accomplishment made even the bland food taste delicious. Tomorrow she would tell Dr. Dupont what she'd found, but first she wanted to share the good news with Alice. Her roommate would be as thrilled as Evelyn.

She finished her meal and carried her dishes to the

kitchen, then headed to the recovery ward. Alice wasn't there. The beds of Sergeant Dennis and Joel stood empty as well.

Guessing the three of them must be outside, Evelyn ducked out the back and strode onto the lawn. She searched for Alice, but the only other nurse she saw among the soldiers was Nurse Shaw. Perhaps Alice had gone to bed early.

She turned toward the nurses' building, to look for Alice in their room, just as a nurse circled the corner of the hospital, pushing a wheelchair ahead of her. Evelyn's eagerness faded to irritation when she recognized Alice and Sergeant Dennis. Alice laughed at something the man said, bringing a frown to Evelyn's lips. Her roommate seemed to be growing more and more comfortable around Sergeant Dennis.

If she could think of an excuse to relieve Alice of helping the man tonight, and in the future, she might be able to prevent any further camaraderie between the two.

Before she could think of a solution, though, she heard Louis call out, "Nurse Gray. Come here."

He waved at her from a small group gathered near the trees on one side of the lawn. Evelyn waved back, happy to see he hadn't gone home yet, but she hesitated joining him, torn between talking with him and rescuing Alice. The boy won out, though. She hadn't seen him the day before like she'd hoped, and there would be time later to sort things out with Alice.

Evelyn walked toward Louis. As she came closer, she realized the group was comprised of several other children. They stood or knelt around someone in a wheelchair. When the man raised his head, Evelyn saw it was

Joel. His eyes held hers as she approached, and a warm smile spread across his face. Her stomach fluttered in response. He was already handsome, but when he smiled like that, he looked the picture of a Greek hero, full of self-assurance and energy, even confined in his wheelchair.

"See what I found, Nurse Gray." Louis grabbed her hand and tugged her forward the last few feet.

Evelyn stopped at the edge of the group and looked down. Near Joel's feet sat a bird's nest with three empty eggs inside. The small eggs were gray in color with brown speckles. Grateful for something—or *someone*—else to look at, she knelt on the grass to study the treasured objects better.

"They're beautiful." She ran a finger over the smooth, glossy eggshells. No wonder Joel and Louis found all things bird related to be so fascinating.

"We're taking guesses as to what type of bird the nest and eggs belong to." Joel lifted his notebook for her to see, the one he'd placed his feather in the day before. "Louis has to translate, though."

Evelyn smiled into the four unfamiliar faces peering at her. "Who are your friends, Louis?"

Louis introduced the other four boys, but their names disappeared from Evelyn's memory as quickly as he said them. Instead her attention was drawn to the toughened look in their young eyes and the stains and holes in their grubby clothing. They reminded her of the first time she'd seen Louis. Had it really been eleven days since she'd met the boy? He had become a significant part of her daily life at St. Vincent's. Much like Joel.

She glanced at him and found those hazel eyes watch-

ing her intently. Too intently. Would he read her
thoughts? She blushed at the prospect and stared down at
the nest again.

He was different from Ralph in many ways, and yet
she liked him, probably more than she should. What if he
didn't return her feelings? She wasn't sure which would
be worse—falling for him and having him decide they
shouldn't marry, or living in a marriage where she was the
only one who felt real love.

Joel's voice interrupted her mental quandary. "What is
your vote, Nurse Gray?"

"My vote?" she repeated.

"For what type of bird the eggs belong to."

"Oh." She pried her gaze from the eggs to Joel's
amused look. The memory of touching his face returned
full force. What would it be like touch his face not out of
duty, but out of love? Would it feel as jolting and wonderful as touching his hand? She gulped as she realized Joel
was still waiting for an answer.

"I...uh...don't know. What are the other guesses?"

Joel read them off to her, pointing to each boy as he
stated his vote. The boys smiled shyly at her. Like Louis,
they sported dirt on their thin faces and had no shoes on
their feet. A swell of motherly compassion filled her. If
only there were more she could do for these boys, as Dr.
Dupont's wife was doing in their village. There had to be
some way to feed them, to help them, to let them know
the world wasn't entirely devoid of kindness and love.

An idea brought her to her feet. The boys could cut the
material she'd found into bandages, in exchange for bread
or vegetables for their suppers.

"My guess is the same as his." She pointed to one of

the boys, who grinned when Louis translated her words. "And now I've got to see the hospital administrator, Sister Marcelle, about something." Louis's mouth turned down, in obvious disappointment at the shortness of her visit. She ruffled his hair as she walked past him. "I'll be back. I may have found a way to get all of you a little more food."

All four boys perked up at the word *food*, especially when Louis translated the rest of her words. Hopefully they would stick around long enough to see the fruition of her plan. She hoped Joel would stay, too. She wanted more time with him, despite her conflicting thoughts about him.

"Corporal Campbell?" She pressed her slightly shaking hands together.

He glanced in her direction, an unreadable expression on his face. Could she break down the wall that guarded his feelings, help him see she was beginning to like him?

Her heart raced a little faster as she said, "Please don't leave either. I'd like to be the one to help you with walking today, if you haven't exercised too much already."

The smile he gave her made her pulse quicken even more and eased any worry she felt over her boldness. "I'll be here."

\* \* \*

The other boys left for home before Evelyn returned, though Louis assured Joel they'd be back the next day. After his friends had gone, Louis entertained himself near Joel's wheelchair by looking through the bird notebook.

Joel noted the careful, almost worshipful, way the boy turned each page. Here was a child as captivated with birds as he was.

The only other thing Louis seemed to care about as much as food and birds was Evelyn, and Joel couldn't blame him. The nurse was beginning to rank quite high on his own list of interests. He watched as she walked across the lawn right then, her movements graceful, her face lit with a smile. In her arms she carried a bundle of cloth.

Joel nudged Louis's knee with his boot. "I think Nurse Gray has brought us something."

The boy looked up. "What is it?"

"I'm not sure."

Louis set the book on the grass and hopped up. "What did you bring, Nurse Gray?"

"Some old sheets," she called back.

Louis scowled, making Joel laugh. "Let her explain," he told the boy. "It may prove to be better than you think."

Evelyn set the cloth near the wheelchair. "I have permission, Louis, for you and the other boys..." She looked around, her face clouding with confusion. "Where did they go?"

"Home," Joel said. "But they promised Louis to come back tomorrow."

The boy cocked his head and eyed the sheets. "They want to see your surprise. But they will not like a bunch of sheets."

"These sheets"—Evelyn playfully tweaked Louis's nose—"are a way for you and your friends to have food from the hospital kitchen." She lifted the corner of one of the sheets for the two of them to see. "If you cut the sheets into strips for bandages, Sister Marcelle has promised to have Cook give you something for your supper."

Louis's demeanor brightened at the news. "All right, Nurse Gray. We will cut."

"Would you like to start now?" Evelyn asked. "Is your mother expecting you home for supper?"

A bleak expression settled on the boy's face. "*Non.* I already had a little food. And *ma mère* likes me here. She thinks I do not know she cries after I leave." He ran a hand under his nose.

Evelyn knelt beside Louis and wrapped his thin body in a hug. "She wants you here because she knows you're with friends, Louis. Isn't that right, Corporal Campbell?"

Joel leaned forward in his chair. "I'm sure your mother will be real proud to hear you're helping out at the hospital. Especially doing something so important. Just think, Louis, the bandages we cut will be used on soldiers all throughout the hospital."

The boy pulled back from Evelyn and turned to face Joel. "Like you?"

Joel chuckled. "Like me."

"That's right." Evelyn shot Joel a look of gratitude over Louis's shoulder and mouthed the words *thank you*. He nodded back. They made a rather good team. "Even if you've already eaten, Louis," she added, "I bet there's still something in the kitchen for you to take home. Maybe even some sweets."

"Really?" Louis grinned.

"Let me show you how to cut these first." Evelyn removed a pair of scissors from her pocket. A folded piece of paper fell to the ground as she withdrew her hand.

"You dropped something." Joel pointed at the paper.

Evelyn glanced from him to the ground and blushed. "It's only a letter." She shoved it back into her pocket, then began tearing the sheet into smaller sections.

Her reaction made it easy for Joel to guess who had sent the letter. Was it the last one she'd received from Ralph? Is that why she kept it with her, as a reminder of him? The idea rankled, though he knew it shouldn't. She wasn't his to be jealous over.

"Got an extra pair of scissors? I think I can help, even one-handed." Joel wanted to prove to her he could be useful. Any minute now, he expected one of the other nurses to come wheel him back to the hospital. If he was doing something, though, he might be able to have more time with Evelyn, even if it meant having Louis along as company.

"If you're sure…" Evelyn pulled a second pair of scissors from her pocket and handed them to Joel.

Once she explained how she wanted the material cut, Joel went to work. It was slow going, with only one good hand, but he wouldn't give up trying. Out of the corner of his eye, he watched Evelyn as she helped Louis. The boy's first bandage came out as jagged as a saw blade, but she praised his effort.

"Keep going, Louis," she instructed. "You're doing well. You, too, Corporal."

The compliment pleased him until he realized his grin had grown as wide as Louis's. He forced his mouth into a frown. He wasn't an infatuated schoolboy, though he couldn't deny he was beginning to like Evelyn. Such a re-alization only heaped more guilt on his already troubled conscience. He needed to help her, for Ralph's sake; liking her wasn't part of the bargain. What would his best friend say about Joel's growing attraction for his girl?

He shook his head. He needed to respond—and think about—Evelyn with complete neutrality. If only she'd stop surprising him, as she had with the feather yesterday. Her thoughtfulness toward him and her compassion toward Louis and the other boys were fast wearing through his defenses against admiring her.

She certainly had a way with these children. He might deem marriage as the last possible way to help her, but if they did marry, was it fair to consign her to a life with only one child? Evelyn deserved a husband who could provide her with a whole houseful of children whom she could care for and teach, just as she was doing with Louis.

The notion of her marrying someone else left him more unsettled and annoyed than he wanted. He frowned at the material beneath his scissors. Why should he care if she chose a different man to be her husband?

"Would you like me to take over, Corporal? You're scowling at that cloth like you want it to surrender."

He cleared his throat, reining in his misguided irritation. "No. I've got it."

"All right." She shot him an impish smile before turning to Louis. "Look how much you've done already, Louis."

An irrational desire to show up the boy, especially one-handed, overtook him, and Joel doubled his efforts to cut the material. At last Evelyn announced, "That's enough for today. It's getting late. Let's get your sweet, Louis."

Joel finished cutting the piece on his lap, then relinquished his scissors to her. He bit back a triumphant smile when he saw his own pile was larger than Louis's.

"I'm impressed, Corporal." Evelyn added his pile of cloth to Louis's and the rest of the uncut material. "Clearly you are a man of many talents."

Her compliment shouldn't inspire as much pride as it did. "Should I walk back, instead of having you push the chair?" he asked, noting her full arms.

"If you're up to it. Either way, I'm afraid if I don't have you back in the recovery ward soon, we'll both be in trouble." Her tone was light, but Joel didn't miss the meaningful look she gave him as she spoke. If they wanted more time together in the coming days, he would have to relinquish a walk around the lawn with her tonight.

"I can walk, if Louis doesn't mind pushing the wheelchair."

The boy's black eyes widened. "Can I?"

Joel laughed. "Sure, kid."

He rose to his feet with the help of Evelyn and his cane. She fell into step beside him, while Louis pushed the chair.

"You've improved in the last few days." Her tone held a note of appraisal.

"I'm hoping by next week I won't need the chair to get around."

"You'll be walking back and forth before you know it. Then you'll be off to the convalescent home." Instead of a smile, her lips appeared to tighten at the thought. What about his leaving made her frown? Did she harbor the same attraction for him that he felt for her? Joel schooled his expression to keep from revealing the absurd hope.

"What is a con-ves-scent home?" Louis swerved the chair one way, then another.

"Convalescent," Evelyn corrected. "It's a place soldiers go to finish resting and getting better before they return to the front lines."

"You mean you have to go fight again?" Louis stared in wonder at Joel. "Are you scared?"

He considered the question as he took one careful step after another. "A little. Most times I don't think about it. In the past I've prayed and put my trust in God. I suppose I'll keep on doing that." Though God's plans for his life were leaving Joel more and more confused of late.

"We'll pray, too, won't we, Nurse Gray?" the boy said over his shoulder.

Evelyn's posture stiffened, but she responded, "We certainly will."

Her obvious discomfort reminded him that he knew nothing of what she thought about religion and God. Unlike Nurse Thornton, he'd never heard Evelyn mention the subject.

"Maybe the corporal will come see us again, too." Louis rolled the wheelchair backward so he was beside them again. "Wouldn't that be great, Nurse Gray?"

She tipped her face in Joel's direction, halting his steps as effectively as if she'd held on to him. His gaze fell to hers and stayed there as if tethered by some unseen force. The openness and vulnerability in her large, dark eyes did funny things to his heart.

"Yes, Louis." Her voice had grown serious, reflective. "I hope we'll see much more of Corporal Campbell."

The urge to take her chin in hand and kiss those red, full lips nearly conquered him. He checked it just in time by gripping his cane and forcing his feet to move again.

He liked her, yes, but nothing could come of it. Though he didn't condemn Evelyn for her choices, he'd expected to marry someone who shared a similar moral code and a faith in God. He also wanted to live near his family, and Evelyn wasn't likely to leave her ailing grandparents to move to another state.

Most of all, Evelyn deserved a relationship built on honesty. She'd been forthright with him; Joel ought to be the same with her. But he couldn't. If he told her the truth surrounding Ralph's death, he would forfeit any chance of aiding her and her child.

"I'd like to see more of both of you, too." It was the truth, but he couldn't quite muster a smile after he said it. The familiar regret over Ralph's death pressed hard against his chest and lungs and soured his mood.

Would he ever be free of the consequences on the battlefield that day? His decision, or the lack thereof, had cost him his best friend, and ironically, now endangered his friendship with the lovely woman Ralph had left behind.

# Chapter 9

Joel kept in step beside Nurse Thornton as they circumvented the far edge of the lawn. His stride wasn't anywhere near his former gait, but he could feel strength returning to his right leg.

His gaze sought out Evelyn, overseeing the cutting of bandages by Louis and the other boys. He wished he were walking with her instead. But Evelyn had informed him they needed to spend time apart today to avoid attracting suspicion. While Joel agreed with her, he still couldn't help watching her and wondering what Louis had just said to make her laugh.

He stole a glance at Nurse Thornton, plodding silently along beside him. Not surprising, her own gaze lingered on someone else, too—Sergeant Dennis seated in a lawn chair with his injured knee resting on another chair. Joel nearly laughed out loud. He and Nurse Thornton both wished they could be with other people, but rules and decorum had stuck them together for today.

Joel slowed his footsteps as he studied the faces of those outside. Were there other soldiers hoping for a friendship to blossom with a certain nurse? How many hearts would be broken when these soldiers moved on? He didn't condone Evelyn and Ralph's way of doing things, but he could understand how the thought of separation had likely driven them to act differently than they might have otherwise. A similar sense of urgency filled him. He wanted to spend as much time with Evelyn as he could, especially with his transfer to the convalescent home looming ever closer.

"Are you ready to turn around?" Nurse Thornton asked.

Joel stopped and considered how far they'd come. If they turned back now, perhaps he could convince Nurse Thornton to leave his wheelchair near Evelyn. "All right."

As they retraced their path, Joel felt someone watching them. Sure enough, Sergeant Dennis kept throwing glances their way. "Is Dennis treating you well?"

The red-headed nurse blushed and darted a look in the sergeant's direction. "Yes, he is. Thanks to you, Corporal."

"What do you mean?"

"I told him what you said about he and I being good friends. How that isn't exactly against the rules." A smile softened her face. "Once this awful war ends, we talked about finding each other. I told him where I'd be in the States."

"Did he agree to your plan to be friends?"

She nodded, her green eyes alive with happiness. "He really is sweet, once you get to know him."

Joel chuckled. "I'll take your word for it."

"What about you and Nurse Gray?"

"I'm not sure what you mean." He feigned sudden interest in placing one foot in front of the other.

"You two have been spending time together, too. I assumed you'd set your sights on a friendship with her." Nurse Thornton shrugged, her gaze moving past him to where Evelyn sat with Louis and the other boys. "I think it might be good for her. Don't tell her I told you, but there've been nights I've heard her crying before she falls asleep. I worry about her."

Joel cleared his throat. Was Evelyn still in love with Ralph? Was that why she cried at night? Or had she done that before Joel came to the hospital?

"She's an excellent nurse and a genuine person," he said with as much nonchalance as he could muster. "We may have struck up a friendship, but that's all for now."

He wouldn't say more and risk betraying Evelyn's secret to the other nurse. Fortunately, Nurse Thornton let the matter slide. They returned to his wheelchair, and he managed to get himself into the seat without assistance. A small victory, but he felt pleased with himself all the same.

As she pushed him across the grass toward the hospital, Joel tried to think of how to get himself near Evelyn. His mind remained void of a good excuse. Any justification to be near her would contradict what he'd told Nurse Thornton about him and Evelyn only being friends. He would have to resign himself to seeing her tomorrow.

At that moment a young voice called out, "Corporal! Come see what we've done."

Joel grinned. Louis had unknowingly given him the

perfect reason to join their group. He'd have to remember to thank him later.

Nurse Thornton stopped his chair. "Would you like to go over there?"

"Sure." He prided himself on keeping his voice casual.

She wheeled him in the direction of Louis and the others. "Maybe Nurse Gray can bring you back inside when you're ready."

Was that amusement in her voice? Joel let it go without comment. He would get to spend time with Evelyn today—and right now, that's all he cared about.

\* \* \*

Evelyn closed the primer on her lap, trying to ignore the increase in her pulse at Joel's appearance. "Good job, Pierre. You're learning fast."

A smile illuminated the boy's face, and he stuck his chest out in pride. She'd been teaching Louis and the other boys to read English from the old primer. Louis and Pierre, who also knew a little English, had caught on the fastest. A sense of accomplishment and excitement had overtaken Evelyn at seeing their progress. The reading also gave them something to do when they grew bored with cutting bandages.

They'd nearly made it through all the material she'd found in the attic. Already some of the bandages they'd cut had been put to use in several of the wards.

"What do you think of our pile, Corporal?" Louis pointed to the bundle of bandages in the middle of their semicircle.

"Very impressive," he said, exchanging a smile with

Evelyn. Her stomach churned in a way that had nothing to do with the baby. "It appears you've been busy in other ways, too." He motioned to the book in her lap.

Evelyn held it up. "It's an old reading primer I found when I was scouting for bandages."

"Look what I can read." Louis took the book from her and opened it toward the beginning. He read one of the sentences in a halting voice, but he managed to get all of the words correct.

"Well done, Louis." Joel clapped his hand against his knee by way of applause. "I see you have a great teacher."

Evelyn's cheeks warmed at the compliment, but she didn't want him to know his attention flustered her. Rising to her knees, she surveyed the boys' handiwork. "Just a little more today, gentlemen."

Louis groaned and flopped onto his back against the grass. "I cannot cut anymore, Nurse Gray. Can we do something else?"

"Like what?" She wanted to finish this project, and yet she understood the boys' restlessness. They'd been diligently cutting the material for more than an hour.

"A game! What do they play in America?"

Evelyn thought a moment. "We could play hide-and-go-seek."

Louis jumped up. "Yes." He translated their conversation for the other boys. They scrambled to their feet, too, their expressions full of anticipation.

"May I play?" Joel asked.

"It might be hard to hide your wheelchair," she teased.

He gripped one of the chair arms with his good hand. "Then I'll leave it behind." Using his cane and the chair for support, he climbed to his feet.

Evelyn's eyes widened. He was growing stronger and stronger, but the game would require more than walking. "Are you sure?"

"I have long held the title for hide-and-go-seek king."

She bit back a laugh. "Is that so? Do you mean here among the other soldiers or at home?"

Joel pretended to scowl as he advanced a step toward her. "At home, of course. It's a title I'm not ready to relinquish yet, even for an injured leg. Just make sure whoever's *it* counts for a good long while."

Her laughter broke through at his request. "Very well." She turned to address the boys. "It appears Corporal Campbell will be playing, too." All four of them cheered. "Now who would like to be *it*? You'll need to count to fifty. That should give us, and the corporal, plenty of time to hide."

After Louis interpreted the instructions, Pierre raised his hand to be the finder. Without waiting to be acknowledged, he covered his face with his hands and began counting in French.

"Go, go," Louis cried as he and the other boys scattered.

Evelyn stood still, unsure where to hide. Should she follow Joel or let him fend for himself? He was already moving with fairly steady steps, even with his cane, toward the trees bordering the lawn. She decided to follow, though she'd hang back in case he didn't want her help.

Pierre had passed the number twenty. After that, Evelyn didn't know the numbers in French. Ahead of her, Joel disappeared into the woods. Evelyn hurried after him.

When she reached the edge of the trees, she glanced

over her shoulder to see if Pierre was finished counting. With her gaze focused behind her rather than on the ground, Evelyn didn't see the tree root until it was too late. She stumbled forward and would have fallen onto the hard ground if a firm hand hadn't grabbed her elbow and pulled her behind the giant tree.

"Careful," Joel murmured in her ear. His steady hold on her arm meant she was standing against his chest.

Her heartbeat ricocheted at his nearness. His warm, solid presence at her back both unnerved and relaxed her. It felt so wonderful to stand in his semi-embrace. *Is that because I'm missing Ralph or because I'm falling for Joel?*

"Thank you. I'm all right." She took a deliberate step to the side, though mere inches still separated them.

"Is he done counting?" Joel kept his voice low.

Evelyn listened, but she couldn't hear much over the rapid pounding of her pulse in her ears. Perhaps she shouldn't have followed Joel. "I—I think so."

"It's terrific what you're doing for Louis and the other boys." His eyes shone with blatant admiration. Could her heart beat any faster? "You're quite the natural teacher, with the bandage project and helping them learn to read, too."

Evelyn lowered her gaze to the root she'd tripped over rather than continue to stare at her gallant rescuer. "It's mostly Louis and Pierre who've been interested in reading, but they've caught on well." She slid a few more inches away from him, finagling her feet around the gnarled roots. Breathing was difficult with Joel so close.

He shifted to lean his shoulder against the tree trunk. "Is something wrong?"

She pressed her lips together and shook her head.

"Are you angry at me? For coming over to the group, instead of staying away like we talked about?"

Evelyn flicked a glance at those hazel eyes. "No, not at all."

Silence reigned for several heartbeats, then she felt his finger beneath her chin. He gently prodded her head upward until she had to look at him. Her stomach flip-flopped as she peered fully into his handsome face. Light fuzz covered his chin and jaw. He needed another shave. A strange, irrational thought that she must be the one to do it filled her mind.

"Are you afraid of something, Evelyn?"

*You.*

She kept the word sealed inside as her thoughts spiraled like a tornado. What if he didn't reciprocate these growing feelings? What if he decided not to marry her next week? There'd been times over the last few days when she thought Joel was beginning to soften toward her, even like her. She'd notice a lingering look from him or a smile, but they would disappear as quickly as they came and his manner would return to its usual, kind aloofness. Perhaps she ought to be asking him a similar question. What was *he* afraid of?

"I'm fine, really." She swallowed hard. "Just a bit tired is all."

Instead of releasing her chin as she expected, Joel lowered his gaze to her mouth. The rush of sound in Evelyn's ears grew as thunderous as a windstorm. Was he going to kiss her? Should she let him?

*Yes*, her heart cried. She wanted him to kiss her, had dreamt of this moment.

She held her breath as Joel leaned forward. Closing her eyes, she waited for his lips to reach hers. Would his kiss be as glorious as she'd imagined? Or better? She felt his breath brush her chin, sending her stomach into another frenzy of flutters.

The sudden blare of horns dropped like a bomb into the quiet of the trees, obliterating their shared moment. Evelyn opened her eyes and turned toward the hospital. "More wounded soldiers."

Joel straightened, robbing her of the warmth of his closeness. "Which means more surgeries."

His disappointed tone had her hopes soaring heaven-ward again. Did it mean he cared? "Yes, it does. Will you watch after Louis for me?"

"I don't profess to be as good a teacher as you, but I'll try."

"Thank you."

She turned to go, but Joel caught her hand, stopping her retreat.

"Evelyn?"

"Yes?" She wished she didn't sound so breathless. Wished she didn't have to leave him.

He released her hand to brush her cheek with his thumb, heating her skin with the tender touch. "Good luck."

Louis and Pierre bolted toward them, signaling the end to their private conversation. "Ambulances," Louis said, gripping his knees as he caught his breath.

"I need to go." Evelyn squeezed Louis's shoulder. "You boys be good." She waved good-bye and hurried across the lawn. Dr. Dupont would be waiting. It was time to be a nurse, and not a woman falling in love.

She drew in a deep breath of the sun-soaked air, attempting to steady her emotions. Her face felt overheated from more than the weather. Evelyn lifted her hands to her flushed face and couldn't help but smile. Maybe Joel hadn't given her a real kiss, but he had caressed her cheek. She could be content with that for now.

# Chapter 10

Evelyn leaned against the cool stones of the hospital. Dusk had finally fallen, bringing a slight breeze that relieved the warmth of her face. She longed to unbutton her collar, but it wouldn't be proper. Instead she removed her nurse's cap and lifted her coiled hair off her neck. The sweat turned icy against her skin and she breathed out a sigh of contentment.

She'd worked a total of twenty-three hours assisting Dr. Dupont with surgeries. The only break she'd had since the previous evening when they'd received a new group of soldiers was the four hours she had slept this morning.

Her back and feet felt stiff and achy after so many hours of standing. Evelyn rubbed at the muscles of her lower back as she peered at the empty back lawn. She wished Joel were outside. She missed talking to him, and Louis, too. Her day no longer felt complete without seeing both of them, even if she did find great satisfaction in the hard work.

"Maybe tomorrow," she muttered, pushing away from the wall. They had at least one more surgery to perform tonight.

A movement drew her notice as she walked around the corner of the hospital. A nurse was pushing a soldier in a wheelchair, rather rapidly, in Evelyn's direction. Which nurse was out this late in the evening?

A familiar loud laugh floated through the air— Sergeant Dennis.

Evelyn frowned. *Please don't let it be Alice with him. Please don't let it . . .*

"Oh, Evelyn." Alice waved. "Could you hold the door open for us?"

Irritation scrubbed across Evelyn's skin, but she moved to get the door. "You two are out late." She didn't bother to hide her accusing tone.

Alice had the good sense to blush, but her chin tipped a little higher, too. "We ended up walking farther than expected. The sergeant's knee is improving well with all the exercise."

Evelyn chose not to comment as she let them pass by and shut the door. Dr. Dupont would require her assistance very soon, but she couldn't leave without talking to Alice first. Her roommate's shift was over, which meant Alice would be coming back this way.

She paced the grass as she waited. The movement worked some of the soreness from her muscles and kept her from rushing in and confronting Alice in front of everyone.

What was Alice thinking, fraternizing with a soldier, especially when she'd been so against such things? Evelyn couldn't understand what had changed the girl's mind.

She stopped and shook her head. That wasn't true. What had persuaded Alice was likely the same thing that had persuaded Evelyn to break the rules—an attentive soldier.

Evelyn swiped her cap across her damp forehead as she resumed her pacing. If she could go back to the day by the sea when she'd met Ralph, would she make the same choice? To leave the group and spend time alone with him? *Yes.* The answer came without hesitation. Meeting Ralph hadn't been the problem—it was giving in to their fear of being separated when their leave was over. She couldn't change that decision now, but she could stop Alice from making a similar mistake.

The door clattered open and Evelyn spun around. "Alice."

Her roommate yelped, one hand rising to her throat. "You scared me, Evelyn. What are you doing here?"

"I could ask you the same question."

Alice closed the door. "What do you mean?"

"Why were you out late with Sergeant Dennis?"

"I told you. We walked farther than—"

Evelyn waved away the thin excuse. "That's what you would tell Sister Marcelle or one of the other nurses. *I* want to know why you were out late with him."

"I don't know why you're angry. It isn't like anything improper happened."

"No? You being out with him this late suggests otherwise." Evelyn tempered her tone from frustration to cautionary. "I don't want you to get into trouble, Alice. And you will, if you keep this up."

Alice shook her head. "Why are you so determined not to believe me? Nothing is going on. He and I are friends; that's all."

"There's where it starts," Evelyn murmured. She wasn't even sure Alice heard her, which was probably for the best. She didn't want to have to do any explaining. "If I were you, I would ask to work in a different ward. You don't know what you're getting into." She started for the back door, but she stopped when Alice spoke again.

"You don't understand. I like him, Evelyn. And he likes me." The pleading in Alice's voice provoked Evelyn's knowing compassion, but she smothered it under her anger. "I promised Corporal Campbell and myself that I wouldn't let it go beyond friendship. And I won't."

"Corporal Campbell?" Evelyn whirled around. "What does he have to do with this?"

"He's the one who encouraged me to get to know George better."

"George?" They were on a first-name basis?

Alice ducked her head. "Sergeant Dennis."

Evelyn rubbed her tired eyes. Alice's words made no sense. Why would Joel encourage something between Alice and the sergeant when he knew Evelyn's history? She would ask him the first chance she got. "I still think you're better off staying away from him. You can't be sure of his real intentions—"

"You don't know him," Alice threw back. "And who are you to lecture me on something like this? You think I haven't noticed how you and Corporal Campbell have managed to spend more and more time together?"

The heat that flooded Evelyn's face had nothing to do

with working in the warm hospital this time. "It isn't like that."

"Exactly. How about you worry about your private doings and I'll worry about mine."

With that, Alice marched toward the nurses' building, leaving Evelyn shaken. Tears of frustration and regret stung her eyes. She'd only meant to help. She hadn't meant to incur her friend's anger or discover that Joel supported the couple's friendship.

"Nurse Gray?"

Evelyn looked up to see Dr. Dupont standing in the doorway.

"Are you ready?" he asked. "The patient is being brought down now."

Unable to trust her voice, she nodded. She followed the surgeon inside and down the stairs to the surgery rooms. Her body still felt weighed down by exhaustion, but now her heart felt just as heavy.

\* \* \*

Joel eyed the path through the woods that Louis had sprinted down. It wouldn't be easy traversing it with his cane, but he welcomed a change of scenery. He was tired of the four walls of the recovery ward or the confines of the back lawn. He needed something else to occupy his time and energy, and keep him from wondering how much longer it would be before he saw Evelyn again.

It had been two days since they'd joined Louis and the other boys in their game of hide-and-go-seek. Two days since he'd touched the smooth skin of her cheek. He hadn't intended to caress her face, until she'd looked at him with those big, dark eyes full of vulnerability.

Hidden away as they'd been behind the tree, he'd longed to kiss away whatever had caused the furrow on her brow, to taste the sweetness of those slightly parted lips. The arrival of the ambulances, though, had made such a thing impossible. So he'd settled for touching her face instead. That didn't mean Joel hadn't given plenty of thought to what might have happened had he seized the moment to kiss her sooner, if he hadn't hesitated.

Was he ready for what a kiss would mean for both of them?

"Come on, Corporal," Louis hollered from somewhere up ahead.

Joel planted his cane on a piece of level ground and stepped onto the path. He kept his gaze riveted to the ground as he walked forward. Louis's progress in the reading primer had gone well, but he and the boy had both grown bored today. When Louis suggested visiting some of his favorite bird-watching spots, Joel had abandoned the reading lesson for the call of the woods.

The air around him felt cool and held the scent of moldering plants. Joel paused to glance at the leafy canopy overhead. He'd spent many happy hours as a kid playing with Tom and Livy in the trees bordering their farm or exploring by himself.

"Are you coming?" Louis appeared up the trail, then bounded ahead with a laugh.

Time stopped and seemed to race backward as Joel stood there, unmoving. Instead of a young French boy calling to him, it was his brother Tom, trying to beat Joel in a footrace to their secret spot. In his mind's eye, he sensed Livy behind him, her girlish voice full of pouting, "Wait for me, boys!"

He, Tom, and Livy. They'd always been a close trio—fighting, loving, playing, and defending each other. He'd expected it to be that way forever. What would it be like to go home now, with Tom gone and Livy married and living far away? For the first time in his life, Joel felt a measure of real loneliness.

Unshed tears filled his throat and he coughed hard against them. He couldn't look back, couldn't stare the loss straight in the face. This war had changed so much about his life, but he had to keep running forward. Or at least shuffling along.

Straightening, he locked the emotions back up and proceeded down the trail again. "I'm coming, Louis."

* * *

"Love to...Ma...and Pa...and all the young'uns," the soldier dictated in a whisper, his face contorted with pain.

Evelyn dug her fingernails into the palm of her free hand to keep from weeping onto the sheet of stationary in her lap. Beyond the soldier's labored breathing, the only other sound in the surgical room was Dr. Dupont penning his notes about the soldier's emergency surgery into the ledger.

"Anything else you want me to tell them?"

"Sorry...I didn't..." He sucked in a gulp of air and twisted his head to look at her. His tortured gaze was difficult to meet, yet Evelyn didn't dare glance away. "Didn't...make it...hhh—"

His sentence ended in a sigh. Evelyn scrambled up from her chair, her eyes focused on the soldier's peaceful expression. "Doctor?"

Dr. Dupont jumped up from his chair and hurried over. He checked the young man's pulse, then shook his head. "He is gone." His voice cracked on the last word as he pushed the soldier's eyelids shut. When he spoke again, his tone was firm, in control once more. "Will you please record the time of death, Nurse Gray?"

Sorrow cut through her as Evelyn walked over to the table, sat down, and picked up the surgeon's discarded pen. She would follow the surgeon's example and not dissolve into tears. "I'm ready."

"Time of death," Dr. Dupont announced in a solemn voice, "is seven thirty-nine p.m. on this, the fourth day of August 1918."

Evelyn wrote the time and date, then shut the ledger. Dr. Dupont drew the sheet over the soldier's face. The finality of that act nearly undid her resolve not to cry. Somewhere, only two short weeks ago, someone else had drawn the sheet up over Ralph's still form. A wave of nausea, which she hadn't experienced in days, rose into her throat, as bitter as her sadness. She clamped her lips hard against it until the feeling passed.

"Could we have done anything else?" she asked the silent room.

Dr. Dupont approached her and placed a gentle hand on her shoulder. "That is a question that will eat you up inside. It is what I asked when I learned my daughter's village had been taken by the Germans." He lowered his hand to his side, his voice weary. "Could I have done anything else to protect her? But the answer then is the same one I will give to you, Nurse Gray. We did our best with what we had."

She tried to take solace from his words, but she kept imagining the devastated faces of this boy's family when they learned he'd died. And not on the battlefield but in a hospital, bereft of the needed supplies and medicines that might have saved his life.

"Is there anything else you need, sir?"

The doctor removed his glasses and wiped them with his surgical coat. "No. Go get some sleep. There will be work enough tomorrow."

With a nod, Evelyn left the room without looking back at the sheet-covered figure on the operating table. Was there anything else she could say to ease his loved ones' grief? Perhaps she could tell them how their son and brother had died courageously, even after recognizing his life was slowly slipping away. Even when the emergency surgery hadn't prolonged his journey on earth as they'd all hoped.

Guilt and regret ate at her conscience as she made her way out of the hospital. They had done all they could for the soldier, and yet if there'd been more supplies on hand... She didn't want to dwell on such unanswerable notions—as the good doctor had admonished—but she felt powerless not to.

The warm evening wrapped itself around her as she stepped outside. Evelyn shivered at the change in temperature from the coolness of the surgery ward. As usual the lawn was occupied with patients and nurses and a few of the sisters, even at this hour. Evelyn searched the scattered group for any sign of Louis, but she didn't see him. She released a relieved sigh. As much as she missed

him, she feared she wouldn't be able to fake cheerfulness
tonight.

She stood for a moment, deliberating between going
straight to bed or not. She hadn't seen much of Alice
since their argument two nights ago—her roommate had
either been asleep or on duty when Evelyn had stumbled
into their room to catch a few hours of sleep in between
surgeries.

Eyeing the nearby woods, Evelyn turned and headed
for their promising solitude. She didn't want to make
amends with Alice right now or speak with anyone. She
saw Joel out of the corner of her eye. He was seated
on a lawn chair, with no wheelchair beside him, looking
healthy and handsome. He'd clearly made more progress
in her absence. In five more days, he'd be leaving for the
convalescent home.

The realization tore at her already grief-stricken heart.
Alice's revelation about him from the other night echoed
in her mind: *He's the one who encouraged me to get to
know George better.* A spark of anger leapt inside her.

When Joel lifted his hand in greeting, she marched
past without acknowledging him. She kept walking until
there were only trees surrounding her. Alone at last, she
sank onto the ground, not caring if she got her uniform
dirty, and wept over the death of a young man she didn't
even know.

*  *  *

Joel watched Evelyn disappear into the trees. Clearly
she hadn't seen him wave. Something was bothering her,
judging by the distraught expression on her face and the

exhausted droop of her shoulders. Should he leave her alone or go after her? He didn't like the idea of another day passing without seeing her.

"I think I'll go for a walk," he said, interrupting the story Sergeant Dennis was telling the captivated group of soldiers seated around them.

No one spared him a glance. Joel stood and proceeded with unrushed steps in the direction Evelyn had gone. He didn't need to arouse suspicion. Yet the thought of being near her again, and hopefully coaxing a smile from her, propelled him forward at a quicker pace.

His leg had grown much stronger from all his recent exercise. He'd even made it all the way to Louis's home in the village and back to the hospital yesterday without too much pain afterward. Physically he was nearly ready for his departure to the convalescent home, although that meant a much greater absence from Evelyn.

Joel reached the woods and slipped into their inviting shade. He searched the faint trail and the trees on either side, but he couldn't see Evelyn. Farther up the path, he spotted her brown head among the greenery. She was sitting on the ground, her nurse's cap off. Above the rustle of the leaves and the distant call of a bird, he heard the soft sound of crying.

He slowed his steps, suddenly reluctant to interrupt her. Was she grieving over Ralph, or was something else upsetting her? Despite all they'd talked about at length—their families, her nursing, his life before the war, his interest in bird-watching and sprinting, her interest in helping Louis—he still had little idea what made her sad.

Her palpable gloom broke his hesitation. He couldn't

leave her now, not without trying to help. He drew near, his boots and cane drumming the hard-packed dirt. Evelyn glanced over her shoulder at him, then looked away.

"What do you want, Joel?" Her voice exuded sorrow but also a hint of anger.

"I wanted to see if you're all right."

She sniffed. "I'll be fine."

Silence beat against his ears. Maybe he should have stayed away. "Is something wrong?"

"I said I'll be fine." She rose to her feet, cap in hand, and wiped at her tear-stained face. "How's Louis?"

"He's doing well. We made it a little further in the reading." Joel studied the dark brown curl that had fallen over her eye. He loved that wayward curl, although it teased him to test its softness, to brush it gently to the side of Evelyn's perfect brow. "He took me to his home yesterday."

Surprise flitted across her face. "Oh? How are things there?"

Joel thought of the small cottage and the nearly empty cupboards he'd glimpsed when Louis's mother had rushed about to make him a cup of coffee. "He and his mother do their best. She told me, with much translating from Louis, that he talks quite a bit about you. She's grateful for the work you've given him at the hospital and the food it's provided."

Evelyn folded her arms as if suddenly cold. He wanted to put his arm around her, but her rigid posture warned him to give her space. "Thank you for doing that. I wish I could do more."

"I've thought the same. Maybe there are other small tasks he could do around the hospital to keep earning the extra bread and things." Joel risked another step closer. "In the meantime, is there something I can do to help you?"

Instead of softening, her expression hardened. "You mean like what you've done for Alice and Sergeant Dennis?"

"What are you talking about?"

"Alice told me you encouraged a relationship between her and the sergeant. Is that true?"

Was this the source of her anger? Joel straightened to his full height, though his leg was beginning to complain at standing still. He had nothing to hide or be ashamed of. "I think they're good for each other."

Evelyn frowned. "Even if they can't be together until after the war?"

"They're content to wait."

"Unlike me and Ralph, right?"

Joel looked back the way he'd come. Following her had definitely been a bad idea. He'd hoped to comfort her, not elicit an argument. "That isn't what I said or meant, Evelyn. Alice—Nurse Thornton—has reassured me that she and Sergeant Dennis are only friends. I don't believe there's anything wrong with that friendship, so long as they stick to the rules, just as we're doing."

Her shoulders relaxed a little, but she didn't unfold her arms. "Maybe you're right. But I worry for her. I don't want her to make the same..." Her voice broke on a sob and she covered her mouth until she regained composure. "I—I watched one of our patients die tonight." When she lifted her chin, her gaze was full of anguish.

"I'm so sorry, Evelyn."

"Dr. Dupont and the rest of us did what we could, but

the emergency surgery didn't help. He died while dictating a letter to me, for his family."

Unable to resist comforting her any longer, Joel narrowed the space between them. He leaned his cane against a nearby tree and opened his good arm to her. She released a strangled cry and buried herself against his shoulder. He tucked his arm around her waist.

"I feel so responsible." She pressed her cheek to his shirt, her tears dampening the material. Could she hear the rapid beating of his heart? How long had he wanted to hold her close like this—minutes, days? "If we'd only had more supplies, more medicine, maybe he would have lived."

"Maybe, but you can't know that."

"The doctor says we can't dwell on what might have been, but I can't help it. I don't know how to make the guilt go away."

Joel tightened his grip around her, knowing all too well what she meant. He didn't know how to assuage his own remorse either, especially when he was holding his best friend's girl close enough to smell the faint scent of roses in her hair and feel those soft curls graze his chin.

"Did he suffer?" Her words were soft but full of pain.

"Who?"

Evelyn tipped her head back to look him in the eye. "Ralph. I want to know." She licked her lips. "I have to know."

He shut his eyes and pressed his forehead to hers, her grief mingling with his own. Her complete trust in him to answer this most painful of all questions sent hope sweeping through his carefully guarded heart, lay-ing open the wounds inside. If she could trust him, then he ought to trust her enough to reply honestly.

"Please, Joel," she whispered into the silence. "Tell me. Did he suffer?"

Opening his eyes, he cleared his throat. "If he did, it was very short. I don't think he was conscious until we arrived at the field hospital."

"Did he say anything else before he died?"

"I think he wanted me to find you."

Her dark eyes widened. "Really?"

Joel nodded, unable to say more. If he shared any more of the memories, he would tell too much and then he'd lose her. Despite the openness and trust on her beautiful face at this moment, Joel knew she'd never forgive him if she learned he was responsible for putting Ralph in harm's way. And losing Evelyn would be like losing Rose all over again, only worse. His feelings for her were growing in a way they never had for his high school sweetheart.

Evelyn reached up and placed her hand alongside his cheek. He tried to resist leaning into her touch, but it was futile. She offered him a tear-filled smile. "Thank you. For being Ralph's friend... and for being mine."

The desire to kiss her filled him, even stronger than the other day. He released her waist to rub his thumb over those tantalizing lips. They felt as soft and supple as he'd imagined. Evelyn inhaled a quick breath, her eyes staring directly at his. It would be so easy for him to claim his kiss, and yet he couldn't take advantage of her grief. Especially when a good portion of it wasn't just for the soldier who'd died tonight, but for Ralph.

He lowered his hand to his side and stepped backward,

creating needed distance between them. "We'd better head back."

Evelyn dipped her chin in agreement. She no longer appeared sorrowful but disappointed. Did she want him to kiss her? If so, what did that say about her lingering feelings for Ralph?

After brushing the tears from her face once more, she secured her nurse's cap back on her head. "I should probably go first. You can follow in a few minutes." She walked past him, then turned and placed her hand on his arm. "Thank you again, Joel. For listening to me and for helping Louis. I'll see you tomorrow?"

"Same time, same place," he said in jest as if they were really courting.

Her mouth curved upward in a genuine smile. "I may not be able to come walking in the afternoon, since we might have more surgeries. But I'll meet you here once I'm off in the evening."

"I'll be waiting."

She waved good-bye and moved back up the path toward the hospital. Emptiness settled into his chest. He didn't feel quite as content when they weren't together.

Joel ran his hand over his face and picked up his cane. How could he have allowed himself to fall for the wrong girl? If Ralph had lived, it would have been him holding Evelyn tonight as she cried. Not Joel. She and Ralph would have married, and Joel would have been left to find some other girl after the war. The thought depressed him as he retraced his steps back toward the hospital. *But I am here, with her. So what do I do, Lord?*

He had only five more days to figure it out.

# *Chapter 11*

Think you can keep up?" Evelyn called over her shoulder.

She was keenly aware of Joel coming up the path behind her. His nearness brought the prickle of awareness along her skin, the increased thudding of her pulse, the twist of her stomach that was both unsettling and pleasant. The feeling wasn't foreign—she'd experienced it with Ralph—but it was different with Joel. Was it stronger, deeper? She couldn't say, but the emotion had only increased as they'd met in the woods the last two evenings to walk and talk.

"Are you issuing an order?"

She laughed at his determined tone and breathed in deeply of the forest scent. Nowhere else did she feel such peace. If only these past few days could last forever. But Joel would be leaving for the convalescent home in two more days—and he still hadn't given her any indication of whether he planned to marry her or not.

Evelyn blew out a sigh. She didn't want to spend their remaining time together worrying, but she couldn't keep her fears completely at bay. At night especially, she often lay awake for an hour or two, thinking. With one hand cradling her stomach, she would imagine what it might be like to be married to Joel.

There'd been times the last week when she sensed his growing affection for her, when she felt certain he would agree to her plan. And yet something held him back. He was being cautious for some unknown reason, and that frightened her the most.

"Come on, Joel. You can't expect to get stronger if you can't—"

He caught her from behind with surprising strength, his arm around her rib cage. "You were saying?" he murmured in her ear.

Evelyn's heartbeat thrummed loudly in her ears. Could he hear it? Was this the moment he'd declare his feelings, his intentions? She turned slowly in his grip until she stood facing him within the circle of his arm. The look of desire in his hazel eyes made her breath catch. He had to love her, but would he admit it?

Perhaps if she confessed her feelings first.

"Joel, I..." Fear stole the moisture from her mouth. What if he didn't feel the same about her? She wet her lips.

He released her waist and reached up to stroke her cheek as he'd done the other day. Evelyn shut her eyes as she pressed her face into his touch. His recent actions seemed to suggest he cared for her a great deal. He had also become a good friend to Louis, which endeared him to her all the more.

Opening her eyes, she summoned her courage to speak the truth. "I loved Ralph..." His hand froze on her cheek and the familiar caution entered his eyes. Evelyn hurried to explain. "We only knew each other a week, but if he'd lived, I believe we would have been happy."

Joel fell back a step, frowning, his jaw locked like iron. She was making a mess of this, but she needed it all said in order to help him understand her feelings now.

Evelyn took hold of his hand and ran her thumb over the masculine lines. "What I'm trying to say is that as much as I cared for Ralph, and still do to some degree, I..." She forced her gaze to meet his. The guarded expression was still there, but the muscles in his face had begun to relax. "I think I'm falling in love with y—"

A noise in the brush behind them interrupted her declaration. Evelyn whirled toward the sound. Was someone following them? Had her words been overheard? Sweet relief washed over her as she realized the intruder was likely Louis.

"Louis?" she called. "Come on out."

The boy didn't appear, but the crack of branches disrupted the quiet of the woods again.

"Maybe he's hoping we'll play hide-and-go-seek again," Joel said with a smile.

"You're probably right." She set off down the trail, Joel following behind. "All right, Louis. We'll come find you."

Evelyn peered on either side of the path for a glimpse of the dark-headed imp. He'd hidden well. She turned to tell Joel that she would strike out into the trees to look for the boy, when she saw a figure step onto the path ahead of them.

She spun to face Louis. "There you..." The words died in her throat.

The person standing less than ten feet away was not Louis. A young man stared back at Evelyn, sporting a bandage around one eye and dried blood near the middle of his German uniform. However, it was the gun pointed at her chest that brought icy prickles of fear coursing through her veins.

*   *   *

Why had Evelyn stopped? Joel glanced over her head to see a soldier blocking the path ahead of them. Maybe someone else from the hospital had discovered their path through the woods. He lifted his hand in greeting until he saw the German uniform and the pistol aimed at Evelyn. His heart ceased beating for a moment, then began pumping faster as he realized they were at the mercy of a deserter.

Joel shot a look at Evelyn, standing as still as a statue. He had to get between her and that gun. For the first time since coming to the hospital, he wished he still had his weapon. How was he supposed to protect Evelyn without it?

Keeping an eye on the soldier, Joel took a step forward. The young man immediately barked out, "*Halt!*"

Joel stopped. He let his cane fall to the ground and lifted both arms in the air, at least as well as he could with the left one still in a sling. When he felt certain the soldier wasn't going to shoot him right away, he lowered his arms.

How had the young man ended up here, far from the

trenches? Were there others nearby, or had he struck out alone? Uncertainty brewed to anger in Joel's gut. How dare this soldier pull a gun on them. Hadn't he and Evelyn suffered enough at the hands of the German Army? The lifeless faces of Tom and Ralph loomed large in his mind. He'd lost more than his two best friends in the last few months. His dream of a large family had been ripped from him, too.

His good hand formed a fist as he contemplated how quickly he could spring forward and pound the guy to the ground before the gun was fired. He pressed his feet into the path in preparation.

The young man's hands shook where he gripped the gun and his uncovered eye was wide with fear. Joel guessed he couldn't be much older than fifteen—the same age as his brother Allen back at home. The realization had Joel uncurling his fist and relaxing his stance ever so slightly. He'd served long enough at the front lines to know it wasn't a place for someone who was only a kid.

He sent a silent and fervent plea heavenward for help, then moved to Evelyn's side. He wouldn't let anything happen to her, even if it meant jumping in front of a bullet.

"*Halt*," the young man repeated. He took a menacing step forward.

*Talk to him.*

Joel didn't question the inspired thought. "You hurt?" he asked, touching his forehead.

The soldier didn't respond.

"You need a hospital. *Krankenhaus.*"

The young man dropped the pistol a few inches. "*Krankenhaus?*"

Joel nodded. "The *Krankenhaus* is back that way."
He pointed over his shoulder. "They will give you help.
*Hilfe.*"

"Please," Evelyn coaxed, speaking for the first time
since they'd stumbled upon the soldier. "We can help you
at the hospital. Fix your wound." She touched her stomach to indicate the bloodied spot on the young man's coat.

He studied them through his one eye.

"Let's get you some medical care and food at the
*Krankenhaus*. Okay?" Joel hazarded a step toward the
young man. What was his story? Had he wanted to fight?
Did he have a family back in Germany?

At Joel's movement, the soldier hoisted the gun, its
barrel still aimed at Evelyn. His face hardened once more.
He gestured to the bandage around his head with his free
hand, then at them, all the while speaking in rapid German that Joel didn't understand.

"We only want to help—to *hilfe*." Joel held out his
hand. "Come with us."

His gaze locked on the young man's. The boy might be
a complete stranger, but the pain, grief, and fear in his visi-
ble eye were a familiar companion to Joel. Which emotion
would win out? Would the soldier come to the hospital or
shoot them out of panic? Joel's muscles tensed, ready to
spring in front of Evelyn the moment the gun fired.

The soldier finally broke eye contact to frantically
search the trees. The next moment he pitched headlong
into the brush at the side of the trail.

Joel shielded Evelyn with his back, in case the young
man fired the gun as he ran away. After a minute, the
noise of crashing footsteps faded and the forest resumed
its former stillness.

"Joel?"

He turned at the plaintive whisper. Evelyn's face had drained of color and her shoulders were trembling. He pulled her to him, wrapping his right arm around her for warmth. She clutched the back of his shirt with both hands.

"I—I've never been so scared." She shuddered.

"It's okay," he murmured against her hair. "Everything's okay now."

He released her waist to run his hand over her silky curls. Now that the danger had passed, exhaustion replaced his earlier adrenaline. What would become of the young man? Hopefully he wouldn't end up shot. Joel cringed at the thought.

Evelyn shifted, lifting her chin to look at him. "Are you all right?"

Her dark eyes, full of openness and concern, caught and held his attention. She might have been killed, or at the very least, seriously wounded if the soldier had fired his pistol. The realization made Joel's stomach twist in horror. He didn't want to imagine Evelyn hurt or, worse, out of his life for good.

Telling himself he needed to be certain she was fine, he cupped her face with his hand and caressed the returning color to her cheek. Her skin felt warm and velvety beneath his fingers. The yearning to kiss her rushed over him, and this time Joel didn't have the willpower to squelch it. Not after what they'd just been through.

He bent forward and brushed his lips against hers, enjoying the way they yielded to him. When Evelyn didn't pull away, he deepened his kiss, pouring all his fears and hopes into his touch. Evelyn kissed him back with equal adoration, her hands moving to rest against his chest. How could he have ever considered leaving this place without a promise to return to her?

Joel released her mouth long enough to kiss her nose, her eyelids, her forehead, before claiming her lips again. In that moment he felt free of guilt and grief. The war, the deaths of Tom and Ralph, his near departure from the hospital all faded away as he kissed Evelyn.

Several long minutes later, he eased back. He couldn't bear to relinquish all contact with her, though, so he brushed the curl from her brow and let his fingers linger on her face. If holding her the other day had felt natural, then kissing her was surely what he was meant to do forever.

"Marry me, Evelyn." He chuckled at his own abruptness and tried again. "Evelyn Gray, will you be my wife?"

Her eyes widened. "You mean that?"

He caressed her lower lip with his thumb. "Every word. I'll make certain this baby wants for nothing."

Instead of the happiness he expected, her expression clouded and she glanced away. "The baby, of course."

Lifting her chin, Joel kissed her quickly. "You know I mean you, too. I don't want to leave here unless I know you're going to be waiting for me."

Some of the apprehension in her eyes disappeared at his reassurance. "Will you be able to come back before you return to the front? For the wedding?"

"I should have at least a day. But we might want to find someone close by to perform the ceremony. Maybe the village priest or something."

"Do you want it performed in a church?"

He nodded. "Is that all right with you?"

She hesitated, then dipped her chin in agreement. "I suppose that's all the planning then. Unless you can think of anything else we need to discuss."

*Tell her about Ralph.*

The unexpected thought set Joel's heart thumping as fast as it had been minutes ago. He ought to share everything with her, before they left the intimacy of the woods, before she fully agreed to marry him. He cleared his throat. "There is one other thing..."

"Yes?" She peered up at him, expectation written on her face.

The words stuck in his throat like a piece of meat too large to swallow. How could he dash her happiness and incur her anger or hatred? How could he confess to being responsible for Ralph's death—the very event that had brought him to this point and had enabled him to ask Evelyn to marry him?

Evelyn frowned at his silence. "Is something wrong?"

He shook his head as he slipped his hand into hers. "You forgot something. I don't believe you said 'yes'— officially."

A smile smoothed out the worry lines. "Yes, I agree to marry you, Joel."

"I'm glad to hear it." He planted another lingering kiss on her lips. "We probably ought to get you back. Would you mind getting my cane?"

She picked up the cane where he'd dropped it and handed it to him. "Thanks for agreeing to help." She blushed again. "I mean, for asking me."

The gratitude and admiration emanating from her cut straight through Joel, resurrecting his guilt. Thankfully she went ahead of him up the path, so she couldn't see the shame he felt certain burned on his face. He hated the idea of starting their life together with a haunting secret between them, but he wasn't about to lose the woman he'd suddenly discovered he cared for more than anyone else in the world.

# Chapter 12

The creak of the bureau drawer opening and shutting pulled Evelyn from sleep. She couldn't have been asleep for more than a few hours—she'd spent most of the night thinking about Joel's departure today.

She opened her eyes to find Alice bolting for the door, carrying her clothes and shoes. "Alice?" Evelyn called out, rising up on one elbow.

The only response came from the solid click of the door. With a sigh, Evelyn dropped back onto the bed. She felt horrible for hurting Alice's feelings, but her roommate refused to let her apologize. Alice was either gone when Evelyn awoke in the morning or asleep when Evelyn came in at night. If they passed each other in the hospital, she acted as if Evelyn weren't there.

Evelyn still worried about her, but she'd observed Alice's interactions with Sergeant Dennis and had found their outward friendship to be above reproach. She'd hoped to tell Alice so, but that seemed more and more un-likely as the strain between them dragged on.

Throwing off her blanket, Evelyn sat up and explored the bump of her stomach. It felt a little larger today than the day before. Thank goodness Joel was going to marry her in two weeks. Everything was working out well. That is, if she could get through bidding Joel good-bye today.

She dressed and ran a brush through her curls. After placing her nurse's cap on her head, she paused to stare at herself in the bureau mirror. Her hair and eyes were the same coffee color as they'd always been, her skin the same milky tone, though slightly tanned from her time outdoors.

Other than her burgeoning stomach, she looked no dif-ferent than she had three months ago when she'd met Ralph, but she felt much older inside. She was going to be a mother in less than six months. There were other changes as well—she'd lost one love and gained another, stronger one. At least she hoped her and Joel's love would prove to be stronger.

She still wasn't certain how much he cared for her, even after last night when they'd said good-bye in the pri-vacy of the woods. She'd all but admitted to loving him the other day, but he hadn't yet returned the sentiment. The reticence she'd sensed in him had not completely dis-appeared either, despite the adoration she felt in his kisses or the way he looked at her.

Did he truly want to marry her, or was he doing it out of obligation to Ralph? Was Joel's desire to be a father the real reason he'd asked her to be his wife?

Evelyn's stomach twisted with nervousness at the unanswered questions, but she was determined to put on a good face for Joel. She was scheduled to help with a surgery in one hour. Joel's ride to the convalescent home was due to show up before then. If the vehicle arrived on time, she'd have a chance to see him one last time before he left the hospital.

Evelyn pulled on her shoes and left the room. She made her way to the dining room for breakfast, more out of habit than from being hungry. Alice wasn't around. Evelyn suspected her roommate had either eaten quickly and left or skipped the morning meal altogether for more time with Sergeant Dennis. He would be leaving for the convalescent home, too.

Evelyn nibbled at her eggs and fried potatoes, then gave up the idea of finishing her meal. After depositing her half-empty plate in the kitchen, she exited the hospital through one of the rear entrances. Her plan was to conceal herself at the front corner of the building, where she could see Joel but wouldn't attract the attention of anyone else.

She rounded the side of the building but stopped short when she saw Alice perched in the very spot she'd expected to wait herself. Evelyn considered moving to a different corner, but she threw out the idea. The uneasiness between her and Alice needed to end, especially since Evelyn would be leaving the hospital once she and Joel married.

Stepping softly, she walked toward Alice. Her roommate stood with her back to Evelyn, her left shoulder pressed against the stone wall.

"I thought you might be here, too," Alice said without turning. Her voice held no anger, only resignation.

Evelyn came to a stop beside her. She could see Alice had been crying. Her roommate's sorrow tore anew at her guilt. She understood Alice's pain—she, too, must bid good-bye to the man she loved. But unlike Alice and Sergeant Dennis, Evelyn would see Joel again in two weeks.

"I'm sorry, Alice." Evelyn gazed down at the grass. "I was wrong to accuse you of anything improper with Sergeant Dennis." She licked her lips as she searched for the words that would convey her sincerity but not incriminate herself. "I was worried about you for reasons that don't matter now. I also didn't want you to get hurt. But I've watched the two of you this last week. And even though it's clear you care very much for each other, I saw nothing improper."

Alice turned toward her. "You mean that?"

Evelyn lifted her head and nodded. "He's lucky to have someone as loyal and true as you. I sincerely hope things will work out for both of you once this war is—"

Her sentence was cut off by Alice's tight hug. "I'm sorry, too, Evelyn. I never should have let my anger get the better of me." She released Evelyn and stepped back. "I couldn't understand how you could fault me when you were acting the same way with Corporal Campbell, but that didn't justify what I said. I didn't realize the two of you love each other just as much as George and I do."

"You think Corporal Campbell is in love with me?" The question slipped from Evelyn's lips before she could call it back.

Alice chuckled. "Don't you think so?"

"At times, yes." She didn't want Alice to know how much she both feared and lived for Joel's answer to that question.

Looping her arm through Evelyn's, Alice gave her

shoulder a playful bump. "I'm sure he does. Whenever I
went walking with him, his eyes always sought you out."

Evelyn let Alice's words seep into her heart and give
her hope.

The sound of gravel crunching beneath tires drew
her notice to the front of the hospital. An ambulance
shuddered to a stop, and the drivers hurried to help
several wounded passengers disgorge themselves from
the back. The buzz of conversation floated through the
morning air.

Evelyn waited beside Alice for a glimpse of Joel.
Would Louis come to see him off as well? He'd told her
yesterday that he would. She let her gaze sweep the trees.
Sure enough, the dark-haired boy burst from the woods
and sprinted toward her.

"Did he leave yet?" Louis asked, his breathing hard
from running.

Evelyn shook her head. "Any minute now."

"Hello, Nurse Thornton." Louis offered Alice a
friendly wave. He'd come to know several of the nurses
and sisters over the last few weeks.

"Hi there, Louis," Alice said. "Did you come to see
Corporal Campbell off?"

With a nod, Louis slipped his hand into Evelyn's. She
gave it a gentle squeeze. She might be losing Joel for a
few weeks, but thankfully she still had Louis—at least for
a little while longer.

Alice tightened her grip on Evelyn's arm as Sister
Marcelle walked to the waiting truck, followed by Joel
and Sergeant Dennis. The three exchanged pleasantries,
then Sergeant Dennis shot a look in their direction. He
winked at Alice. She waved her free hand in farewell.

"I won't cry; I won't cry," Alice whispered as the sergeant disappeared into the back of the vehicle. "We will survive this, won't we, Evelyn?"

She didn't answer. It was Joel's turn to depart. Evelyn kept her gaze fastened on him as he shook Sister Marcelle's hand and hoisted his bag onto his shoulder. With slow but sure steps, he walked with his cane toward the truck. One of the drivers waited to help him inside.

*Please look over. Please look over.*

Evelyn held her breath. Would Joel acknowledge her or would he count last night as their good-bye? She'd asked the same question three months ago with a different soldier.

Time seemed to spin in reverse. Instead of standing outside a quiet hospital, she was standing in the noisy, crowded train station. Ralph stood on the bottom rung of the train steps with that devil-may-care grin on his face.

"I'll see you again," he shouted, not caring who heard. "I promise, Evelyn."

It was the last time she ever saw him.

Panic gripped her heart, hard enough that her chest hurt. Would something happen to Joel, too? Might this be her last time seeing him? Losing Ralph had been a devastating shock. How would she go on if Joel were ripped from her life, too?

"Evelyn?" Alice nudged her in the ribs. "He's looking at you."

Evelyn squared her shoulders against her worry. Joel wouldn't be fighting again for another few weeks. They would both be fine until then.

While the driver placed Joel's cane and bag inside the truck, Joel stood watching her. She smiled, hoping the wordless gesture would convey all she felt for him. Louis waved vigorously beside her. Joel returned the boy's wave, but he kept his gaze locked with Evelyn's.

For one brief second it was as if they were back in the woods with no one else around. Evelyn could feel the firm press of his lips against hers, the warmth of his hand on the small of her back. The memory vanished as the driver helped Joel into the truck and dropped the canvas flap. He was gone.

Evelyn waited with Alice and Louis until the truck rumbled back down the drive and disappeared behind the trees lining the main road in front of the hospital.

"Will we see him again?" Louis asked when the three of them turned around and headed for the back lawn.

Evelyn squeezed his hand again. "I believe we will, Louis."

She wanted to tell him she and Joel would be married in a few weeks. But that meant admitting she was leaving, and Evelyn wasn't ready to voice that yet.

"Life is going to be mighty dull." Alice rested her head on Evelyn's shoulder. "Who am I going to yell at now?"

Evelyn laughed. "You are welcome to yell at me. It's better than your silence."

Alice lifted her head. "I know. I'm sorry, Evelyn. I don't know what I'd do without your friendship."

"Me, too," she managed to say over the lump in her throat. She would miss Joel the most when she left France, but Louis and Alice would be close seconds. She pushed away her sadness and smiled at Louis. "Let's see what job Sister Marcelle has for you today."

She wouldn't dwell on the fourteen days she had to en-dure until she saw Joel again or how she'd bear to say good-bye to everyone at St. Vincent's when she left for good. Today she would be grateful for the absence of fear, and the knowledge she and her baby would be taken care of once Joel returned.

*   *   *

As the ambulance drove away from St. Vincent's, Joel wished he could see out the back flap so he could get one more look at Evelyn. Not that he needed it. He had sketched, though rather poorly, her face in his notebook the night before. While lifeless pencil didn't capture the pool of feeling in her dark eyes or the vivacity of her smile, he figured it was the next best thing to a photograph in helping him remember her face.

"Think they'll let us go earlier than two weeks?" Dennis asked from his seat on the bench across from Joel's. "My knee's just fine. I bet I only need a week in that convalescent home."

Joel shrugged. "Maybe. Why are you suddenly so eager to get back to the trenches?"

It was Dennis's turn to act nonchalant. "Just want this war over with, that's all. The sooner we end this thing, the sooner I can get back here."

"You'll miss the sisters that much, huh?" Joel teased.

The sergeant grunted. "I don't think it's a secret who I'm hopin' and prayin' to see again."

Joel shifted on the wooden bench as the hardness bit into his right leg. It was going to be a long ride. "Did she say she'd wait for you?"

"I haven't asked her yet." Dennis's face turned a shade of red, but he was grinning. "But if things don't wind down soon, I'll come back here when I get leave in another few months."

Joel gave an absent nod in response. At least he'd see Evelyn in two weeks. After that, though, it wouldn't matter when he got leave. Evelyn would be home with her grandparents and preparing for the baby's arrival. The thought of a lengthy absence from her brought a tangible ache to his chest.

"Nurse Gray gonna wait for you?" Dennis asked. He flashed a cocky smile when Joel feigned confusion. "Don't go denying that you want her to. I seen the way you two would sneak off into the woods when you thought no one was looking." He held a hand up as Joel started to protest. "I'm not sayin' you weren't a gentleman. Just that you're as gone over her as I am with Alice."

Joel couldn't help smiling at his friend's intuitiveness. Did he dare confess his and Evelyn's plan? He wanted to share his good news, and Sergeant Dennis couldn't spoil their secret, now that they were leaving the hospital.

"Actually I'm going to marry her."

"I knew it. She can wait with Alice, once I ask her."

Shaking his head, Joel chuckled. "No. Not at the end of the war. I'm going to marry her in two weeks when I'm released from the convalescent home."

Dennis rested his arms on his knees, his eyes wide. "You're serious? And she's fine with gettin' sent home because of it?"

Joel chose his next words carefully—he could divulge his surprise, but he wouldn't betray Evelyn's. "Her grandparents aren't doing well. She'd like to be home with them for whatever time they have left."

"Well, congratulations, Campbell." Dennis leaned across the space and shook Joel's hand with one of his giant ones. "Wish I'd thought of that. Though I don't think Alice would've agreed to up and leave."

"I think you're right."

"That Nurse Gray must really love you—to be discharged like that, even if she does want to care for her grandparents."

Joel smiled to himself. Evelyn had declared her feelings right before they'd confronted the renegade German soldier in the woods. Any fears he had about living in Ralph's shadow had disappeared with that confession.

"That's a long time not to see your wife," Dennis added. "Good thing she knows how much you love her, too."

The smile on Joel's face faded into a frown as the import of his friend's words settled like a weight around his shoulders. He twisted on the bench to face forward, wishing he had a window to look out.

Thankfully Dennis didn't question the sudden end to the conversation. Instead the sergeant leaned his head back against the side of the vehicle and shut his eyes. Joel followed suit, but sleep wouldn't come.

He hadn't told Evelyn he loved her, at least not out loud. His actions the last couple of weeks might have shown it, but he hadn't given voice to the sentiment.

It was no mystery why he hadn't said those words yet. His persistent guilt over Ralph's death had kept him from admitting how much Evelyn meant to him. If he didn't say it, then he wouldn't be hurt if she ever found out the truth and despised him for it. But as Dennis had wisely reminded him, Evelyn needed to know how much he cared—how much he loved her—before she returned to the States.

*I'll tell her the minute I see her again.*

He wouldn't divulge everything. Telling her he loved her would be monumental enough. He didn't want to ruin it by revealing his secret or, worse, have her refuse to marry him once she heard it.

The familiar discomfort at keeping something from Evelyn threatened to destroy his logic, but he fought it back with memories of her enticing lips, her sweet-smelling hair, her expressive eyes.

In two weeks' time, they'd be husband and wife. The thought reduced any lingering guilt to a mere prick at the back of Joel's mind. Easily replaced by happiness so keen he wanted to shout it to the world. Surely the day he returned to St. Vincent's to claim her as his bride would be soon enough to tell Evelyn that he loved her. As deeply and passionately as he'd ever hoped to love.

# Chapter 13

Evelyn, come quick," Alice said, bursting into their shared room. She was smiling, in spite of her flushed face.

Evelyn chuckled at Alice's exuberance as she finished putting on her shoes and stood. Her stomach twisted with the same cramping sensation she'd experienced the night before. She inadvertently touched the bump hidden beneath her dress. *Was something wrong with the baby?* She quickly pushed the worrisome thought away.

"Is the hospital on fire?" Evelyn teased. She faced the mirror to put on her nurse's cap.

"No," Alice managed to get out between breaths. "The supply trucks finally arrived!"

Evelyn spun around. "They have?" She pressed her hands to her mouth. Laughter, laced with pure relief, escaped her fingers. "I can't believe it."

"Come on." Alice waved for her to follow.

They hurried down the stairs and outside. Evelyn filled her lungs with the fresh morning air. The good news brought a smile to her lips, the first real one she'd experienced in several days. She hadn't realized how much she would miss Joel. Had it only been four days since he'd left? It felt twice that long, but Evelyn clung to the knowledge he'd be back in ten more to marry her.

She and Alice rounded the front corner of the hospital. Two trucks sat in the driveway, their flaps pulled back to reveal stacks of boxes inside. Grateful tears filled her eyes, momentarily blurring the scene before her. Finally the wounded soldiers would have the proper care they needed.

If only the supplies had come a week sooner...

Evelyn amended the thought, too happy to dwell on what might have been. More supplies on hand could have possibly saved the life of the young soldier who'd died, but as Dr. Dupont had said, they had done the best they could with what they had. Thankfully what they had now would include sufficient bandages and medication.

She stood behind Alice in the growing line of nurses and sisters helping to unload the supplies. The smiles and easy laughter among the staff reminded Evelyn of Christmastime—but this year it had come in August. She couldn't think of better gifts, unless someone had slipped in real chocolate or American newspapers with the supplies.

Accepting the box she was handed, she carried it toward the hospital, passing Sister Marcelle on the way in.

"See how the Lord has rewarded your tenaciousness?" Sister Marcelle gestured to the box in Evelyn's arms.

Evelyn blushed. "It wasn't me."

"Not you alone." Sister Marcelle gave her a conspiratorial smile. "But your ingenuity with that old material certainly helped us get by for a few more weeks until He saw fit to bless us. He truly does come through in our extremities, does He not? Though seldom on our timetable."

Evelyn brushed aside the sister's words with a nod and went to set her box in the growing pile inside the open space of the hospital entryway. Her gaze sought out Sister Marcelle, cheerfully overseeing the unloading, as she returned for another box. The woman certainly had a lot of faith, but more than that, Sister Marcelle had genuine hope that God would provide.

As a child, Evelyn had felt that sort of optimism in the Lord. Until her father died. Without her parents, she'd given up trying to believe God would watch over her. Instead she'd come to rely on herself. Her decision to be with Ralph had only further alienated her from God.

Was it too late to change her heart? Could God truly have been working through her, as Sister Marcelle continued to profess, even as imperfect and doubting as Evelyn was? Was He watching out for her by bringing Joel into her life at the moment she needed him most? The possibility added to the optimistic feeling blooming in her heart.

She collected another box to carry in. This time, though, the short walk from the supply truck to the hospital was accompanied by the sudden renewal of the cramping in her abdomen. Evelyn forced herself to breathe through the mild pain. She probably shouldn't be hefting boxes, but she didn't want to draw attention to herself by not helping either. If she carried only those boxes that weighed very little, though, she could surely keep the cramps from worsening.

After discarding her second box, she moved back out-

side to the truck and discreetly asked one of the drivers
which boxes contained only bandages. He pointed to several sitting beside the truck. Evelyn piled two of the
featherlight boxes on top of each other and carried them
inside. She paused beside the stairs to catch her breath
when the pain came again. This time she selected only
one box when she returned to the truck. The less she did,
the more likely she could get the ache to go away.

As she'd hoped, her slowness went unnoticed and allowed her to carry fewer boxes than the others. Once both
trucks had been emptied, Sister Marcelle made quick
work of dividing the supplies among the wards. Evelyn
and Alice were assigned to take new supplies to the recovery ward, then another set to one of the surgery wards.

Evelyn selected the lightest boxes again and stacked
three of them on top of each other. The sooner she finished carrying things, the sooner she'd feel better.

A blur of movement and a thatch of dark hair alerted
her to Louis's presence even before he reached her side.
"Good morning, Louis. Look what we got today..." Evelyn let her words trail off at the distraught look on the
boy's face.

"Nurse Gray, you have to come. Please." Louis loosened one of her hands from around the boxes and tugged
on it. "*Ma mère* is sick. Too sick to get out of bed."

"Oh no." She glanced at the grandfather clock in the
entry and stifled a groan. She had only fifteen minutes
before she had to assist Dr. Dupont in surgery. While
standing seemed a better activity than lugging boxes in
her present condition, she wished she could rest beforehand.

"I wish I could come, Louis. But I can't." She hated

the crestfallen expression that leaked into his dark eyes. "I'm due to be in the surgery ward after we unload these boxes. I can try and come when I'm finished. All right?"

Louis gave a courageous nod, though his gaze shifted to the floor. Going down on one knee, Evelyn bit back a gasp at the stab of agony below her belly. Why wasn't the pain going away? She felt someone watching her and glanced up to see Alice waiting for her.

Planting a false smile on her face, for Louis and Alice, Evelyn set down the boxes and brushed a lock of black hair off the boy's forehead. "Tell me quickly about her symptoms."

Louis ran a hand beneath his nose. "She is hot but says she is cold, even with a blanket. She does not want to eat or drink." He lifted his chin to look Evelyn in the eye. "I am scared, Nurse Gray."

*I am, too.* The cramps were increasing in magnitude with every minute and becoming harder to ignore. She needed to lie down, but what excuse could she give to be free of her duties? She couldn't simply disappear without an explanation.

She swallowed back her own fear and pulled Louis into an embrace. "You are very brave, Louis. You must keep being brave." She released him and gripped his shoulders. "Do you know how to make tea?"

He nodded.

"Good. Make some tea for your mother and spoon as much of it into her as she'll let you. You can also wet a cloth and place it on her forehead. I will try to come as soon as I can."

"Okay." He jutted his small chin, then turned and sprinted out the front doors. Evelyn lifted her boxes and followed Alice through the hospital in the direction of the recovery ward.

"What's wrong with his mother?" her roommate asked.

"It sounds like influenza. I'll check on her as soon as I'm done with—" She sucked in a sharp breath through her teeth.

"Is something wrong, Evelyn?"

Evelyn shook her head. *It's going to go away—I just need to lie down.*

Her eyes sought out the bed in the corner as they entered the recovery ward, even though Evelyn knew the patient lying there wasn't Joel. How was he getting along at the convalescent home? Did he think of her as much as she thought of him?

After helping Alice unload the boxes in the supply closet, Evelyn trailed her upstairs to gather the supplies for the surgery ward. By the time they descended the stairs to the basement, sweat beaded on Evelyn's forehead. She felt hot and clammy.

"I'm going to slip into the bathroom," she said once they had the boxes inside the supply closet. "I'll be right back."

Alice gave an unconcerned nod and opened the first box. Evelyn forced her feet to move at a normal pace to the bathroom, despite a sudden buzzing in her head. Once inside she sank to the floor, her knees drawn up to her chest to ease the pain.

She stared at the wooden planks of the floor as she tried to breathe normally. One shoe had come unlaced amid the flurry of activity. She bent forward to tie the lace, but she froze at the sight of a bright crimson spot between her shoes.

The sisters were meticulous when it came to a clean hospital. No one would have missed mopping up blood like this. Besides, it was too bright to be old.

Evelyn rose slowly to her feet. Another spot appeared, then another. Terror as chilling as winter crashed over her. Her knees buckled with the force of it and she crumpled back to the floor. A tortured cry hurtled from her lips to the opposite wall at the thought of losing her baby. The bathroom began to tip and spin around her. She squeezed her eyes shut against the dizzying movement.

*Please, make it stop. Please let the baby be fine.*

"Evelyn?" Alice tapped on the door. "Are you all right? I thought I heard you say something."

Somehow she hauled herself to her feet, though she gripped the door handle to keep from losing her balance again, and opened the door. She would have to leave the blood spots and hope someone else assumed they'd simply been overlooked when the ward had been scrubbed down.

"Can you help me back to the nurses' building?" she pled through clenched teeth. "I...don't think I can make it there on my own and I need to lie down."

Alice's eyes widened with surprise, but her reaction was quickly replaced by her nurse's demeanor. "Of course. Let's get you to bed. You're looking really pale."

Evelyn draped an arm around Alice's shoulders, grateful no one else was in the ward yet. She could slip away unnoticed for now. Her relief ended as quickly as it had come in the wake of the pain and fear clawing at her insides.

Managing the stairs and the long walk across the lawn depleted what little energy she had left, but she was determined to ride out her discomfort in the privacy of the nurses' building. Their ascent up the flight of stairs to the second floor took twice as long as normal. Every few steps, she made Alice pause in their progress. Her roommate patiently did so, thankfully keeping whatever questions she had to herself.

Evelyn directed Alice to help her into the bathroom. Once on the floor, she laid her head against the planks, grateful to no longer be moving.

"There's one more thing," she murmured. Alice knelt down beside her. "I need you to take my place in the surgery ward today. Can you get someone to cover for you in the recovery ward?"

"Yes. Is there something I should tell the doctor?"

"Tell him..."

The awful truth pushed forward in her mind, but she fought it back. She wouldn't even think it. If she did, her heart would irrevocably break.

"Just tell him I'm ill." It could be true. There was still a chance the baby would be fine.

Alice placed a hand on Evelyn's forehead. "You're not feverish, but you feel sweaty. What are your other symptoms?"

*Agony. Terror. Heartbreak at the thought of losing my baby.*

"Some cramping." Her voice did nothing to betray the turmoil roiling through her mind and body. "I'll be fine."

"I'll get a cloth for your head." Alice rose to her feet, but she stopped at the door. "Why don't I bring some towels, too? I think you've started your regular bleeding. There's a trail from here to the stairs and a mark on the back of your dress."

So much blood. Too much. Tears leaked from Evelyn's eyes and she squeezed them shut. If only Joel were here, to wrap her in his strong arms, to steal away her dread and pain with his kisses.

"What's wrong?" The creak of the floorboards and a hand on her shoulder told her Alice had returned to her side. The compassion in her friend's tone was Evelyn's undoing.

"I'm miscarrying," she whispered before her voice broke on a sob.

"Y-You're pregnant?"

"Yes." She opened her eyes to Alice's astonished expression.

"Who's the father?" Alice asked in a gentle tone as she removed Evelyn's crushed cap and set it aside.

"His name was Ralph Kelley. He was killed in the same battle that brought Corporal Campbell here." Speaking their names aloud filled Evelyn with renewed anguish. "They were best friends, you see."

"Oh, Evelyn." Alice reached for her hand. "I don't even know what to say. I'm so sorry."

Evelyn gritted her teeth—the pain was beginning to move with greater force into her lower back. "Don't worry about me," she said in a tight whisper. "Thank you for helping with the surgery."

Alice jumped to her feet. "I'm coming back to check on you the minute I can get away. All right? Let me get those towels before I go."

A glimmer of comfort, and relief at telling someone else her secret, shone through Evelyn's fears for a brief moment. She wasn't alone in all of this—Alice would help her.

Alice left the bathroom and reappeared a few minutes later with three or four towels in her arms. She positioned all but one underneath Evelyn. "Here, you can bite on this." She pressed the last towel into Evelyn's hand.

"What for?"

"My mother had two miscarriages and four children. She said biting the towel helped her deal with the pain. How far along are you?"

Evelyn tried calculating the weeks in her head, but her mind felt fuzzy. "Thirteen, maybe fourteen weeks."

"That's going to mean more blood."

"I know." The woozy feeling from earlier bathed her again, reminding her of the night she'd sliced her hand and Joel had bandaged it. What would he think if he knew she was experiencing something infinitely worse than a small cut?

"Are you sure you don't want me to tell anyone?" Alice asked. "I could talk to Dr. Dupont."

"No. Please just cover for me."

Alice squeezed Evelyn's hand where it clutched the towel. "I'll be praying for you, too. And I promise I'll be back."

Alice's absence brought the press of silence. The nurses' building was largely deserted during the day, while those on the day shift worked at the hospital and those on the night shift slept. Evelyn welcomed the quiet, but she hated the feeling of isolation it brought.

The stabbing cramps reached to her knees now. Her muscles felt as if they were being twisted tighter and tighter. She sensed the flow of blood increasing. Clamping her teeth down on the towel, she let out a groaning sob that the material thankfully muffled.

Would Joel still want to marry her if she lost the baby? Wasn't that his main reason for asking her to be his wife, despite all his tender looks and fervent kisses? The uncertainty filled Evelyn with a piercing loneliness she hadn't felt since her father's death. Would she lose Joel, the man she loved so dearly, along with her last tangible connection to Ralph? All her bright hopes and dreams for the future—a future that until this morning had included Joel and a baby—were slipping away and she could do nothing to stop them.

*   *   *

"Nurse Gray?"

The masculine voice penetrated the numbing cloud shrouding Evelyn's mind. How long had she been lying here on this hard floor? She lifted her eyelids and found Dr. Dupont peering down at her. Alice stood behind his shoulder.

"I—I'm sorry, Doctor." Had he seen the blood? "I'll... I'll be back in surgery..." Her voice faded when he shook his head.

"You will worry about no such a thing." The dark eyes behind his glasses exuded concern and kindness. "Nurse Thornton told me everything. You have already lost a lot of blood. I am going to carry you to the surgery ward, then we will perform a dilation and curettage."

Before Evelyn could argue or agree, the doctor gently hoisted her into his arms. "We will have to go through the woods to avoid being seen."

"What about the... mess?" Her voice sounded so weak and quiet, even to herself.

"I'll clean it up as soon as we're done in surgery." Alice's face registered her worry as she covered Evelyn with a blanket.

Dr. Dupont carried her down the stairs and outside. The movement jostled her pain-riddled body, but Evelyn gripped the towel in her hand as hard as she could to keep from crying out. The doctor cut toward the trees and into the shade of the forest. Evelyn shut her eyes as dizziness threatened to overwhelm her.

Sunshine on her face and the crunch of gravel underfoot told her the moment they left the woods to traverse the drive in front of the hospital. She expected them to enter the main doors at any minute, but instead Dr. Dupont continued walking.

"There is a cellar entrance that is not used much," he explained quietly in her ear.

Soon the warm afternoon air gave way to the cool interior of the basement. Evelyn shivered and opened her eyes as the doctor carried her into his now vacant surgery room. He carefully placed her on the operating table.

"Let me rest and I'll be fine," she protested. "I—I don't want you to use any of our new supplies."

Dr. Dupont came to stand at her side. "You need this procedure, Nurse Gray. Please allow me and Nurse Thornton to help you. You cannot go without this. Not with how far along the baby was and with how much blood you have lost already." He rested his hand against her arm, bringing warmth to her shivering body. "I told you once you remind me of my Bridgette. Since I cannot help her, please allow me to help you."

His fatherly tone renewed her tears, but Evelyn felt compelled to say, "I made a mistake…"

The doctor shook his head, his eyes full of compassion. "This unfortunate turn of events today is not because of your mistake. It is what it is, and nothing more. And now we must stop your suffering and prevent something far worse from happening."

She hated the idea of them using supplies and medication on her that were meant for the wounded soldiers. She hadn't fought bravely at the front; instead she'd broken the rules. If she'd only gone home weeks ago and bravely faced her grandparents' disappointment, perhaps she would still have the baby.

*But then I wouldn't have come to know Joel.*

The thought brought her only temporary comfort. Her body felt as if it had turned against itself. "All right," she whispered in defeat. "Go ahead."

Alice moved to stand at Evelyn's head. "Here's the chloroform," she said in a calm voice.

She rested the mask an inch above Evelyn's face and applied the chloroform to the gauze. Evelyn forced herself to take long, even breaths. Lying flat on her back heightened the awful pain.

"You're doing great, Evelyn," Alice soothed. She replaced the chloroform mask with the ether one. "Everything's going to be okay."

Evelyn clung to those words, though she knew nothing would ever be okay again. The happy scenes she'd daydreamed of her and Joel and the baby back home together in Michigan would never be a reality. Twice now her greatest dreams and wishes had been yanked from her grasp. Fresh tears spilled from her eyes just before the anesthesia pulled her down and away from the horror of the morning.

# Chapter 14

I brought you some supper," Alice announced with a hopeful smile.

Evelyn eyed the bread and meat Alice set on the bedside table, then turned to face the wall again. She'd memorized every line and crack. "Thank you, but I'm not hungry."

Alice blew out a sigh and sat down on the edge of Evelyn's bed. "You need to eat sometime, Evelyn. Won't you at least try the bread?"

Evelyn wanted to yell at Alice to go away, to stop checking on her. But even in the midst of her apathy, shock, and morphine-controlled pain, she was conscious enough to keep a civil tongue. Alice had been nothing but kind and solicitous. And so had Dr. Dupont.

After Evelyn had awaken from the surgery the day before, the doctor had carried her back to the nurses' building and given her strict charge not to leave her bed for two days, other than to use the bathroom. Alice later relayed how Dr. Dupont had told Sister Marcelle and the other staff that Evelyn was quite ill and needed rest.

"Okay," she said with a sigh. "I'll try the bread."

Alice beamed as if Evelyn had agreed to smuggle Sergeant Dennis into the hospital. She handed Evelyn the hard roll, but she made no move to leave.

"I promise to eat it." Evelyn took a bite as proof. She wanted to be left alone again, to not have to think of conversation, to not have to think at all.

"Good. How's the pain today?"

Evelyn shrugged. "Bearable."

What she couldn't manage was the hole in her heart. The pain there hurt worse than anything else she'd experienced in the past two days. Her baby was gone, leaving behind a deep hollowness inside her. Even her arms felt bereft, as if they, too, were mourning the loss of ever holding an infant. Tears, her constant companion, dripped down her cheeks.

"What can I do, Evelyn?" Alice brushed aside some hair from Evelyn's forehead and handed her the still damp handkerchief Evelyn had dropped onto the bed earlier. "Do you want to talk?"

"No." Evelyn shook her head. "I don't know." She dabbed at her wet face. "Maybe."

In between bites of bread, Evelyn told Alice everything—meeting Ralph, learning she was pregnant, discovering Ralph had been killed, her proposal to Joel, and his eventually asking her to marry him.

Alice remained quiet as Evelyn talked. Only her facial expressions, which vacillated between surprise and sympathy, showed what she might be thinking. When there was nothing left to tell, Evelyn wiped away the last of her tears. The tightness in her chest had eased a little at sharing the total burden of her secrets with someone else besides Joel.

"I can't believe all this was going on and I never knew." Alice shifted on the bed to rest her back against the wall.

"I needed to keep it that way, although it doesn't matter now."

"No wonder you were worried about me and Sergeant Dennis."

Evelyn nodded. She'd finished her bread, but she couldn't stomach anything else.

"What will you do now?" Alice asked, her voice full of compassion.

It was the question that had plagued Evelyn since waking from the surgery. "I...I don't know."

"Aren't you still going to marry Joel?"

Evelyn closed her eyes. His handsome face rose in her mind, the hazel eyes, the boyish grin. "How can I? He asked me to be his wife largely because of the... the...baby." The word cut through her throat and her heart.

"But he loves you. I'm sure of it."

"He never said it." Evelyn opened her eyes and peered up at the slats of the ceiling, the underside of the floor above. That's how she felt—turned inside out with grief, scarred with self-reproach over what she might have done differently to keep the baby.

If she'd refused the night shift or hadn't carried any boxes, would the baby still be alive? She hated these questions. She could hear Dr. Dupont's reminder of their futility, but she felt powerless to stop them.

"Besides, maybe losing Joel and"—she couldn't bring herself to repeat the word *baby* out loud again—"and not being pregnant are my punishment."

"Evelyn, that's not true. We all make mistakes. God still—"

"Nurse Gray? Nurse Gray?" a frantic young voice hollered. The shouts were accompanied by the slap of bare feet against the stairs.

"Louis?" Remembrance dawned on Evelyn at the same instant Alice jumped up and walked out the open door. *Louis's mother was sick and I promised to come.* A new round of guilt flowered inside her. She physically couldn't have helped him yesterday, but she still felt horrible for letting the boy down.

"We're in here, Louis," she heard Alice call down the stairs.

Evelyn struggled to a sitting position just as the boy burst into the room, followed by Alice at a more sedate pace. His hair stood up on end, and his clothes looked as though he'd slept in them. "What's the matter, Louis? Is your mother any better? I'm so sorry I couldn't—"

Louis hurled himself across the room, straight at Evelyn. She bit back a cry of pain as he landed next to her on the bed. He buried his head in the crook of her neck and began to weep. Evelyn wrapped her arms around him as she gave Alice a questioning look. Alice shook her head in equal puzzlement.

Evelyn attempted to tamp down his thick, black hair. "What's happened?" she asked softly.

"She is gone," he sobbed into Evelyn's nightdress.

"Gone? You mean…" Evelyn froze, her hand unmoving on his head. *No. Oh please, no.*

Louis dipped his chin. "She is dead, Nurse Gray. She died today. I made her drink the tea and gave her blankets and told her stories, but I couldn't make her well..." His voice broke on a sob.

Evelyn felt incapable of speaking. No words were sufficient anyway. Instead she held the boy tight as regret seared her mind. If only she'd been able to do something for his mother, or at the very least, had been there with Louis through the awful ordeal.

"I'm so sorry, Louis." Alice sank onto her own bed. "Does anyone else know?"

"*Ma mère* told me to get Madame Heroux." He sniffed and ran the back of his hand under his nose. "The old lady came, but she made me leave the room. When I came out, she said *ma mère* was gone. She sent me for the *pasteur*. He and Madame Heroux talked like I was not there, so I left."

"Oh, Louis," Evelyn said, finding her voice at last. "I am so very, very sorry."

Louis put his arms around Evelyn's neck, nearly crushing her breath. "Can I stay with you? *S'il vous plaît?*"

"For a while." Evelyn eased his hold around her throat. "But I'm sure the *pasteur* and Madame Heroux will be worried if you don't return soon. Perhaps I could..."

Alice guessed at what she was going to say. "No, you need to stay in bed. I'll talk to Sister Marcelle and see what she advises."

"Thank you, Alice." Evelyn sent her friend a look of gratitude over Louis's head.

Alice gave her a quick smile. "What are friends for?"

Not for the first time, Evelyn felt a surge of appreciation that she and Alice had mended things between them.

She would not have survived the last two days without Alice's help.

Once her roommate left, Evelyn scooted toward the wall so Louis could sit beside her against the pillow. She kept her arm wrapped around him. He laid his head on her shoulder and sniffed again.

"I'm sorry I wasn't able to come help your mother, Louis." Thankfully she couldn't see his eyes; she hated to think of the disappointment or accusation she might find there. "I...got very sick yesterday, and even missed the surgery I was supposed to help with."

Louis's head shot up. "Are you going to die, too?" His voice bordered on sheer panic. He needed her now more than ever, with his mother gone. Evelyn rested her hand against her empty womb. Perhaps she needed him, too.

"No, Louis, I'm not going to die." *At least not on the outside.* "I'll be back to work soon, but I'm sorry I wasn't there."

He gave a halfhearted shrug. "It does not matter. She is dead and I am alone."

His attempt at bravery nearly broke Evelyn's heart anew. She twisted to face him and gripped his shoulders. "It's okay to cry and feel afraid, Louis. I did that when my father died and I was almost an adult. But you must never, ever think you're alone."

"'Cause I have God with me?"

The sincere question pierced straight through Evelyn's chest. She wasn't able to answer in the affirmative for herself yet, but she had no doubt Someone was watching over Louis. Why else would she have met him?

"Yes, Louis. Because God is with you, and because I

will be with you as long as I can. And Nurse Thornton and the sisters at the hospital."

"And Corporal Campbell."

Tears threatened again and Evelyn forced a cleansing breath through her nose to drive them back. Joel might not want to marry her anymore, but maybe he would keep in contact with Louis.

"I miss her," Louis said. "It hurts bad, right here." He placed a hand over his chest.

Evelyn hugged him tight. She could no longer keep from weeping. Her chest hurt fiercely, too. She'd wanted so much to be Joel's wife and a mother, and now she wouldn't be either. At least hugging Louis gave her empty arms something to hold.

Neither of them spoke again, but Evelyn felt a bond being forged between them as they silently cried out their grief together. Sometime later, Sister Marcelle pushed through the partially open door.

"Come in," Evelyn said. She hurried to wipe the moisture from her cheeks.

"How are you feeling, child?"

*Does she know what I've been through?* Evelyn wondered, a prick of alarm knotting her stomach. The open sincerity on Sister Marcelle's face belied Evelyn's fear, though.

"I promise to be back to work as soon as I'm able."

Sister Marcelle waved away her words. "I am not concerned with you shirking your duty, Nurse Gray. Far from it." She stepped to the bed. "Now, young Louis. I am sorry to hear of your mother's passing. Do you have any living relatives nearby?"

Louis shook his head.

"I see." Sister Marcelle folded her hands within the long sleeves of her dress. "Then I would like to offer you a home here at the hospital, for the time being." Louis sat up straight at the announcement, and Evelyn gave his shoulder an encouraging squeeze. To have him here and taken care of was her greatest wish right now.

"If you are willing to continue assisting us in various tasks, I will see that Cook gives you regular meals and you may sleep in one of the attic rooms." Sister Marcelle gave him a kind smile. "Would that sort of arrangement please you?"

"*Oui*." Louis glanced at Evelyn. "Can I eat with Nurse Gray and say *bon nuit* to her when I go to bed?"

Sister Marcelle tipped her headdress forward in a thoughtful nod. "As long as you do not disrupt Nurse Gray during her assignments, I have no objection to you taking meals with her. As far as bidding her good night, I don't believe that would be sufficient, do you, Nurse Gray?"

Evelyn studied the sister's neutral expression. "It wouldn't?"

"I think a hard worker and a gentleman such as Louis," Sister Marcelle said, her mouth twitching with a smile, "deserves to be tucked in at night."

"*Merci*, Sister Marcelle." The boy jumped up from the bed and threw his arms around the sister's waist. Sister Marcelle appeared momentarily startled, but her face softened as she hugged Louis back.

"We must leave Nurse Gray to her rest now, while you and I walk back to your home. I want to share our plans with the *pasteur* and find out when he wishes to hold the funeral." She offered her hand to Louis, who slipped his

small one into hers. "He may also know of a family or
two who have lost their homes to the war and may ben-
efit from living in yours. Since you will be here with us,
Louis."

His exuberance had drooped at the news of returning
home, but he stuck out his chin in an obvious effort at
courage. "I will be back soon, Nurse Gray. Get better." He
gave her a limp wave with his free hand.

Evelyn waved back. "I'll be waiting for you."

He and Sister Marcelle walked out of the room, leaving Evelyn alone once more—just as she'd wanted. But
the quiet grew large and suffocating. The sooner she
could return to her work in the hospital, the better. At
least she would have Louis to help occupy her hours off.
And she wouldn't have to say good-bye to him or Alice or
Sister Marcelle now. That knowledge eased her anguish a
little.

As hard as it might have been to leave these dear people, she would have done it a thousand times over if it
meant keeping her baby. If it meant keeping her last remaining connection to Ralph. If it meant keeping her
hopes and dreams of marrying Joel and having a family.

Fresh tears coursed down her face as she slid back
beneath the covers. She pulled them over her head. Hopefully sleep would block out—however temporarily—the
torrent of emotions she couldn't escape while awake.

\* \* \*

Joel strode through the front doors of the château and
jogged up the grand staircase. Everything about this private residence boasted wealth—from the fine food to the

walls covered with paintings to the large room he and Sergeant Dennis shared.

He reached the landing and paused to catch his breath. He'd attempted running only the last couple of days, but already, strength was returning to his right leg. His arm was on the mend, too, and he'd soon be able to give up wearing the sling. He might be stiff and a little sore at night, even lying on his comfortable bed, but the walks—and now the slow runs—around the grounds were improving his overall stamina.

After traversing the next flight of stairs, he walked down the hallway to his room, grateful he could shave and wash up anytime he liked here. He ran a hand over the stubble on his face, thinking of the night Evelyn had given him a shave. Though he hadn't realized it at the time, he'd started to fall in love with her that night.

*Only seven more days till I see her again.* The thought brought a whistle to his lips. He entered his room to find Sergeant Dennis reading at the desk.

"You spend more time with that Bible now than I do," Joel teased. "I'd say you need to get yourself your own copy."

Sergeant Dennis glanced up, a sly grin on his face. "Don't forget I outrank you, Campbell. Maybe you oughta find yourself a new copy."

Joel laughed as he walked through the open door of their private bathroom. He was pleased to see that Dennis's enthusiasm for spiritual things hadn't waned in the week away from Nurse Thornton. If anything, the sergeant had been more vigilant about studying, taking advantage of the times Joel wasn't reading the Bible himself. His own faith had slowly been returning the last few weeks, but he'd gladly shared the book with his friend.

Removing his shirt, he set out his shaving things. He was becoming more and more adept at shaving with one hand. "Did you find out what day you're leaving next week?" Joel called over his shoulder.

"Next Saturday. What about you?"

"Friday—just like we'd hoped." Things were going exactly as he and Evelyn had planned. He smiled at himself in the mirror as he applied the soap lather.

"Wish I'd gotten the same day as you. Then I could've stood up as your best man," Sergeant Dennis said. "I plan on goin' down there myself with my free hours. Will you tell Alice that?"

"Sure thing." Joel began sliding the razor across his face.

By this time next week, he'd be married to the woman he loved, and in another couple of months, they would have a baby. Maybe a son—a precocious one like Louis. Joel had to admit he missed the boy, especially since he'd discovered some new birds during his time at the château. Perhaps he'd loan his bird book to Louis and collect it back on his next leave.

Maybe Evelyn would have a girl. A beautiful, dark-eyed girl. Joel wouldn't mind a daughter.

Of course, boy or girl, the baby might look like Ralph.

Joel frowned in the mirror as he rinsed off his razor. He didn't want to think about Ralph right now. It only succeeded in dredging up the guilt he'd nearly buried beneath good rest, exercise, and thoughts of Evelyn.

*I can't change the past*, he told himself, staring at his reflection. But he would do everything in his power, once he and Evelyn were married, to care for her and her child. Surely that would erase any lingering remorse and responsibility he felt over Ralph's death.

His rationale made sense, but Joel couldn't shake the feeling in his gut that he should have told Evelyn everything before leaving the hospital. He felt like a coward, and he hated that feeling.

He hurried to finish shaving, then put his sweaty shirt back on. "I think I'll take another run around the grounds," he announced as he stepped back into the room.

"All right." Sergeant Dennis didn't even look up from his reading.

Joel hurried down the stairs and back out the main doors, eager to hear the gravel crunching under his feet as he drove everything from his mind but pushing his body as hard as he could.

# Chapter 15

Evelyn blinked, trying to remember which tool Dr. Dupont had requested. She couldn't blame her muddled mind on the morphine anymore.

Dr. Dupont studied her intently from behind his glasses. He'd expressed concern about her returning to work too soon. She needed to focus more and reassure him that she did not need to go back to bed. The two and a half days she'd spent in that small room, minus her attendance at Louis's mother's funeral, had nearly killed her. She couldn't stand the quiet or the isolation. It gave her too much time to think, to ask herself fruitless questions, to wonder how to break the news to Joel about the baby.

Before the doctor could repeat his request, Evelyn recalled what he'd asked for. She handed him the tool and forced her stiff lips to lift into a smile. He cocked an eyebrow but didn't say anything. Thankfully another nurse was present or Dr. Dupont might have pressed Evelyn for answers to how she was feeling. And that would be her downfall.

She crammed her emotions down deep inside and concentrated all her efforts on the surgery at hand. At least it wasn't life-threatening. She could handle assisting the removal of a soldier's tonsils.

Once the procedure was over, Evelyn set about washing blood from the surgical tools and scrubbing down the room. Her gaze wandered to the bathroom and the last time she'd been in there. Remembering brought the shadowy echoes of panic she'd felt that day, and suddenly her lungs struggled for breath. While the doctor spoke with the other nurse, Evelyn slipped out the cellar entrance Dr. Dupont had pointed out the other day.

The afternoon sun had been obliterated by thick gray clouds, and the air hung heavy with the promise of a summer rainstorm. Evelyn pressed her back against the stone wall and forced herself to take even breaths until the horrible memories fled.

"Nurse Gray?" Louis called out as he bounded around the corner of the hospital. A basket swung wildly from his hand. "The doctor said I would find you here."

Evelyn blushed. "Only for a minute. We just finished with a surgery. I should get back, Louis."

The boy shook his head. "Dr. Dupont said you could come on my..." He scrunched his face. "What did you call it when we ate on the grass?"

"A picnic."

"Yes, he said you are to come on my picnic." He hoisted his basket in the air. "Cook made it up, but it smells good."

Something akin to pleasure warmed Evelyn's heart at

Louis's clever idea and the doctor's foresight. She hadn't fooled Dr. Dupont with her feigned composure after all.

"I think a picnic sounds lovely. Where shall we go?"

Louis twisted his head in one direction, then the other. "How about there?" He pointed to a break in the brush and trees that bordered the lawn. Evelyn nodded and followed her young rescuer to his chosen spot.

They sat down on the grass, and Louis plunked the basket between them. "I am hungry," he declared, grabbing a loaf of bread for himself. He gobbled a bite as Evelyn fished out some bread and cheese for herself. The memory of the last time they'd shared a meal like this returned full force into her mind. She'd been pregnant—and sick—that day.

Evelyn fought the urge to cry. Would she ever stop weeping or battling tears? "What job did you have today?" she asked after sampling some cheese.

Louis paused in devouring his lunch. "Washing windows." He made a face. "But I get to stand on a ladder to reach the high parts."

Evelyn allowed a soft chuckle. The sound was foreign and felt as if it must have come from someone else. She cut a glance at Louis. He appeared to be adjusting well to living at the hospital, though at night when she came to tuck him in, he often confided through his tears how much he missed his mother. Evelyn didn't have the heart to tell him it would be a long time, years perhaps, before the ache lessened. Was that how it would be for her, without her baby, without Joel?

Louis finished his bread and started in on his cheese, but several moments later, he stopped chewing and cocked his head. "Are you sad, Nurse Gray?"

Evelyn swallowed the morsel in her mouth and did her best to appear less sorrowful. "Why do you ask?"

He broke off a tiny bit of cheese and squeezed it between his fingers. "Dr. Dupont said something sad happened to you last week, but I am not to ask. I promised. He said Cook would give me no sweets for a week if I broke my word." He lifted his chin and studied Evelyn. "You look like *ma mère* after Papa was killed. But you are not going to die, too, right? That is not asking, okay?"

Sliding over, Evelyn placed her arm around him. She could relate to his fear of her leaving him. "You haven't broken your word, Louis." She pulled him close. "And no, I am not going to die. I am perfectly healthy."

He visibly relaxed. "I am sorry you are sad."

"That may be true at other times. But do you know what?"

Louis glanced up. "What?"

"You help me not be sad."

"Really?"

"Yes."

His face brightened at her words and he scrambled onto his knees. "Guess what Cook made last night?" He didn't wait for Evelyn to answer. "Fudge."

Clearly there'd been more in the truck the other week than just supplies. Evelyn peered into the basket. She'd longed for real chocolate for months. Louis removed a napkin from a small plate, revealing four brown squares.

"Real fudge? This is the perfect picnic."

Louis picked up the plate and held it out to her. Evelyn took a piece of fudge and bit into it. While it didn't taste exactly like the fudge from home, it was better than any sweet she'd had in ages. "Delicious."

That was all the prompting Louis needed. He popped
two in his mouth before Evelyn had swallowed her first
piece. As she reached for her second, a large raindrop
splattered on her hand. Another hit her apron. She finished off her fudge and climbed to her feet.

"Come on, Louis." She grabbed the basket, just as
the scattered drops became sheets of rain. She darted
for the building and Louis followed. Evelyn ducked
down the cellar entrance, which provided some shelter
from the downpour. She looked at Louis and couldn't
help a genuine laugh. "We're soaked."

Louis grinned and gave his head a good shake, sending
water flying in all directions. Removing her drenched
cap, Evelyn shook out her hair, too. She would definitely
have to change before she returned to her duties. She eyed
the still pelting rain, an idea forming, then she smiled at
Louis.

"Do you know what you do when it rains at a picnic?"
Louis shrugged.

"You play tag." She touched Louis's arm and darted
back into the rain, calling over her shoulder, "You're *it*,
Louis. Now you have to chase me."

He laughed and started after her as she raced through
the rain. She sprinted to the driveway, but she slowed her
steps when she reached the front lawn so Louis could
catch up.

"I got you, Nurse Gray." He slapped a hand against her
back before running off. The joy on his face brought Evelyn a twinge of happiness.

She turned and dashed after him. Back and forth they
chased each other across the grass—first one *it* then the
other. Evelyn couldn't remember ever being so wet, but

the coolness of the rain, the fresh smell of the damp earth, and the sweetness of laughter in her throat felt exhilarating.

Out of breath, and a little sore, she stopped and lifted her face to the cleansing drops. The water slid down her face and off her chin, but this time, it wasn't tears. She felt Louis's hand slip into hers as she stood there. Gratitude for the simple moment melted some of the hard numbness that had encased her heart the last week. A feeling of thankfulness grew and became words in her mind, almost like a prayer.

*Thank you for Louis. Thank you for the rain. Thank you for a reason to smile, if only for a few minutes.*

Down deep she still felt the hollowness of losing the baby, but this moment in the rain gave her hope that someday she would feel more whole.

"Race you to the surgery wards," Evelyn said, tipping her head in the direction of the cellar entrance. It was probably time to get back.

Louis let go of her hand and raced away. "I will beat you, Nurse Gray." His adorable grin reappeared.

Evelyn followed at a slower pace. She'd done enough running. The rain felt colder now that their tag game had ended, but she had to admit she'd enjoyed herself. Ahead of her, Louis disappeared down the cellar steps. Evelyn collected her neglected cap and the picnic basket and pushed through the heavy door.

"You certainly did beat—"

Dr. Dupont stood there, a hand on Louis's shoulder. "Did you have a nice picnic?" he asked.

Evelyn wrung water from her apron. "We did, though we got caught in the rain."

"It is all right, Nurse Gray," Louis said. "I told him about tag."

She blushed, though the doctor's gaze reflected only amusement and compassion, not censure. "Yes, well, I need to get back to work, Louis."

"Actually, Sister Marcelle would like to see you." Dr. Dupont peered down at Louis. "You, too."

"Is everything all right?" Evelyn studied the doctor's face as her stomach twisted painfully with fear. What did Sister Marcelle want? Had someone told her the real reason for Evelyn's three-day absence from work?

"No need to worry." The doctor gave her a pointed look that brought Evelyn some relief. He, at least, hadn't revealed anything. "She said she had news, which concerned the two of you."

"Should we change?" She glanced at Louis and couldn't help laughing again. He looked like a drowned kitten, and she was certain she hadn't fared much better.

Dr. Dupont shook his head. "She asked you to come the moment you returned."

Evelyn blew out a sigh and held her hand out to Louis. "Let's go then. Wet and all."

She led him up the back stairs. With each step, their shoes made squishing noises, which set Louis laughing. Soon Evelyn was giggling, too. When they reached the door to Sister Marcelle's office, she paused to smooth her damp apron and take a deep breath.

"Can you keep a straight face?" She gave Louis a stern look, but he wouldn't have it. His lips creased. He clapped his hand over his mouth to hide his smile.

Evelyn fought back another set of giggles as she knocked and waited for the sister to invite them in. Once she did, they stepped into the room and Evelyn shut the door behind them.

Sister Marcelle turned away from the window and smiled. "Ah. Here are two of my favorite people."

"The doctor said you wished to see us." Evelyn didn't spare a glance at Louis. If she did, she might not be able to keep from laughing again.

"Yes, thank you both for coming." Sister Marcelle went to her desk, but she didn't sit. Instead she set her fingers on a sheet of paper lying there and shifted it back and forth, back and forth. She cleared her throat.

The head sister had always exhibited a calm, controlled demeanor, but clearly she was distressed today. The worry Evelyn had felt downstairs returned with greater intensity. Whatever the news, it wouldn't be pleasant. Evelyn squeezed Louis's hand and risked a quick peek at him. He, too, must have sensed the discomfort in the air. His earlier smile had been replaced by a tight frown.

"I will get right to it." Sister Marcelle placed her palm flat against the paper and lifted her chin. "I received word this morning that you are being transferred, Nurse Gray."

"Transferred?" Evelyn echoed, reeling back as if slapped. "To where?"

"The front lines. A truck will be here tomorrow to take you and Dr. Dupont to your new assignment."

"And me." Louis stood tall, his small chest puffed out. "I am going, too."

"I am afraid that is not possible, Louis." Sister Marcelle came around the desk. "You will need to stay—"

"No." He pulled his hand from Evelyn's grip and

twisted to face her. "I can come with you, Nurse Gray. I can help. I can."

Evelyn's heart felt as if someone had twisted it full circle. How could she leave Louis behind, and yet what choice did she have? She had no legal claim on the boy, and she would not put him in danger by taking him with her to the front.

Kneeling, she took both of his hands in hers. "Louis, you can't come with me. You know that. It's much too dangerous. You have a home here, with Nurse Thornton and Sister Marcelle and all the others."

Several tears slipped down his clamped jaw. The determined light in his black eyes reminded her so much of Joel that it hurt. "But you will not be here," he argued in a fierce tone.

"For a while, yes—"

"No," he repeated. Yanking his hands from hers, he darted past her and flung open the door.

"Louis?" Evelyn rose to her feet and started after him, but Sister Marcelle called her back.

"Let him go," she said in a gentle voice. "I knew he would need some time to accept the change. I will look in on him in a bit."

"Thank you." Evelyn longed to follow him, to bury her own head beneath a pillow and sob. She had thought her time for good-byes had passed with the loss of her baby, and now it was sooner than she'd expected.

"I am sorry you cannot stay, Nurse Gray. You will be greatly missed, and not only by Louis."

"Do you think there is a chance I could be transferred back?"

The sister lifted her hands in a helpless gesture. "I suppose it is possible. In the meantime, we will have the boy write to you, and you are always welcome to come here on leave."

Evelyn pinched the bridge of her nose. A headache was forming. Her next leave was still weeks away. "You—you will look out for him?"

Sister Marcelle nodded. "While a hospital is not the best place for a young boy, he is welcome to stay here as long as he likes."

"I wish I could do more for him. He is..." Evelyn let her voice trail off. Was it silly that she and Louis were the closest thing to family either of them had now?

"He is a good boy and loves you very much. I do not think your bond is one that will be severed with time or distance." Sister Marcelle's voice was soft, almost wistful. "Nor do I think it a coincidence that you met one another before his mother died."

Evelyn studied the sister's lined face. "You are very good with him."

Sister Marcelle smiled, but it held a bit of sadness. "I had two younger siblings I looked after and adored. My brother died at four years old, and I have not heard from my sister in years. She felt I was throwing my life away when I decided to become a Sister of Charity. We had always planned to marry brothers, become mothers ourselves, and live beside each other. I hope she has fared well through this war." She glanced at her hands, then straightened her shoulders. "As I said, I will look in on Louis soon."

"Thank you, Sister Marcelle." Evelyn meant so much more than the sister's help with Louis. Sister Marcelle's story gave Evelyn a rare look at the woman's private life and the heartache she hid behind her perpetual smile. "Is there anything else you need?"

Sister Marcelle shook her head. "You may to return to your work."

Evelyn left her office, but she hesitated beside the stairs. She wanted so much to talk to Louis now, though he was likely still angry with her. Hopefully they could resolve things before she left tomorrow.

Recalling that Dr. Dupont was also leaving, Evelyn went back downstairs. She was needed in the recovery ward soon, but first, she had something to say to the surgeon. She found him in his surgery ward, going over the ledger. He glanced up when she walked in and set his book aside.

"Did you know?" Evelyn demanded. "That I was going to be transferred to the front? Is that why you let Louis take me on that picnic, knowing all the while I was going to have to leave him behind?" Her voice cracked with emotion, and she pressed her hand to her mouth to keep from crying.

"I did not know. Sister Marcelle only mentioned I was being transferred. She did express sorrow at losing her best nurse, too, which I suspected meant you." He removed his glasses and wiped them on his lab coat. "I allowed the picnic because you needed something happy and pleasant, Nurse Gray."

Evelyn turned away, her face hot. "I'm sorry. Forgive me for jumping to conclusions. You've been nothing but kind. It's just that..." She swallowed back her tears, but they would not obey. "How can I leave him? He's as much mine as..." She couldn't bring herself to finish the sentence. If she did, she feared the pain of losing her baby would rise up and render her useless to everyone, including Louis.

She heard the sound of the doctor crossing the room. He came to a stop in front of her and took her hand in his. "You can. And you will."

"But how? I won't be here to know he's all right. That he's fed and warm and happy."

Dr. Dupont's eyes glistened with moisture. "I thought the very same thing when I learned the Germans had taken over Bridgette's village."

Evelyn wiped at her wet face, guilt replacing her anguish. She shouldn't complain. At least Louis had someone kind to look out for him, even if it couldn't be her for some time. The good doctor had no way of knowing how his daughter was faring.

"Do you know what has kept me from going mad with worry?" he asked.

"What?"

He patted her hand. "Prayer, Nurse Gray. At times like these, it is only God who can keep the burden of fear and remorse from crushing us. Do you believe that?"

She sniffed and glanced at the floorboards. Did she believe God would help her and Louis? Maybe not so much her, but she didn't doubt He would watch over this little boy who'd become as near and dear to her as anyone. Except perhaps Joel.

Fighting the sting of memories when it came to Joel, Evelyn nodded. "I will try to remember that."

"Good." He released her hand and offered her a compassionate smile. "I am somewhat relieved to hear you are going to the front, too. They need both our skills and I want our best nurse assisting me."

"Thank you."

He returned to his books and Evelyn left the room. She made her way to the recovery ward, where she threw herself into the work of assessing patients, helping others to walk around the lawn, and wheeling others outside in their chairs. The keen attention to her tasks kept her mind from wandering too often to things she didn't want to dwell on, such as the transfer or her miscarriage.

By the time dinner rolled around, she was ready to drop from exhaustion, though she was glad she'd made it through the past several days without morphine. She would need all the stamina she possessed to be a nurse at the front.

Evelyn entered the bustling dining hall, but to her great disappointment, she didn't see Louis. She sought out Sister Marcelle, seated at one of the tables, hoping the sister would know where the boy had gone. The head sister informed her that Louis had eaten earlier. Evelyn's distress cut deeper—she and Louis typically ate their meals together. Sister Marcelle told her she'd talked with the boy that afternoon and was confident he understood the impossibility of accompanying Evelyn to the front.

*He must still be angry, though*, Evelyn thought, if he'd avoided eating with her. She finished her dinner quickly, then headed upstairs to Louis's room in the attic. The two of them had created a nice, snug room, complete with a lamp, a makeshift bookshelf out of crates, and the iron bedstead Evelyn had discovered on her perusal of the top floor. They'd also brought his grandmother's books, a pocket watch of his father's, and two of his mother's quilts from the little cottage to serve as tangible, happy reminders of his family. The room also had a radiator, which would keep Louis warm in the coming cold months.

She found Louis in bed, reading his copy of *Around the World in Eighty Days*. He flicked his gaze at her as she entered the room but didn't speak. Evelyn sat down on the bed beside him.

"You've read quite a bit," she said, noting the number of pages he'd made it through.

He shrugged, his eyes still focused on his book.

"Are you ready for me to blow out the lamp?"

Louis shook his head.

Evelyn straightened the corner of his blanket and stood, frustration and hurt weighing heavily on her. She couldn't force him to talk, though she wished her last night with him might have gone differently.

"Good night then, Louis. Sleep well." She walked to the door. "I'll see you in the morning."

"Evelyn?"

Surprise filled her at hearing him use her first name. He'd always called her Nurse Gray. She turned back, relieved to have the strained silence broken. "Yes?"

He shut his book, though he still wouldn't fully look at her. "You will not forget me, will you?"

Evelyn pressed her lips hard against the rush of emotion crawling up her throat. She crossed the room in three strides and sank onto her knees beside his bed. "Of course not. I could never, ever forget you, Louis. I'm going to write you and I'll come see you the minute I can. All right?"

His chin wobbled with unshed tears before he threw his small arms around her neck and held tight. "I do not want you to go."

"I know." A few tears escaped her own eyes, despite her efforts to appear strong. "I don't want to go either. But we're going to make it through this, Louis. We will."

He drew back and wiped his runny nose on his sleeve. "Will you come back?"

"Yes. I promise I will come back for you." She hugged him again and pressed a quick kiss to his forehead. "Now get some sleep. Tomorrow is a big day for both of us."

Louis slid under his blanket, and Evelyn blew out the lamp. "Good night, Evelyn."

"Good night, Louis."

She left his room and shut the door behind her. When she reached the stairs, she sank down and wept, one hand covering her mouth to keep from being overheard by Louis. Once her shoulders ceased to shake with sobs, she dried her face with her apron. She needed to get to bed, but there was something she needed to do first.

Lowering her chin, she offered a quick but fervent prayer. Something she hadn't done in ages. A prayer not so much for herself, but for Louis.

*Please, God. Please let me keep my promise to him. He's gone through so much already. Please let me make it back to him. I am all he has now…and he is all I have, too.*

She studied her hands where they rested in the lap of her well-used apron. She'd used her hands to assess, and aid, and comfort so many soldiers. And yet her greatest happiness had come in using these same hands to love, and hold, and care for the boy in the room down the hall. In spite of all the tragedy she'd experienced in the last month, Evelyn could no longer deny God had stretched out His own Almighty hand to bring her and Louis together, just as Sister Marcelle had hinted at earlier.

Her own plans had never included mothering an orphan boy as a nurse in France, but Louis's presence in her life had become a beacon in the midst of a sea of sorrow. Could that have been God's plan all along, to bring the two of them together before they truly needed each other?

Evelyn rose to her feet. Fatigue plagued her body, but something akin to hope had sprouted anew inside her heart. And this time, she didn't plan to let it go so easily.

# Chapter 16

"Did you decide what you're going to do about Corporal Campbell?" Alice asked, handing Evelyn a pair of socks.

"Yes." She placed the socks inside her suitcase. There were only a few more things to pack.

"That doesn't sound promising."

Evelyn went to the bedside table and picked up the envelope lying there. "I need you to give him this." She held it out to Alice.

Alice glanced at the letter. "You aren't going to marry him, are you?"

"I can't." Evelyn dropped the envelope onto Alice's bed and resumed packing. She didn't want to think about Joel right now—not when her heart already felt near breaking at having to say good-bye to Louis and everyone else today.

"Why not? He loves you, Evelyn."

"That's your opinion." Evelyn frowned at the apron she was folding. "Maybe he did, in a way, but there was always this hesitation underlying his words and his kisses. The main reason he asked me to be his wife is because I could provide him with the child he could never have." A rush of emotion stilled her fingers as it often did when she thought of her baby. She forced a deep, steadying breath. "Since I'm no longer pregnant, our arrangement is void."

"But you love him," Alice countered. "Regardless of the baby."

Evelyn gripped the sides of her suitcase, turning her knuckles white. "That doesn't matter now."

Alice exhaled a long sigh, but she gave up arguing, to Evelyn's relief. "Do you want me to mail it to him?"

"No. He leaves the convalescent home in three days. It wouldn't get there in time." An image rose in her mind of Joel striding up the gravel drive, expecting to marry her, expecting her to still be carrying her child. "He's planning on coming here. Will you please see that he gets it?"

"All right." Alice picked up the letter and placed it on top of the bureau. "I still can't believe you're going to the front lines."

Evelyn murmured agreement.

"Do you want to?"

Alice's question made Evelyn turn around. "What do you mean? It isn't like we have a say in where we're sent."

"I know. But most of the nurses here want so much to work at the front."

"Do you?"

Alice pursed her lips, then shook her head. "Not now. I'd rather be here, where George can easily find me."

Evelyn twisted back to face her suitcase. "Would you marry him if he asked, before the war is over?"

"No." Alice passed Evelyn the remaining pile of clothes waiting to be packed and sat down in their place. "I'd miss nursing, but it's more than that. I didn't want to be home while all my brothers were off fighting. Mama's probably going crazy with all of us gone, but I thought doing my part over here would be better than seeing her fret over the boys. What about you? Would you have been sad to leave all this behind if you had married Joel?"

Picking up her nurse's cap, Evelyn fingered the material. It didn't look nearly as pristine as it had in the beginning. "I'm glad I don't have to be too far away from Louis. But I don't know that I love nursing the way you do. It's always been the expected course for my life, with my father being a doctor." She thought of Sister Marcelle asking her, weeks ago, if she enjoyed nursing. Perhaps the sister had guessed at what Evelyn was only now realizing.

"I don't regret joining the Nurse Corps," Evelyn quickly added, "or coming over here to help our soldiers. Look at all the wonderful people I've met." She smiled at Alice, though her mind soon filled with memories of Ralph and Louis and finally Joel.

"What would you do instead?"

Evelyn shrugged. "I don't know. I enjoy helping people, but I'm not sure nursing is what I want to do after the war." Maybe there was something else she could do to help others, like Dr. Dupont's wife turning her home into a refuge for children.

A knock sounded at their door. Evelyn glanced over her shoulder to find Sister Marcelle standing there, holding Louis's hand. He smiled at Evelyn, but she knew him well enough now to know the action was a bit forced.

"The truck is here," Sister Marcelle announced.

"I'm finished packing." Evelyn shut her suitcase and glanced around the room. Her corner looked bare and lonely now. She straightened the hem of her blue coat, hefted her luggage, and faced her small audience. "I guess it's time then."

The four of them traipsed outside and across the lawn to the front of the hospital. A few nurses and soldiers called "good-bye" as Evelyn walked past. Dr. Dupont was loading some of his things into the truck with the help of the driver. Evelyn set her suitcase on the ground. Now came the moment she'd been dreading since getting the news of her transfer yesterday.

Alice stepped forward first and embraced Evelyn. "It won't be the same without you here. We'll all miss you. Write when you can and I'll do the same."

Evelyn hugged her back. "I will." She couldn't say more without dissolving into tears, and she'd resolved to stay strong for Louis's sake.

When Alice stepped back, Sister Marcelle took her place in front of Evelyn. The sister lifted both of Evelyn's hands and held them in hers. "You have been a gift and a blessing to us, Nurse Gray. Please come visit as soon as you are able. I promise we will not put you to work, at least not right away." She smiled at her own joke, then leaned close, her next words spoken in a low voice. "God has not forgotten you, child. He is working through you and for you. Remember that."

Evelyn gave her a grateful smile as the sister moved to the side. Louis raced straight at Evelyn and clasped her around the waist. She ran a hand over his thick, dark hair. After a long moment spent swallowing and fighting back tears, she knelt down to look him in the eye. "Be good, all right? Listen to Sister Marcelle and Nurse Thornton. And don't tease Cook."

Louis gave a solemn nod.

"I'll see you in about a month."

He threw himself at her again and Evelyn held him tight. "I will pray for you, Evelyn," he whispered in her ear.

"I will pray for you, too, Louis." And she meant it.

She climbed to her feet and Louis bravely returned to Alice's side. The other nurse draped her arm around his shoulders.

"Are you ready, Nurse Gray?" Dr. Dupont asked.

She wanted to say "no" and instead hide in the woods where she and Joel had kissed, where the future had been so full of promise.

Her gaze moved to the great trees bordering the lawn. *Good-bye, Joel.*

Even though she didn't speak the words out loud, a physical ache filled Evelyn at their finality. She wouldn't be here when Joel came back, when he learned the baby was gone, when he discovered she'd released him of his bond. If only she'd known that evening in the woods the other week was to be their last together. She would have hugged him tighter, kissed him longer, memorized every detail of his face and smile. He might not have loved her back, but he'd cared enough for her to show her that loving someone after Ralph was possible.

With a last look at the hospital and the three dear faces before her, Evelyn turned to face the doctor. "I'm ready."

\* \* \*

When the gray turrets of St. Vincent's came into view, Joel jumped off the farmer's cart, too excited to continue on at the meandering pace.

"*Merci*," he said, giving the man a few coins.

The old man tipped his worn cap at Joel and clucked to his pony. Joel walked toward the hospital, but at the drive, he picked up his pace. Two weeks away from Evelyn had felt like two years. He couldn't wait to touch her beautiful face and kiss those wonderful lips. In a short while, she would be Mrs. Joel Campbell. He broke into a jog until he realized he didn't want to arrive for his wedding sweaty and smelling.

He slowed his steps as he neared the hospital. No place, except home, could be dearer to him. And to think how he'd despised being here at first.

Outside the main doors, he paused to straighten his cap and jacket. He'd taken extra time this morning shaving his face and combing his hair, in hopes of looking his very best on his wedding day.

*Here we go.*

Nerves mixed with eagerness in his gut as he opened one of the doors and stepped into the grand entryway. A sister glanced up from her spot at a table in the corner.

"May I help you?" she asked, her French accent thick.

"I'm here to see Nurse Gray. Evelyn Gray."

The sister frowned. She probably didn't approve of a soldier requesting an audience with one of their nurses. But everything would be made proper in a few hours.

"I am sorry, but Nurse Gray is not here."

Joel fell back a step. Had Evelyn gone to see the village preacher ahead of him? "I'll wait then." He scanned the entryway for a chair.

The sister stood and came around the table. Joel realized, as she came closer, that what he'd read as possible disapproval had become sympathy. "Nurse Gray is not coming back. She was transferred three days ago."

Transferred? The word bowled him over with all the strength of a tank. Evelyn was gone? "Did she leave a note of some kind?"

"Not that I am aware. I am sorry."

Joel was conscious of waving away her apology before walking back out the doors, but he felt as if he were moving through the thick mud at the front. Evelyn wasn't here. He moved down the drive, heading back the way he'd come, but he hadn't gone far when he stopped and looked around. What should he do now?

He stared at the gravel underfoot. What about their plans? What about *his* plans—to tell her how much he loved her? Evelyn had feared this very thing happening, but their marriage was supposed to prevent such a transfer. Removing his cap, Joel ran a hand through his hair. Why would she leave without a word to him?

"Corporal!"

Joel spun around to see Alice hurrying toward him. His relief at seeing the other nurse revived his strength. He met her halfway up the drive. "Where is she, Alice? Why didn't she send me word?"

Alice gripped his arm as she caught her breath. "She knew there wouldn't be time. She only found out the day before she left."

"Where did she go?"

"To the front."

A prickle of apprehension crawled up Joel's spine. Typically the nurses were kept out of harm's way, but he didn't want to think of Evelyn anywhere near a battle, especially being pregnant. Couldn't she have told everyone the truth instead of leaving, especially since he was coming to marry her and make things right?

"She told me to give you this." Alice held out an envelope.

Joel glanced at it. Something in her tone and the way she wouldn't quite meet his eye made him want to decline taking the letter. "What happened? Did she change her mind?"

"You'll have to read her letter." Alice pressed it into his hand and gave his arm a reassuring squeeze. "When you're done, come around to the back of the hospital. We can at least feed you. Louis will want to see you, too."

Joel managed a nod, then crossed to the trees at the side of the drive. He dropped to the grass and tore open the envelope. Curving, feminine handwriting met his gaze. His heart beat faster with uneasiness as he began to read.

*Dear Joel,*
  *By the time you get this, I will have left for the front. I'm sorry I am not there in person to give you this news. What I share next, though, I'll admit I'm grateful I won't have to tell you face-to-face. There is no easy way to relay it, so I will simply state what happened. A few days after you left for the convalescent home, I had a miscarriage.*

The cold hand of shock wrapped itself around Joel's neck and he swallowed hard. Evelyn had miscarried her baby? The thought of her in pain tormented him. Had she

kept her pregnancy a secret during the ordeal? Had anyone helped her?

> *Dr. Dupont and Alice—who both know about Ralph
> and the baby now—were more than helpful during
> those dark days. I would not have made it through
> without them or Louis.*
>
> *In light of what has happened, I am withdrawing
> my agreement to marry you. I can't provide you
> with a child, as we'd planned, and I no longer need
> a husband to avoid disappointing my grandparents.*

Joel shook his head and gripped the paper tighter.
What was she thinking? He loved her, with or without the
baby. Didn't she know that?

Reality crashed over him like a wave. Evelyn didn't
know the extent of his feelings for her. He'd held on to
them as tightly as his guilt and had lost the woman he
loved because of it.

> *Please know how much your friendship means to
> me. I wish you all the best now and after the war.
> I hope you will bear me no ill-will. Let us part as
> friends and always look upon our shared time at St.
> Vincent's with the fondest of memories.*
>
> > *Sincerely,*
> > *Evelyn*
>
> *P.S. If you're able, please write Louis or come
> see him when you get your next leave. His mother
> died and he is now living at the hospital. I know any
> contact from someone he knows and likes would be
> appreciated.*

Without really thinking, Joel wadded the letter into a ball between his hands. His jaw clenched with frustration and hurt, but the feelings roiling through him soon gave way to gut-wrenching remorse. For Evelyn, for himself. Resting his arms on his knees, he hung his head in defeat. He'd come back with hope and excitement for the future. He'd never suspected that future had already slipped between his fingers.

"Corporal!"

Joel lifted his head to find Louis running toward him. The sight of that familiar face would've solicited a smile from him if he hadn't just read Evelyn's devastating letter. The boy slowed when he reached Joel's side and stuck his hands in his trouser pockets.

"Hi there, Louis."

"*Bonjour.* Can I sit with you?"

"By all means." Joel gestured to the grass.

Louis sat down, his shoulder resting against Joel's arm. "Did you hear she left?"

Joel didn't need to ask who the boy meant. "Yes." He discreetly set the crumpled letter in his pack, out of sight from Louis. "Did she say when she'll be back?"

"In about a month. I wish she was still here. Nurse Thornton does not tuck me in like Evelyn did. But I am trying hard not to tease Cook and to work hard."

One corner of Joel's mouth quirked up at Louis's admission, but it fell just as quickly. "I heard about your mother. I'm sorry."

The boy plucked at some grass. "I wish she were here, too." He shot a sideways glance at Joel. "I think of Evelyn as *Maman* Evelyn sometimes. Do you think that is all right? *Ma mère* will not care, will she?"

Joel cleared his throat over the swell of sympathy and gratitude settling there. *Thank you, God, that Evelyn had Louis here with her—that they have each other.* He might never hear the word *father* directed at him, but at least Evelyn had someone who thought of her as *mommy*, even if she was no longer pregnant. "I imagine your mother doesn't mind at all, and I'm sure Evelyn would be happy to know you think of her in that way."

"Are you going to marry her?"

The question sliced through Joel, renewing his guilt and bitter disappointment, though he could tell from Louis's innocent tone that the boy didn't know his and Evelyn's previous plans. "I'm not sure, kid. How come?"

"Because I saw you kissing the night before you left." He grimaced in a way that made Joel chuckle.

"Ah." Joel ripped off a blade of grass and fingered it. Should he explain? "I like Nurse Gray a lot, but I'm not sure she likes me as much." *At least not anymore.*

"She likes you," Louis said, making a pile with his grass.

"How do you know that?"

He shrugged. "Because she told me so."

"When?"

"The other day." He pulled more grass and added it to his stack. "She could not read to me because she had to write you a letter. She looked sad when she was all done, so I asked her why. She said the thing she told you was hard."

Joel glanced at the boy's bent head, trying to squelch the faint stirring of hopefulness inside him. "That's when she said she liked me?"

Louis nodded. "'If it is hard,' I asked her, 'does that mean you do not like the corporal anymore?' She said, '*Non*, it is hard because I do like him.'"

Could Louis be right? Joel wanted to believe him, wanted it more than anything he'd ever wanted.

"So," the boy stated, "you must marry her."

"Because we kissed?" If only things could be that simple between him and Evelyn.

Louis shot him a scathing look. "No. Because God brought her to you and to me."

The words, spoken with the sureness and innocence of a child, lodged in Joel's mind and heart. He'd foolishly thought he was the one in control, the one making plans and doing what he could to fulfill those, when it had been God all along. Though he'd lost his brother and his best friend, God had still led him to the woman he loved more deeply and fervently than he'd hoped to ever love a woman. God's plans had proven much better than his own in bringing richness and happiness to his life.

*And like a fool, I drove Evelyn away with my guilt and fear of losing her in the first place.* Joel lowered his chin in shame. He should have told Evelyn everything before he'd left—he could see that now.

Could he have saved Ralph's life by insisting his best friend go with the other group? Perhaps. But hadn't Dr. Dupont told Evelyn that asking "what might have been" was useless?

Joel thought of his younger brother—cheerful, charismatic Tom—who'd died while attempting to save a fellow soldier. Hadn't Ralph done something similar by choosing to be a loyal friend and stick to Joel's side as he'd always done in battle?

*Greater love hath no man than this, that a man lay down his life for his friends.*

In light of Ralph and Tom's deaths, the simple verse of scripture took on a deeper personal meaning. Tears pricked his eyes, and Joel was powerless to hold them back as the grief he'd held inside for so long finally broke free.

After a few minutes, he felt a small hand pat his arm. "It is all right, Corporal. I cried, too, when *Maman* Evelyn left. But she promised she would be back."

"Then she'll be back," Joel said, wiping at his wet eyes with his thumb.

The real question was would Evelyn take *him* back? Especially once he told her everything about Ralph's death. Just because he felt relieved of the burden he'd been carrying didn't mean Evelyn would feel the same. There was the real possibility she'd reject a second proposal of marriage from him.

And yet he had to try.

Reaching into his pack, Joel pulled out his bird notebook. "I want you to have this, Louis. Will you take good care of it until I come back, with Evelyn?"

Louis glanced at the notebook, then up to Joel's face. "You are going to bring her back, for good?"

"If she'll let me."

Louis grabbed the book and jumped up. "Hurray! *Maman* Evelyn is coming back to stay!"

With a chuckle, Joel climbed to his feet. "Hold on, kid. I've got to find her first."

"Nurse Thornton and Sister Marcelle know where she is."

"I guess we'd better go talk to them then." Joel hefted his pack and slung it onto his shoulder.

Louis hopped from one foot to the other. "Will you bring her back today?"

Joel wished he could say "yes." He wanted nothing more than to find Evelyn, confess what he hadn't, kiss her soundly, and bring her back to the safety of the hospital. Then he'd marry her, if she would have him. "I wish I could, Louis. But I get my orders tonight and leave first thing for the front lines in the morning."

The boy's enthusiasm faded to a frown and he kicked at a pebble with his bare foot. "What if you do not come back and neither does Evelyn?"

Kneeling down, Joel put his hand on Louis's shoulder and waited for him to lift his head. "As soon as we're pulled off the line to rest, I'll go after her. I promise. I will do everything in my power to get her safely back here."

Those black eyes, which ironically looked similar to Evelyn's, stared back at him. "If you do come back, Corporal, and marry *Maman* Evelyn, does that mean I can call you *mon père*?"

Joel coughed to clear his throat. He wouldn't start weeping all over again, even if these were tears of joy. "I would be proud to be called your father."

He stood and led Louis by the shoulder toward the hospital. God willing, he'd find Evelyn and convince her to marry him—and soon. Joel looked down at Louis, bouncing even as they walked. Perhaps there was even a way he and Evelyn could have the family they'd both dreamt of, after all.

# Chapter 17

Ready to brave the mud to dinner?" Evelyn's tent mate, Janet Rutledge, arched her eyebrows, her blue eyes sparkling with amusement, as she pulled on a coat.

Despite the complete exhaustion weighing down every one of her muscles, Evelyn couldn't help smiling. Janet never seemed to run out of optimism, despite the long hours, the awful food, the incessant mud, or the brutality of the wounds they saw every day at the evacuation hospital.

"I just need my coat," Evelyn answered.

She walked past the operating tables to the other side of the large tent. She'd almost forgotten what the tops of the tables looked like without wounded soldiers lying on them. Grabbing her coat from where she'd stowed it early that morning, she drew it on and followed Janet outside.

A cold breeze made Evelyn shiver, and she pulled her coat tighter around herself. Another two weeks and it would be October. She'd been at the front lines for almost a month. It felt much longer. How was Louis doing? She hadn't received a letter yet, though she guessed the mail was backed up as usual. Her thoughts turned to Joel next. Was he all right? How close was his regiment to the evacuation hospital? Every time she assisted Dr. Dupont or the other surgeons, Evelyn would hold her breath until she was certain the dirty face of the soldier lying on the table wasn't Joel's.

She pushed her incessant worries to the back of her mind and trudged along behind Janet. They headed up the hill toward the woods, where the kitchen tents were kept. Her shoes sank above her ankles in the thick mud as she walked, eliciting a sigh from Evelyn. Mud was as constant as the wounded here at the front.

She and Janet reached the brow of the hill and entered the trees. Another minute brought the kitchen tents into view. Lanterns cast the silhouettes of those inside against the canvas walls, reminding Evelyn of the shadow shows her grandfather used to do using a lamp and a sheet. The murmur of conversation and the steam from hot coffee wrapped itself around Evelyn as she and Janet slipped inside.

Armed with a plate of food and a cup of coffee, Evelyn took a seat across from Janet at one of the tables. The meat, whatever it might be, was no longer hot and the coffee wasn't much better, but as hungry as she was, Evelyn ate what she could. What she wouldn't give for her grandmother's cooking or even the blandness of Cook's meals at St. Vincent's.

Tears stung her eyes as she stared down at her plate. Her work in the surgery tent kept her hands and mind too busy to think of anything else. However, memories of

Joel, Louis, or the baby would sneak in at a moment's rest or at night before bed.

"We could pretend it's steak." Janet pointed with her fork at Evelyn's half-eaten dinner. "With mashed potatoes."

Evelyn recognized her friend's attempt to pull her from her sadness—it wasn't the first time. She needed to stop thinking about the past and focus on the present.

"What about freshly baked rolls?" Evelyn added, joining in Janet's game. "With real butter and strawberry preserves."

Janet murmured agreement. "And for dessert, apple pie."

Evelyn shook her head. "I'll take chocolate—real chocolate." The mention of her favorite sweet prompted the memory of Louis's picnic with the fudge and how they'd chased each other in the rain afterward. Only one week more, and she'd be given leave. Then she'd be able to see Louis and Alice and Sister Marcelle again.

*But not Joel.*

Even though weeks had passed since she'd last seen him, Evelyn could remember nearly everything about his face, his kisses. She might have released him from their agreement to marry, but she couldn't release him completely from her heart.

"How do you do it, Janet?" she asked, needing a new direction for her thoughts.

"Do what?"

Evelyn waved her fork to encompass the tent and its other occupants. "How do you stay cheerful in a place like this?"

To Evelyn's surprise, Janet didn't laugh or smile as

Evelyn had expected. Instead the other nurse lowered her gaze as she pushed her food around her plate.

"I'm sorry," Evelyn said. "I don't mean to pry—"

Janet shook her head, that customary smile lighting her face for a moment. "You don't need to apologize. I'm just not sure how to answer." She set her fork down. "I chose misery and guilt in the past and my life suffered because of it. Now I choose cheerfulness and my life is blessed."

Evelyn sampled a large bite to keep herself from questioning Janet further, though she wanted very much to know what the other nurse meant. The two had worked together and shared a tent for three weeks, but Evelyn still knew very little about Janet.

"I was married," Janet said, her voice low, "to a wonderful man. We had a beautiful little boy."

Evelyn glanced at Janet's hand—she wore no ring. She'd never mentioned having a family either. What had happened to them? Evelyn ate slowly, both curious and anxious at what Janet's story might be.

"My husband suspected the United States would enter the war long before we actually did. He was older and knew he wouldn't be able to enlist, so he encouraged me to become a nurse. That would be our family's contribution to the war effort." Janet pushed her half-eaten meal to the side and cupped her hands around her mug. "I'd always liked helping others, and I enjoyed nurses' training."

"Didn't you miss your family?"

Janet looked down into her coffee. "Very much. But I came home as often as I could." She visibly swallowed, and Evelyn thought she saw Janet's hands tremble slightly as she brought her mug to her lips and took a drink. "One day, about two years into my training, I got word that there'd been a fire. I rushed home...only to find I was too late. The fire took both my husband and my boy."

Evelyn covered her mouth with her hand as sympathy and sorrow rushed through her for her friend. She might have experienced the agony of losing a baby and being separated from those she loved dearly, but she hadn't been married with a family. "I'm so very sorry to hear that."

The other nurse shrugged, though the unshed tears in her eyes caught the lantern light and glistened. "It was a very dark time for me. I quit nurses' training and went to live with my parents again. For weeks I didn't leave the house. I kept thinking if I hadn't pursued nursing, I could have saved them. I was bitter and angry." She glanced at Evelyn. "Then one day, our neighbor came over, in hysterics. Her daughter was very ill. I overheard her talking with my mother and something in me snapped to attention. I had the woman take me to her daughter."

"Did she get well?"

"Yes." A soft smile lifted Janet's mouth. "All that training flooded back and I was able to help her, over the course of a few days, to fully recover. That experience saved me." She brushed strands of blond hair beneath her nurse's cap. "I realized I had a choice. I could choose to continue my course of isolation and bitterness. Or I could choose to find joy, despite the horror I'd lived through. I'd tried the first way and was miserable, so I figured I would try the second."

It was Evelyn's turn to move her food around her plate. She didn't need Janet's story to remind her there were things she still clung stubbornly to, instead of nourishing the fledgling faith she'd rediscovered. "So you came over here?"

Janet nodded. "I finished my training, joined the Army Nurse Corps, and came to France. Which has been such a rewarding experience."

"But wouldn't you rather have your family than nursing?" Evelyn regretted her question at once. "I—I didn't mean—"

"No, I understand." Janet waved away her explanation. "Yes, I wish I still had my husband and my boy, and I will probably never stop wishing that. But I realized I could still use the gifts and training God had blessed me with to bless others." She looked Evelyn in the eye as she added, "From the ashes of my grief, He gave me opportunities I might not have had any other way."

The simple admission pierced straight through Evelyn's heart, and she struggled to hold back her own tears. "Thank you—for sharing all of that." Evelyn braved a smile for her friend.

Janet returned the gesture. "You're welcome."

They finished the rest of their meal in companionable silence.

"You ready to head back?" Janet asked.

"Back through the mud."

Janet laughed as they cleared their dishes and stepped back out into the cold, black night. Evelyn didn't worry about seeing, though. She could find her way back to the tents in total darkness.

Gritting her teeth against the chill, she followed Janet through the woods to their tent. Once inside, she lit a candle, then she and Janet grabbed their canteens and went to fill them. When they returned to their tent, Evelyn placed her canteen under her pillow. By morning it wouldn't be so frigid, and she'd use it to wash up quickly before going to breakfast.

She shivered into her night clothes, pulled on her wool socks, and scrambled into her sleeping bag. As the last one dressed, Janet blew out the candle. The other cot squeaked as Janet settled into it.

Evelyn stared up through the dark in the direction of the canvas ceiling. Normally she fell asleep within minutes of climbing into bed, but tonight, she found herself strangely awake. She thought over her friend's experiences and, for the first time since coming to the front, felt compelled to share her own.

"Janet? Are you still awake?"

"Yes."

Evelyn inhaled, then let the words out in a rush. "I was pregnant up until a few weeks ago. I had a miscarriage."

"How awful." Janet's voice, full of compassion, floated through the darkness. "And your husband? Where is he?"

Rolling onto her side, Evelyn was grateful Janet couldn't see the blush heating her face. "I'm—I'm not married. The baby's father was killed in battle two and a half months ago. We met on leave. When he heard about the baby, he promised to marry me as soon as he could, but…" She fisted her hands against the rise of emotion in her throat. There was so much more to unburden. "I met his best friend, though. He was brought to the hospital after being wounded in the same battle that killed Ralph."

Evelyn went on to share the events of the past few months. The more she did, the easier it became. She told Janet everything about her relationship with Joel—from that first meeting to telling him in the letter they no longer needed to marry. She talked about Louis and the motherly instincts and joy she felt caring for him. The details of the miscarriage were the hardest to relay, but Evelyn managed to voice them, despite the tears that dampened the corner of her pillow.

When she ran out of things to say, Evelyn flipped onto her back and gripped the sleeping bag tightly between her hands. What would Janet say? Would she condemn Evelyn's choices?

"That's quite a lot to go through," Janet finally said. Her cot creaked as she shifted her weight. "I'm sorry to hear you've spent some time in the same hopeless place I was in."

Evelyn twisted her head to peer through the dark in Janet's direction. "It's not the same, though. A lot of this I brought on myself, Janet."

"Ahh." Evelyn could hear the soft smile in Janet's voice. "Much of my heartache was my own creation. Like I told you earlier, I blamed myself for not being where I thought I should have been—with my family. Difficult things, whether of our own making or not, can still bring hope and happiness to our lives. If we choose to embrace them."

Janet's counsel seeped down into Evelyn's soul, just as the cleansing moisture from the heavens the day she and Louis had played in the rain. Her friend's words were clear echoes of things Sister Marcelle and Dr. Dupont had both tried to share, about God working through her and the importance of letting go of questions about changing the past.

"Look what's come from meeting Louis," Janet said. "You may have lost one child, but it sounds to me as if you've gained another."

Evelyn sniffed and wiped her wet cheeks with the edge of the sleeping bag. It was the same conclusion she'd come to before leaving the hospital. "I don't think I would adore him more if he were my own flesh and blood."

"What about Joel Campbell?" She sensed the smile had returned to Janet's face. "I do enjoy a good love story and yours sounds very promising."

Evelyn gave a bitter laugh. "I told him it was over, Janet. I can't give him the child he wants. Why would he want to marry me now?"

Her friend laughed, but the sound wasn't condescending. "A man doesn't go to the trouble to propose if he doesn't hope for more than a child from a woman. If the arrangement had been all business, he would have accepted your proposal instead of wanting to issue one of his own."

Evelyn mulled over Janet's explanation. Could her friend be right? Could Joel still love her, even if she was no longer pregnant? She released a frustrated groan. "What have I done? I practically told him I didn't love him anymore, which couldn't be farther from the truth."

"So tell him."

"You mean write him again?"

"Yes."

Evelyn fiddled with the edge of the sleeping bag. "I don't know where he is right now. What if he's already . . .

put our relationship behind him? What if he wants nothing to do with me?"

Janet's cot creaked again. "You won't have the answers to those questions unless you try to contact him. Besides, we can probably figure out where his regiment is stationed."

"I'm afraid I don't deserve happiness with him."

"Whether we deserve God's bounteous blessings or not, He wants to give them to us." Janet's voice, though quiet, carried conviction and strength. "But we have to step away from the sorrow and hurt to embrace that goodness. He won't force us to come."

Evelyn lay silent for a minute or two, pondering over their conversation. She felt lighter and more peaceful than she had since coming to the front. And she knew to Whom she needed to express appreciation.

*Thank you, for bringing Janet and Joel and Louis and Ralph into my life. Thank you, for the hope and happiness You gave, even when I wasn't aware of it.*

"Thanks for your help, Janet."

The modesty and shyness were evident in her friend's simple reply: "You're very welcome, Evelyn."

"I think I'm going to do it," she said, sitting up. "I'm going to write to Joel." She shivered as the cold air draped itself around her thinly clad shoulders, but she didn't mind the frigid temperature now. "Since I have leave next week, I'll try to find out where he's stationed and write him a letter."

"I think that's an excellent plan."

A real smile lifted Evelyn's mouth at the prospect of seeing Joel again, of telling him how much she still longed to marry him. There was the possibility she'd driven him away for good, but she would take her chances and see. Sliding back down into her sleeping bag, Evelyn shut her eyes. But sleep took some time in coming as her mind filled with happy memories, new plans, and renewed faith.

# Chapter 18

Joel climbed out of the truck, his knees almost giving way beneath him. His injured leg had started to bother him a few days earlier, but the middle of a battle hadn't been the time to focus on his wounds. The promise of rest in this French village meant he could keep his leg propped up—if he didn't have something more important to do.

After hastily eating his hot dinner, he shaved the light beard from his face and washed the mud and stench of the trenches off himself and his uniform. The wool hadn't completely dried before he dressed again, but Joel couldn't stand to wait another minute.

Obtaining permission to leave wasn't hard to come by. Joel simply had to return by the following evening. Plenty of time to get to the evacuation hospital where Evelyn was stationed and back to his squad. He descended the stairs of the house where he and his men were staying and crossed the entry to the front door.

"Aren't you coming to the YMCA performance?" Private Wiseman, one of his squad members, asked from inside the parlor.

Joel shook his head. "Sorry, Wiseman. I've got something more pressing."

Private Wiseman shrugged and blew out a puff of smoke from his cigarette. "Suit yourself. I heard the girls singing tonight are prettier than the last group we saw."

The soldier's words brought a forgotten memory to the front of Joel's mind. He'd asked Ralph to come see a similar performance at the beginning of the summer, more for something to do than anything else, but Ralph had declined. *"I don't need to see a stranger's pretty face—I've got a much better girl to think about."* It was one of the many times he'd talked of Evelyn and showed how much she'd changed him, even though their time together had been short.

*Thanks, buddy*, he thought, shooting a smile at the sky as he stepped out of the house. *For trusting me with her.*

Procuring a ride back to the front proved the hardest task of the evening. After asking around, Joel learned of a supply truck making a run near Evelyn's evacuation hospital. The drivers were more than willing to allow him to ride with them, as long as he made himself a spot in the back. Joel rearranged some boxes and folded himself into the back of the vehicle. With a rumble, the truck jerked forward and soon left the village behind.

The drive wouldn't be longer than a few hours, but his already agitated leg would likely not fare well in a bent position for that long. Still, it didn't matter. A sense of urgency dulled most of his pain. All he cared about at the

moment was finding Evelyn and telling her that he still
wanted to marry her—if she'd have him.

*   *   *

Evelyn sat upright on her cot, her heart pounding. Something had pulled her from her pleasant dreams. She took
a steadying breath and tried to relax. The noise was likely
a truck or someone dropping something nearby. She
couldn't have been asleep for long, judging by the darkness outside the tent. A steady influx of wounded the last
week had kept her and Janet busy until almost midnight
every night.

What had she been dreaming about? Evelyn searched
her mind. She'd been back at St. Vincent's with Louis,
but Joel had been there, too. She slid back down into
her sleeping bag and shut her eyes. Tomorrow—or rather
today—she would be given leave. Her pulse leapt again,
from excitement this time. She couldn't wait to hug Louis
and Alice and find out where Joel was stationed. Though
she hadn't written her letter yet, she knew every line she
planned to pen to him.

*Just a few more hours.*

An ear-splitting *bang* jerked Evelyn from her sleeping
bag again and sent her heart crashing against her rib cage.
The sound wasn't a truck or a dropped object.

She swung her legs over the side of the cot. The cool
air in the tent sent shivers up her spine. "Janet! I think that
was shellfire, but it's awfully close."

"You're right."

"I'll go see what's going on." Evelyn pulled her outdoor uniform over her nightgown for speed and warmth.

She pushed her arms through her coat and had one of her rubber boots in hand when a whizzing noise sounded outside the tent. "Did you hear that?"

"What?" Janet was pulling on her own boots.

"It sounded like—" Her words were drowned out by another bang that sent her and Janet scrambling to the ground. Evelyn covered her head with her arms. A memory snagged in her mind as she tried in vain to slow her racing pulse. Some of the wounded soldiers referred to shellfire as "whizz bangs" because of the noise they made.

Janet gripped Evelyn's elbow and helped her to a sitting position. "We'd better see if they're evacuating the patients."

Evelyn wet her dry lips. "Right. We can do this." *Don't think about your leave. Don't think about Joel and Louis.*

The murmur of conversation and the hasty fall of footsteps reached her ears from outside the tent. Evelyn climbed to her feet as someone rapped a knuckle against one of the tent poles. "Nurse Gray? Nurse Rutledge?"

Evelyn recognized the voice of Chief Nurse Rowena Sheffield. "We're awake," Evelyn and Janet replied together.

"We're evacuating all the patients to the kitchen tents, to get them out of range of the shells. Will the two of you help with the abdomen and head wound tents?"

Evelyn swallowed hard. "Yes. We're coming."

"Good." Nurse Sheffield moved on.

Evelyn hurried to finish putting on her rubber boots and hat, then followed Janet out of the tent. Outside the moon lit up the hurried movements of nurses, doctors, orderlies, and those patients who could walk. All were moving in a steady stream toward the safety of the woods, up the hill and behind the evacuation hospital.

Janet led the way through the river of people toward the abdomen tent. Evelyn stuck close behind her. "There ought to be a stretcher," Janet said, "that we can—"

The whizzing noise came again. Where would the shell drop? "Get down," Evelyn said to Janet, yanking her friend's arm. They crouched on the ground until the deafening *bang* sounded over the hospital.

Janet stood, urgency and determination evident in the movement. Evelyn followed suit.

Around the hospital others were climbing to their feet as well. Nurse Sheffield called everyone to attention. "Sergeant Tanner here is going to help us evacuate as safely as possible. He'll tell you when to drop. But don't move until he gives the 'all clear.' Now, let's go."

Evelyn ran after Janet to the abdomen tent. Inside they found an empty stretcher. They situated it next to one of the occupied cots.

"All right, soldier," Janet said with perfect calmness. "We're going for a little ride."

Gripping the man's feet, one in each hand, Evelyn assisted Janet in getting the young man onto the stretcher. They hoisted him into the air. Evelyn's arm muscles strained at the weight. After maneuvering their way out of the tent, she and Janet started in the direction of the hill.

They hadn't gone far when Evelyn heard the sergeant shout, "Drop!" She and Janet lowered the stretcher to the ground and bent over the patient, their arms covering their heads. The bang cracked over the hospital and Evelyn cringed at the sound. How did these men run headlong toward such noises?

She waited until she heard the "all clear" before she lifted her end of the stretcher, and she and Janet continued on. They had to stop twice more, to crouch down and wait for falling shrapnel, before they reached the bottom of the hill.

Being at the head of the stretcher, Janet ascended the muddy hill first. Evelyn felt the staggering weight of the young man tip toward her as the stretcher angled downward. The mud dragged at her boots as they slowly ascended the incline. Evelyn concentrated on keeping her feet from sliding in the muck. Sweat began to form on her neck, making her wish she'd left her coat behind.

Near the top, one foot slipped, sending Evelyn to her knees in the mud. She managed to keep her end of the stretcher from joining her, but she lost her hat in the process. She'd have to find it later.

"Are you all right?" Janet asked in a winded voice.

Evelyn stifled a groan and hauled herself onto her feet. "I'm fine."

Once they breasted the hill and reached the woods, they were able to pick up their pace. It took only a few minutes more to reach the kitchen tents. Several other tents were hastily being thrown up to give the men protection from the cold.

"Which ward is he from?" Nurse Sheffield asked as they approached.

"Abdomen ward," Evelyn answered.

"Place him over there." The chief nurse pointed to one of the new tents. Evelyn and Janet carried the soldier to the tent and gently moved him from the stretcher to the ground.

"You'll be inside soon," Janet said, pulling the man's blanket up to his chin.

Evelyn lifted her end of the empty stretcher, and she and Janet rushed back through the woods to the hill. She half slid, half jogged through the mud to the bottom. As they neared the hospital, Evelyn heard the yell to "drop." She sank to her knees beside Janet and held her breath as she waited for the "all clear." Once the call came, Evelyn clambered up and ran with Janet back to the abdomen ward. They loaded the next patient onto their stretcher and left the tent a second time.

The way to and up the hill took less time this round—partly because the soldier on the stretcher was a spry young man, and partly because she and Janet were becoming more proficient at navigating through the mud. The sweat on Evelyn's back and forehead turned icy in the chilly night air, and her legs and arms began to ache with the exertion of holding the stretcher higher to climb through the mud. She pushed through the discomfort, though, blocking it out with thoughts of how quickly they could get the patients out of the abdomen and head wound wards.

She and Janet took their patient to the appropriate tent and returned for another injured soldier. Then another, and another. The shellfire faded into the background as Evelyn focused on each small step of the evacuation. *Leave the tent. Rush until the "drop" signal. Wait. Jump up. Rush forward until the next "drop" signal. Wait. Jump up. Hike the hill. Ignore the mud. Place the patient near the kitchen tents. Repeat.*

When all of the patients had been cleared from the abdomen ward, Evelyn followed Janet to the head wound tent. This ward was located closer to the hill, which meant she and Janet were able to evacuate three of the patients in half the time it had taken them to travel with one from the abdomen ward.

"We're almost done," Nurse Sheffield announced when they placed their third head wound patient inside one of the tents.

"Do you think anyone's been hit?" Janet asked as they scrambled back through the mud with the empty stretcher between them.

"I don't know."

Evelyn didn't want to think about it. Is this what Joel experienced each day at the front? Wondering which of his buddies wouldn't be returning? She hated to think of anything happening to the other members of the medical staff or the patients at the evacuation hospital, even if she didn't know any of them as well as she did Janet.

Before long, there was only one patient left for her and Janet to evacuate—a soldier who insisted on walking, though he needed both nurses to support him. Grateful not to have to heft the stretcher one more time, Evelyn didn't protest the young man's stubborn request. Instead she and Janet helped him hobble outside.

They made it nearly to the hill before they had to lower him between them when Sergeant Tanner yelled, "Drop!" His commands were sounding hoarser by the minute. Hopefully the other tents were almost all evacuated, too, and Sergeant Tanner would be able to take cover in the woods along with everyone else. He had surely saved many lives with his expertise and loud calls.

"All clear!"

Evelyn elevated the soldier to his feet with Janet's

help. They made it to the hill and started trudging their way upward through the mud. Even without the stretcher, the ascent was slow going as they half lifted, half dragged the young man. At the top, they paused to rest.

Evelyn sucked in great gulps of air. Soon she would be safe inside the kitchen tents and she could remove her coat. Maybe even catch a little more sleep, once the patients were attended to, before she left for St. Vincent's.

Thoughts of the hospital spurred an idea. "Do you think you could carry him the rest of the way?" she asked Janet. "Someone ought to get the supplies from the surgery tent. We're going to need them." She hated the idea of anything happening to the precious medical supplies after knowing what it was like to go without.

"All right." Janet shifted the soldier's full weight to her own arms, and Evelyn slipped out from underneath his grip. "As soon as he's situated, I'll come help you."

"Okay."

Evelyn slid back down through the mud to the bottom of the hill and took off at a clopping run toward the hospital. She made it into the surgery tent before the holler to "drop." The ceiling of the tent was pockmarked with holes from the shrapnel, which let in enough light to see by. She remained crouched until a muffled "all clear" reached her ears. As she stood, a dark figure rose up from the corner. Evelyn screamed—her mind racing back to the day in the woods when she and Joel had stumbled onto the young German deserter.

"It's all right," a male voice said. An orderly stepped closer and Evelyn put a hand to her chest to slow her racing heartbeat. She recognized him now. He was one of the men who brought soldiers into the surgery ward; his name was Theodore or Teddy, as most people called him. "I'm just getting supplies."

"Me, too."

"I haven't gotten to the stuff over there." He pointed to the opposite side of the tent before turning back to fill the box he'd set on one of the operating tables.

Evelyn crossed to the other supply cupboard. She couldn't find a box, but a water pail would suffice for transporting the things they needed. Dumping out the little bit of water inside, she used some bandages as cushioning and added in medicine and needles. Twice she heard the yell to "drop," and she paused to shelter her head.

"My box is full," Teddy announced after several minutes. "You wanna make the run back up the hill together? Or try to get more supplies from one of the other wards?"

Evelyn tucked a few more tins and bottles into her pail and stood. "Let's take these up. They'll be needing them soon."

She shadowed Teddy as he exited the tent, but once outside, Evelyn stopped. An eerie silence cloaked the hospital. Where was Sergeant Tanner? Had he finally gone up the hill with the rest of the staff and patients?

"Are you coming?" Teddy asked, turning back to look at her.

"I think we're the last ones. Sergeant Tanner isn't calling out instructions anymore."

Teddy frowned and glanced up at the sky. "Probably 'cause the shellfire's stopped."

Wariness filled Evelyn's stomach, but she didn't wish to stand there and end up being left behind in the deserted hospital. Teddy started walking the tent line. Evelyn made it only a few steps after him when a horrific *boom* crashed nearby. She dropped to her knees and hunkered over her pail, her arms over her bent head. Something hot scraped her left arm. She cried out at the pain and gingerly touched her arm with her right hand. It felt sticky with blood.

Wooziness threatened to claim her captive, but Evelyn fought it off by pressing her lips as tightly together as she could and filling her lungs with full breaths of air through her nose. She hadn't lost her arm; the shrapnel had merely grazed it. She'd be fine. They just needed to get to the woods.

Lifting her head, she looked for the orderly. Where had he gone? "Teddy?" she called out. "Teddy?" There was no response. Keeping low to the ground, now that she knew the shelling hadn't ended as he'd predicted, she slid her bucket along the ground with her good arm. Had he left her during the shelling?

Her pail struck against something hard and she stopped. In the faint moonlight, Evelyn saw a pair of boots, toes pointed toward the sky. There was no torso attached. Shaking, she bent over the bucket and wretched into the dirt. She'd seen soldiers who were missing limbs, but never one blown to pieces in front of her.

When there was nothing left in her stomach, she drew a trembling hand over her mouth and crawled a little farther. She found Teddy's upper body a few feet away.

"Teddy, can you hear me?" Another bang made her duck her head, but this one sounded farther down the tent line. After a long moment, Evelyn scrambled to the orderly's side. Teddy lay face up, his eyes open wide. Evelyn checked for a pulse, though she wasn't surprised when she didn't find one. He'd been killed instantly.

She fought hard against the alarm clawing up her throat in the form of a scream as she closed the man's eyes. She had to keep going. It was up to her to bring the supplies to the others.

In spite of her rattled nerves, Evelyn forced herself to search the dirt for any of Teddy's supplies that might have survived the blast. They would need every drop of medicine and every needle. Surely someone—most likely Janet—would come along soon and help.

She scooted away from Teddy and found a tin of medicine and a bottle of something. Sliding the bucket alongside her, Evelyn inched forward, her unscathed arm outstretched. She continued to feel along the ground for any supplies, moving forward in the semidarkness, until suddenly the earth gave way beneath her. She pitched headlong into black nothingness.

*A shell crater*, Evelyn thought, with horror, before she hit the muddy ground below, her right leg pinned under the rest of her body. Pain shot up from her ankle and Evelyn let out an anguished cry. She sat upright in the mud and tried to feel around her ankle. She couldn't tell if she'd broken it or not, but judging from the ache, she guessed the ankle was sprained.

Another shell exploded, this one also sounding farther off. Still, Evelyn hunkered down in the mud to avoid the shrapnel. The pungent smell of sulfur filled her nostrils. After a long pause, she lifted her head again. She needed to get out of here—now. She trudged her way through the squishing mud on hands and knees to the side of the crater, and attempted to scramble out. Her muddy boots slid beneath her, refusing to grip the earth underfoot. For every few inches she managed to climb forward, she slid several more backward. Her ankle throbbed from the effort, but Evelyn did her best to ignore the pain.

She felt as though she'd been crawling forever, but the hole was surely no more than six feet deep. At last she was able to reach out with one hand and grip the earth near the edge of the crater. New beads of sweat formed on her forehead as she dug her knees into the crater's side to get a better hold. After another minute of slipping and clawing with no success at freeing herself, she released her hand and slid back down the crater wall.

Once her heart rate slowed a bit, Evelyn tightened her jaw over the pain in her arm and ankle. Time for a second try. She backed up, to get a faster start, and charged at the crater's side. Halfway up, her boots slipped out from underneath her. She landed on her stomach at the bottom of the hole again.

"Come on," Evelyn groaned, driving a fist into the mud. She had to get out of here, but how? The despair tightening her chest became a lump in her throat, and hot tears stung her eyes.

More shellfire burst overhead, forcing Evelyn to press herself against the side of the hole. She could taste grit in her teeth, and her boots were full of mud, making her socks squish about in her shoes. The mire coated her hair, her dress, and most of her face. But she wouldn't give up. If she stayed in this hellhole, she might not live through the remaining shellfire.

As soon as she deemed it safe, Evelyn hauled herself up again. Her sprained ankle was useless now, so she used her arms to drag the lower half of her body up the side of the crater.

A foot or so from the top, she could go no farther. Her flailing boots and scraping hands could not find ground. The exertion proved too much for her wounded arm as well. With a cry of defeat, she twisted onto her back and allowed herself to slide down into the hole.

Tears mingled with the mud on her face, but she had nothing to wipe away either one. She was good and stuck, unless someone came along.

"Help!" she screamed. "Help!"

Her only answer was an ear-shattering boom. She covered her head with her arms and closed her eyes. Who was she kidding? Certainly not herself. Everyone else was in the safety of the woods. She wasn't even sure if Janet was still coming—something must have kept her at the kitchen tents. There was no one to help her.

She pictured Louis's face in a few hours when she didn't show up at the hospital for her leave. Who would care for him if she was gone? And what about Joel? She hadn't told him yet how much she still loved him.

In that moment, with death a possibility at any second, Evelyn's mind cleared of all her muddled thoughts and fear. She knew exactly what she wanted to do with the rest of her life, if she ever escaped this hole. A way she could still be a mother and give Joel a family, if he was willing to marry her.

"Please, God," she whispered, her heart both troubled and hopeful. "If You see fit to let me live and keep my promise to Louis, I'll take the path You want. I'll live with greater faith. Please, just let me live."

# Chapter 19

The closer he came to the evacuation hospital, the more pronounced the shellfire became. Not even the fearful thrumming of Joel's own heartbeat could drown out the awful noise of the whizz bangs. Was Evelyn out of harm's way?

He broke into a run the last quarter mile, despite the ache it brought to his leg after the drive to the front. But he ignored all thoughts except the one that pounded in his brain with each step—*Find Evelyn; find Evelyn.*

As he drew near the line of tents, motion off to his right snagged his attention. There were people moving into the woods at the top of the hill. Relief rushed over him. They were evacuating; Evelyn was safe.

He changed direction to follow them. Reaching the bottom of the hill, Joel plowed upward through the mud. So much for cleaning his boots and uniform earlier. He came alongside a nurse and a soldier who'd reached the top.

"Do you know where Nurse Gray is?" he asked the nurse.

She glanced over her shoulder at him. "I haven't seen her. But I think we're the last to evacuate."

He hurried past them up the trail, following the stream of people moving through the woods. As he passed each group or pair, he asked the same question. "Have you seen Nurse Gray?" No one had.

Before him, the trail widened into a clearing with half a dozen tents set up. The place was teeming with people and activity. Where would he find Evelyn? Joel moved to his left and asked a nurse kneeling beside a man on a stretcher, "Nurse Gray?" She lifted her chin to look at him and shook her head.

Joel moved to the next nurse and the next. Evelyn had to be here somewhere. He didn't want to poke his head into the tents, but after several long minutes with no success, he gave up feeling embarrassed and entered one of the tents. Dim lantern light threw shadows against the walls. He scanned the room for Evelyn but didn't see her. Ducking back out, Joel tried the next tent. Evelyn wasn't in that one either. Perhaps he ought to start asking again.

No one knew where she was in the third tent, but in the fourth, a tall, blond nurse stood up at Joel's call for, "Nurse Gray? Has anyone seen Nurse Gray?"

"I have. I'm her tent mate, Janet. She went to get some supplies from the hospital."

"Has she come back?"

"I don't know. I meant to go help her, but one of our patients started hemorrhaging and we had to stop the bleeding first." Janet looked around the crowded tent. "Did you try the other tents?"

"There are two I haven't checked."

She frowned. "I'll come with you."

"Nurse Rutledge?" another nurse called out.

Janet turned. "I'll be back in five minutes."

Joel followed her out of the tent. "I'll take that far one. Do you want to take that one?" He pointed to the other tent he hadn't checked.

Janet nodded and hurried away. Joel made his way across the clearing to the farthest tent. He ducked inside, but none of the four nurses were Evelyn. They didn't know where she'd gone either. Concern began to uncurl once more in the pit of his stomach. Maybe Janet had found her. He retraced his steps and met Janet coming out of the other tent. By the look on her face, he knew the answer to his unspoken question even before she shook her head.

"You don't think she's still down..." Joel let the words fade away as he turned in the direction of the evacuation hospital. Though he couldn't see it, there was no mistaking the continuous barrage of shellfire beyond the trees.

"We've got to find her." Janet's panicked voice mirrored the trepidation churning in Joel's gut. She started forward, but Joel stopped her with a hand to her arm.

"I'll do it. You're needed here. I'll come back..." He swallowed back the rush of acid in his throat as possible scenarios flew into his mind of what awaited him below. "I'll find her," he announced in a firmer tone.

Without waiting for Janet's response, Joel rushed back along the trail through the woods. He reached the brow of the hill and plowed downward through the mud. Toward the bottom, he had to put his hand out to stop his sliding descent, but once his boots hit more solid ground, he began running again.

He neared the first of the tents just as a shell exploded. Joel threw himself on the ground and waited, hating every second he wasn't searching for Evelyn.

When he felt it was safe to move again, he jumped up and flung back the flap of the first tent. "Evelyn?" he called. There was no answer.

He sprinted to the tent opposite the first. Sticking his head inside, he yelled her name again. He couldn't see much beyond the dark outlines of cots, but no one answered his call.

Joel darted to the next tent and repeated Evelyn's name, with still no response. Where could she be? The tent he came to after that had caved in. He lifted the tent flap to find a jumbled mess of furniture. Could Evelyn be trapped in here? He pushed his way inside, calling for her. Another shell explosion made him wedge himself beneath a table for protection. Did Evelyn know to stay low, wherever she was, away from the shrapnel? He could only hope so.

"Please let me find her, well and safe," he prayed in a whispered voice. "Let me have the chance to tell her what she means to me. Don't let it be too late."

After what felt like hours, though it couldn't have been more than a few minutes, Joel climbed out from under the table. He did his best to explore the rest of the tent, hoping and praying his outstretched hands wouldn't touch anything human. Once he was satisfied Evelyn wasn't there, he left that tent and moved on to the next. Before ducking inside, though, a faint cry for "help" sounded in his ears. Joel whirled around, searching the area for the source of the sound. It came once more, but he couldn't ascertain the direction.

"Ev-vel-lyn—" His shout was drowned out by more shellfire. Joel dove to the ground beside the tent and covered his head with his arms. He was certain he'd heard a voice. His heart beat painfully against his ribs as he waited, muscles tensed, to move again. If she was alive, why hadn't she gone back up the hill yet? Was she hurt or trapped? He hated not knowing.

As soon as he dared, Joel scrambled to his feet and shot down the line of tents, shouting, "Evelyn? Evelyn, where are you?" He paused long enough to listen for a response. When none came, he clenched his jaw in frustration. *Help me, please, Lord.*

He turned to his left to try another tent, though he didn't think the voice had come from inside one of the canvas structures. It hadn't sounded muffled, just weak. "Evelyn?"

"Help!"

Joel spun toward the sound. It was more distinct now and coming from somewhere ahead of him. Was it Evelyn? "Hold on," he called out.

The person wasn't inside a tent, so what had prevented him or her from escaping? Joel's mind skittered away from an image of Evelyn torn up and lying in the dirt, unable to move. He strained to see better in the half-light. Twenty feet away he caught sight of a dark patch of ground, where the earth seemed to give way.

A crater!

Joel ran forward. A mud-filled crater could be a death trap. He'd heard of men drowning in them. "Evelyn?" he called again as he dropped to his knees by the hole.

"Joel? Is that you?"

Relief at hearing her voice washed over him with such

intensity Joel was grateful he wasn't standing anymore. She was alive.

Before he could help her out, another shell plummeted into a tent down the line. "Get down!" he screamed as he flattened himself against the ground. Something flew past his head, and he ducked his chin to his chest.

After a long agonizing moment of waiting, he peered down into the crater. He couldn't see much, but below him, a dark form crouched near the side. "Evelyn, lift your arms. I'm going to pull you out."

"What are you doing here?"

"Getting you out of this blasted hole," he said, his voice gruff with emotion as he reached out for her. "Give me your arms."

She obeyed at once, placing her hands in his. Joel reached for her forearms, then he set his jaw as he began pulling her up. His muscles strained, but he kept at it. Finally her head appeared, followed by her mud-covered face. He was so grateful to see her that he almost let go. Once he yanked her free from the hole, she collapsed beside him, her breath coming as hard as his.

"What happened?" he asked, hovering over her.

"I came to get supplies. There was an orderly here, too—Teddy. We left together, but he was...was killed right in front of me." He could hear her teeth chattering.

"It's okay." He rubbed her arms vigorously to warm her and relieve the shock he heard in her voice, but she cried out in pain. "What's wrong? Are you hurt?"

"I twisted my ankle when I fell in the hole, and my arm..."

Joel peered at the arm she touched. He could make out her torn sleeve and something dark there. "It looks like some shrapnel grazed the skin," he said, gently probing the area, "but it didn't enter your arm."

"Told you that you'd make a good nurse," she murmured, despite everything she'd been through.

He wanted to kiss her, good and long, right then. But they weren't out of danger yet. "I'll settle for good soldier. Now let's get you out of here before—"

As if reading his mind, more shellfire shattered nearby. Joel used his body to shield Evelyn. "When it's time to move," he whispered near her ear, "I'm going to carry you."

"And then what?"

The stroke of her breath against his neck resurrected the rapid firing of his pulse. He swallowed, forcing himself to concentrate. "Then we run to those woods, where you've got some serious explaining to do, Evelyn Gray."

He sensed more than saw her half smile, but it was enough to infuse new energy into his already complaining muscles. Shooting to his feet, Joel scooped her up into his arms and ran down the line of tents. The stiffness in his right leg increased as he sprinted as hard as he could. His steps faltered, and one knee buckled. He held tight to Evelyn to keep from dropping her as his knee hit the ground.

Using all his strength, he managed to get his feet back under him. More shellfire thundered behind him as he neared the end of the tent line. This time Joel refused to stop and wait. Praying they'd avoid the shrapnel, he carried Evelyn past the last tent and toward the hill. As if in anger at their escape, the sky opened up and the hospital was suddenly pummeled with shell after shell. If their retreat had taken even one minute longer...Joel shuddered at the thought.

He plowed up the hill, though the mud slowed his steps. Tightening his hold on Evelyn, he pushed himself toward the top. When he reached the path above, he paused to catch his breath. He glanced down at the evacuation hospital below, which now lay cloaked in silence. They were safe.

*Thank you, Lord.*

Tears of gratitude stung his eyes as he cradled Evelyn more snugly to his chest. "Don't ever do that again, all right?"

She pressed her forehead into his neck and whispered back, "I won't; I promise." After a long moment, she lifted her chin. "You can put me down if you'd like. I can hobble from here."

Instead of releasing her, he hoisted her higher in his arms. "Not on your life, Nurse Gray. I didn't go through all this to let you go that easily."

She chuckled but made no further protest. Joel carried her through the woods to the tents. Nurses and orderlies swarmed them as he strode into the lit clearing. Janet was among them, looking more than a little relieved to see the two of them alive. A barrage of questions hit them about what had happened down below.

Evelyn told them about collecting the supplies with help from Teddy. In a voice that trembled with emotion, she announced to the hushed group that the orderly had been killed when they tried to come back to the woods and she'd fallen into the shell hole.

"The supplies! I left them behind." She glanced up at Joel, the question in her dark eyes unmistakable.

"No," he barked. He tempered his tone to add, "Someone else can go get them, now that the shellfire is over. You need to stay here."

Janet directed him to carry Evelyn into one of the tents. Reluctantly he released his hold on her and set her gently onto a chair.

"We need to get you cleaned off." Janet waved a hand at Evelyn's mud-covered face and uniform. "If you'll wait outside," she kindly told Joel.

He hesitated, not wanting to leave Evelyn. Being near her reassured him that she was indeed safe. Besides, now that they were out of danger, he needed to share what he'd come all this way to say.

"Why don't you go get the two of you some coffee?" Janet suggested.

"All right." At least it was something to do while he waited for Evelyn. He looked down at her. Even mud-splattered, she took his breath away, especially with the way she was watching him so intently.

"Thank you, Joel." She reached out and gripped his hand.

He shrugged off her thanks. "Promise me you won't go back down there?"

She smiled—it was the same beguiling smile that had claimed his heart the first moment he'd seen it. "I promise."

"I'll get that coffee."

With that, he forced himself to exit the tent. He crossed the clearing and ducked into one of the kitchen tents. The two tables inside were half filled, despite the unearthly hour, with nurses, doctors, and a few patients who could sit.

"Corporal?"

Joel turned and saw the surgeon from St. Vincent's hospital seated at one of the two tables. "Doctor…"

"Dupont," the man finished. He stood and came around the table. "What brings you out here, especially on a night like this?"

Heat infused Joel's neck. He felt as if everyone in the room were listening. Would the doctor report him for breaking the rules?

Now that he wasn't running for his life, and Evelyn's, exhaustion stole over him and he no longer cared what anyone else thought. The woman he loved was alive and he could finally tell her what he'd kept back all these weeks. Nothing else mattered.

Straightening to his full height, he kept his gaze trained on the doctor as he answered. "We were pulled off the line yesterday, so I thought I'd come see Nurse Gray. I arrived in time for the fire show down below."

Instead of contempt, Dr. Dupont's eyes shone with approval behind his glasses. "I heard just now of your rescue of Nurse Gray. Was she hurt?"

"Her ankle is sprained and some shrapnel split the skin on her arm, but other than that, she's fine."

"I am most glad to hear it."

"Dr. Dupont?" an orderly called as he entered the tent. "We need you, sir."

The doctor excused himself and Joel went to collect two mugs of coffee. He took a seat at one of the tables and cupped his hands around his mug to warm them.

As he sipped his drink, he listened to the murmur of conversation around him. Several nurses, including the chief nurse, came up and offered their gratitude to him for helping Evelyn. He responded with a polite tip of his head. He didn't like all the attention; he simply wanted to talk to Evelyn, alone, before his mounting nerves got the better of him.

A commotion at the tent flap drew his attention. Evelyn entered the tent, leaning on Janet's arm. Her hair and face were free of mud and glistened with water, though her uniform was still spotted in places. A blanket had been draped around her shoulders.

Joel stood to help her. "I've got some coffee for you."

"Sounds wonderful," she murmured as he assisted her onto the bench, her back to the table.

"You can manage from here?" Janet asked with a smile.

Evelyn nodded. "Thanks for helping me, Janet."

The blond nurse smiled again, then slipped out of the tent. Evelyn accepted the mug Joel handed her and took a long sip.

"Not the best, but it tastes heavenly right now." She peered up at him. "I can't thank you enough for finding me. What made you come here?"

Joel stalled by taking another drink of his coffee. Again he felt as if every set of ears in the tent were trained on their quiet conversation. He couldn't confess his love to Evelyn right here in front of all these people.

"Do you mind if we go outside?"

Evelyn glanced around the tent. "No."

After draining his cup, Joel helped Evelyn to her feet. He offered her his arm to lean on and took her coffee mug in his free hand. They proceeded slowly out of the tent. Once outside, he searched the clearing for a secluded place to sit. Past one of the tents, he spied a fallen log. The lantern light reached to the foot of the log, but the rest of the spot was mostly veiled with shadow. They'd be near the commotion, yet not easily overheard.

"How about over there?"

Evelyn glanced in the direction he indicated and nodded. Joel led her across the clearing with measured steps to avoid straining her ankle. When Evelyn was situated on the log, he took a seat on a rock opposite her, their knees almost touching. He handed her the coffee again. She shivered in the cool air and drew her blanket tighter around her shoulders with one hand as she took a sip.

"Here, take my coat." He removed it and placed the coat over the blanket.

"Thanks." She stared down at her cup and gave a self-deprecating laugh. "I still can't believe you're here. When I heard your voice, I thought I was dreaming."

Joel took courage from her words. Thinking his arrival was a dream had to be a good sign. At least until he told her everything he needed to. He cleared his throat and shifted on the rock.

"I . . . got your letter."

She lifted her gaze to his but didn't say anything.

"I'm sorry about the baby." When she glanced away, he knew she'd misunderstood the reason for his apology. "I'm sorry you had to go through that, Evelyn. That I wasn't there to help in some way."

She shrugged, despite the strain on her face. "Like I said in the letter, Alice and Dr. Dupont helped a great deal. And I'm fine now."

Did she mean about the baby or about them? He frowned, hoping it wasn't the latter. Didn't she think about him every day and every hour as he did her? Didn't she still wish to be together as he did? Didn't her heart leap at being close to him as his did at being near her again?

"*Are* you fine?" he pressed.

"I'm not sure what you mean."

Joel pushed his hand through his hair—he'd lost his cap somewhere during his search for Evelyn. This wasn't going quite as he'd pictured. "Look, I'm botching this all up. But the fact is I came here to find you and tell you something I should have a long time ago."

"Yes?" She took another drink of coffee, then set the mug on the ground near her feet.

"There's something I need to tell you about the day Ralph died." The memories washed over him, but they no longer held the power to cripple him. He'd fully let go of the guilt, even if he didn't know what Evelyn's reaction would be.

"What is it?" she asked, her tone both wary and curious.

"We were concerned about a possible ambush, so I decided to divide the squad in two. I figured our chances of survival against the Germans would be better that way." His shoulders slumped as the weight of that decision bore down on him again, but it didn't crush him like he'd thought it might at voicing the words out loud. "I asked Ralph to lead the other group, but he refused. Said we made a better team. I didn't push it. You know how Ralph was once he made a decision." He sought her agreement, but she sat silent, watching him intently.

"We set off, making it up and over the hill with no difficulty. Then everything turned chaotic. The Germans hit our small group with everything they had." Joel swiped his hand over his face at the recollection and felt Evelyn's hand touch his knee. Maybe she would forgive him after all.

He looked down and cupped her hand in his, his thumb tracing circles over the back of her hand. "I've re-lived that day over and over again. If I'd insisted Ralph go with the other group, he would have lived. He would have made it back to you." He blew out his breath, both fearful and relieved, to have the complete truth between them at last.

"Why didn't you tell me before?" Her tone was gentle, not reproachful.

Joel glanced at the tents. "I couldn't. The guilt was too great. Especially when I started to fall for you. I thought you'd hate me if you knew the truth."

Evelyn leaned forward. "And now? Do you still harbor that guilt?"

"No." He finally met her gaze. How he loved those vibrant eyes of hers. "I realized after I read your letter I'd been wrong to hold back the truth. It was actually Louis who helped me let go of my regret."

"Louis?"

"He said God brought you to him…and to me." Joel tucked a damp curl behind her ear. "He's right, too. All this time, I thought I was the one with the plans, but God had better ones in mind." He grazed his thumb across her cheek, relishing the softness of her skin. "Can you ever forgive me, Evelyn?"

She lifted his hand from her face and pressed it to her lips, resurrecting the rapid thumping of his heart. "There's nothing to forgive, Joel. I wish you would've told me everything sooner, but I'm not angry with you."

"You're not?" He struggled to concentrate on her

words as she stroked each of his knuckles, then ran her warm fingers up his vein lines, beneath his shirtsleeve, to his forearm.

"No." Her fingers stilled against his arm. "But there is something I need to confess."

He nodded for her to go on. His heart ricocheted in his chest, but not from her touch this time. He sensed he would know in the next few moments whether she would accept him again or not.

"I meant what I said in my letter, at least at the time. But I don't feel that way anymore." She resumed drawing imaginary lines up and down his hand and arm. "I know I can't give you the son or daughter you wanted, but do you, could you possibly still..." She let the question fade away as she glanced at him. The earnest hope on her beautiful face gave him all the answer he needed.

Freeing his hand, Joel placed it against the back of her wet hair and drew her close. He rested his forehead against hers. "Do I still love you? Do I still want to marry you?" He smiled when her breath snagged in her throat. "Yes, Evelyn. To both."

He lowered his chin, capturing those delectable lips at last. They tasted every bit as sweet and inviting as he remembered. This time, he kissed her without hesitation, without guilt. He tangled his fingers in her hair as he pressed his mouth more firmly to hers. Evelyn circled her hands around his neck.

He lost track of time, his focus caught up in kissing her, until the murmur of distant conversation finally registered in his mind. They weren't entirely alone, even out here. With much disappointment, Joel released her.

"I won't get leave again for another two months or

so, but we could marry then." He locked his fingers with hers and rested their joined hands on his knee. "That is, if you're still okay with being discharged."

"I don't mind, but I won't wait eight more weeks to marry you." Her eyes shone with playful determination. "I think we've waited long enough."

"You do, huh?" He chuckled, tugging her closer. "So what do you have in mind?"

In answer, she leaned forward and pressed her lips to his in another long kiss. "I want to marry you today," Evelyn whispered against his mouth before sitting back.

"Today?" he echoed, warming to the idea. Even if they'd been up all night, the thought of finally being married to Evelyn drove any remaining exhaustion from him. They'd have less than twenty-four hours to spend as husband and wife, but that was better than waiting weeks to marry her.

"What time do you have to be back with your men?" she asked.

"Nine o'clock tonight."

"What time is it now?"

Joel consulted his wristwatch. "Five thirty."

Evelyn rewarded him with such a radiant smile he thought his heart might explode with joy. "Perfect. I'm officially on leave in thirty minutes."

She bent toward him, clearly intent on another kiss, but Joel stopped her with a finger to her lips. Her eyes widened.

"I still need to officially ask you—again." He searched the ground for something to put on her finger, since he didn't have a ring. A loose thread on his coat caught his eye and he broke it free of the fabric. Going down on one knee, he tied the string around Evelyn's ring finger. "Not the most permanent, but it'll do."

He lifted her hand and peered into her dark, soulful eyes. "Evelyn Gray, will you do me the honor of agreeing to be my wife—for the second time?"

"Yes," she said, her answer barely out of her mouth before she launched herself into his arms.

He laughed and held her tight, overjoyed at the thought that very soon he wouldn't have to let go so quickly.

"There's one more thing." She sat back and twisted the string on her finger. "I want to adopt Louis, Joel. I mean, I want us to adopt Louis. I'm sure that's what he wants. He hasn't any family now and I couldn't leave him here when I go back to Michigan. To me, he's like…"

"A son."

A hopeful smile spread over her face. "You feel the same?"

Joel nodded, remembering how Louis had asked to call him "father" once Joel and Evelyn married. The simple, childlike gesture had done more to ease Joel's disappointment over never fathering a child of his own than anything else. If he and Evelyn couldn't have children, they could at least be Louis's family. "I'd be proud to call him my son."

"Oh, thank you, Joel."

They shared another lengthy kiss, then Joel helped her to her feet. Ideas were forming rapidly in his head—ideas for where they could hold the wedding and where they could spend some time alone together before he had to return to his duties as a soldier. Perhaps Dr. Dupont could help him carry out the plans.

"I've got some things to do, but I'll be back very soon."

"You're leaving?" Disappointment clouded her face. "What are you doing?"

Joel caressed her cheek. "Can't a man who's about to get married have a few surprises up his sleeve?"

She gave him a reticent smile. "All right. But you promise you'll be back?"

"I promise. Just give me two hours, at the most, to get ready." Joel scooped her up into his arms to carry her back to the tents. Evelyn let go a startled cry, but she was laughing. "Can you wait a little longer to become Mrs. Joel Campbell?"

"I've waited weeks now. I suppose I can last a few more hours."

"Just don't go back down to the evacuation hospital."

Evelyn pressed a kiss to his cheek; he could almost see the wheels turning in her mind. "I won't. Don't worry about me. A bride has to have a few surprises of her own."

He laughed again, relishing the feeling of lightness and purpose he felt for the first time in months. Ignoring the curious glances of those they passed, he carried Evelyn to the door of the tent he'd first brought her to. He set her down and gave her a quick kiss on the forehead.

"I want to talk to Dr. Dupont before I leave, but I'll be back no later than seven thirty."

"I'll be waiting." She cupped his face with her hand for a moment.

He stole one more kiss, then hurried toward the kitchen tent, where he'd last seen the doctor. There was a lot to do in a short time, but he'd never felt happier. In a few hours, Evelyn would finally be his wife.

# Chapter 20

Evelyn studied herself in the hand-held mirror Janet had managed to rummage up from somewhere, along with some hairpins. Under her friend's deft hand, Evelyn's dark curls had become a pretty arrangement at the nape of her neck, fit for a bride-to-be.

"It's perfect," Evelyn murmured, to keep from disturbing those eating breakfast at the other end of the table.

Janet smiled down at her. "You look very pretty."

"Even in uniform?" Evelyn teased.

An orderly had agreed to fetch Evelyn's stuff from the evacuation hospital. He reported that her and Janet's tent had withstood the barrage of shellfire, with only a few holes as evidence of what had happened. Evelyn had changed out of her dirty outdoor uniform and nightgown into a clean jersey dress. Although not white or ornamented, the simple gown, without its usual apron, and the fancy hairstyle helped Evelyn feel more like a bride.

"What time is it now?"

Janet glanced at her watch. "A quarter past seven."

Evelyn's pulse leapt at the announcement. Joel would be here soon. She'd already informed Nurse Sheffield of her plans. While the chief nurse expressed regret at losing Evelyn's help at the front, she offered sincere wishes for Evelyn and Joel's happiness.

Dr. Dupont entered the tent as Evelyn set down the mirror. "I hear you are leaving us, Nurse Gray."

"Yes, sir."

"I spoke at length with your corporal. He is a good man and a very lucky one to be marrying such a lovely and accomplished young lady."

Evelyn blushed at his compliment. The remark touched her deeply, especially since the doctor knew so much about her past. "What did he ask you before he left?"

The doctor wagged a finger at her. "You will not get his secrets out of me."

She laughed and stood, one hand holding the chair to support her injured ankle. "Thank you, Dr. Dupont...for everything." He would know what she meant, even if she couldn't say it out loud with so many listening ears. She shook his hand with her free one. "I wish you all the best. I'll be praying for your family."

"Thank you. A letter from Bridgette made its way here yesterday, though it was sent many months ago." His voice wobbled with emotion. "I am pleased to say I am the grandfather of a healthy little girl."

"Oh, I'm so happy for you."

When she released his hand, the doctor gently gripped Evelyn's shoulders and placed a kiss on each of her cheeks. "Your father would be proud, Nurse Gray," he said in a low voice that she alone could hear. His eyes peered straight into hers.

A lump rose in Evelyn's throat as the truth of his words penetrated straight to her heart. Her father would be proud and her grandparents, too. She had made mistakes, yes, but she was no longer living in sorrow and hopelessness. She was embracing the life God had blessed her with.

Brushing at her wet eyes, Evelyn stepped back. This was only the first of many good-byes. How would she stand them all? "I'd better go."

"*Au revoir*, Nurse Gray." The doctor lifted her suitcase and handed it to her.

She gripped the handle and braved a smile. "*Au revoir*, Dr. Dupont."

Other nurses called "good-bye" as Janet helped her to the tent door. Evelyn waved to them before ducking out the tent flap. Outside, she paused. Bidding Janet farewell for good would be as difficult as it would be with Alice and Sister Marcelle. She'd never imagined she would meet some of her dearest friends here in France.

"I'll help you to the hill," Janet said.

Grateful for a few minutes more with her friend, Evelyn linked her arm through Janet's as she hobbled along. Sunshine dappled the path before them and Evelyn took in a cleansing breath of the cool morning air.

"What will you do after today?" Janet asked.

"I suppose Louis and I will go home to Michigan."

"Do you wish you could stay?"

Evelyn threw a glance over her shoulder at the tents she could barely see through the trees. "Yes, more so than

I thought. It would be nice to stay nearby since Joel has leave again in two months. But you know the rules. I'll be discharged very soon."

"Maybe something will work out so you can stay awhile longer." Janet gave her arm a hopeful squeeze.

They reached the brow of the hill and stopped. Evelyn peered down at the road below. No sign of Joel yet, but he still had a few minutes to go before his promised arrival. She set down her suitcase and hugged Janet tight.

"How can I thank you enough for your help?" She let go of her friend to peer into her face. "Joel and I are getting married largely because of you and the things you said the other night."

"It's me who must thank you, Evelyn."

"What do you mean?" Evelyn couldn't think of anything she'd done to help Janet, at least not to the extent her friend had done for her.

Janet brushed some blond hair from her face, her eyes locked on something in the distance. "You helped me see that love and family might still be a possibility for me—again. Who knows?" She shrugged. "You'll write, won't you?"

Evelyn nodded and hoisted her suitcase. She and Janet had exchanged addresses. The sound of a horn floated up to them. Evelyn turned to see a truck waiting on the road below. "I wonder where in the world he found that."

She gave Janet one last hug, then slowly descended the hill, doing her best to avoid spraining her other ankle or stepping in the mud. It wouldn't do for the bride to appear with dirty shoes.

"Good-bye, Evelyn," Janet shouted, her arm lifted in a wave.

Evelyn waved back as her feet met level ground again. "Good-bye," she called over her shoulder.

She limped toward the truck, her excitement making her wish she could move faster. A man stepped from the truck. Her smile spread wider, until she realized it wasn't Joel.

"Sergeant Dennis?" Evelyn stopped. Her heart leapt into her throat as concern washed over her. Where was Joel? Had the sergeant come to relay bad news? "What's happened?" she demanded.

Sergeant Dennis removed his hat and wiped at his forehead. "The dang truck got caught in the mud a ways back. But don't be tellin' Campbell that. He promised to tan my hide if I was late to pick you up."

Relief rushed in to take the place of her fear. "So you're my ride. How did you . . ."

"Had a few favors to call in," the sergeant said with a grin. He helped her walk around to the other side of the truck and climb inside. Once he returned to the driver's seat, he fiddled with the gears and the truck jerked forward.

"Where are we going?" Evelyn asked as they headed down the road.

"To St. Vincent's."

A thrill shot through her. "Is that where Joel is?"

Sergeant Dennis nodded.

"Your helping us has nothing to do with seeing Nurse Thornton again, does it?"

Red crept up the sergeant's neck. "I told Corporal Campbell I'd be his best man." He shot her a sideways look. "But it don't hurt that Alice is there, too."

Evelyn laughed. George Dennis was a good man. She

was glad he and Alice had become such close friends, despite Evelyn's objections in the beginning.

"We could make it a double wedding," she teased.

His face turned as dark as his neck. "Nah. Alice wants to keep nursing until the war's over. But I'm goin' to ask her to be my girl today. You know, wait for me, official like."

"I think that's a wonderful idea."

Comfortable silence filled the cab between them. Evelyn listened to the noises of the truck and watched the countryside moving past. Each turn of the wheels brought her closer to Joel and to her wedding. Before long, her eyelids began to droop as the previous night of little sleep caught up with her.

Sometime later, she jerked awake when the truck shuddered to a full stop.

"We're here," Sergeant Dennis announced.

Evelyn peered out the window at the familiar stone walls and turrets of St. Vincent's hospital. She felt as if she'd come home. She touched her hair, reassuring herself all the pins had stayed in place even as she dozed. Satisfied, she lifted her suitcase to her lap and waited for the sergeant to open her door. When he did, she climbed out and smoothed the front of her dress.

She allowed him to assist her to the hospital's main doors. But instead of helping her walk in, he took her suitcase and set it inside the door.

"Aren't we going in?" she asked, confused.

The sergeant shook his head. "We're needed in the church."

He offered her his arm again and they walked around the side of the hospital. As they passed the nurses' building and crossed the expansive lawn, memories flooded

Evelyn's mind—both pleasant and painful. She would always cherish this place.

Her heart beat faster with anticipation as they reached the ancient church. Sergeant Dennis held the door open for her.

"Will you walk me down the aisle, Sergeant?" Evelyn asked. "Not just for tradition's sake either." She gave a light laugh. "I don't think I can do it on this ankle."

The sergeant looked surprised. "It would be an honor, Nurse Gray."

Evelyn shuffled ahead of him into the cool interior of the church. Her eyes took a few seconds to adjust to the dimmer light. Once she could see, she realized the building was already half-full with sisters and nurses, including Alice and Sister Marcelle.

Up front, beside the pastor, stood Joel. Though she'd seen him just a few hours earlier, Evelyn's pulse quickened at the sight of him. He looked so tall and handsome in his mud-free Army uniform. And that smile, directed straight at her, made her stomach churn with pleasant butterflies.

"Evelyn!" Louis shot down the aisle and threw his arms around her waist. "You are back."

She hugged him tight. Tears of joy filled her eyes at seeing him again. "Oh, I missed you, Louis."

He broke free of her embrace to show her the notebook he clutched in one hand. "I kept the corporal's book for him, like he told me to. Until you came back. I have been so careful with it and only drew a few pictures inside." Evelyn recognized Joel's bird book as Louis showed her a drawing he'd made.

"That's very good—"

"Now that you are back, we will be a family and all look for birds together."

Evelyn hated to steal away the grin from his young face. "Well, you see, Louis. Corporal Campbell has to go back to being a soldier, and you and I—"

"Will be staying with us at the hospital," Sister Marcelle interjected, "as long as you like."

Evelyn blinked in surprise at the sister. "What about my being discharged?"

Sister Marcelle placed her hand on Evelyn's arm. "You may be released from active service with the Army Nurse Corps once you are married, but we could still use your help." She glanced at Joel, who was coming down the aisle toward them. "Besides, I hear your husband-to-be has leave in a few months. It might be nice to stay close so you can see him sooner."

"Say you'll stay, Evelyn," Alice said from her spot next to Sergeant Dennis. "It hasn't been the same without you here."

Evelyn gazed into the earnest faces around her and laughed. "All right then. Looks like you and I are staying for a while longer, Louis."

The boy gave a whoop as Joel came up to them. His nearness set Evelyn's heartbeat racing with anticipation again. "Go and sit down, Louis," she gently directed. Sister Marcelle led the boy back up the aisle.

"What are we celebrating back here?" Joel asked, amusement in his hazel eyes.

"Louis and I are going to stay on at St. Vincent's for a while longer. At least until after you get leave."

"That's an excellent idea. But I think we need to get married first." He tipped his head in the direction of the pastor. "The poor man's been waiting since I woke him up an hour ago." Leaning closer, he whispered in her ear, "And the cottage I rented for the day should be just about ready as well."

Evelyn blushed, even as excitement shot up her spine at the thought of being alone with Joel, as her husband this time.

He kissed her quick on the cheek. "Are you ready?"

"Yes."

Alice handed her a small bouquet of wildflowers as Joel returned to his spot beside the pastor. Evelyn fingered the colored petals—they would look pretty, dried and pressed, in her flower book at home.

One of the sisters struck up a wedding march on the little organ. It was Evelyn's cue.

She linked her arm through Sergeant Dennis's and they started slowly up the aisle. For a moment, she wished her father were walking next to her and her grandparents were seated in one of the pews. But as her gaze took in the happy faces around her—Louis, Sister Marcelle, Alice— she realized these people were as dear to her as her own family. And in a few minutes, she and Joel would become a new family themselves. She locked her eyes with his and returned his brilliant smile as she took her place beside him.

*     *     *

Evelyn leaned against Joel, her hand clasped in his. They turned onto the gravel drive leading to the hospital, their footsteps crunching in the early evening quiet.

"Don't you wish we could go back?" She glanced over

her shoulder, though she knew she couldn't see the little cottage they'd spent the day in.

Joel lifted their joined hands and kissed her knuckles. "Yes, very much."

"I suppose it wouldn't do to miss the lovely dinner they're making for us, though."

"Probably not." Joel chuckled. "Besides, Sergeant Dennis and I have to head back soon."

"I know." She refused to focus on the imminent farewell; instead she wrapped the happy memories of the day around her like a quilt. She felt so blessed, so loved. "I'm grateful Sister Marcelle is letting me and Louis stay."

"Me, too. It'll be easier getting through the next two months, knowing you'll be here waiting for me when I get leave again." He smiled down at her in a way that made her stomach flip-flop. She hoped the next eight weeks would speed by. "What will your grandparents say about our marriage and about Louis?"

"I think they'll be happy for us." She kissed his cheek in reassurance. "It's my other idea I'm worried about. I'm not sure how they'll react."

"What idea is that?"

They were almost to the main doors of the hospital. Evelyn stopped and turned toward him, her heartbeat picking up with fresh excitement. "I want to turn my grandparents' big farmhouse into a home for boys like Louis. Those who've lost their parents or have run away from home. Like that boy you once told me about, who lived with your family."

"Les?"

"Yes. I want to provide them with a place to stay and work and be loved for as long as they need it." She looked at Joel, hoping he would approve. Everything inside her told Evelyn this was her new life's work, but she would need Joel's help to make it happen, even if it wasn't until the war ended and he was finally released to come home. "What do you think?"

Instead of answering, Joel set down her suitcase and cupped her face between his hands. He pressed a firm kiss to her lips. When he pulled back, he left her delightfully weak in the knees.

"I love you, Evelyn." He rubbed his thumb over her lips. "And I love the idea. I don't know that we can find Les, but I'm sure there are plenty of other boys who could use a good home."

One of the front doors crashed open, and Louis dashed toward them. He threw an arm around each of them, his face lit up with his usual grin.

"You are back," he said. "I have been waiting and waiting."

Evelyn tousled his hair. "Are you ready for dinner? Did you see what Cook made?"

Louis nodded. "But I cannot tell. It is a surprise."

"Let's go inside then," Joel said with a laugh as he picked up her suitcase. "I'm starving."

He held one of her hands and Louis latched on to the other as they moved toward the hospital doors. Louis stopped just before they crossed the threshold. "So this will be our home now, *Maman* Evelyn?"

Hearing that sweet word—*maman*—directed at her filled Evelyn's soul to overflowing with joy. "For a little while, but there's something I want you to remember." She smiled at him, then up at Joel. "Wherever we are together, that is home."

# Epilogue

*October 1919*

Evelyn glanced up from peeling potatoes at the sink as Louis and five-year-old Aaron raced into the kitchen, brandishing the wooden guns Evelyn's grandfather had made Louis the previous Christmas. "Outside, boys," she directed.

They tore out the back door, slamming it shut behind them. Evelyn's grandmother chuckled from her seat at the table, where she was knitting winter hats for all the boys at the farm.

"Things aren't as quiet as they used to be for you and Grandpa," Evelyn said with a chuckle. She brushed a curl from her face and returned to her task.

"It's nice not to have things so quiet."

"Really?" Evelyn set down her knife to study her grandmother. She'd been saddened to find both of them looking so frail when she and Louis had arrived home last December before Joel was released to join them in the States. Yet her grandparents had welcomed the idea of opening their home to other boys in need of help. To Evelyn's surprise, the whole venture had seemed to renew their health, instead of speeding up its decline.

Her grandmother's knitting needles paused. "I haven't seen your grandfather so happy in years."

"What about you, Grandma?"

Her wrinkled face lifted into a smile as the knitting needles resumed their quiet clicking. "I am a great-grandmother now. I have nothing to complain about." She looked up from her work, her keen gaze on Evelyn. "I'm proud of you, Evelyn. You have a good husband and son, and you are raising a whole passel of boys to be good men, too."

Evelyn brushed at the corners of her eyes with the back of her hand. Telling her grandparents all that had transpired during her time in France hadn't been easy, but they had reacted to the news with the same loving kindness she felt in her grandmother's words at this moment.

Joel stepped through the back door, a bushel of apples in his arms. "How are my two favorite women?" He placed a kiss on Grandma's cheek as he passed her chair. Evelyn's grandmother grinned.

He set the bushel of apples on the counter, then came to the sink and kissed Evelyn firmly on the lips.

"Is that the last of the apples?" she asked when he stepped back.

"Just about. The older boys think they can get one more bushel, maybe two."

"Good. I think Grandma and I will make apple pie tomorrow." Evelyn rinsed another potato as she glanced out the window. The red and gold leaves clinging to the trees matched the colors of the sunset.

A movement drew her attention and she looked to see a lone figure walking up the road in the direction of the farm. The young man had a knapsack over his shoulder and appeared to be about sixteen years old. He glanced at the farmhouse and came to a stop, his blond hair lifting with the evening breeze.

Something in his face brought a spark of hope and excitement thrumming inside Evelyn. Could her letters have finally found the person she'd been seeking ever since she'd returned to the States?

"Joel, I think we'll need to get out that other bed frame tonight."

Joel came up behind her and looked out the window. "I'll go meet him," he said with a smile.

Evelyn kept her eyes focused on the young man. A minute later, Joel appeared on the road. He approached the boy with his hand outstretched to greet him, then he froze. Evelyn held her breath. The young man stumbled forward and Joel clasped him in a tight hug.

"Oh, thank you, Lord," she breathed, dropping the potato in the sink. "I'll be right back, Grandma."

She hurried out the back door and through the short side gate. Joel released the boy and led him toward the house. Evelyn met them on the road.

"Who do we have here?" she asked, though she suspected the answer already.

Joel grinned. "Les, I want you to meet my wife, Evelyn. Evelyn, this is Les."

"Pleased to meet you, Les." She shook hands with the young man. "Welcome to our farm."

A faint smile erased the hesitant look on Les's face. "Thank you, ma'am."

"Why don't you go on up to the house and wash up? We'll be eating soon. The kitchen's right through there." She pointed at the back door.

Les nodded and strode to the gate. Evelyn watched him a moment longer, then turned to Joel. He was studying her intently.

"What?" She laughed.

He took both her hands in his. "How did you find him? I didn't even think his mother knew where he was."

Evelyn shrugged, though she couldn't stop beaming. "It took a lot of letters and patience, but I finally found a woman who had hired him to work in her store a while back. I wrote and told Les about our home here and invited him to come. To be honest, I wasn't sure he'd even—"

He ended any further attempt at explanation with a long kiss that set Evelyn's pulse racing. "Thank you, Evelyn. For marrying me, for finding Les, for giving us a family with Louis and all these boys."

Joel put his arm around her waist as they walked back toward the brightly lit house. On the front porch, her grandfather sat in a rocker, whittling at a stick, while two of the younger boys listened to his stories. Ahead of her and Joel, Louis and Aaron jostled each other good-naturedly as they entered the kitchen behind the older boys. Through the open door, the trill of her grand-mother's laughter and the murmur of many voices spilled out, encircling Evelyn. She couldn't imagine happier sounds. With the warmth of Joel's hand on the small of her back, she climbed the stairs and stepped inside.

Nora Lewis left America behind when
she lost everything in the Great War.

What she'll gain in a new land is more
than her heart ever imagined . . .

Please see the next page for a preview of

*A Hope Remembered*.

# Prologue

*Iowa, May 1920*

Nora led the strangers into the parlor, their footsteps sounding unusually loud against the polished wood floor. Her gaze swept with approval over the tidy room and settled on the upright piano. It looked a bit forlorn without its usual sheet music or adornment. She'd removed the two photographs from off the top yesterday—one of her parents and one of herself as a young girl—in preparation for the young couple's arrival.

"What a spacious room," the woman said, her hand resting on her protruding belly. Her husband draped his good arm around her shoulder, the other hanging lifeless at his side. Wounded in France, he'd informed Nora in his letter of inquiry about the farm.

"Perfect for all those children we're going to have." He pressed a kiss to his wife's forehead.

Nora looked away, steeling herself against the emotions their happiness provoked. If Tom Campbell had survived the Great War, this would have been their home.

Tom would've been standing here, kissing her, and she wouldn't be trying to sell the place.

"The kitchen is through there." Nora forced a cheerful tone to her words she didn't quite feel.

The couple moved past her and stepped into the large, sunny kitchen. Nora followed. She rested her hands on the back of one of the chairs. How many times had she sat here rolling dough for her mother or eating meals with her parents? While those memories had nearly been replaced by more recent ones—sitting alone, her dog Oscar lying near her feet—the ones from her childhood were still alive.

"The place comes with all the furnishings?" The young man's eyes were trained on the icebox. Nora recalled the day her father had brought it home in the wagon—a birthday gift for her mother.

"Yes."

"You don't want to take any of it with you?"

Wanted to, yes, Nora thought, but it wasn't possible. "The place I'm moving to in England is also furnished."

The young man turned to look at her. "England, huh? Heard things haven't been good there since before the war. I would've thought more of them would be coming here, than anyone going there."

"I inherited some property."

"A big manor house, huh?" He chuckled. "I met a bunch of those rich Brits overseas. Decent guys, though most of them never worked a day in their lives before the war."

Nora watched his wife fingering the red-checked curtains over the window. She'd helped her mother sew those a few years back. "It isn't a house, actually. It's a cottage—on a sheep farm."

"Can we see the upstairs?" his wife asked, eagerness in her voice.

"Of course." Nora motioned them ahead of her, back into the parlor. "There are three bedrooms."

The couple started up the stairs, but Nora paused, her foot on the first step. Did she want to stand by while the two of them, nice as they were, looked at and touched the things that had once been her parents? The things that were hers but wouldn't fit into her suitcase?

"Take all the time you need," she called up to them. "I'll be outside."

She slipped out the front door. The slam of the screen behind her was a comforting and familiar sound. Nora moved down the porch steps and across the yard. Oscar trotted up to her side, his tail wagging. She stopped to rub the soft, brown fur between his ears, wishing she could take him with her. The old hound dog would detest being cooped up on a ship, though, and Tom's younger brothers had already consented to taking care of him.

Nora crossed the road running in front of the farm and slipped beneath the shady limbs of the giant, oak tree that stood like a sentinel before the fields. Oscar moved off to explore the nearby brush.

For the first time since the couple had arrived, Nora felt like she could breathe normally. She circled the trunk to look at the heart Tom had carved into the bark years earlier. Lifting her finger, she traced the smooth, weathered outlines of the heart shape and the letters whittled inside: TC + NL.

Tom had kissed her for the first time under these leafy branches. She'd bid him goodbye in the same place, the day before he and his brother Joel had left to fight in the war. This tree had also been privy to Tom's promise to marry her when he came back and Nora's anguish when she'd received word he wasn't returning.

She lowered her hand to her skirt pocket and removed the envelope tucked there. She'd memorized every word—about her being the next of kin to inherit Henry Lewis's sheep farm in England's Lake District.

She'd nearly written her great-uncle's solicitor back and declined the offer. She had a home and a life here. Her dearest friend Livy, Tom's sister, lived a few hours' drive away. What more could Nora want? Yet the idea of traveling somewhere beyond Iowa took hold in her mind and wouldn't leave her alone.

For the next week as she milked the cow, fed the animals and tended the farm, the notion of a fresh start consumed her every waking thought until she finally relented and wrote a letter of acceptance. Only then did she feel a measure of peace.

"I don't know anything about sheep, Tom," she admitted in a half whisper as she smoothed the envelope containing the solicitor's letter. "I'm not afraid, though. I need to go." She splayed her free hand against the grooves in the bark. "I think God needs me to go."

A movement across the street caught her eye. The couple was exiting the house. Nora pocketed the letter and stepped swiftly toward them.

"Everything's just lovely," the young woman said.

"We'll take it," her husband announced as Nora came to a stop below the porch. "How soon can we move in?"

Nora swallowed the tug of sorrow at her throat and managed a tight smile. "You can move in next Thursday. I'll leave the key under the mat."

They settled on a price, which was a few hundred dollars less than what Nora had asked for, but she'd expected that. After all, she could only do so much with running the place alone. The young man promised to bring the money over tomorrow morning.

"Do you have family there? In England, I mean?" The young woman allowed her husband to help her down the porch steps.

Nora shook her head. "Not anymore." With the death of her grandfather's brother, she no longer had any living relatives.

"Then why go?" Genuine concern shone on the other woman's face. "If I had this place, I don't think I could leave it for the unknown."

Nora glanced at the oak tree and the unseen heart imprinted there. This had been her home for twenty-three years—she'd never known another. So many dreams and hopes had been sown and lost here. Could she uproot herself from a comfortable existence to live in a foreign country, to work at something she knew little about? Would a life in England prove better than a life here?

*Fading recollections and isolation are not much of a life*, her heart reminded.

She turned her attention back to the couple. This time Nora did not need to infuse her response with feigned confidence. "I believe I'm ready for an adventure." The words sunk deeply into her soul and sent a tingle of excitement unfurling in her stomach.

"Judging by the state of things here, Miss Lewis, I think you'll do well on your sheep farm." The young man extended his good hand toward her. Nora shook it firmly and offered the two of them a genuine smile. "We wish you all the best across the Pond."

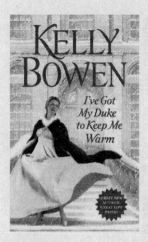

## *Fall in Love with Forever Romance*

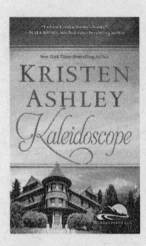

### KALEIDOSCOPE
### by Kristen Ashley

When old friends become new lovers, anything can happen. And now that Deck finally has a chance with Emme, he's not going to let her past get in the way of their future. Fans of Julie Ann Walker, Lauren Dane, and Julie James will love Kristen Ashley's *New York Times* bestselling Colorado Mountain series!

### BOLD TRICKS
### by Karina Halle

Ellie Watt has only one chance at saving the lives of her father and mother. But the only way to come out of this alive is to trust one of two very dangerous men who will stop at nothing to have her love in this riveting finale of Karina Halle's *USA Today* bestselling Artists Trilogy.

## Fall in Love with Forever Romance

**DECADENT**
**by Adrianne Lee**

Fans of Robyn Carr and Sherryl Woods will enjoy the newest book set at Big Sky Pie! Fresh off a divorce, Roxy isn't looking for another relationship, but there's something about her buttoned-up contractor that she can't resist. What that man clearly needs is something decadent—like her...

**THE LAST COWBOY IN TEXAS**
**by Katie Lane**

Country music princess Starlet Brubaker has a sweet tooth for moon pies and cowboys: both are yummy—and you can never have just one. Beckett Cates may not be her usual type, but he may be the one to put Starlet's boy-crazy days behind her... Fans of Linda Lael Miller and Diana Palmer will love it, darlin'!

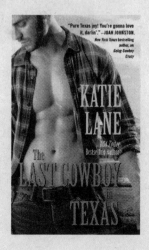

*Fall in Love with Forever Romance*

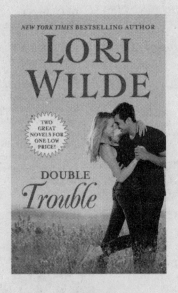

**DOUBLE TROUBLE**
by Lori Wilde

Get two books for the price of one in this special collection from *New York Times* bestselling author Lori Wilde, featuring twin sisters Maddie and Cassie Cooper from *Charmed and Dangerous* and *Mission: Irresistible*, and their adventures in finding their own happily ever afters.